PRAISE FOR *108*

"Captivating and conscious. Seamlessly weaving the metaphysical and metaphorical into a story of our current, pressing environmental realities, *108* reminds us of our innate connection to the world around us and opens our eyes to the truth that pulses underneath our everyday existence. A rich and radiant journey of awakening, healing, and empowerment, this eco-thriller vibrates with insight, leading us into a deeper alignment between ourselves and Earth. A new and compelling kind of climate fiction!" —Dr. Sue Morter, author of bestseller *The Energy Codes: The 7-Step System to Awaken Your Spirit, Heal Your Body, and Live Your Best Life*

"A needful story. A tender story. A gripping adventure. *108* entertains, but it also contains the seeds of personal and societal change. We can do more together than we can alone. This debut eco-thriller from Dheepa R. Maturi stirs my inner 'peaceful warrior.' I love this book. I think you will, too." —L.L. Barkat, author of *Earth to Poetry: A 30-Days, 30-Poems Earth, Self & Other Care Challenge*

"A gripping, mesmerizing, and ultimately *hopeful* tale about climate change—a story with an important message for all readers. *108* describes a world reeling under the impacts of climate change—a world of which we can already see the early signs. It reminds us of the power that lies within all of us to forge a better future when we work with each other, as found families, communities, and collectives. This book is a must-read for everyone concerned about the precarious future of our world in the era of the Anthropocene." —Harini Nagendra, professor of ecology, public speaker on nature and sustainability, and author of *Nature in the City: Bengaluru in the Past, Present, and Future* and *The Bangalore Detectives Club*

"Dheepa R. Maturi's thrilling and hopeful debut novel has it all: an ecological crisis of global proportions, a pulsing web of energy that connects every living thing, and a woman who must harness her power to stop the destruction of the Earth. I couldn't put it down. I needed to know what happened next to Bayla Jeevan, a refreshingly unique heroine who solves problems through meditation, yoga, and skilled fighting. In *108*, Maturi's imaginative writing lights up the strands in the web, a necessary and beautiful reminder that we're all connected." —Sarah Layden, author of *Imagine Your Life Like This* and *Trip Through Your Wires*

"Dheepa R. Maturi has given her readers a powerful and engaging debut novel. In an Earth-spanning chronicle set in 2040, *108* features a battle between Zed, an agricultural chemicals billionaire whose actions will destroy all arable land on Earth, and Bayla. Drawing power from the life force of the natural world, *108* combines Indian mysticism with modern technology. Evocative of the hit film *Avatar*, it is a compelling page-turner with many fascinating dimensions in time and geography. The complex and surprising ending leaves this reader hopeful of a sequel." —Michael Decter, author of *The Fulcrum*

"In this all-too timely eco-thriller, Dheepa R. Maturi employs a compelling mix of hard science, philosophy, ritual, and mysticism to weave a vivid and chilling picture of what will befall us if we don't address climate change now." —Barbara Shoup, author of *About Grace* and *A Commotion in Your Heart: Notes on Writing and Life*

108

108

AN ECO-THRILLER

DHEEPA R. MATURI

Published by GFB™, Seattle
www.girlfridayproductions.com

Produced by Girl Friday Productions

Design: Paul Barrett
Production editorial: Reshma Kooner
Project management: Abi Pollokoff

Source: mantra texts from *Pūrṇa Vidyā: Pūjā & Prayers* by Swamini Pramananda Saraswati and Sri Dhira Chaitanya (Pūrṇa Vidyā Trust, 2000); interpretations by Dheepa R. Maturi.

A special thank-you to Usha Ramaswamy and Philip Kocovski for assistance with translations and notations in Sanskrit and Croatian, respectively.

Image credits: cover © Shutterstock/kungfu01; Shutterstock/tongo51; Shutterstock/Peace Studio Creations

ISBN (hardcover): 978-1-964721-76-7
ISBN (paperback): 978-1-964721-77-4
ISBN (ebook): 978-1-964721-78-1

Library of Congress Control Number: 2025900869

First edition

To my mother,
Sunantha Sreenivasan Rammohan
1948–2021

I miss you.

PROLOGUE

She placed her hands on the soil.

She felt the pulse of the forest. She felt its pain.

Its edges had been pushed and consumed. Its roots were breaking.

"We need you!"

She heard the call, closed her eyes, and coaxed her awareness southward and westward across the land, until it surfaced in a grove of axlewood trees.

Black liquid poured into the edges of her vision and spread toward her.

"Now!"

It was too late.

She wailed as the liquid pierced her flesh and bone, and surged through her body.

CHAPTER 1

BAYLA

September 2040—San Francisco, California

The scent of jasmine caught Bayla Jeevan off guard.

She never allowed herself to think about the land where she'd grown up, but here she was, daydreaming of axlewood groves and haldina plants and, yes, jasmine. And of a woman, unfamiliar and yet . . .

Stop it, she scolded herself.

Her eyes scanned the room. The interns sat working at their desks while the rest of the staff exited the Environment Wire news agency. Most were heading to La Cantina next door before going home.

"Weren't you here just a few nights ago?" Braden Turner had stepped out of his glassed-in office and was looking at her with concern—or was it amusement?

She winced. "Someone needed to switch. It's okay—really."

"Well, keep an eye on the board." He tipped his head to indicate the electronic monitor mounted nearby. Originally installed to track fire activity in Northern California, it now showed an office-evacuation prompt at least once a week.

The overhead purifiers kicked into high gear as they labored to scrub the day's accumulation of toxins from the office air. Bayla jerked her thumb toward the EtherScreens and spoke loudly: "I'd better . . ."

Braden answered through the din. "Yep, go ahead. See you in the morning."

She nodded and turned away, making a show of adjusting the EtherScreen projections but watching from the corner of her eye as Braden walked toward the door.

For the next eight hours, she'd be working alone.

Bayla scanned the screens. Taking in twenty-four rotating screens of environmental data at once required sharp concentration, but she was used to it. A few times per month, midlevel researchers like her monitored overnight information and siphoned it to the appropriate interns. They, in turn, pushed their findings up the writing and editorial chain.

Bayla's hands flowed through the air in front of her. The EtherScreen technology allowed her to manipulate the displays and information by gesture alone, with no physical touch required.

On one screen to her left, the Global Monitoring Lab released the latest spikes in atmospheric carbon dioxide over the Arctic Circle. That was Ethan's area. She swept the data to him for examination.

She grimaced at eyewitness photos of New Yorkers skirmishing around bread trucks, attacking hapless drivers. Rani could handle that—*sweep*. Immediately, an e-zine headline popped up on the same screen: "NYC mayor's office plants evidence of food crisis." Sighing, she pushed it to the trash folder.

On her right appeared the Census Bureau count of persons displaced from the South Florida coastline. Usually that information would go to Kwame, but Tara was already analyzing similar numbers along the entire East Coast. *Sweep.*

The same display rotated to satellite images of the latest lethal heat wave moving across South Asia. She flinched a little, then swept the information to Min-Lee.

Minutes, then hours, slipped by as Bayla continued to review and sweep, review and sweep. When she began to yawn, she stood to stretch and ward off her sleepiness.

There it was again—a whiff of jasmine.

Stop it, she admonished herself, shaking her head in an effort to push away the daydream. What had triggered it again?

"Bayla!"

Her eyes widened, and she sat down hard. She dug her fingernails into her forearm.

That voice.

Craning her neck, she looked around. At the far end of the floor, the interns sat bent over their desks. One was snoring, his head buried in his arms. The only other sounds were the hum of EtherScreen projections and the whir of air purifiers.

"Bayla, we need you!"

Yes—it was her father's voice.

She hadn't heard it in fifteen years.

Bayla gasped as the news agency blurred and faded, and she found herself standing amid dense foliage, heavy moisture pressing against her body. Fear gripped her belly, and her breathing accelerated. *What's happening? Where am I?*

Sounds, sights, smells began to populate around her. The call of cicadas. The trunks of banyans. The breath of jasmine.

I know this place!

She'd tried hard to forget it.

She turned in a circle, absorbing familiar details of the land in which she'd spent the first twelve years of her life. Reaching out, she touched the bark of an axlewood tree, and then another, and another—she was inside a grove.

Glancing at her hands, she gasped again. Threads of light emerged from them, connecting her to the tree she was touching, and the next tree, and the next, entwining her with the entire grove. Looking down, she saw that they emerged from her entire body—arms, torso, legs, feet—and wove into all the other threads.

Yet she didn't feel restrained. The threads were bolstering, fortifying her.

And they were *familiar*. This had happened to her before—but when? Before the memory could surface, the threads lengthened, then split like vines, moving in whatever direction she looked, joining her to everything she could see.

"Bayla! Look down!"

She obeyed without thinking, peering into the dark soil. The threads of light followed, pushing through the ground and interweaving with the root structures that anchored the grove and spread outward for miles. She bent and examined the individual roots, perceiving the gossamer between them, lacing the whole system together. She smelled loam and life.

Her fear could not coexist with the wonder of it all, this web of light surrounding her and extending both earthward and skyward.

Closing her eyes, she listened. The web pulsed and reverberated, rendering its own music. Like the terrain, the music seemed familiar to her, and she rode the melodies like waves.

"Bayla, we're here."

She spilled out of the rise and fall of sound.

We?

Looking around at the web, she saw a tiny orb a few feet away from her, a point brighter than the threads surrounding it. She looked down at her own body. She, too, existed as one sphere of light within the web. Concentrating, she peered around and saw more bright spots—only ten at first, then twenty, fifty, a hundred, maybe more.

Somehow she knew: they were all people, just like her.

But who were they? What did they want?

"Bayla, we need you!"

The bright spots united into one intention—striving and straining together, to do . . . *something.*

Then she saw it—black liquid, thick and viscous, pouring and spreading all around her. It pooled and sank into the ground, burning as it went. She recoiled, because she felt it in her own body, too. The black liquid beaded around the threads and slid into her, piercing her skin, biting her bone. She dropped to her knees.

The hiss of acid blurred the swell of song. The reek of smoke covered the scent of soil. Her vision became shadowed.

"Now, Bayla!"

She drew a ragged breath, focusing on the chaos around her.

Suddenly, she understood. They—whoever they were—wanted to stop the liquid, and they wanted her help.

But what could she do? She attempted to thrust her hands into the soil, to block the liquid and push it back, but she could no longer move. Fixed in place, she could only watch.

No! she tried to shout, but her voice caught in her throat.

It was too late.

She watched the liquid push through land and water, bleeding farther and farther outward, past her line of sight.

When at last her limbs jolted into motion, she collapsed to the ground. *No, please, I can't—I can't bear this!*

Curling into a ball, she writhed, drawing rattling breaths and gripping the scorched soil around her.

She looked up, shocked, as the soil cooled into laminate beneath her hands. The buzz of insects became the whir of air purifiers. She was surrounded again by EtherScreens. The threads of light had vanished.

It had felt too real to be a dream. Could she have been physically transported to the forest?

That makes no sense.

The devastation and loss she'd witnessed flashed through her mind. Her gut lurched at the possibility—the certainty—that somehow she could have prevented it.

And why—why my father's voice?

CHAPTER 2

BAYLA

"Are you okay?"

Startled, Bayla blinked at the intern standing before her, looking at her with concern. "Wha-what?" she stammered.

"I was walking by, and you were just staring at the wall."

Bayla shot to her feet, then sat again, catching the desk as she tilted. She clutched her stomach in dread. "Something's happened, Ethan. Something terrible. Get Min-Lee—she's on South Asian stories. And I need you, too, and whatever other interns are still here."

"Bayla, what's going on?"

"I'm not sure. There's been some kind of accident—maybe an oil spill or a chemical leak. A bad one, in southwestern India, near Prithvi Forest, I think. Check the news feeds for the surrounding cities and all our sources on the ground nearby."

"Where did you hear—"

"All of you, *right now!*"

As Ethan dashed away, Bayla pulled up three real-time satellite feeds. Given the scale of what she'd witnessed, the details would surely show up there.

Nothing.

She double-checked the time stamps on the images.

Current.

Well, many government organizations took satellite imagery, not to mention hundreds of private companies, and she had all the agency's EtherScreens at her disposal. She began to open feeds and data from around the world. Five interns were now searching as frantically as she was.

As the hours passed, though, she noticed their pace slowing. Glancing at them from time to time, she saw their questioning looks and then their frustration.

It doesn't matter, Bayla thought to herself. Some incident *had* occurred. She just didn't know what it was—yet.

She continued searching, looking up in surprise when the office lights brightened to daytime mode. Staff members were returning. An entire night had passed.

She looked across the room. The interns were talking to their teams, probably explaining what Bayla had instructed them to do. Feeling more and more eyes on her, she broke into a sweat. How she hated that feeling—everyone staring as though something was wrong with her. Over the years, she'd learned to adapt—clothes, gestures, accent, expressions—in order to avoid those looks.

Was it possible that she'd been mistaken? That it had been a dream?

But she'd never had a dream so detailed, so *real*—and never a dream featuring her father's voice, just as she remembered it, clear as day.

"Bayla?"

She looked up; Ethan was standing in front of her again.

"We're not finding anything," he said.

"Keep looking."

"Okay, but—"

"Text me when you find it."

Ignoring Ethan's bafflement, Bayla stood up and began to move toward the exit. She had to leave and clear her head.

"Where are you going?" he called after her.

"I'll be right back."

At the front of the building, Bayla pushed the doors open and stepped outside. Dry heat assaulted her. She tried to take a deep breath and immediately started coughing. She'd forgotten to check the air-quality rating before rushing out of the office. She felt in her pocket: *Please, please, please.* There. Pulling the mask out, she adjusted its disposable filter and slipped the straps over her ears. Nevertheless, she continued to cough for a full minute.

Few other people were outside. The sky was red with haze from the latest outbreak of wildfires to the north. She missed the grasses and linden trees that had lined the sidewalks until a few years ago. Watering into the ground was now forbidden, and everything green had shriveled. In the past, she would walk four blocks to Kendall Park when she needed a break from work, but now, there was no point. The last time she'd been there, it had been as brown and gray as the rest of the city.

Her phone buzzed. It was a text from Braden, already back at work. She wondered if the man ever slept.

Please come to my office.

Bayla tensed. She was regretting her behavior. In the light of day and as the minutes passed, her strange experience no longer carried the weight of reality. She looked at her hands. *Threads of light? Really?*

Why hadn't she calmed herself, slowed down, and verified

the incident before involving the interns? With the amount of disinformation in the media, Environment Wire was fighting hard to ensure accuracy, and she'd always tried to live up to that commitment.

Turning on her heel, Bayla retraced her steps. When she stepped onto the agency floor, she tried not to notice her co-workers' mystified looks. Not that she could blame them—she'd caught a glimpse of herself in the glass entry doors. She looked bewildered, her clothing disheveled, her hair a mess. As she made her way to Braden's office, she pulled her long curls out of their elastic band and twisted them back into a neat bun.

In front of his door, she stopped, touching it lightly. Braden was only four years her senior, but he'd already ascended to second-in-line to the bureau chief, overseeing most agency operations. What would he say to her? Ever since his promotion, he'd tried to transfer her from the research team to the journalism department whenever she submitted her written analyses. *This is excellent, Bayla. What are you still doing in research?*

Bayla sighed. He'd stop asking after this.

At last she knocked.

"Come in."

Braden turned toward her from the window, and she winced at the seriousness of his expression. He gestured toward the overstuffed vinyl sofa and waited for her to take a seat.

"Looks like you had a rough night. Want to tell me what happened?"

Bayla sat but couldn't respond. Looking down, she pressed her index finger into the sofa arm where she saw a rip beginning.

When she didn't answer, Braden continued. "The interns

tell me you saw documentation of a spill in South Asia, but they haven't been able to corroborate it. *At all.*"

Bayla cringed. There hadn't been any documentation. She'd acted on impulse, convinced that whatever she'd experienced had been real. What had gotten into her?

She wrapped her arms around herself. "I'm sorry, Braden. I really believed it happened."

Braden looked at her for a few moments. "You know, the overnight shift can mess with people's heads." He consulted his laptop. "And it looks like you've done . . . *eight* this month alone."

Her face flushed, and she lifted her chin. So what if she spent a lot of time at work? It kept her mind from wandering where she didn't want it to go. *Until today,* she thought.

Anyway, Braden was a workaholic himself. She looked down at the heavily indented couch, where he often slept in order to meet deadlines.

"I'm not sleep deprived. I just . . . I just made a mistake."

Braden's lips pressed into a line. "Yes, you did—a mistake I don't expect from someone at your level, with your experience. We all have to react fast to push information out before our competitors do, but we're known for our factual accuracy. This was a rookie mistake, and . . ." His voice trailed off.

He looked at her as though waiting for her to speak, but she couldn't. At last, he sighed. "Bayla, what convinced you?"

"I don't know!" she blurted, digging her fingernails into her forearm. She closed her eyes and remembered being sprawled across the soil, feeling the heat emanating from it.

Wait a minute. Heat. She looked up. "Braden, listen, I need to check the infrared heat-sensor readings from Alsa Corp's close-orbit satellites. Maybe Ethan could—" She stopped, noting the skepticism in his gray eyes.

"I'm going to get the interns started on something else," he said. "For now, why don't you head home."

She nodded miserably, then stood and turned toward the door.

"Bayla?"

She turned back.

"Do you need some help, or—"

"No!" she exclaimed. "Sorry," she continued after a moment. "I'll be fine. Thanks." Despite her embarrassment, despite everything, she appreciated his concern.

Back on the Environment Wire floor, she saw staffers furtively glancing her way. She grabbed her messenger bag and dashed out of the agency.

Walking toward the train station, she took deep breaths but regretted them immediately as she began choking. The city air was thickening into soup. She dug into her pocket again for her mask. Where had it gone?

An incoming train rumbled, and she ran the length of the platform. Scurrying inside just before the doors closed, she swung onto a seat, then leaned over her knees, coughing and gagging from her sprint through the haze without a mask. Fortunately, the train's air purifier was working, and her spasms soon quieted.

Despite her disgust at the sticky seat, she felt lucky she'd caught this train. With the departure of so many people and companies from the city, far fewer trains were running, and many were canceled at the last minute for maintenance. Often, they never made it back on the schedule. She glanced at the oxygen tanks in the corner, now required in every compartment. So many people had breathing problems these days.

For years, Environment Wire had been reporting such changes, both the everyday details and the large-scale events.

All of them had initially shocked and horrified Bayla. Now she felt only a constant, low-level hopelessness, kept at bay and at a distance because she witnessed them through the EtherScreens of Environment Wire, where she spent most of her time, even on weekends.

Was that why her experience last night had felt so real? Nothing had separated her from what was transpiring. Instead, she'd existed right in the middle of it, touching the soil and trees, watching a many-layered destruction occurring before her eyes.

She'd felt everything in her own body—the burn of that peculiar liquid sinking deep into her cells.

Bayla dropped her head into her hands.

There was more to it than that.

She felt certain that the experience, whether real or in her mind's eye, had occurred where she'd grown up, at the edge of Prithvi Forest—the place she avoided thinking about, even to the extent of trading away South Asian research assignments to others. It was the place that reminded her she had no control or choice in her life.

She felt the old surge of anger and anguish, and tried to calm herself with long, wide breaths. Instead, she found herself feeling more agitated.

Exiting the train, she made her way toward a vending machine, where only two sealed masks remained. She swept her phone across the sensor to purchase both. Tearing one package open, she pulled the mask over her head, then placed the second on the lap of the man sitting crouched at the station exit, hacking into his hands. He gave her a tired nod.

Bayla began walking to her apartment, then, inexplicably, started to run as fast as she could, pounding the sidewalk with her feet, trying to escape that feeling, that bitter cocktail of powerlessness and grief. At last, she stood panting and coughing in front of her building.

The patches of grass on either side of the door were dead, and the landscape shrubs had become stalks of straw. The building itself, deteriorating from heat and ash, looked far shabbier than when she'd moved in five years ago. Some faraway corporate office received her rent by automatic bank transfer, and no one seemed to be maintaining the grounds anymore.

As she stepped inside, Bayla dropped her messenger bag on the floor by the door. Switching off her phone, she tossed it onto the entry table, one of the few utilitarian pieces of furniture in the boxy one-bedroom with gray-beige walls. Looking over the bland space, she felt a sudden twitching, like she wanted to shrug out of her skin, out of her life. She clenched her fists and let out a long shout.

Entering her bedroom, she rummaged through the closet until she found a long staff of tamarind wood in the back corner, the last gift her father had given her. She hesitated, then grabbed it and stomped back to the living room.

Though it had followed her to each place she'd moved, she hadn't brandished it for a long time. Bracing it horizontally before her now, Bayla visualized her old *kalaripayattu* sparring practice. Many scholars believed that all Eastern martial arts had sprung from this one, indigenous to South Asia.

Taking a deep breath, she worked through a warm-up sequence and then through a basic routine, regaining her form gradually as she twisted and spun, moving faster and faster until she felt the sweat stream from her forehead and down her face and back.

When she finished, she brought the staff in front of her again to a resting posture, enjoying the combined feeling of strength and exhaustion in her limbs and the lightening of her dark mood. Unbidden, an image of her father came to her—how he bowed his head in gratitude after every training session with her.

But she didn't feel gratitude.

Instead, she felt the energy and power she'd just generated ebbing away. She could almost see herself shrinking.

Tossing the staff into the corner by the front door, she reentered her bedroom, knelt at the dresser, and opened the bottom drawer. Pushing aside some clothing, she lifted out a green box.

She didn't open it.

Instead, she sat with her hand on the lid. Inside were mementos from her old life—not many, because she'd left so abruptly and without realizing she wouldn't return. Unconsciously, her hand moved up to the pit of her throat, touching the pendant she always wore there. The knot in her stomach tightened.

At last, she opened the box and took out the letter she'd discovered in her suitcase a few days after her arrival in the US fifteen years ago, at age twelve. She'd read that letter daily during her first month away from home, and then less and less often as months, then years, passed. A few times, she had marched the letter to the dumpster but, for some reason, hadn't been able to toss it in.

The paper had softened and torn a bit at the crease. A delicate hand-drawn bayla flower in the corner was barely detectable.

She hadn't read the letter in years, but she did so now.

Little Flower, I feel as though I am sending my heart away. You aren't safe here, and you're not safe with me. Do not try to contact me or look for me. Please trust me. When I can, I'll bring you home, and we'll be together again. Then I'll tell you everything.

But he hadn't. He hadn't come.

CHAPTER 3

AATMANJI

Campsite, Western Ghats, India
Thirty minutes. He'd had only thirty minutes to prevent thirty years of effort from unraveling.

And he'd failed.

Aatmanji clenched his fists and shouted his frustration. The woman next to him looked up in surprise.

He took her hands and looked into her eyes, an unusual shade of green against her dark skin, and then at the dramatic white streak coursing down the right side of her black hair. He wanted to utter words of comfort—both for her and for himself—but none came.

"I'm sorry, Aanvi" was all he could manage.

Aanvi shook her head. "Listen to me, Aatmanji. It's not your fault."

For millennia, southwestern India's topsoil and trees had anchored this entire ecosystem, along with its water cycles and flora and fauna. Their interrelationship had kept the land viable and warded off the desertification that had occurred throughout much of the world.

His unit had battled for decades to keep the ecosystem healthy, but now . . . now . . . Looking down at the ground, he cringed. He hadn't been prepared for the devastation he'd just witnessed, for the chaos and cacophony, the cessation of voice and vibration. He shuddered. It had sounded like flesh sizzling and creatures screaming, and then . . . nothing.

Nothingness.

Long ago, the Seven Sages predicted a catastrophe, one that humanity would inflict upon itself. Was this the beginning of that catastrophe?

If so, the Sages had also provided a way for humanity to prevent its own destruction.

He thought of the work his unit had been doing for so many years.

Would they be ready?

CHAPTER 4

AP WIRE

NEW AGROCHEMICAL TESTED IN
SOUTHWESTERN INDIA

VAYU CITY, INDIA. Global agrochemical conglomerate ZedChem conducted
a test pour of its newest formula,
FZ5, in an area of farmland in southwestern India. According to ZedChem
spokeswoman Lyn Tran, FZ5 will force
exponential growth from the treated
topsoil.

Topsoil is often compared to a
layer of skin anchoring all life on
the planet, containing intersecting
ecosystems full of organic matter.
Over centuries of human history, the
conversion of natural grasslands and

forests into agricultural land gradually degraded that topsoil.

By early 2020, 65% of the world's existing topsoil was rendered infertile or fully washed away. Then, in the late 2020s and early 2030s, massive waves of desertification destroyed half of what remained, endangering the world's food supply and dislodging citizenry from homelands that could no longer produce crops.

Today, only twenty zones around the world have retained their topsoil and are now responsible for 95% of food production in the world. There are concerns that the topsoil in those zones will also diminish, as it is under tremendous pressure to meet global demand.

One of those twenty zones, also the test location for FZ5, is in southwestern India. Due to an educated populace committed to environmental sustainability, enlightened government officials, and social and financial support for farmers, it has preserved the largest area of topsoil in the world, with the highest levels of organic content. Efforts in the area included returning to traditional agricultural methodologies such as crop diversity, intercropping, and natural pest deterrents, as well as reforesting land to redevelop root systems that hold topsoil in place.

However, according to Krakun Zed, ZedChem's CEO, such preservation actions are ineffective and backward-looking. "Modern chemicals hold the answers and the way forward. FZ5 has been under meticulous development by our scientists for over a decade. The formula removes any need to change agricultural methods or procedures. FZ5 will make soil produce like never before."

The test pour was officially conducted by ForwardChem, now revealed to be ZedChem's newest subsidiary. The history of the area shows that ZedChem, originally founded in Croatia, tried to establish a presence in southwestern India in the 2010s but encountered a series of obstacles, from government roadblocks to public condemnation. Eventually, ZedChem departed the country entirely after a massive factory fire in 2015.

Mr. Zed took over company leadership from his father, Harvat Zed, growing ZedChem into a truly global presence, gobbling up almost sixty

other independent companies in the
process. Mr. Zed is regarded as one
of the top 25 industrialists of this
century, reportedly possessing wealth
in the hundreds of billions.

According to spokeswoman Tran,
ZedChem is satisfied with its test run
and has now scheduled a large-scale
release of FZ5 in one week.

"ZedChem will revolutionize modern
agriculture," Tran declared. "We will
make Earth's remaining soil produce
like never before. We will save the
food supply."

11:05 a.m.

**TEXT from Braden Turner to Bayla
Jeevan:**

did you see AP wire? here's the link.

12:30 p.m.

**TEXT from Braden Turner to Bayla
Jeevan:**

new agrochemical test in southwestern
india. was that the incident you were
talking about?

3:15 p.m.

TEXT from Braden Turner to Bayla Jeevan:

but not a chemical or oil spill. so wouldn't have shown on satellite photos.

7:04 p.m.

TEXT from Braden Turner to Bayla Jeevan:

where r u? did you see the link?

2:15 a.m.

TEXT from Braden Turner to Bayla Jeevan:

?

CHAPTER 5

BAYLA

I'm a child again, cradled in my favorite axlewood tree, held aloft by the interlocking boughs. They rock me, and the branches touch my face like gentle fingers. I see a woman, familiar somehow, approaching on the ground, looking for me. I lean forward, waving my arms, trying to get her attention, but my body slips through the boughs. I fall straight through the ground, into gooey blackness. Sludge invades my lungs, and I try to scream. . . .

Bayla gasped and opened her eyes. Her hands flew to her throat as though she were choking, and then she relaxed. *Just a dream.*

I think.

She turned to the clock—4:00 a.m. Awakening at this time seemed hardwired into her body, for as long as she could remember. Bayla sat up, swung her legs to the side of the bed, and spoke the mantra she recited daily before her feet touched the ground:

samudravasane devi
parvatastanamaṇḍale
viṣṇupatni namastubhyaṃ
pādasparśaṃ kṣamasva me.

She'd always loved the meaning: *Mother Earth, draped by oceans, adorned with mountains, forgive me for stepping upon you with my feet.*

After showering, she entered her walk-in closet, which she'd repurposed as a yoga and meditation space when she'd moved in. Her clothes hung instead on a few freestanding racks near her bed.

When she'd left India, young and dazed and grieving, these practices had been her only solid ground. She'd always felt grateful for the stability they'd provided, making her body ready to serve her and her mind focused and alert. They allowed her at least to begin her day with clarity and calm.

Readying herself at the front of her yoga mat, she moved through 108 sun salutations, welcoming the day, feeling the surge and buildup of energy from the movements. After that, she began the classical *yogāsanas*, the postures taught by the First Yogi to the Seven Sages, preserved and passed on for thousands of years.

It was her favorite part of the day, occupying only the present moment, temporarily separated from her frustrations at work and her irritations with people. Today, though, she was having difficulty maintaining that separation. The past she'd pushed away for years was drawing her out of the moment, whispering for her attention.

She found herself wondering exactly when she'd learned

this combination of yoga, meditation, and breathing exercises. She couldn't remember those first lessons as a child at Tulā School, but she certainly remembered the teachers walking through the large hall, adjusting students' postures and limbs—none too gently when they'd needed repeated reminders.

The teachers' words now echoed in her mind.

Remember: only precise geometric configurations invite the flow of energy.

Remember: yoga encompasses more than physical postures and movements.

Remember: you must not resist your practice but, rather, welcome it.

Her mind wandered to the Tulā School rooms, all integrated with the outdoors—the walls of bamboo, mats of straw, scents of incense and jasmine. She thought of the grounds, full of color and vibrancy emerging directly from the land.

No. I don't want to remember.

Clearing her head yet again, she knelt in *vajrāsana*, sometimes called the diamond pose for the firmness and strength it lent the body, and began a *kriyā*, a process combining physical postures, breathing techniques, and meditation. Finally, she ended her practice with alternate nostril breathing, to balance the *iḍā* and *piṅgala* of her body, the feminine and masculine energies existing in every human being, and to unite them with the *suṣumna* energy along her spine. It was a practice intended to bring all the energies coursing within her body into balance.

Balance in all things—body, mind, Earth, cosmos, the teachers always said. Indeed, *tulā* in Tulā School was the Sanskrit word for "balance."

When she finished, she sat in silence. For a few minutes,

she savored a feeling of completeness and wholeheartedness. She knew, though, that the feeling would fade soon after she left this little room. Try as she might to prevent it, her mind would begin to spin and her heart would shrink. Despite her wish not to, she would push people away.

So Bayla waited, allowing the completeness to inhabit her a bit longer.

At last, she stood and placed her hand on the door. She felt the events of the previous day pushing against it—her forest vision, her frantic search for answers, Braden's puzzlement. And her father's voice, gentle yet resonant, the voice she hadn't heard in so long.

Suddenly, she slipped back to the floor, and her body curled into itself. She clenched her fists and squeezed her eyes shut, but tears broke through.

Oh, Appa, why—why did you send me away? How could you leave me so alone?

CHAPTER 6

BAYLA

Bang, bang, bang!

Bayla looked up, startled. Someone was pounding on the front door of her apartment. Dashing her tears away with the back of her hand, she glanced at the clock—it was a little after 7:00 a.m. Who would be here so early in the morning?

Exiting the walk-in closet, she approached her front door and swung it open.

"Braden! What are you doing here?"

He seemed relieved. "Bayla! I was getting worried—I kept calling, but you never answered your phone. Didn't you get my texts?"

Bayla shook her head. "I turned it off." She picked up her phone from the entry table where she'd tossed it. When she turned it on again, she heard the *ping, ping, ping* of notifications.

"Did something happen?"

"Can I come in?"

She looked over her shoulder at her apartment, then turned back to him. "I . . . I guess."

Gesturing for him to follow, she walked into the living room. She perched on the arm of the sofa and read the link Braden had texted her earlier. Glancing up, she noticed he'd removed his mask and seated himself.

His expression was apologetic. "Hope you don't mind my coming by. I looked up your address in the company directory, and I thought I'd stop by on the way to work."

Bayla shook her head. "Sorry, I . . ." Her voice trailed off as she continued to read the news clip.

"So, was that the incident you were talking about yesterday?" Braden asked, after a few minutes.

She closed her eyes and considered—yes, her strange experience must have occurred during the test time. And the test had happened on the agricultural lands bordering Prithvi Forest, as she'd originally thought.

"Yes, it's the same, but . . ." How could she tell Braden that she'd actually *experienced* the test pour herself—and that it had felt like an apocalypse, not a small trial run for a beneficial agrochemical, as the company's CEO seemed to indicate. Bayla looked at the article again. "ZedChem," she said aloud.

She slid off the arm of the sofa and walked to the EtherScreen projector positioned on the dinette table. Near the setup was a small window box crowded with plants—the only spot of color in the room. They consumed much of her precious water allotment, but they were the only thing in her apartment that made her feel that she, too, was alive. As she passed it, she brushed her fingertips along the greenery.

Sitting down, she ran a search and began scrolling through the results.

"You know—" Bayla jumped at Braden's voice close to her ear. She hadn't realized that he'd come to stand behind her and read over her shoulder. "Sorry—didn't mean to startle you.

We'll have to check all the facts and sources, but the press coverage is positive so far. There's so little agricultural land left, and the food shortages are increasing. And this . . . this FZ5 is supposed to make the existing soil produce more."

Bayla didn't answer.

"So, this is good, right?" Braden continued, his face brightening. "Obviously, you must have seen a minor source as events were unfolding and you followed it. You were right about the event, just not your evaluation. But it's often like that in our job—we have to chase information quickly. As far as I'm concerned, you're vindicated." He paused. "You still seem upset."

Bayla turned to him. He looked exhausted. She considered how he'd been trying to reach her throughout the day—and night, she noted, glancing down at the text chain—to let her know her story had been real. It was kind of him.

She felt a longing to confide in someone, to share the confusion of the last twenty-four hours. Would he understand?

"You know," she spoke haltingly, "I grew up near that test pour, right in Prithvi Forest—at a place called Tulā School."

"You're kidding."

"I"—Bayla paused and clutched her stomach—"*left* fifteen years ago. A few weeks after I got here, I learned that Tulā School had burned to the ground, and everyone there had died—my whole family."

Braden looked at her in shock.

"For years, I tried to find out more, but I couldn't. I just heard the same thing over and over, whomever I asked—that the place had burned. Finally, I just gave up. I couldn't bear to think about it anymore."

Leaning back in her chair, she covered her face with her hands.

After a few moments, Braden knelt in front of her, tugged her hands from her face, and held them. "I don't know what to say. I'm so sorry that happened to you."

She felt a rare moment of relief, leaning into the support of another person. Making up her mind, she took a breath. "Braden . . . this is going to sound weird, but I . . . I *experienced* that test pour. It was happening, all around me, and . . ." Bayla choked as she remembered the liquid sinking deep. "And then . . . and then I heard my father's voice. It was so real—like he was next to me, talking to me."

She looked at him and winced. He had that look, the one she dreaded, the look that confirmed how odd and different she was. She pulled her hands away. "You don't believe me," she stated, her voice flat.

CHAPTER 7

AATMANJI

Campsite, Western Ghats, India

Aatmanji scanned the clearing, with its thatched dwellings and bamboo gathering halls and thriving gardens, as well as the foliage pressing in—the axlewood groves, the banyan overhangs, the teak and laurel and flame-of-the-forest trees.

He thought of the liquid spreading through the forest, poisoning the diverse fungal system woven through the underlying soil structures. Those fungi facilitated the exchange of nutrients, information, and support among the plants and trees. When they perished, that communication mechanism would fail.

Communication mechanism, he thought. Cold and technical words for what he'd always heard as song. If that music ceased, the entire forest would soon follow.

Three months ago, he'd heard that ForwardChem, an agrochemical company, had established itself on the outskirts of nearby Vayu City with the intention of developing a new product. Soon, the details had reached him—how quickly and how far the chemical would spread through land, burrow into soil, bleed through water. How it would bond instantly with whatever it touched and could never be flushed away.

"I thought we'd have a year before they released it," Aanvi murmured. Aatmanji nodded. Usually they had time to work with local and government contacts, to educate local farmers and suppliers and supporters, to thwart the agrochemical company's plans. It was the unit's usual plan of attack for these recurring situations, and it had worked well in this part of the country, here in southwestern India.

But then a warning had arrived, specific and urgent:

> Test pour imminent. Coordinates to
> follow.

Those coordinates had pointed to the farmlands bordering Prithvi Forest. The place he considered home.

With the clock ticking down, he'd known that only one person could stop what would transpire there.

Daksha.

At first, Daksha had responded to his call, and then she was . . . gone.

Aatmanji now turned to Aanvi. "What happened to her? Where did she go?"

Aanvi sighed and shook her head. "There's no way to know. Daksha doesn't answer to us, or to anyone. You know this. She's different—and she leads a different kind of life."

"I . . . I called to Bayla." Aatmanji's voice cracked, and Aanvi placed a hand on his shoulder. "Maybe I shouldn't have."

"Aatmanji, you had no choice. When Daksha disappeared, you had to reach out to Bayla. You had to try."

Aatmanji closed his eyes. "I thought she might be able to do what was needed—even without fully understanding, even without training. But she wasn't ready. She was terrified. She doesn't understand her capabilities . . . and I never prepared her."

Aanvi looked at him, and he knew they were remembering the same incident, long ago.

***

Aatmanji stood before the group. The Tulā School students sat cross-legged before him, flanked by the residents. Out of the corner of his eye, he spotted Aanvi sitting between her younger brother and sister, both visiting during a rare break from their work. Aatmanji smiled at Aanvi's joy in being reunited with her siblings.

"In the name of the Seven Sages, I greet you all. As you know, the Seven were tasked with spreading the wisdom of the First Yogi across the globe. If that wisdom is forgotten, humanity will suffer the loss. Each of you plays a vital role in keeping that wisdom alive."

He paused and looked at each of the students in turn. All of them were learning to perceive and tune in to the web of life. Students began training in this particular practice at age sixteen.

On Aatmanji's signal, the adults sat in silence and deepened their concentration, envisioning the web of life, revealing it, holding it steady. Minutes, then hours, ticked by as the students slowly tuned in, learning to see and feel themselves within that web.

Suddenly, they all felt a pulse.

The web shimmered.

To everyone's surprise, a little flame seemed to leap into the web, twinkling, gleaming . . . dancing.

They watched intently. While all of them remained im-mobile points of light within the web, the little flame instead moved through it with ease, thread to thread, end to end.

After a few moments, the flame seemed to draw them all together and lead them en masse—bound in purpose, rising, turning, advancing, diving.

A school of fish.

A swarm of bees.

A flock of birds.

At last, they separated, individuated, and opened their eyes. Bayla, age eleven, sat cross-legged in the middle of the group, her dark curls wild, her hazel eyes wide, her golden face smiling.

"It was fun!" she whispered loudly to Aatmanji, before jumping up and running off.

Aanvi looked at Aatmanji and then at the awestruck faces of the students and teachers. Approaching him, she whispered, "Aatmanji, she's just like her—just like Daksha."

***

They were silent for a few moments.

"Aatmanji." Fear prickled in his belly as he anticipated Aanvi's words. "We've lost our margin of time, and we don't have a choice. We need to bring her back."

She paused for a moment, then spoke firmly.

"If Daksha can't be found, then Bayla is our only hope."

CHAPTER 8

BAYLA

Braden looked uncomfortable as Bayla continued to stare at him. "Uh, well, it's just that . . . if your father died, how could you have heard his voice?"

"I don't know—I don't know—it doesn't make any sense."

Braden spoke gently. "Bayla, I don't understand what happened to you at work, but listen. I was looking through the online log, and you sent some South Asian news to Min-Lee before all this happened. Is it possible it triggered some memory just before you saw the info about the test pour, and you connected them in your head?"

Bayla looked away. What had possessed her to confide so much? They weren't friends—they were colleagues.

Edging away from him, she stepped toward the window box and contemplated the leaves of the plant farthest to the right, a hibiscus. Unlike the rest, it seemed fragile and sickly, its leaves tangling with the others as though struggling to support itself.

When she didn't answer, Braden approached and touched

her shoulder, startling her again. "It sounds like you have some things to work through—things from your past. Maybe . . . maybe you should take some time off to do that."

Her eyes flashed, and she pulled away. "Are you telling me not to come in to work?"

"No, not at all, it's just—"

"Thanks for coming here to check on me," she interrupted, her voice cold. "And I'm sorry—this won't happen again. Let me walk you out."

Bayla moved toward the door in an effort to shepherd him, but he didn't seem to be following her. She turned back. He stood rooted to the spot, looking surprised by her abruptness.

At last, he followed her. As he reached for the doorknob, Bayla spoke. "Maybe . . . maybe you're right." He turned. "About time off, I mean," she finished.

He nodded. "I'm guessing you have vacation time saved up. Now that I think about it, I'm not sure I've ever seen you take a vacation."

"I . . . I don't like having free time." She turned her head away from him. "It makes me think about the past."

"I'll let HR know. And Bayla?"

"Yes?"

"Whatever you find, I hope you know—it doesn't have to define you. You're so much more than your past."

Bayla looked at him, uncertain how to respond.

"And if there's any way I can help, just let—"

"No," she interrupted. "No. I have to do this on my own."

Braden reached for one of the dark curls that had escaped the bun in her hair, and tucked it behind her ear. He held her gaze. "Good luck, Bayla. I'm rooting for you."

She blushed and nodded, then watched as he slipped on

his mask, opened the door, and walked to his car, parked at the curb in front of her apartment building. When he waved, she felt warmth rush into her ears.

Shutting the door, she leaned against it and dropped her head.

The memory that had been bubbling broke through the surface—her child-self running into a clearing next to Tulā School, where a group of people sat meditating. For fun, she'd stepped into the middle, closed her eyes, and seen a web of shining strands, each meditator an orb within it. She'd felt such joy—she'd wanted to pull them together, embrace them all at once, gather them up in her heart.

So she had.

She'd swept them up, and together they'd traveled through that web, anywhere she wished to lead them. They'd soared through treetops and slid down the trunks. They'd romped to the edges of the forest and looked toward the mountains, then the farmlands. They'd dived into the river, through its clear waters, and touched the stones at the bottom.

Bayla sighed and walked back to the EtherScreen, pondering that day long ago. There was so much she still didn't understand, but she knew two things for certain. She *had* experienced the ZedChem test pour in real time. And she *had* felt people surrounding her, all urging her to stop the pour, to prevent it from spreading, to step up and act before it destroyed the land beneath her.

This time, she hadn't been able to move. But as a child, she'd gathered up those people, those orbs of light, and they'd moved, turned, twisted together.

A school of fish.

A swarm of bees.

A flock of birds.

A swell of individuals, moving in unison, spinning upward, sideways, downward, before leaping to the sky, reaching to the sun.

They were many, and they were One.

CHAPTER 9

DAKSHA—AN INTERLUDE

She gasped, and her eyes opened.

She lay sprawled on a forest floor—the forest of her earliest memories, her first home before she'd wandered south as a child.

What happened?

She remembered.

Aatmanji had called her, and she'd pushed her consciousness to Prithvi Forest.

She cringed, remembering the black liquid that had seeped into the ground. She hadn't been able to stop it, so, instead, she'd pulled the liquid into herself—absorbing, processing, consuming it.

Agony.

Now, retching and vomiting, she pushed herself into a seated posture, waiting for the spasms to subside.

Wait. Something's wrong.

She fought her panic as she looked around. Her surroundings were the same—foliage, roots, branches—but she no longer felt connected to them. She could not feel them breathing with her. She could not hear the sounds that had anchored her throughout her life.

She could not see the threads.

A web of light flickered just out of her reach, dimming, re-appearing, and flickering again. But she no longer felt entwined within it.

It was a sort of blindness—a blankness wrapped in silence, emptiness, separation. The isolation terrified her. She took long, wide breaths to calm herself.

Then she saw it, at the edge of the emptiness.

A little flame.

She gazed at it for a few minutes, its light pure and true.

Yes. It was time.

The decision made, she stood up. She wore a simple tunic and pants and carried only a satchel and a walking stick.

She began to walk toward the little flame.

CHAPTER 10

CHAADI

Shara Forest, Lebanon

Chaadi Darius heard applause and stuck his head out of the communications tent. A woman smiled and beckoned to him. "Come have a look!" she called.

Chaadi grinned. It had taken the better part of three weeks, but the Oxford-based archaeological team had stabilized the entrance point to the temple. He sprinted toward Evelyn Beckwith, the PhD candidate leading the effort, picked her up, and swung her around. "You did it, Evie!"

She laughed as he set her down, then grabbed his arm. "Let's go!"

Chaadi trailed her into Shara Forest. He was still surprised by the dry heat, so different from the cool, wet mountain air that had once pervaded the area, anchored by acres of cedar forest. Now, what little forest remained was under strict protection of the Lebanese government, as well as organizations like UNESCO.

They approached the temple, and Evelyn made her way

down two roughly hewn and uneven steps, gesturing for Chaadi to follow.

He glanced back at the rest of the team setting up the study stations, noting some resentful stares. *Understandable,* he supposed. After all, he was just a volunteer supporting computer connectivity at the site, but his friendship with Evelyn gave him priority access.

Bracing his hands, he stepped down after her, and they both stood before the entrance to a dark chamber. Evelyn leaned forward and beamed the flashlight around.

She gasped. "The chamber—it's intact! Even with all this wreckage outside." She passed him the flashlight and made way for him.

Chaadi's skin prickled in anticipation. Leaning forward, he felt cold, dank air against his face. He swept the beam from left to right and back again. Yes, it was just as he remembered it—a perfectly circular stone chamber, about fifteen feet in diameter, with alcoves carved into the wall at regular intervals. Turning the beam upward, he gazed at the low-domed ceiling, nine feet at its highest point, with an intricate lotus carved at the center. He remembered Grandfather's voice:

Look at the ceiling, Chaadi—that lotus is not native to Lebanon. Can you guess the origin of the temple's design?

"Coming through!"

Chaadi and Evelyn moved to either side so that the lighting specialist could pass through with floor spotlights. As they waited, Chaadi peered inside with the flashlight. He could almost see his eight-year-old self, learning from Grandfather how to sit cross-legged in a meditation posture, with his palms turned upward on his thighs. Of course, he'd fidgeted like a typical child, but Grandfather had never reprimanded him, only offered encouragement.

Don't worry, it will come with time and with practice. For now, just sit and watch your breath. Remember what the Seven Sages taught: turn inward for stability, balance, wisdom.

A click sounded as the floor lights illuminated.

"Come on," Evelyn said, stepping over the threshold. Chaadi followed, and people entered behind them, discussing schedules, photography, documentation. He walked the chamber perimeter, as Evelyn issued instructions. Chaadi knew she wanted to complete the basic setup before the local crew demanded time off for lunch.

Again, Grandfather's voice echoed in his head. *This is a special place, Chaadi. The Seven Sages journeyed from the Himalayas, spreading their wisdom and building these temples all over the world. I am the caretaker of this one, and you will be the caretaker after me.*

I don't understand, Grandfather. Why is the temple special?

I'll explain when you're older.

But it was not to be. Suddenly, Chaadi could not catch his breath. *Oh no.* He recognized the signs of a panic attack, seeing fire in his mind's eye, hearing explosions. *Deep breaths. Deep breaths. It happened a long time ago. It's not happening now.*

***

Grandfather burst into the house and grabbed his hand. Together, they rushed to the temple, with twelve-year-old Chaadi asking questions the whole way. His grandfather, wheezing as he ran, couldn't respond.

When they entered the chamber, Grandfather spoke at last, between heaving breaths. "Chaadi, dear child, I wish

I'd told you everything sooner, and now there's no time."
Dragging Chaadi to the wall, he pointed to an indentation
and knelt next to it. "Do you remember the Earth mantra I
taught you?"

"Yes."

"Watch." Grandfather bent close to the indentation, whispered the mantra, and pointed.

Chaadi's mouth dropped as a red marking revealed itself
on the wall, then faded after a few seconds. "What was that?"
he asked, wide-eyed.

An explosion sounded outside the temple, and they both
turned toward the sound. "What's happening?" Chaadi gasped.

"Listen carefully, Chaadi—someone is trying to destroy this
place. I have to stop them."

"What do you mean?"

"You do it—say the mantra—right now." Chaadi knelt and
whispered the mantra just as his grandfather had done, and
watched the marking reappear.

"Good. If something happens to me, you need to find them.
Promise me," he demanded, pointing to the marking.

"I don't understand, Grandfather—find what?"

"Promise me!"

"Yes, I promise, but what am I supposed to—"

Another explosion sounded, louder this time. Chaadi
jumped. His grandfather looked at the chamber entrance, panic
in his eyes, then pulled Chaadi forward.

"Look here—it's a false wall. See the passageway? Go all the
way through—run fast, then climb the steps at the end. Don't
stop until you're outside. Go—go now."

"But . . . but aren't you coming with me?"

The explosions became deafening.

"Now!"

Chaadi ran down the passageway but stopped short. I must go back for Grandfather. *He heard cracking noises and looked around in dismay.* What if the tunnel collapses while I'm inside? *Sprinting to the end, he raced up the steps and emerged into the open air. Turning, he saw fire erupt and heard a thunder of sound. The entire structure shuddered, and Chaadi watched the surrounding trees and rocks launch into the air and collapse upon it.*

He screamed. "Grandfather!"

***

"Are you okay, Chaadi?"

He gulped and opened his eyes. Evelyn was kneeling beside him. He realized he'd been crouching on the floor. Catching his breath, he exhaled and stood unsteadily. "Yes, fine," he murmured.

Evelyn's eyes showed curiosity and concern. "Why don't you go get some rest? We're closing down for the day anyway. I hoped we could start again in the evening, but the local crew wants to wait till tomorrow. It's been a hard month of excavation—everyone could use a break, I think. But I'm so excited!"

Chaadi smiled at her enthusiasm.

"Evelyn!" a voice called from the entrance. "Margo says we have to move the photography area. Would you come have a look?"

"Be right there." She stood up, then turned to Chaadi again. "Meet me outside, okay?"

Chaadi nodded and watched her walk toward the entrance. Moving along the wall, he looked for the indentation he remembered. *There.* Kneeling in front of it, he glanced behind him to ensure that nobody was watching, then whispered:

samudravasane devi
parvatastanamaṇḍale
viṣṇupatni namastubhyaṃ
pādasparśaṃ kṣamasva me.

He smiled as a red marking became visible, just as he remembered. Pulling out his cell phone, he took a photo as it began to fade. *Got it.*

He thought about his escape on that terrible day, fifteen years ago. Was the back passageway still there, or had it caved in during the explosion? He stood and began to look for it.

"Coming, Chaadi?" Evelyn's voice sounded from the entrance. "Margo's shutting off the lights."

Next time, he thought.

***

Back in the tent he was sharing with Evelyn, he turned on the miniature generator, opened his laptop, and pulled up CloseView, the new application that archaeologists used for detailed examination of artifacts. He hesitated a few moments before uploading the photo he'd taken.

Was he really going to do this—open the door to the worst day of his life? As the explosions sounded again in his mind, he squeezed his eyes shut, then sighed. The memory—and his panic—had returned more and more frequently over the years, demanding his attention.

His English mother and Lebanese father had met in college, married at the local chapel, and moved to Beirut. After both died in an automobile accident, Chaadi, at age five, had moved in with his grandfather in a small mountain town bordering Shara Forest.

Chaadi had loved living with his gentle grandfather. At times, he thought Grandfather's death had affected him even more than his parents' had, due to its utter inexplicability. No one had ever given Chaadi a reason for the explosions.

Within a week, Chaadi had been sent to Croydon, England, to live with his mother's great-aunt, a brusque woman who'd urged him, at age twelve, to put the past behind him. While grateful that she'd opened her home to him, Chaadi had done everything he could to leave it as soon as possible, graduating early from school and attending Oxford with the help of scholarship money and income from a patchwork of local jobs.

He'd studied complex computer networks, intuitively grasping the rapidly evolving field, then dropped out of college, finding plenty of consulting work without a degree. Whatever his sharp intelligence did not bring him, his charm and good looks seemed to supply, including a wide circle of friends. Per his aunt's advice, he'd put the past behind him.

Or so he'd thought.

One night three years ago, at a concert with his then girlfriend, a stereo speaker had malfunctioned and burst into flames. Chaadi had sunk to his knees in terror, struggling to breathe. He'd had panic attacks before, but this was by far the worst. After three more incidents in as many weeks, he'd sought a therapist.

The therapist had suggested that his unwillingness to face his past might be contributing to his panic attacks. He'd begun to wonder again about the events of that day in 2025, and about his grandfather's mandate: *You need to find them.*

Beep.

Chaadi looked up. The upload was complete. It had taken much longer than expected—probably some issue with the satellite uplink. Taking a deep breath, he enlarged the photograph on the screen, looking closely at the red marking.

Was it a symbol?

No, it had the look of letters—but not in any script he recognized.

What now?

He pondered. The lotus carving. The Sages. The Himalayas. The mantra.

Sanskrit. It must be Sanskrit. Even though he'd learned the Earth mantra verbally from Grandfather, he'd never seen it written. Chaadi pulled up Sanskrit alphabet charts on a university website, and his face fell.

No, they weren't Sanskrit letters.

Sighing, he continued to scroll through the website, reading about notations used during the time India was a trade and economic powerhouse, before colonists had descended upon it like locusts.

A trade and economic powerhouse . . .

What if they were numbers?

Locating a table of Sanskrit numerical notation, he looked again at the marking and grinned.

Yep!

Three *numbers*, stacked vertically.

One.

Zero.

Eight.

CHAPTER 11

CHAADI

Chaadi referred to the table of numbers again. Yes, he'd gotten it correct, but "108" didn't mean anything to him.

Might as well start at the beginning. He scanned the Google references—mostly articles on India, Hinduism, and yoga philosophy: 108 sacred texts called the Upanishads, 108 beads on a prayer garland, 108 energy points within the human body.

All intriguing, but nothing explaining why the number was associated with this temple—or why it was significant in the first place.

He leaned back and closed his eyes, trying to recall whether Grandfather had ever mentioned it, but the only number he could recall was "seven"—the Seven Sages. Searching again, he learned that seven sages were mentioned in myths and legends all over the world, from Egypt to China, Greece to India, usually as keepers of ancient wisdom.

His grandfather's story had jibed with one of the Indian versions of the legend—that the Sages had come from the

Himalayas and traveled all over the world, sharing the wisdom of their teacher, the First Yogi, and building temples like the one Evelyn had just excavated.

Chaadi sighed. What did any of that have to do with the number "108"?

He set the laptop next to him and lay back on the canvas cot with his arms behind his head. *Find them,* his grandfather had said. What had he meant? Was he telling Chaadi to find more numbers?

There wasn't enough information, and he didn't know where to look next. Perhaps he should return to the temple, look for other markings, other clues. He didn't think Evelyn would mind if he went back to the site on his own.

Where was she anyway? Probably conferring with the rest of the team, and he didn't want to disturb her. Regardless, he knew the location of the main light switch at the site—he'd seen Margo disconnect it on the way out.

Opening the flaps of the tent, Chaadi looked around but saw no one. Those not involved in a meeting were probably getting a bite to eat or some well-deserved rest. He stepped outside. The wind had kicked up, and at last he felt some coolness and a touch of moisture in the air.

At the temple site, he made his way down the makeshift stairwell fashioned by the crew. Reconnecting the switch for one of the floor lights, he stepped over the threshold and looked again at the walls and dome. How fortunate that the chamber had survived the initial blast back in 2025—and what a testament to ancient engineering.

He returned to the place where he'd seen the marking. Kneeling in the correct spot, he whispered the mantra. The marking appeared as expected.

Chaadi bent closely to examine it before it faded. Were there any other markings near it? No, nothing he could detect, but maybe—

"How do you know about the marking?" The voice was gruff, gravelly.

Chaadi jumped up and spun around. A petite Indian woman in her forties stood there, staring at him. Her body seemed composed entirely of angles, her figure wiry, her facial bones prominent. He met her eyes, and her glare seemed to pin him in place and render him silent.

"Are you one of them?" The question sounded more like a demand.

"One of whom?" Chaadi asked.

She didn't wait for an answer. She lunged toward him and grabbed the side of his neck.

"Hey, what are you doing?" he choked out, struggling to throw her off, shocked at the thin woman's strength. Despite his efforts, she plunged her thumb at an angle into the side of his neck. Chaadi gasped and fell to his knees, unable to speak.

Leaning over him, the woman raised her arm again. Was she going to kill him? With effort, he tried to maneuver away from her, when a loud sound made both of them turn toward the entrance.

The woman sprang up and stood above him. Chaadi cowered as he waited for the next blow, but nothing happened. When he looked up again, he was alone. *Where did she go?* He saw a quick motion several feet away. She'd gone down the old passageway!

How had she known about it?

Chaadi froze. Explosions again, coming closer and closer. He looked up as the entryway shattered. Was this really happening again? He fell to his side and curled into a ball as the sounds around him grew more deafening. Dirt and stone began to dislodge from the dome and fall onto his face, and he blinked to clear his eyes.

No. I can't do it. I can't go through this again.

Gathering his strength and struggling to his feet, Chaadi turned toward the stairwell he'd come through. It was fully blocked. He'd have to find the back passageway again. But was it still open at the other end? He gasped, hearing another explosion.

He had no choice.

Coughing, he stumbled in the direction the woman had gone, looking for the point of entry.

There!

He sprinted through the passageway, looking back at the clouds of reddish smoke advancing toward him. His eyes widened in shock when he saw a wall looming in front of him, rather than the steps he remembered. Reaching the wall, he banged on it frantically. Looking backward, he felt the tunnel shudder.

Chaadi turned to the wall again. There had to be a way out—there had to be. After all, the woman who'd attacked him had used the same passageway, and she wasn't there now.

His eye caught a shaft of light to the side. *So that's how she got out.*

Chaadi dashed toward it, climbed up over the rock, and squeezed through a narrow hole. He emerged from the tunnel, gagging from the smoke. He tripped and hit his head, and the world went dark.

***

Chaadi groaned as his eyes regained focus. Struggling, he sat up, rubbing his neck where the bony woman had jabbed him and his head where it had hit the ground. How long had he been unconscious?

His ears were ringing. He sat up stiffly, holding his left arm, which must have taken the brunt of the fall. Blinking, he looked around. He was on his cot, back in his tent. How had he gotten here?

He turned toward the other cot and took in a breath. Evelyn was sitting there, watching him with a look he couldn't interpret.

"Are you okay?" Her words had an edge to them.

"Evelyn, there was a woman there! I was looking around the temple, and . . ."

"Yes, I know, Chaadi. I was there when you spoke with the security officers and the police."

"Police? I spoke to the police?"

"You really can't remember?"

He shook his head. "Evie, what happened?"

She looked at him for a moment without speaking. "Someone planted old mining explosives. I didn't know those existed anymore—there's nothing left to mine. I don't know how they did it without our noticing. You mentioned a woman, but they can't find anyone matching your description."

"Is it—the temple—is it . . ."

Evelyn dropped her head. When she spoke, her voice broke. "The temple's gone, Chaadi, all of it. The entire inner structure collapsed."

Oh no. He lay back on the cot, bringing the heels of his hands to his eyes. *It's gone. The temple's gone.* He'd been working his way back to it for three years, sure that it held something for him—resolutions, answers.

"Chaadi, you should have told me that you witnessed an explosion as a kid and that your grandfather died because of it. I spent months researching events in this area, but that explosion was never officially recorded." Evelyn's voice lowered as she spoke, almost to herself. "I wonder if Dr. Das knew about it. Maybe that's why he . . ." Her voice trailed off.

"Wait, who?"

"Mohan Das, from the University of Chennai. I told you about him. He's on that joint commission—the one that gave us so much trouble about excavating. Professor Tauck had to pull strings to move the project forward quietly."

"But how did *you* know about that first explosion?" He choked a bit. "And about my grandfather?"

She gave him a sharp look. "Chaadi, you just explained everything to that officer—how you escaped through the tunnel you remembered from 2025. And then I helped you back to the tent."

"I can't seem to remember."

Evelyn crossed her arms, and her voice hardened. "You used me, Chaadi. You steered me toward this site without telling me you had your own agenda. That you were trying to figure out your own family history."

"Evie, I didn't use you—at least, well, I didn't mean to. I thought we both had something to gain. I could learn about my past, and you could get original research for your doctorate."

"Well, congratulations. Now neither of us will get what we want."

"What do you mean?"

"The site's been closed off. Permanently. The Lebanese government is sending us home, and they're mad as hell—another chunk of the cedar forest was destroyed because of the explosion. Our team is salvaging whatever equipment it can."

"I'm so sorry—I didn't mean for any of this to happen. I never thought . . ." He stopped, seeing her tears and feeling her frustration. He felt horrible.

She came to stand in front of him. "Why did you think you couldn't tell me? You didn't have to manipulate me—I would have helped you, and . . ." She broke off and stared at him. "You know what? It doesn't matter. I want you to leave. Roger will have the jeep ready in an hour, to take you back to Beirut. You can catch a flight home from there."

"Okay, Evie. Okay." He groaned as he pulled his aching body to standing, and he reached toward her, taking her hand. "I really am sorry."

She pulled her hand away, turned, and exited their tent. Chaadi dropped back to the cot.

How could he make Evelyn understand? He couldn't possibly have shared with her what had happened to him as a child. It was a kernel deep within him, and the rest of his life had layered upon it. It was *his* story. He'd wanted to unearth it, to rediscover his connection to Grandfather, to understand what had happened and what he'd been tasked with.

But he'd failed.

CHAPTER 12

CHAADI

With his duffel now packed, Chaadi opened his knapsack and began collecting his electronics. As he reached for his laptop, his finger grazed the screen, and the display revealed the search results for "108"—a search now at an end.

How could he learn the connection between "108" and the temple if the temple had been destroyed?

He thought of the woman who had attacked him. Would the police find her? Had she planted the explosives, and if so, why had she done it? And could she be connected to the first explosion, back in 2025, as well? She'd known about the back passageway, after all.

Chaadi looked toward the tent flaps, still open after Evelyn's exit. Remorse and disappointment gripped him. She was right, and he had to be honest with himself. He'd manipulated her into studying the temple for his own reasons.

Three years ago, he'd left his therapist's office convinced that facing the past could quell his panic attacks, feeling ready to try. Almost immediately, his phone had beeped an alumni notification for an Oxford lecture on Lebanon's depleted cedar forests, including Shara Forest near his childhood home.

It had seemed like a sign.

At the lecture, he'd met Evelyn Beckwith, an archaeology graduate student who'd asked so many questions of the presenter that the audience had begun to groan. Afterward, he'd charmed her into joining him for coffee and learned she was seeking a new direction for her research.

Did you know there was a temple on the edge of that same cedar forest? he'd asked. *I grew up near it.* She'd been intrigued at first, then fascinated as she'd heard more. Within a month, she was tapping into Oxford's considerable resources and contacts to further her research. Despite those contacts, she'd had to battle for permission to excavate.

Why had that professor whom Evelyn mentioned, Mohan Das, worked against the excavation? And was it possible the professor had known about the first explosion in 2025, as she'd speculated?

Chaadi looked at his watch. He still had twenty minutes before the jeep departed. Pulling up the University of Chennai website, he found the man's profile page: "Professor of Ecological and Environmental Anthropology." Chaadi hadn't realized that such a field existed—exploring the relationship between people and the physical environment. Chaadi read further; the professor's main area of interest was agricultural impacts upon forests and soil over time.

Das's list of papers and prizes was impressive, not to mention his various board and commission memberships. Chaadi scanned the long list and then saw it: Joint Commission on World Climate Defense. Evelyn had mentioned a commission resisting the temple excavation; this must have been the one, given that Das was a member.

Chaadi completed the online contact form: "Professor Das: Could we speak about the temple excavation near Shara Forest in Lebanon? It's urgent." After sending the inquiry, he sat looking at the "Message Sent" screen. Chaadi doubted that the professor would answer anytime soon; he'd have to keep checking his email during the trip back to England.

As if in response to his pessimism, his laptop beeped within a few minutes. Maybe his luck was changing.

> TO: Chaadi Darius
> FROM: Professor Mohan Das
>
> I am available at this link now.

Chaadi clicked through immediately. After a few seconds, an Indian man in his sixties appeared on the screen, portly and balding, yet dignified looking.

"Mr. Darius, listen to me." The man's expression was severe, his voice cold. "I'm the head of the joint commission. After we evaluated your excavation proposal, we concluded that the environmental impact would outweigh any cultural benefits." His voice grew icier. "As I've told your team—*repeatedly*—this excavation cannot proceed. We will not change our decision, and you need to stop inquiring."

Chaadi was confused. Clearly, the man's information was not up-to-date. "Well, sir, the excavation already started, and—"

"*What?* Are you sure?"

"Uh, yes, almost a month ago."

Das jumped up and began to pace. "I should have gone to Lebanon to make sure." He began muttering to himself. "I should have gone myself—why, why didn't I?"

Chaadi was taken aback. When Evelyn told him that Professor Das had resisted the excavation, Chaadi had assumed academic or organizational politics were at play. But this man seemed genuinely distressed, as though the news affected him personally.

"Professor Das . . ." Chaadi stopped, feeling reluctant to upset the man further. "I hate to tell you this, but you should know there's been an explosion, and . . . and the temple's been destroyed . . . completely. The entire inner chamber." Chaadi's voice caught, pain and disappointment sharp in his belly.

Das gasped and, for a few moments, did not seem able to speak. He placed a hand on his desk, as though trying to steady himself. "How did it happen?" he murmured.

"We're not sure. The authorities are looking into it. There was a series of blasts, just like, just like . . ." Chaadi couldn't finish, feeling his gut tighten.

Das dropped his head into his hands. "I was afraid this could happen. You don't know what you've done."

"But . . ." Chaadi wasn't sure what to say. He had so many questions for this man but doubted he'd receive answers right now. He waited a minute before speaking again. "Um, Professor . . . ?"

At last, Das lifted his head and spoke harshly. "How dare you circumvent the commission's decision? You people think you have the right to go anywhere you want and take anything you want. Some things should not be poked and prodded by those who don't understand—academicians like you who want to analyze them from a position of superiority—"

"Wait, wait a minute, Professor. I assure you, this team isn't like that—I know their leader personally, and she's dedicated to learning from ancient structures. Anyway, I'm just a volunteer—and it's definitely more than an academic interest for me."

Das's forehead wrinkled. "What do you mean?"

Chaadi took a breath. "Sir, do you know anything about '108'?"

Das froze. "What did you say?"

"There was a marking inside the temple. Please, just have a look—I'm opening the file in this telelink now."

Chaadi watched as Das examined the file. He could tell the man was trying to compose his face into calmer lines, but his agitation was apparent.

"How . . . how did you know about the marking?"

"My grandfather taught me how to reveal it, just before he died. I came back here to try to understand his last words to me, to understand why the temple was so important to him, and—"

"Your grandfather?" Das looked disbelieving.

"Caveh Darius. He was my father's father." Chaadi saw the recognition on the man's face. "You knew him, didn't you?" Chaadi asked excitedly. *How wonderful to meet an acquaintance of Grandfather's!*

"I knew *of* him."

"Oh." Chaadi's face fell. "But you *do* know about my grandfather's connection to the temple, don't you? You know about the explosion back in 2025? The one that killed him?"

"Yes, I do—a terrible tragedy." He lowered his voice. "But I'm not at liberty to talk about it."

"What do you mean? Please listen, Professor Das. I was there during the explosion. Just before my grandfather died, he told me to 'find them.' And I think it has something to do with '108.'"

When Das still wouldn't answer, Chaadi felt exasperated but tried to convey his sincerity and earnestness. "I assure you that I'm just trying to understand. My grandfather was the caretaker of the temple and told me that I was supposed to take his place afterward."

Das appraised Chaadi closely and, after a brief silence, seemed to come to a decision. "I know someone who can give you some answers. But you'll have to come here to meet him. To India."

"Meet whom? Who is he?"

For some reason, Das lowered his voice until it became barely audible. "His name is Aatmanji."

CHAPTER 13

AATMANJI

Campsite, Western Ghats, India

Aatmanji and Aanvi looked up as a girl about fifteen years old rushed into their midst, panting from her sprint. Aatmanji smiled at her. "What is it, Lali?"

"Aatmanji," the girl said, recovering her breath and extending an arm toward him. "There's a call on the satellite phone."

"Who is it?"

"It's Professor Das."

Aatmanji frowned. He took the phone from Lali and waited for her to move a sufficient distance away.

"Mohan, what is it?"

"Aatmanji . . ."

He could hear the distress in Mohan Das's voice, and he tensed.

"It's the Shara temple. They've excavated it . . . and the inner chamber's been destroyed."

"What? How can that be?" After the explosion in 2025, the unit's engineers had examined the site and determined that the inner chamber had remained intact within the wreckage.

They'd left it alone, with the intention to return and reenter the chamber at the right time.

"The chamber was intact when they started. But there was a *second* explosion yesterday. I've been trying to get through to you."

"A second explosion . . . ?"

"Apparently, a woman was present just beforehand. I've been following the investigation, but they haven't been able to find her."

"Do you think she was responsible?"

"I don't know." The professor groaned. "Can you believe it, Aatmanji? They started excavating, despite the commission's decision and without my knowledge. I should have gone to Shara myself. I could have stopped them—or done *something*. That was my task, and you trusted me."

"Mohan, please calm down. We're all doing our best—and if someone intentionally harmed the site, what could you have done? Anyway, there's something larger at play right now, and we just don't understand it yet."

"What about the other site—"

"Let's not discuss that right now."

"Understood." Das paused. "Aatmanji . . ."

Aatmanji sensed his hesitation. "What is it?"

"I'm bringing someone to meet you."

"You're doing what?" he asked, astonished by this breach of protocol. The unit always kept his location—in fact, his existence—a secret.

"He was volunteering with the excavation team, and—"

"One of the excavators? Oh, Mohan, why would you bring him to us?"

"Wait—please listen. He knew about the marking. He showed me a photo he took before the temple was destroyed."

When Aatmanji didn't answer, Das continued. "Don't you understand? He *knew* how to reveal it."

"Mohan, how could he possibly . . . ?"

"He's Caveh Darius's grandson. His name is Chaadi."

Aatmanji drew in a breath. "Do you believe him?"

"I talked to him, and I do. You won't believe the resemblance. And Caveh gave him an instruction—a directive, really. So this is Chaadi's legacy, too."

"I see. Okay, Mohan, contact Bose to coordinate your arrival."

"Yes, Aatmanji."

Aatmanji discontinued the call and looked toward Aanvi, who had been listening to his end of the conversation.

"The Shara temple?" she questioned.

He looked at her, nodded, and relayed Das's information.

Aanvi was silent for a few seconds. "We always thought that temple would be there when we needed it—and we really need it now." She sighed.

"I know, my dear, I know."

After a few minutes, Aanvi spoke again. "Did you know Caveh Darius had a grandson?"

Aatmanji shook his head.

"He may have a part to play in all this." Aanvi looked at Aatmanji and spoke pointedly. "Events are coming to a head. You see it, don't you?" He nodded, knowing where her words were leading. "As I told you, it's time—time for you to contact Bayla. We need to bring her here and tell her everything."

When he didn't respond, she touched his shoulder. "Aatmanji? Did you hear me?"

He looked at her. Technically, they were coleaders of this unit, but she'd absorbed most of that responsibility so he could travel between the units. It suited Aanvi, the mantle of leadership, with her regal bearing and her strength and wisdom.

He took her hand and pulled her palm to his cheek. Aanvi looked surprised for a moment, then closed her eyes, relaxing into his touch. They'd decided not to marry, for a variety of reasons.

When she opened her eyes, her expression was gentle but expectant.

At last, Aatmanji spoke. "Can we risk it, Aanvi? You said they shouldn't come together—she and Daksha."

"They won't. We can't even *find* Daksha."

"And is it safe for me to contact her again?"

Aanvi closed her eyes, and he watched with an admiration bordering on awe. Aanvi possessed an ability of the Ancients, an ability that had provided their unit with special insights, that had guided them through many dilemmas.

"Yes," she said at last. "The timing is correct."

Aatmanji watched Aanvi rise to her feet. She was tall and large boned and moved with fluidity and grace. She looked down, where he was still seated. "And it's time you relocated, Aatmanji—for your own safety. You've spent far too long in one place."

"Yes, I know. I'll leave tonight."

"I'll join you tomorrow. Goodbye, my . . . friend." She stepped off the straw mat.

"Aanvi." She turned back with a questioning look. He lowered his voice. "I'll miss you."

The corners of her mouth turned up a bit, and she spoke equally softly. "What's gotten into you today?"

He sighed. "Thinking about all the choices I've made."

CHAPTER 14

AP WIRE

NEW AGROCHEMICAL GARNERS CRITICISM

NEW DELHI, INDIA. Formula FZ5, touted
by global chemical conglomerate
ZedChem as a miracle aid for the
planet's remaining farmland, encountered immediate public-relations
trouble after its test pour on the
agricultural areas bordering Prithvi
Forest and Vayu City in southwestern
India.

The test pour was conducted by
ForwardChem, ZedChem's newest subsidiary. Just before resigning,
ForwardChem's chief chemical engineer, Dr. Jala Sharma, released a
series of reports on FZ5's toxicity
and apparent dangers.

ZedChem spokesperson Lyn Tran continues to assert that FZ5 will revolutionize modern agriculture, forcing the planet's remaining agricultural land to produce more food, more quickly. "This formula is a godsend. The global food crisis is accelerating, and ZedChem is the only company doing something about it."

By contrast, Dr. Sharma urged ZedChem to "keep this agrochemical off the market until extensive testing can be conducted. Not only does the formula render farmland useless after a few years, it also sinks into the mycelial layers of forests, eventually killing them. We have a responsibility to . . ."

———

AGROSCIENCE NEWS

SHARMA'S DATA VINDICATED

Our team has found the data on FZ5, released by ForwardChem's former chief chemical engineer, Dr. Jala Sharma, to be substantiated and credible.

FZ5 is demonstrably detrimental—and, ultimately, fatal—to the health

of soil, specifically the mycelial
layer undergirding the forests.
Ignoring this data would be foolish
and self-destructive.

Given what we've learned, allowing this chemical to be dispensed
throughout the world without additional testing would be an outrageous
. . .

CHAPTER 15

ZED

ZedChem branch outside Vayu City, India

Jala Sharma had been a wrench in the works.

Within minutes after the test pour, the chemical engineer had released negative reports about FZ5, and the information had traveled globally with alarming speed.

Sharma's stellar credentials had made her a natural hire for this new branch of ZedChem, but she'd apparently suffered a crisis of conscience, disregarding his ironclad rule against revealing company research. Now, because of this whistleblower, he'd had to re-vet all ZedChem employees and triple physical and network security worldwide. It was a time intensive and costly process.

Zed grabbed the arm of the blond woman standing next to him and swung her toward the EtherScreen projection. "Look—look there—or are you blind?" Marja flinched and cowered.

"I know," she whispered. "I am trying to work faster, but—"

"What?" he barked. "Speak up. Why am I still seeing so much positive press about Jala Sharma?" He pointed at a list of scientific articles referencing Sharma's research and denouncing FZ5.

Of course, given the toxicity levels of all ZedChem formulas, he expected negative press. In fact, he had as many employees assigned to disinformation deployment as to product development. Each new formula was launched with a proactive campaign to dilute facts and defuse public indignation.

There were so many ways to derail opposition—denying toxicity with false proof, directing attention to irrelevant issues, defaming those who disagreed.

Zed released Marja's arm and stretched his neck and shoulders forward, trying to suppress the spasms in his upper back—he knew they would migrate and worsen as the hours progressed.

He gritted his teeth. Until now, everything had proceeded like clockwork. For the past ten years, FZ5 had been developed in closely guarded secrecy. In the meantime, he'd established ZedChem infrastructure in twenty locations worldwide, negotiating with or threatening or bribing governments and private industry, as needed.

He'd invested more than half of his wealth in FZ5, but it would be worth it in the end.

Zed had overseen the test pour himself, right here in southwestern India. He'd witnessed the media celebration—with the help of his staff—of FZ5's promise to save the world's food supply.

Now, though, his disinformation team was working frantically to defuse Jala Sharma's published data and analysis. Moreover, Marja had not moved quickly enough to attack Jala personally. It was this last area in which Marja usually excelled—character assassination. Indeed, Jala Sharma's reputation should have been shattered by now.

He pondered Marja's lagging competence—perhaps it was time to . . . redistribute her. But she had other uses—specifically, taking care of his physical needs. He could obtain women anywhere, but it was convenient to have someone at his beck and call.

Zed now eyed her with distaste. She was gaining weight, pushing out of her tight clothes. Again, he grabbed her arm, shaking her, but she knew better than to cry out. "You have one job. Destroy Jala Sharma's reputation. Go do it." She nodded and scurried toward the door.

He watched Marja leave, his eyes narrowing. Perhaps there was an easier way to deal with Jala Sharma. He would talk to his security detail.

Zed stood to stretch, pushing his neck forward, unable to relieve the pain in his back. He gripped the edge of his desk as his spasms rekindled and surged through his torso. *Fight,* he thought to himself. *Fight the pain.*

He'd been diagnosed with reflex sympathetic dystrophy in his early teen years. At the time, he'd recovered physically from a bad fall down a staircase resulting in multiple broken bones, but his pain had persisted. According to the doctors, it was an autoimmune disorder, but Zed had come to think of it less like a disease and more like an enemy inhabiting him. He wanted to shout at it, stab it, kill it.

Doubling over, he gasped as his agony crescendoed. Opening a drawer, he struggled with a syringe and injected himself with shaking hands. After a minute, the pain relented, its peaks softening, and he sat back in his chair, exhausted.

He dropped his head to his desk as a memory came to him: Matej sitting with him during his worst bouts of pain. *I love you, Krak—remember that.*

Zed felt his old anguish spark and meld with the spasms in his body.

In the early 2010s, Father had tasked him and his younger brother, Matej, with establishing ZedChem's Indian operations near Vayu City. They'd struggled for almost five years, encountering one obstacle after another.

Father had berated them mercilessly. *This country is full of farms, and you morons can't turn a profit on agrochemicals.* The curses became a refrain: *You are weak—you are pathetic— you are unworthy of a company like ours.*

But Father had no patience for Zed's pain. The bullying had worn on Zed, making him coil and shrink. Not on Matej, though, who had remained joyful, his laughter light. *Krak, don't listen to Father.*

And then Matej was dead.

One night, to preempt Father's wrath, Matej remained behind in the empty ZedChem building, completing work Zed had left unfinished due to a worse-than-usual attack of spasms. A fire had caught Matej unawares. The entire operation had burned.

Zed had been inconsolable.

Immediately after Matej's death, ZedChem had abandoned its Indian operations, and within a year, Father had died, the last word on his lips directed toward Zed:

Shame.

Zed had taken over his father's company. Given the power of global electronic connectivity, his pain and physical condition had not limited him. He'd pushed ZedChem across the world, deploying newer and faster-acting agrochemicals, doubling, then tripling, the company's reach and profits.

Zed smiled. *FZ5.* With its complicated formulation and intricate dispensing mechanism, it would take at least a decade for another company to reverse engineer it. But they were unlikely to try. Twenty simultaneous chemical pours would activate tens of thousands of contracts across the world and generate a spectacular and swift flow of income to ZedChem.

Within a few years, he'd have wealth beyond anything his father could have imagined. He closed his eyes, relishing what was to come.

But a thought stirred, against his will.

How can I prove myself to a dead man?

CHAPTER 16

AATMANJI

Campsite, Western Ghats, India

Aatmanji sat cross-legged in a meditation posture, his palms resting upward on his thighs. He began to envision a space between himself and the problems pressing on him.

Gradually, he found his way to stillness.

As his perception opened, he observed the threads around him, connecting him to every bit of life on the planet, connecting every human being to one another, though imperceptible to almost all of them. A web of life. A web of light.

As his perception deepened, the supposedly solid objects in his line of sight began to flicker, showing their true composition, the waves of energy and fields of information underlying each particle and cell within them. This was the quantum realm of existence, unreachable by the five basic senses of a human being.

Like Aanvi, Aatmanji had an ability that some of the Ancients had possessed. His was the power to call through that web and communicate with others in simultaneous meditation with him—and sometimes with those who simply possessed deep receptivity. There was no geographic limitation to his ability; physical location was irrelevant in the quantum realm.

But it had been *Daksha's* ability, different from both Aanvi's and his own, that had so profoundly opened up the unit's opportunities for action. Daksha could move freely within that web, gather them all up, and direct them as she pleased. With her, they moved as a collective.

A school of fish.

A swarm of bees.

A flock of birds.

It had empowered them to protect land and forests, soil and water—to do the work to which he'd dedicated his life.

Aatmanji breathed deeply. Soon, he inhabited only the present moment, and there he remained.

When he opened his eyes at last, he relished the feeling of vigor and intensity. It surprised him when people regarded meditation as inertness or passive withdrawal. Those people also seemed to consider a spiritual life as one of retreat and disinterest.

They could not be more wrong.

He was at his most aware, most alive, in a meditative state. And to him, a spiritual life required full and wholehearted engagement with the world, grounded in balance and consciousness and connection.

Aatmanji stood and walked toward the shelter he'd been occupying, in order to pack his few belongings for travel. It would be the latest in a long series of moves between sites, cities, even countries, ever since the first one fifteen years ago, after Tulā School's destruction.

What a terrible year 2025 had been for all of them. Bayla's sudden departure, necessitated by circumstances. The invasion of Tulā School and the loss of so many of their group. The first attack on the Shara temple in Lebanon. All of these had followed the death of Aanvi's brother and sister the preceding year.

Aatmanji saw movement out of the corner of his eye, looked up, and smiled at the man hurrying toward him. Over forty years ago, the unit had helped Bose, a farmer, revitalize the soil on his lands and rebuild its organic content, acre by acre. After passing the farming mantle to his son, Bose had joined Aatmanji's cause. Since then, he'd served Aatmanji with love and dedication, accompanying him wherever and whenever he traveled, attending to his daily routine.

"Ah, perfect timing, my friend. Would you please pack up the jeep? I'd like to leave within the hour." He took Bose's arm. "Come, walk with me so we can plan the next—" Aatmanji stopped short, noticing the anxiety on Bose's face. "Bose, what is it? What's wrong?"

Bose placed a hand on Aatmanji's shoulder. "I came to find you. To tell you."

"Bose, what's happened?"

"We've learned more about the test pour—Associated Press has it now. Aatmanji . . . it's Zed."

The name felt like a jolt in Aatmanji's body. He tried to tamp down the dread welling up inside him. His voice shook. "What do you mean?"

"The new chemical company outside Vayu City—you know, ForwardChem, the one that conducted the test pour. It's actually ZedChem."

"But why didn't we hear about it—why weren't we informed?"

Bose sighed. "Our network of contacts isn't as tight as it used to be—we've lost so many people, and many have become unreliable." He lowered his voice. "And we're worried that some are working against us."

"But didn't government officials notice? They're the ones that ousted ZedChem the first time, and they've kept a watch on incoming chemical operations."

"Things are changing, Aatmanji. You know we don't have the same influence. Many of the officials who helped us back then are gone, and the new ones aren't as sympathetic. It looks like one of them was bribed to let ZedChem into Vayu City under the name of—"

"ForwardChem," Aatmanji finished. Bose nodded.

Aatmanji regarded him. "There's more, isn't there?"

Bose nodded. "We've learned that ZedChem is planning a simultaneous pour of FZ5 in twenty locations around the world."

"My God, Bose!"

Aatmanji knew instantly which twenty locations would be used. They were the locations of units like his that had been fighting for environmental stability and health, battling for clean soil and water. Their efforts had preserved the last remaining topsoil on Earth, the places that could still grow food from the land.

Now FZ5 would destroy that topsoil, then burrow into the world's forests. Topsoil and trees. Without them, the world could not feed itself.

Aatmanji shuddered, remembering his experience of the test pour—the seepage of poison into the underground ecosystem, the gagging and choking of the interchanges that sustained life.

The finality of the silence.

Aatmanji put his hands to his temples, closing his eyes. This had to be it—the catastrophe predicted by the Seven

Sages. It was a tipping point—*the* tipping point—when the accumulation of centuries of reckless disregard would avalanche, sealing humanity's fate.

He knew what was coming. In fact, it had already begun—the population displacements, the mass migrations, the brawling for basic resources like water. But it didn't compare to the conflicts that would occur when the soil was irrevocably lost and food was no longer available, when human beings clawed and clashed for survival.

Aatmanji passed a hand over his forehead. "How much time do we have? Before they pour in those twenty locations?"

Bose looked anguished. "One week."

One week? Aatmanji gaped. So little time.

"Jala Sharma started pushing out scientific data after the test pour to warn the world, but you know what happens these days—her data is already buried in swill."

Aatmanji sighed. Lately, they were addressing one emergency after another. He was so much older now—and much more tired. And his moments of dejection were increasing in frequency. What was the point of continuing this work when people couldn't see a problem or, worse, turned away deliberately?

He looked at Bose—this dear, kind man who'd dedicated himself to Aatmanji's service. He thought of Aanvi, the woman he'd loved for so long. Of young Lali, growing up on a land now dying. Of all the people battling for their own lives, the lives of others, the life of the planet.

He thought of Bayla, his Bayla, named for the fragrant little jasmine varietal that had permeated every corner of Tulā School. Bayla, too, had seemed to be everywhere at once—on the school grounds, in the gardens, by the river, even in the trees.

Humanity was worth saving.

This was the unit's work—this was the crisis they'd prepared for. He turned to Bose, to remind and encourage him, when he saw Aanvi approaching, her expression grim.

"Did something happen?"

"Jala Sharma. They found her . . . body."

That brave woman, their source inside ForwardChem—*No*, he thought grimly, inside *ZedChem*—was dead.

CHAPTER 17

ZED

ZedChem branch outside Vayu City, India

When Zed looked up, he almost jumped in alarm. An Indian woman stood before him, five-and-a-half-feet tall, her physical frame like a blade. He hadn't heard her enter and approach. How had she gotten past his assistant?

Zed examined her face. He knew this woman—yes, he'd met her once before, fifteen years ago, right here in Vayu City. It was as though his memories of the past had conjured her up.

"What are you doing here?" he demanded.

"I want to talk to you." He recalled the jaggedness of her voice, how it seemed to cut her words as she spoke. Her accent contributed to that impression as well, sounding Indian but also stretched and strained by other languages and dialects. "Well? Out with it."

"He's still alive."

"Who are you talking about?"

She pulled out her phone and swept a photo toward him. Zed looked at the image, and a cinder in his mind reignited.

The photo showed a tall, lean man with long limbs and thick, wavy hair.

Aatmanji. How had he escaped?

"When was this photo taken?"

"A few days ago. By my contact."

The man looked almost unchanged. Unconsciously, Zed looked down at his own body, with its stooped shoulders and limbs twisting against themselves. It was the reason he never allowed photographs of himself.

He stood, rage churning in his belly. "How is this possible? I watched Tulā School burn—I watched them all burn."

She merely looked at him.

"So, where is he?"

"I don't know."

Zed bared his teeth and advanced toward her. "Then why did you come here?"

The woman regarded him without emotion. "You can draw him out—I've found his child."

Zed froze. "His child survived, too?"

"I'll tell you where she is, but I want something in return."

Zed raised a brow, waiting. He was unaccustomed to other people setting terms, but this was an unusual situation.

"Kill them both before you pour FZ5 in those twenty locations."

"Why?"

"That isn't your concern."

Zed almost insisted on hearing her reason but reconsidered. What did he care? "Fine. A deal."

She swept him another photo, this one from a website. It was an employee profile for the Environment Wire news agency.

Environment Wire? He returned to his chair, opened

an EtherScreen, and scrolled. Apparently, this agency collected news and data on environmental disasters. Zed almost laughed. *What's the point?* He estimated humanity's end in 120 years or so, given the rate at which protections were being removed and poison was accumulating in the environment, not to mention the disregard of the populace.

He returned to the profile photo, which showed a woman in her midtwenties, with a solemn, almost severe expression in her large, hazel eyes and with thick, black curls captured in a bun at the top of her head. Her South Asian features looked vaguely familiar, but that didn't necessarily mean they'd met, particularly given her location in San Francisco.

"How do you know that this is his child? So many years have passed, and . . ." His voice trailed off, and he squinted again at the photo, enlarging it to look at the pendant at the woman's neck.

He'd seen it before.

***

"Appa, look, look!" A girl, about twelve years old, ran into a room fashioned out of bamboo and thatch, where Zed stood waiting. She stopped short, eyes wary. "Namaste," *she said.* "Where's Appa?"

He stared at her without answering. Then, looking at the girl's hands, he asked, "What are those?"

The girl's large eyes looked troubled, but politeness seemed to overcome her misgivings. She held up six flowers, their petals somewhat crushed from their journey in her embrace, and her enthusiasm returned. "I'm studying the golden ratio. Look! Look at the spirals on the seed heads!"

What nonsense, Zed thought, furrowing his brow and

frowning at the girl. She retreated a few steps, as though he'd pushed her, then turned to leave.

Zed saw a flash of copper. "What's that around your neck?"

The girl turned back to him and touched her pendant. "I-I've always worn it. I think my father gave it to me."

"Your father is Aatmanji?"

She nodded, then ran off.

***

Zed sat, mulling. Somehow, Aatmanji's daughter was alive and well in the US. He looked at the name below the photo: Bayla Jeevan.

"Stasia!" Zed shouted.

She appeared at the door.

"Get Velky on the line."

"Right away, sir."

This time, Aatmanji would experience Zed's pain, enduring the suffering and loss of the one he loved most.

Zed looked at the woman still standing in front of him. "How do I contact you again?" he asked.

"You don't," she replied. "Find them."

He stared as she slipped through the door. He thought of the day they'd met, back in 2025. Then, too, she'd eluded his security detail, as though the angles of her body had pried open the building's cracks and allowed her to slide through.

CHAPTER 18

AATMANJI

Campsite, Western Ghats, India

Aatmanji groaned as he listened to the details—Jala Sharma found in her apartment, hanged, a note typed onto her laptop: "I falsified my data. I'm sorry."

There is no way she authored that note, Aatmanji thought grimly, remembering the principled woman he'd met just after she'd been hired as the chief chemical engineer of the new agrochemical outfit, ForwardChem, being set up outside Vayu City.

***

"I've been in the field for a long time, Aatmanji, and I think there's something wrong with this company's formula. I just started this job, so I haven't seen everything yet, but the data I have seen isn't making sense to me."

"Why do you think they hired you? You're known for supporting responsible agricultural methodologies."

"Honestly, I don't know. Maybe to give them credibility. Regardless, I know of the work you're doing, and I can help you. You need information, and I'm in the position to feed it to you as I learn more."

"No, Jala. I can't risk your safety."

Jala smiled and put a reassuring hand on his shoulder. "That's not your choice to make, Aatmanji."

***

At last, he'd given in.

Aatmanji thought of the messages that had arrived from ForwardChem over the last few months, explaining the nature of FZ5—how it would bond with everything it touched, and how it would seal and burn the mycelial fibers in the soil, causing them to become inert and isolated.

At first, the treated farmlands would produce better than ever, but only for five years or so. After that, all the existing nutrients would be depleted.

But Jala had gotten one piece of information wrong—the one-year timeline until the test pour. Why hadn't she been informed about the change? Had the company become suspicious of her?

Aatmanji sighed. *A courageous woman.*

The quickness and brutality of her death, the shattering of her reputation at the same time—all matched what he knew of ZedChem and the man at its helm. He shuddered, thinking of how many in their unit had died during the burning of Tulā School in 2025, for Zed's vengeance.

Aatmanji sighed. The human beings in the most pain, suffering the most anguish, were the ones who unleashed the greatest destruction and damage on the world around them. It had been true throughout human history.

And now, Jala was dead.

Aatmanji's stomach prickled.

Bayla.

Could she be in danger again? Zed had reentered southwestern India, more powerful than ever, his eyes and ears trained outward. Information had always had a way of finding Zed. What if Zed had also discovered that he and, more importantly, Bayla were still alive?

***

Aatmanji strode past bamboo dwellings and classrooms, observing students in various stages of yoga and meditation practice, hearing the clack and clang of kalaripayattu *sparring in the distance. He'd been informed that someone was waiting to speak to him in his quarters.*

When he arrived, he was startled to find a giant of a man stationed in front, with a red-blue scar reaching from forehead to chin. The bulk at the man's side suggested a weapon. He watched Aatmanji through narrowed eyes, but did not speak.

Aatmanji edged by the giant and stepped onto the sunny veranda of his quarters, where another man waited. He, too, was broad shouldered but, unlike the guard outside, stooped over and ill at ease. Pain exuded from his limbs and his face— indeed, it was palpable.

Aatmanji observed him for a moment, suspecting an autoimmune disorder. "Thank you for waiting. Won't you join me?" He gestured toward a caned chair and seated himself on another.

The man remained standing and staring. "You? You're Aatmanji?" Contempt dripped from his voice.

"Yes, I am."

"A teacher—of yoga—in the forest," Zed stated flatly, gesturing toward the bamboo walls and thatched roof.

"That's not inaccurate. And you are?"

At last the man lowered himself onto the other chair. "Krakun Zed. Of ZedChem."

Aatmanji tried not to betray anything on his face, but wasn't successful.

"You know of me. I can tell."

Aatmanji nodded briefly.

"You worked against me and my company. You drove me out of the country years ago. Admit it."

Aatmanji chose his words with care. "We'd been working for decades to reclaim the organic content of our soil and to increase its square footage. We were retraining our farmers and educating the public and assisting the government. So when your company arrived, we didn't want to restart the downward spiral."

Zed looked unimpressed. "Is that a yes?"

Aatmanji took a breath. "In short, yes. We did everything we could to push you out because you have no right to poison what all of us use—what belongs to every living creature on the planet."

"You think that justified destroying my personal property?"

Puzzlement swept across Aatmanji's face. "What do you mean?"

"You set a fire at our factory."

"We heard there was a fire, but we certainly didn't set it. We were surveilling that day, and—"

"So, you were on the premises."

"Yes, but—"

"You set the fire that killed my brother. You burned him to death in the middle of the night." The man's face crumpled for a moment, then smoothed. "He died a horrifying death. And I've learned that you are the one responsible."

"Mr. Zed, I'm deeply sorry for the loss of your brother, but I assure you that we had nothing to do with—"

"Shut up." The words sliced the air between them.

Aatmanji looked at Zed with compassion. "Your brother's death was a tragedy. Let me—"

"I said, shut up."

Aatmanji remained silent.

Zed looked at the wall and spoke under his breath. "My brother . . . when Father was—" Zed stopped short, his entire body curling inward as though withstanding a series of shocks.

Aatmanji tried to keep pity out of his eyes. "Perhaps we should talk again at a later time, when you're feeling . . . better."

Zed shot him a look full of hatred. The two men regarded each other for a few moments, and then Zed spoke.

"You killed the only person I loved. You may think you're safe in your little school in the forest, but listen to me. I know who you are. I know where you live. There's no safe place on Earth for you anymore. For any of you." He paused. "Or for your charming daughter."

Aatmanji froze.

Zed looked as though he was enjoying Aatmanji's shock. "Oh, yes, I met your child. So pretty." He pointed at the giant standing at the entrance. "Imagine what he might do to a little girl." He leaned toward Aatmanji and lowered his voice. "I promise, the worst you can imagine—it will be even worse than that."

Aatmanji stared at Zed, his face aghast.

***

Aatmanji shuddered, remembering the threat Zed had directed at Bayla long ago. He couldn't allow Bayla to come to harm, and he'd sent her away the next morning.

Now he felt the same sense of urgency in his gut. *Can this be happening again?*

He looked up and saw Aanvi's direct gaze, and he nodded his head as if in answer. He picked up the satellite phone, stepped away from the others, and dialed a number he knew by heart.

A calm voice answered the phone. "This is Aki Nakamura of the Advanced Technology Agency. How may I help you?"

"Code 789314."

"I'll connect you with the general right away."

As Aatmanji waited, he considered the hundred ways he'd justified—and tortured himself for—his decision to send Bayla away, as well as his decision to involve General Edmond Cartwright in his problems. Cartwright had provided a strategic advantage—he had hidden Bayla well, providing her a new surname and identity.

But he'd also demanded information that Aatmanji had been reluctant to reveal.

A resonant voice boomed over the line. "Hello, my friend. It's been a long time. Too long."

"Hello, Edmond."

"You have some timing—I was just about to call you."

That can't be good, Aatmanji thought, considering all the events coming together over the past days. "Why?"

"You know I set up some alerts when I constructed an identity for Bayla all those years ago. I receive a ping when someone tries to access her driver's license, credit reports, that sort of thing. Until now, they've all been legitimate inquiries, nothing to worry about. But an hour ago, I received a ping from PIERS."

"PIERS?"

"Passport Information Electronic Records System— basically, a vast database of every passport that's ever been issued. An unidentified source was able to access her information."

Aatmanji felt a wave of terror. The timing was too coincidental. "Edmond, I'm worried she might be in danger—the same danger."

Cartwright paused. "Zed? Are you saying he knows she's alive?"

Aatmanji tried to calm his breathing. "Maybe. Yes. And I need your help to protect her—again."

There was silence. Was he sensing reluctance on the general's part?

"Aatmanji, you'll have to update me on what your group is doing. I need to know more if you want me to keep protecting Bayla. That was the deal."

"Yes, Edmond, okay. But first, I need to get a message to her. It has to come from me. Can you send this to her?" Aatmanji typed rapidly into the keypad, then waited for Cartwright's response.

Cartwright did not answer.

Aatmanji waited for almost a minute, then gave in. "Fine, Edmond, I'll tell you what you want to know first. But no names. Agreed?"

"Agreed."

Aatmanji sighed, wondering how to balance it all—his love for Bayla, the needs of the group he led, the needs of the world.

Again, he feared not a single decision he'd made had been the right one.

CHAPTER 19

BAYLA

Bayla opened the kitchen faucet, but only a few drips emerged. She frowned—the city had turned off the water an hour earlier than usual. She took the cooking pot to the water storage barrel in the corner, filled it, and put it on the stove to heat.

Rummaging through the cabinets, she located a tin with a few tea bags and found herself thinking of Tante Sindhu's masala chai, served at Tulā School every morning. Using a pestle, Sindhu would grind cardamom, cloves, cinnamon, and black pepper in a large stone mortar, then sweep the mixture into boiling water along with black tea and freshly grated ginger.

Bayla smiled, remembering Sindhu's particular enthusiasm for ginger root. *Look—look at it! It holds an entire medicine chest!* Sindhu had possessed an encyclopedic knowledge of the properties and uses of plants: supporting digestion, reducing inflammation, relieving muscle aches—an endless list.

Though Sindhu had not been a true family member, Bayla had loved her like one, enjoying her linguistic rotation of English, French, and Tamil. Sindhu had been fluent in all three but preferred French, having grown up in Puducherry, a former French colony in which the language still lingered. Indeed, *tante* was French for "aunt."

Glancing at the window box burgeoning with plants, Bayla remembered walking with Sindhu through the forest when she was just five years old.

Tante Sindhu! There's a giant bug!

Just leave it alone, kutti. Come along.

No, no, I'm too scared. It's looking at me—it wants to bite me! You have to kill it!

Sindhu had looked at Bayla for a moment, then taken her hand and tugged her forward gently, approaching the insect slowly. *Do you see the bend in its back legs? And the little launch pads at the ends? Those help it move more quickly to escape its predators. It wants to live, Bayla, just as much as you do.*

Bayla sighed.

No. I don't want to think about the past.

She took her mug to the dinette table, blowing on the liquid to cool it. Launching the EtherScreen displays, she began to read more about ZedChem. Of course she'd heard of the company—it dominated the chemical industry and was reported to employ questionable tactics.

In fact, it had been responsible for a large number of chemical accidents in recent years, quickly forgotten as newer industrial accidents came to light. An occasional lawsuit against ZedChem or a government investigation would emerge, only to be quashed based on technicalities, or for no apparent reason at all.

Strange that she couldn't find a single photo of the CEO; these days, it was almost impossible to avoid being photographed. How had the man managed it?

And why had ZedChem chosen the agricultural land near Prithvi Forest for its test pour? Though ZedChem was global in reach, she hadn't heard of its presence in southwestern India, one of the few spots in the world that had successfully recovered the natural cycles of its land. From what she'd read in the course of research at Environment Wire, there were few such zones left.

Bayla turned to the considerable number of articles on ZedChem released over the preceding hours. For the most part, FZ5 was being heralded as a triumph during a time of ecological distress and food insecurity. Supposedly, the new agrochemical could increase agricultural production at least tenfold, even up to twentyfold, in order to feed the population.

Mixed within the search results, though, were a few articles about the long-term dangers of FZ5, written by chemical engineer Jala Sharma, PhD, of Vayu City. For a second, Bayla closed her eyes—she remembered the city well. So many people had gone back and forth between Tulā School and Vayu City when she was growing up—teachers, lecturers, students, business leaders, politicians.

Bayla clicked on a video clip posted by a local news organization. Sharma, an Indian woman in her late thirties, spoke into a reporter's microphone:

"Soil is sustained by the mycelial netting that undergirds it. FZ5 doesn't just harm that network—it *consumes and dissolves* it. All those ecosystems within ecosystems in the soil will die within five years. It's happening as we speak, just from the test pour. We cannot use this chemical. It will kill whatever soil we have left. I'll speak plainly: no soil, no food, no way to feed ourselves."

Bayla noted three organizations and several scientists corroborating Sharma's damning conclusions. Bayla ran another search and sifted through the results:

WATCHDOG JOURNAL

SHARMA EXPOSED AND HER DATA DISCREDITED

Jala Sharma is trying to be the woman of the hour, but our reporters have discovered that the good "doctor" has falsified almost all her records. Sharma never graduated from the University of Chennai and never served on the faculty. In fact, at the time of her hiring by a subsidiary of global chemical star ZedChem, every single one of her credentials was forged.

Not only that, the sheaf of research she published—in total disregard for her contract—was unsubstantiated and shoddy, and her corporate supervisors have now proven that her . . .

———

THACKARAY REPORT

ANTI-CORPORATION = ANTI-LIFE

Why is Jala Sharma trying to destroy the man who is trying to save the world?

The disgraced chemical engineer falsified not only her credentials but also her published data, and we must discern her agenda before she causes any more damage to a great company built from the ground up by a small family in a real rags-to-riches story.

Krakun Zed has dedicated considerable resources to addressing the world's hunger crisis, and this woman has acted unconscionably to . . .

———

THE "GET REAL" BLOG: TRUE NEWS OF THE ENVIRONMENT

SHARMA THE ECOTERRORIST: FZ5 HOLDS UP UNDER MISGUIDED ATTACK

Yet another so-called scientist armed with false data is trying to undermine those trying to do an honest day's work. This entire tragic situation shows that environmentalists' positions on the critical issues of today are flawed, fear mongering, and utterly anti-progress.

The next time you hear environmentalists bellyaching about the future, dig in and find their agenda. We have

received information that Sharma has
radical ties, and she was spotted at
a rally in . . .

———

WEALTH-LINE E-zine

**CAREFUL WHO YOU HIRE: 10 WAYS TO
AVOID YOUR OWN SHARMA SCANDAL**

How well are you vetting your incoming employees? These days, scammers
and forgers have more AI tools than
ever at their disposal to perpetrate
fraud upon employers. With just a
few clicks and adjustments, and with
just a few digital files, a criminal
can construct an identity that even
employer watchdogs can't spot as
fraudulent.

Below are our suggestions to avoid
a Sharma Scandal at your corporate
entity . . .

Wow, thought Bayla. The anti-Sharma stories were proliferating.

Bayla turned to the organizations that had initially cor-
roborated Sharma's research and found similar stories about
them—sudden and serious problems with leadership, legit-
imacy, legality. The corroborating scientists had their own
emerging issues—personal scandals, lawsuits, academic dis-
qualifications, aspersions of all kinds.

She pushed back from the table, thinking. A beep sounded—
a news alert—and she looked at the display.

What?

AP WIRE

LOCAL CHEMICAL ENGINEER FOUND DEAD

VAYU CITY, INDIA. Local chemical
engineer Jala Sharma, PhD, was
found dead in her apartment in Vayu
City, India. The longtime professor
served as the chief chemical engineer of ForwardChem, a subsidiary of
ZedChem, the agrochemical conglomerate. ForwardChem's physical plant
is located just outside the eastern
borders of the city, near most of its
agricultural land.

After ZedChem's recent test
release of its new agrochemical FZ5,
touted to be a crop savior during
this time of disappearing farmland,
Sharma released dozens of reports on
FZ5's apparent toxicity, with extensive analysis.

Sharma's credentials made the
world take notice, but this morning
Sharma was discovered dead in her
apartment. Authorities located a
note, supposedly written by Sharma,
that recanted her research and

pointed to suicide. An investigation
is now underway to . . .

At that moment, Bayla heard a hiss and crackle, and she turned toward the kitchen. Had she left the stove on? Dashing toward it, she groaned. The remaining tea had continued to boil, charring against the side of the cooking pot. She grabbed the handle with a towel and tried to turn on the faucet. *Shoot.* She'd forgotten—no water right now.

Hearing the ping of an incoming text, she spoke aloud: "HomePort, play message."

TEXT from ATA External Communication to Bayla Jeevan:

Little Flower, I beg your forgiveness.

Bayla dropped the pot, pulling her toes out of the way just in time.

Only one person called her by that name.

She dug her fingernails into her arm as the soothing voice of HomePort continued to relay the message.

It's time for me to tell you everything.
You are in danger again. Trust Edmond
Cartwright. —Appa

Rushing to her phone, she read the screen. Gripping the table in front of her, she tried to slow her breaths, without success.

Appa is alive?

Her head began to pound.

If he's alive, why haven't I heard from him in fifteen years?

How peculiar it was to receive a text from her father, especially after hearing his voice during her strange experience at work and after reading the letter he'd left her. It was as though she'd conjured him up. Questions flew through her mind.

Is he really alive?

He's going to tell me what happened?

He wants my forgiveness?

Bayla drew a long and ragged breath.

No. Oh no. Since yesterday, she'd allowed tiny holes—Tulā School, yoga lessons, Tante Sindhu—to pierce the dam she'd built to keep her past at bay. Now the dam was crumbling, and other memories were surging through.

She remembered a twelve-year-old girl.

On an airplane with a man she'd never met: She'd begged the stocky, broad-shouldered man with features of stone and eyes like ice to tell her what was happening, where she was going, anything, anything at all. He'd had only one answer: *Your father wants to keep you safe.*

At a boarding school in rural Nevada: She'd looked, disbelieving, at the array of gray cinder-block buildings on a flat tract of land, without any vegetation, without a single tree in sight. As she'd attempted to digest the sudden changes in her life, the loss of trees had seemed to encompass every other loss.

Within a dormitory sealed from the outside: She'd attempted to muffle her anguish as she lay in bed, trying not to disturb the others, desperate for her father, her family, the trees, the sounds of the forest, and the cool night breeze. On the first night, nauseated, she'd run to the front door for fresh air, but it had been locked from the outside, per procedure. She'd vomited on the floor in the foyer.

In a classroom of people who pointed and laughed: She'd

asked questions that her fellow students deemed stupid. She'd spoken with an unfamiliar accent—the British English of Tulā School's teachers. She hadn't been able to fill the varied and often gaping holes in her cultural understanding. Though she'd tried to duck, to blend in, to disappear from notice, they'd always found her.

Bayla was shaking. She got up for a glass of water from the storage barrel and massaged the tightness in her throat as she drank.

She'd been told that her father wanted to keep her safe. Safe from what? Couldn't he have done so without sending her away? And she'd been told that Tulā School had burned, killing everyone within it. But he'd been alive the whole time—for fifteen years.

Bayla read his text again, infuriated by the gentleness of the message, refusing to allow that gentleness to thaw her anger. *No. How dare he? No.*

She felt a wave of nausea. She needed to walk. She needed to think.

Making her way to her front door, she stopped at the threshold, again visualizing the displaced twelve-year-old girl she'd once been.

Over time, she'd distanced herself from that girl, pushing her into a corner of her consciousness. It was easier to reject that girl than to mourn for her. It was easier to berate that girl for weakness and unworthiness than to accept what the world had done to her.

CHAPTER 20

BAYLA

Bayla pulled on her mask, closed the front door, and took to the sidewalk without a destination in mind. Her thoughts were racing. After all these years, her father's text promised answers.

Braden's words came to mind, unbidden. *You're so much more than your past.*

How could he be so sure?

Did she have the courage to face what had happened to her and to surmount it? She felt another wave of nausea. *No, I don't think so.*

She looked at the message again—it indicated she was in danger. *But from what?* she wondered. It also said "Trust Edmond Cartwright." She didn't recognize the name. As she walked, she ran a search, but the results showed more than thirty people.

Returning to the text, she noted it was an external communication of "ATA." Another search:

> The Advanced Technology Agency (ATA)
> is an agency of the United States
> Department of Defense, intended to
> initiate and advance leading-edge
> technologies to support and transform
> the nation's military capabilities,
> particularly AI technology and preci-
> sion weapons. The Cyber, Innovative
> Technologies, and Information Systems
> Subcommittee of the House Armed
> Services Committee has jurisdiction
> over the ATA.

Bayla looked at her prior search results—one of the Edmond Cartwrights on the list was associated with the ATA.

> Edmond Wallace Cartwright began his
> military career as an army physician
> and surgeon, rising to the rank
> of Lt. General as well as Surgeon
> General of the US Army. After his
> retirement in 2024, he joined the
> Advanced Technology Agency, develop-
> ing a variety of technologies related
> to computer-brain interfaces.

Bayla felt puzzled. What would someone from a military agency have to do with her? And how could he possibly be connected to her father?

Another article caught her eye: "Edmond Cartwright: A Military Yogi." Now, *that* could be more illuminating. She scanned the introductory information until she reached the middle:

As an army surgeon, Cartwright witnessed countless soldiers suffering from crippling emotional trauma. He himself had experienced debilitating and long-term PTSD after multiple tours of duty. For many of those soldiers, including himself, pharmaceuticals failed to provide adequate long-term relief. However, no other treatments were offered for psychological ailments.

"During a trip to India, I met a yogi schooled in classical yoga and meditation techniques. He taught me a daily practice, and it changed life as I knew it, from my physical health markers—including resolved allergies and normalized blood pressure and cholesterol—to my emotional stability. It inspired me to try adding alternative modalities to treat soldiers' physical and emotional pain."

Despite his resolution, Cartwright asserts it was an uphill battle. Such methods were disregarded and even belittled in the military. However, when the opioid crisis affected many

recovering soldiers and addiction
rates among them became rampant, many
leaders finally came on board. Yoga
classes and mindfulness and meditation practices became de rigueur on
bases, and research proliferated such
that few could deny their potential
benefits.

Cartwright went on to launch eigh-
teen different wellness programs for
soldiers across the armed services.

Fascinated, Bayla continued to read as she walked. This was certainly not what she'd expected when she'd read Cartwright's ATA profile. Had Cartwright and her father met? Was her father the yogi mentioned in the article? If so, perhaps she'd seen Cartwright during her childhood. She scrolled back up to the bio photo she'd only glimpsed in her eagerness to read the article. The face was rather bland, but the eyes seemed familiar.

She stopped and glanced at her front door—she'd circled back to her apartment without realizing it. Again, she looked down at the photograph to examine it more closely.

Wait, something's not right.

She looked up at her door again. It wasn't fully shut, but she remembered closing it.

Bayla approached the door and, hoping it wouldn't squeak, pushed it open a few more inches and peeked inside. Nothing. Slipping in, she looked around.

She felt a shiver travel up her spine. *I need to call 911.* She gasped and dropped her phone as she caught sight of a tall and sturdy figure turning toward her.

Grabbing her *kalaripayattu* stick from the corner where she'd thrown it earlier, she swung hard across the stranger's neck, then lunged forward, forcing the woman to stumble backward to the floor. Bayla turned to run, but the woman was struggling to speak.

"Miss . . . Miss Jeevan, wait," she rasped. "General Cartwright sent me. I'm Jade Sidaris."

Bayla turned back and looked at her in disbelief. Despite the painful blow Bayla had dealt her, the woman had gotten to her feet and was now holding her hands out, palms forward, as though indicating she didn't mean any harm.

"Did you say C-Cartwright?"

The woman attempted to clear her throat. "Yes, Lieutenant General Edmond Cartwright with the Advanced Technology Agency. He needs to talk to you."

"I know who he is." Well, at least, now she did. "And did he tell you to come inside my house without permission?"

Jade coughed as she responded. "I'm sorry. The door was open. . . . I wanted to make sure you were okay, so I . . ." Her voice was raw.

"I don't understand—what are you doing here?"

"The general thinks you might be in danger, and he asked me to bring you in. So I—"

"So you what? Just walked in here?"

They both froze as they heard a gun cock.

Bayla inhaled sharply, looking at an intruder standing at the entrance to her bedroom—a giant of a man, with a crooked red-blue scar running the length of his face, from temple to jawbone.

Jade spoke calmly: "Hey, man, easy."

The intruder looked at Jade with contempt, gesturing with

his gun. "Shut up. Move to corner," he growled. His accent sounded Eastern European.

Jade slowly backed up, and the man turned to Bayla. "You—you are coming with me." He pointed a finger toward the front door.

"N-no, I'm not."

The intruder pivoted, leveling the gun at Jade's head instead.

"Okay, stop—stop it," Bayla exclaimed.

The man grinned and pointed to the door again. Bayla moved slowly toward it, shuddering as the intruder began to follow her. Suddenly, the gun fired, and Bayla screamed.

She looked back, panicked. Jade had run toward the intruder and moved his arm straight upward, pinning it. *Thank God.*

The intruder suddenly twisted, and Jade struggled with him, causing the gun to drop. She kicked it away. Bayla scrambled toward it, then stopped, stunned, as two armed figures in black body armor rushed through the door. The first of them lunged toward the intruder, who propelled himself backward and skirted into Bayla's bedroom.

The second grabbed Bayla around the waist. She twisted wildly, trying to escape the iron grip. "Let me go—put me down!" she shouted.

"Bayla, it's okay," shouted Jade.

"What's okay?" she gasped. "What's happening?"

She was pushed through the door and into a black SUV with tinted windows. As she scrambled to get out again, the door slammed. Bayla pulled on the handle, but the door wouldn't budge. She lunged toward the handle on the other side. *Locked.*

She began screaming and banging on the divider in front of her. "Let me out of here!"

The divider lowered an inch, and she heard Jade's voice from the passenger seat. "Bayla, everything's fine, please calm down."

"What the hell is going on?"

"I'm not authorized to say, but I promise that it's okay."

"Tell me what's happening!"

"I can't." Jade closed the divider.

"Let me out of this goddamn car!"

CHAPTER 21

BAYLA

As Bayla's fury lessened, her fear increased. She had to think. Where was this woman—Jade—taking her? She didn't seem like a dangerous person, but she also seemed *trained*, the way she'd attacked the intruder. She'd also claimed to be with Cartwright, and her father's text said Cartwright could be trusted.

More worrisome was the other man—the intruder with the scarred face. Who was he? What did he want? She shivered—he'd been waiting in her bedroom. Was he already inside when she'd left the house for her walk, or had he slipped in afterward?

She tried to calm her spinning mind, taking deep breaths, down to the bottom of her abdomen.

Can I call for help? No, her phone was missing.

Can I get out of this car? No, neither handle would open.

Can I see where I'm going? No, the windows were dark.

She heard the murmur of Jade speaking on the phone and pushed an ear to the divider, straining to hear, to no avail.

When the vehicle stopped, Bayla tensed. Jade opened the door, but Bayla did not emerge, shrinking away instead. "Where am I? Why did you bring me here?"

"Bayla, please, I'm not going to hurt you. I told you—General Cartwright ordered me to bring you here."

"Cartwright's here?"

"Yes."

She considered for a moment, then scooted toward the open door, stepped out, and looked around, blinking. They were in a hangar on a tiny airfield, and a medium-sized jet stood nearby. Its door was open, revealing the built-in staircase.

A man strolled forward with his hand extended. "Hello, Bayla. I'm Edmond Cartwright. It's good to officially meet you."

Officially? She squinted at him. "It's you," she whispered.

✳✳✳

Bayla awoke in her Tulā School dormitory to find Sindhu packing her clothes into a small trunk. "Tante Sindhu? What's happening?"

Sindhu whispered, "Shhh. Nothing, kutti, *you're going on a trip."*

"A trip?" she asked excitedly. "Where? Back to the ocean?" During the previous year, they'd traveled to Tante Sindhu's hometown of Puducherry, and she'd seen the ocean for the first time.

"No, not to the ocean. Just wait—Aatmanji will tell you. Now go and get ready—quickly, quickly, okay?"

Bayla sat up to say the Earth mantra before her feet touched the floor. She looked around at the other sleeping girls. "Just me?" she asked.

"Just you."

As she went to get ready, she looked back for a moment. Why does Tante Sindhu look so sad?

Within the hour, Bayla and her father got into a jeep driven by a European man.

"But where are we going, Appa?"

"I'll tell you in a minute, Little Flower."

They arrived at an airfield and entered a plane. When takeoff was imminent, the European man nodded at her father, who closed his eyes for a moment, swallowed hard, then turned to Bayla.

"Bayla, do you trust me?" he asked.

What a strange question—of course she trusted him. How could she not?

He held her face in his hands, kissed her forehead, then buckled her into her seat. "I need you to stay on this plane and do what this man says."

She grabbed his hand. "Wait, aren't you coming with me?"

He winced. "I have to stay here. But you're going to the US." *He reached under the seat across the aisle, pulled out a* kalaripayattu *stick, and laid it at her feet.*

"Wait—stop!" Bayla struggled wildly to release the seat belt, until he placed his hands gently on top of hers to stop her frantic motion.

"Remember, Little Flower—trust me. I'll come for you. For now, I need to keep you safe." He began to move toward the front of the plane.

"Appa!" she called frantically. "Appa!"

He looked at her, his eyes full of remorse, then descended the steps.

***

Yes, this was the same man—the one who'd arrived at Tulā School all those years ago, Bayla thought. Not a European—an American. "You're the one who brought me here—to the US."

She looked down at his extended hand, but did not take it. How could he address her so casually, like they were at a social function? After a moment, he dropped his hand back to his side.

"Why? Why did you pluck me out of my life like that without any explanation? Why did you put me in that stupid school in the middle of nowhere and just leave me there?"

She looked from Cartwright to Jade, and back to Cartwright. Their silence infuriated her.

"Well? And why am I here now? Tell me what's going on," Bayla demanded.

"I know you have a lot of questions—get on this jet, and you'll have the answers."

"If you think I'm getting on that jet with you, you're wrong. You'd probably deposit me in some other godforsaken place and disappear again." The corner of Cartwright's mouth turned up a bit, enraging Bayla.

Suddenly, her fury drained. She felt exhausted. The weight of what she'd carried alone for fifteen years—terror, anger, grief, despair—seemed to push down on her body, pressing her lungs flat, squeezing out all of her breath. She looked around at the airfield.

"I have to get out of here. You can't just keep me."

"Bayla—"

"Am I being arrested or something?"

"No, of course you're not being arrested. You're free to go."

"Fine." She looked around, trying to find the way out, then

realized she had no phone, no wallet. She noticed that Jade was holding a phone in her hand. "Is that mine? Give it to me."

Cartwright nodded, and Jade handed it to Bayla, who snatched it and turned it on.

General Cartwright spoke again. "Bayla, please listen. You're in danger. We think someone is trying to kidnap you."

"Kidnap me? Isn't that what *you* just did?"

"We needed to get you out of your house. We would have questioned your attacker, but he got away. Frankly, I didn't think it would all happen so quickly, so I wasn't adequately prepared. That's on me."

Bayla felt torn. The man's words rang true. After all, there had been an armed man lurking in her bedroom. She shivered. Her father's message had told her to trust Cartwright, but how could she be sure?

Cartwright seemed to sense her hesitation. His brow furrowed, as though he was trying to recall something. "Ah, yes. He told me to tell you something. 'Cashews or cockles.' But I don't know what it means."

Bayla remembered the game from her childhood. Every day, Appa would find her, his fists behind his back, one containing her favorite snack of raw cashews and the other, cockleshells. Even when she chose the wrong fist, he still gave her the cashews. It was a silly memory, just between the two of them, one she might have laughed at under other circumstances, in a different life.

Her father must have spoken to Cartwright.

"As I told you, Bayla, the answers are on this jet. I'm sorry, but you'll have to decide right now whether you're joining us."

She flashed Cartwright a look of exasperation. The central anguish of her life, and he was in a hurry. She turned and looked at the jet. She could see the pilots in the cockpit readying the flight for takeoff.

Could she indeed trust Cartwright? Or her father, for that matter? Or anyone?

Should she walk away? Cartwright had made it clear that she was free to go.

Bayla thought of the last decade and a half, of the excruciating lack of answers. She thought of all the events that had occurred after her vision of the test pour. She thought of the confusion and chaos that seemed permanently lodged in the center of herself.

Now answers were being offered. If she turned away from them, she might never have the opportunity again.

Bayla walked to the jet's staircase and began to ascend.

CHAPTER 22

AATMANJI

Campsite, Prithvi Forest, near the former Tulā School grounds

Walking into the grove adjoining the clearing, Aatmanji leaned into the bark of a sandalwood tree, native to this part of the forest—just one unrepeatable piece of life on a long list of endangered flora. He inhaled the distinctive scent of the bark. Nothing else in the world resembled it, and indeed, it was difficult even to describe its notes and subtleties.

He looked across the stretch of land and trees and then at the adjacent river. Its levels had diminished since his boyhood, but it still flowed strong here in the hills. Closing his eyes, he listened to the chant and chime of the water flowing over rock.

It had been years since he'd been in this area, near the old Tulā School grounds. Aatmanji smiled to himself—how extraordinary those grounds had been, with seamless indoor and outdoor spaces, lush with greenery, lavish with flowers. The school was like a living entity itself, with a breath and pulse that had seemed to match his own. And when it had been destroyed by fire, he'd felt as though part of his own body had burned to ash as well.

He felt a moment of trepidation. To maintain the illusion of his—and, more importantly, Bayla's—death, he had never stayed in one place for more than six months, and had never approached the area surrounding Tulā School. With ZedChem back in southwestern India, perhaps it was not wise to locate their camp here. But he had his reasons, and anyway, they would not remain at the site for long.

"Aatmanji!"

He looked up and saw Shanti, one of the women setting up camp, waving and walking toward him. Aatmanji looked past her, noting that the temporary structures were almost fully assembled. Across from the small sleeping tents were the larger cooking and eating areas, as well as a gathering tent with basic electronic connectivity and communication capabilities.

The problem was that electronics of any kind made them vulnerable to detection. They would need to vacate the area soon. When they did, the equipment would be dismantled and moved, and everything else—the bamboo and thatch and jute—would be left to reintegrate with the earth.

"Bose is at the outer gate, Aatmanji—they'll arrive in fifteen minutes or so. I've set up the tents and chairs you asked for, and tea will be ready when they arrive."

"Thank you." He began to follow her, then stopped to glance at the clusters of trees flanking the river. Trees, topsoil, and rivers had always existed and operated in a natural and mutual interrelationship. The knots of roots and fungi trapped water in the topsoil and released it gradually, feeding the rivers over time. The thick tree cover induced rainfall through transpiration, and the dense root system held topsoil in place so that monsoons could not deplete it.

He thought how ancient legends and myths were often dismissed with derision, without understanding the knowledge encoded within them. The story of Shiva capturing the Ganga River in his matted hair and releasing her powerful waters gradually was a story about the water cycle—the steady, sustained release of water enabled by the tangled roots and fibers of the trees. It was a vast and intricate web of ecological connections—a web of life all around them.

He looked longingly toward the temporary meditation platform that had been assembled over one of the river's narrow inlets, wishing he could spend some time there now.

"Wouldn't you like to answer your messages before Bose arrives?" Shanti had doubled back when he hadn't followed her, and was now pointing to the gathering tent.

Aatmanji smiled at Shanti's diplomacy. "Right behind you," he said, but stopped yet again, hearing the twitter of bulbul birds and catching sight of the red crown of a flameback before it flew farther into the interior. This was one of the most biodiverse areas of the world, these lands bordering the Western Ghats mountain range.

And this particular location, a transition zone between moist and dry forests, and between lower and higher altitudes, was a rich crossroads of plant and animal life. As such, he was surrounded by climbing vines like jasmine, as well as orchids. He saw trees like giant bamboo and palm, as well as pine and eucalyptus.

He remembered the Tulā School students and their intimate familiarity with the flora and fauna of the area. Aatmanji had started the school in the early 2000s as an experiment, an attempt to infuse yoga and yogic philosophy, as well as ecological consciousness, into modern education, to cultivate adults with strong bodies, stable minds, respect for life, respect for Earth.

With such an education, he knew graduates would never equate virtual reality with reality. He knew they would be able to navigate the accelerating technological leaps and increasing social disconnection with consciousness, balance, and a sense of responsibility.

Over time, many Tulā School graduates moved on to work in the nearby towns and cities, entering public office and other positions of leadership. As they did, Aatmanji enlisted them to address a growing environmental threat in the surrounding forests and farmlands: increasing agrochemical seepage into the ecological cycles. Those agrochemicals were disrupting the sustainability of a system that had existed for millennia. As his group grew, they defended land and forests and deployed massive education campaigns and tree-planting projects.

They'd been successful, but the arrival of ZedChem in the 2010s, with the quickest-spreading and highest-concentration agrochemicals in the industry, had been a setback.

Back then, they'd pushed ZedChem out of the area. But to what end? ZedChem had grown and flourished all over the globe and had now reentered southwestern India. What had been the point of his years of labor? And what was the point of continuing to battle corporations, governments, ignorance, and inexplicable recklessness?

He sighed. It was not like him to give in to dejection, but it was happening more often these days. He closed his eyes and thought of Aanvi, who always urged him to live in hope.

"Aatmanji!"

Shanti's call from the clearing pulled him from his reverie, and at last he made his way toward her. There was much to accomplish in the next few hours. Mohan Das would be arriving soon, along with the guest, Chaadi Darius.

Caveh's grandson! Aatmanji shook his head. How quickly time was passing.

And then Bayla, his Bayla, would be arriving as well, soon afterward. He felt the leap in his heart simultaneously with the apprehension in his belly.

Closing his eyes, he concentrated, feeling through the web. Still, he could not sense Daksha at all. Was she okay? He didn't even know how to begin searching for her if she didn't respond.

He remembered the day Daksha had wandered into Tulā School as a child of four or five. Despite months of searching and inquiring, they could not locate any parents or family, and Tulā School had become her home.

Though Daksha had been a mere child, Aatmanji had felt less like her caretaker and more like her steward—providing a stable base for her as she ventured farther and farther into the forest for days at a time, and even weeks as she grew older. In the beginning, he'd sent search parties for her, but he'd eventually given up. Daksha returned only when she wished to. In her teens, she began disappearing for months at a time.

Late one evening, when Daksha was about sixteen, she'd returned to Tulā School.

***

"Daksha, my dear! You're back!"

She didn't answer but, with her head, indicated the bundle she held.

Shocked, he looked down at a swaddled infant, barely a few days old, yet active and alert and burbling. "When . . . Who . . ."

Daksha shook her head, and he didn't press—there would be time to ask his questions. He took the child in his arms and marveled. He'd always lived surrounded by vibrant flowers and plants, by rolling hills and rivers, but he'd never before seen anything as beautiful as this tiny bit of life. Looking into the heart-shaped face with its golden skin and pink cheeks, he loved the little one instantly.

The following morning, Aanvi spoke to both him and Daksha, delivering heartbreaking news.

"You and your child cannot be together, Daksha—it's too dangerous." Aanvi's voice was mournful, her eyes full of tears.

Shock filled Aatmanji. "Aanvi, are you sure?"

He watched as Aanvi closed her eyes and concentrated, knowing she was invoking her ability, one that only a few of the Ancients had possessed, that even fewer people possessed now.

Aatmanji knew she would not make such a drastic pronouncement without the highest degree of certainty.

Aanvi's face clouded with sadness. "I'm sorry. But yes, I'm sure."

"I don't care about myself. But . . ." Daksha looked down at her daughter. "When? When must I leave?"

"The sooner, the better. But it's your decision."

Weeping, Daksha placed the infant in Aatmanji's arms, removed her pendant and chain, and clipped them around the child's neck. She stepped backward once, twice, then turned to the forest.

And she was gone.

***

He'd never seen Daksha again . . . in person, that is. Still, through the web, he always had a sense of her existence, her presence. Over time, he'd learned to call to her, communicate with her. They'd learned to work together, and that had been critical for the unit's activities over the years.

In the meantime, Bayla had grown up at Tulā School. He and everyone at the school, teachers and staff and students, had raised her. When Bayla was eight years old, she'd asked him where her mother was. Aatmanji had anticipated the question, merely responding, "She's gone, my dear, but we are *all* your mother, all of us here at Tulā School." He'd waited to see whether she'd ask additional questions. She hadn't, seeming to accept his answer.

He thought of the striking similarities between Daksha and Bayla, their sculpted features, their dark curls, not to mention their intensity, intelligence, and affinity with the natural world. Aatmanji sighed. In the end, he'd lost both of them.

He looked toward the river again, begging it to bear his grief away.

But how could it?

Aatmanji jumped at the vibration of the satellite phone in his pocket and eagerly read the text from Cartwright. He heaved a sigh of relief. Bayla was safely on the jet and coming to him after more than a decade.

Poor child. She knew only that her father had sent her away and never contacted her afterward. She believed everyone at Tulā School had been lost in a fire.

She might never forgive him, and honestly, he wasn't sure he deserved forgiveness. The best he could hope for was that she'd come to understand what had prompted such a disruption of her life.

Aatmanji felt his heart break again—for his loss of his daughter and for Bayla's loss of . . . everything, really.

He breathed through his tumult of emotions, letting each

one inhabit him before letting it go. All emotions ebbed and flowed; it was crucial to welcome them, but also to remember their impermanence. How hard he tried to ensure that his actions rose from a place of clarity, and not from that transient swirl.

Feeling calmer, he approached the gathering tent, then stopped. His emotions surged again as the memory unfurled: a delicate infant placed in his arms, the fragrance of bayla flowers in the night.

CHAPTER 23

CHAADI

Vayu City, India

When Chaadi exited the Vayu City airport, sights and sounds engulfed him. He struggled to get his bearings through the swirl of languages and crush of traffic and swarms of people. It was late morning, but the haze made it seem like dusk. His eyes began to water, and he felt thankful he'd purchased a high-quality mask before leaving the airport—one of the new "rebreathers" with active air purification

Fortunately, Professor Mohan Das located him almost immediately, put him in a taxi, and was now pointing out the various sights in a city that had become an overnight IT powerhouse after Bengaluru and Hyderabad had fully burst through their seams.

Looking out the window, peering through the haze, Chaadi saw a brand-new highway packed not only with compact cars and scooters but also with a luxurious assortment of electric BMWs and Audis. About half the vehicles were self-driving. They passed gleaming skyscrapers covered with global IT logos and glittering malls inviting shoppers to partake in Valentino and Balenciaga and Dior.

Chaadi wondered why he felt so overwhelmed. After all, he'd traveled often for work and seen bustling cities all over the world. But as their taxi turned onto the crowded local roads, he understood.

It was the contrasts.

Bells clanged from towering temples just beyond the sleek skyscrapers. Oxcarts stood next to Maseratis. Vegetable vendors called from sidewalks in front of the most glamorous hotels he'd ever seen.

It was dizzying. He tried to concentrate on the deluge of information coming from Das. "India has one of the youngest populations in the world," he was saying, gesturing toward the crowds of fashionably dressed twenty-somethings entering call centers and corporate offices to begin work. "It's become an economic power again after its legs were cut out from under it. Let's not mince words—colonialism raped this country. And, after that, corruption was—*is*—a constant challenge."

Chaadi looked at Das, surprised at the man's passionate words after their cold exchange via computer.

Most fascinating to Chaadi, naturally, was Das's discussion of ancient Indian architecture, particularly temples. "Many people think that temples are only places for prayer and ritual. That's not the case."

"What do you mean?"

"Temples were constructed and established in a certain way, Chaadi, in order to preserve certain qualities of energy. Their primary purpose was to invite people to align themselves with that particular energy for a few moments every day. That's why people were taught to sit for a few moments before leaving the temple premises—to promote that alignment."

Chaadi wished they had time to visit one of the many city temples still in operation after thousands of years, but Das clearly had a plan in motion. As they pulled into the driveway of the Easton International Hotel, they were greeted by a lithe gentleman in his late sixties, his manner kindly but also sharp and alert, as though he was absorbing everything occurring around him.

"Welcome, welcome, it's a pleasure to meet you, Mr. Darius."

"Please call me Chaadi."

"Then you must call me Bose." Bose turned toward the professor, and they embraced. "Mohan, how are you?" Bose asked, patting him on the back. "It's been a long time."

Bose led them to a set of armchairs in the lobby, and a server brought them glasses of chilled lime juice. Chaadi gulped one down, and it was refilled immediately. His thirst now dealt with, the aromas of the sprawling buffet and its kaleidoscopic array of foods caught his attention. His mouth began to water.

Bose noticed where his gaze had traveled. "I'm sorry that we don't have time to eat here in the hotel. I just wanted you to have a short break and access to facilities. We need to get moving, but don't worry—I've brought food and water for you."

Leading them to an electric jeep in the parking lot, he gestured them inside, handing each a small jute satchel and a stainless-steel canister of water. Chaadi was intrigued by the little green packets inside the satchel and realized, as he unwrapped them, that his meal was tamarind rice wrapped in banana leaves and accompanied by a spoon fashioned out of some kind of husk.

He smiled. *Perfectly biodegradable.* He looked up at the strip of fast-food restaurants they were passing, the outdoor trash cans bursting and overflowing with empty containers and bottles.

They soon exited the city highways and began driving past stretches of farmland, some of which seemed operational but most of which looked brown and burnt. Bose spoke with Das. "It's becoming harder and harder to reclaim the land. We can't hold the topsoil, so it's becoming desert."

Chaadi listened soberly as Bose described the plight of the local farmers, traumatized by their inability to feed their families and to continue the work of previous generations, the most critical work of human survival—the cultivation, harvest, and distribution of food. The rates of farmer suicides had risen to epidemic proportions decades ago and had not yet leveled off.

After a while, they all rode in silence. Das dropped off to sleep. Chaadi tried to sleep, too, but the jeep made for a rough ride. After an hour, Bose spoke again. "We're entering one of the few areas of forest that's still healthy and thriving." He turned back to Chaadi for a brief moment. "I'm going to lower the windows, and you might not even need that mask." He smiled and pulled his own off with a flourish.

Chaadi stuck his hand out of the open window and felt coolness in the air. Relieved, he removed the heavy mask and relished the ease of breathing without it, down to the bottom of his lungs. He tried to lean back in his seat and enjoy the feeling but soon became nauseated from the jarring bumps and curves as they made their way through the forest interior.

After a few hairpin turns, they slowed and approached a wooden gate, where a woman greeted them and spoke to Bose in low tones. They drove a few minutes longer, then stopped in a clearing. Chaadi got down from the jeep, and Das ushered him to one of the small tents. "Hold on to that water canister—there's a refill station just outside, about ten feet in that direction," he said, pointing. "You might want to get some rest here until Aatmanji can meet with you."

"Okay, sure."

"Chaadi, I'll leave you now—I just heard from a law-enforcement agency in Lebanon. I'm flying there to see what I can learn about what happened. I'll keep you posted."

"It was good to meet you, Professor. Thank you for bringing me here."

"I'm glad that you contacted me—I really am. And I'm sorry I was so short with you."

Chaadi smiled. "No hard feelings."

Das smiled back and ducked out of the tent. Chaadi overheard bits of his conversation with Bose. Das's voice was animated. "I was so excited to hear. When did you find it?"

"Just months ago."

"I must see it before I go—please, Bose."

"Yes, I can take you now—come this way."

Their voices faded.

What was that about? Chaadi wondered.

He lay back on the cot, thinking of the last canvas cot he'd slept on, near Shara Forest. He hoped Evelyn was doing okay after the defeat at the temple. He sighed, feeling that knot of guilt and remorse again.

Chaadi twisted and turned on the cot. He could indeed use a nap, but his mind wouldn't wind down. After a few minutes, he exited the tent and began to wander the grounds. A bamboo platform stood near the river. Everything looked clean and well tended, but this clearly was not a permanent settlement, more like a campsite. The surrounding forest pressed in, as though ready to reclaim the site at the earliest possible opportunity.

The few people he saw were fully engaged in their tasks, mostly related to water collection and tent setup. Noticing a low hill rising to the side, he walked toward it, making his way up the gentle slope. When he reached the top, he surveyed the landscape: the forest, the river, and . . . Was that a satellite antenna? It was—but on the most miniature scale he'd ever seen, and clearly transportable. He looked at it in wonder, so out of place in the greenery, amid the buzz of living creatures.

As he returned to the clearing, he saw a tall and elegant man waiting, his expression pleasant. Chaadi assumed this must be Aatmanji, but the man seemed younger than expected. Das had mentioned that Aatmanji was in his early sixties, but his unlined face and thick head of hair made it difficult to believe.

"*Namaste,* Chaadi." His voice was rich, calming. "I'm Aatmanji."

CHAPTER 24

BAYLA

From the middle of the jet where she'd been seated, Bayla watched Cartwright and Jade conferring at the front. The general lowered his voice and glanced in her direction, and Bayla strained to hear.

"Jade, this is a highly sensitive matter. I'm relying on your discretion. Do you understand?"

"Yes, sir."

"Good. Are we all set?"

"Yes, sir. Ready to go."

Cartwright turned to his right and entered a small chamber with a sliding door that seemed to serve as an office. Jade walked down the aisle and seated herself in the row across from Bayla, buckling her seat belt. Bayla followed suit.

She regarded Jade, who appeared to be of both Black and Asian ancestry. The woman was tall, strong, and fit, with a face that looked impassive for the most part but annoyed at the moment.

Well, she'd hit Jade pretty hard with her *kalaripayattu*

stick. What had Jade expected, though, walking into the house like that?

"Where are we going?"

"The general will tell you," Jade rasped. Apparently, her throat was still hurting.

"So, you're the general's . . . ?"

"Assistant."

"But you were in the military?" The way she'd responded to the intruder suggested it, but Bayla wasn't sure.

Jade gave a brusque nod.

Okay, then. Obviously, Jade wasn't inclined to be forthcoming.

Bayla closed her eyes. She'd flown on occasion for work but never enjoyed it. As the plane took off, her stomach felt like it was tumbling. She encircled her body with her arms. When the jet leveled off, she opened her eyes and was startled to find Cartwright directly across from her. Jade had shifted next to him.

Bayla looked at Cartwright expectantly.

"Do you need anything?" he asked. "Something to drink?"

"Water, please."

Jade stood and went to a supply cabinet.

"General, please don't make me wait any longer. Tell me what's happening. Where are we going?"

He leaned back in his seat, looking at her. "So, Bayla, you were twelve years old when you left India for the US."

"I didn't leave—you moved me."

"Yes, that's so," replied Cartwright. "I placed you in a small Nevada boarding school under the legal guardianship of the headmaster and made arrangements for your tuition and up-keep and, eventually, your US citizenship."

A water bottle appeared at her elbow. Bayla thanked Jade, then turned back to Cartwright with impatience. "General, I *know* all of this—it happened to *me*. You're still not telling me *why*."

"Bayla, we were trying to protect you from someone."

"But who?"

"A man named Krakun Zed."

Bayla stared, open-mouthed. "Are you . . . are you talking about the CEO of ZedChem?"

Cartwright looked surprised. "Yes, that's right. ZedChem is a global agrochemical concern that has—"

"Yes, I'm familiar with it—I've been reading about their recent test pour. But what on earth does Zed have to do with me?"

"More than you can imagine. Back in the 2010s, his company tried to establish itself in southwestern India, outside Vayu City. But during that time, Aatmanji had been working nonstop to protect the area between Vayu City and the Prithvi Forest, to keep it ecologically healthy and viable. He and his unit stopped ZedChem and pushed it out of the area."

Bayla hugged herself tighter as Cartwright spoke the names from her past so lightly: Aatmanji, Vayu City, Prithvi Forest. "I . . . I didn't know that," she managed to say at last.

"One evening, Aatmanji and a few others were on the ZedChem grounds—surveilling, basically. A few hours after they left, a factory fire broke out and killed Zed's brother."

"My God, that's horrible."

"It was. Some years later, Zed confronted Aatmanji, right at Tulā School. He believed Aatmanji was responsible for his brother's death."

Bayla's eyes widened. "I . . . I think I remember meeting him that day."

"Zed threatened you. That's when your father contacted me, and we made a plan to extract you quickly. And just in time. Within the week, Zed sent an armed contingent and burned Tulā School to the ground."

Bayla passed a hand across her forehead. That certainly explained why she'd been rushed out of the country. "But I don't understand—why did my father have to relocate me so far away?"

"I'm the one he asked for help, and that was the place I had the ability to deliver you to in complete secrecy. And as Zed became more and more powerful, it made sense to keep you hidden far from his usual locations."

Bayla wasn't sure if she agreed, but at least there was logic to it, some explanation after so many years without one. There was so much she hadn't known. But still . . .

"I thought Appa didn't contact me because he'd died in the fire. But he didn't die. So why didn't he just explain somehow—send me a message? And why didn't *you*?"

"I'm taking you to those answers."

"What do you mean? Where are you taking me?" Bayla tensed, anticipating the general's answer.

"To India. To see Aatmanji."

"You . . . you know where he is?"

"Yes."

After a moment, she asked, "You've been in communication with him all these years, haven't you?"

"Intermittently, but yes."

"So all this time, he could have told me. I didn't know what happened to my home, my family—and the headmaster at my school couldn't tell me anything." She tried to keep her voice under control, but it shook. "Why? Why would you both do that to me? Why didn't you tell me when I got older? I would have understood."

Bayla detected impatience in the general's sigh. He looked at her for a few moments. "Bayla, does it occur to you that you're looking at only one part of a large and complicated picture? I realize you were hurt very badly, but does it make sense to you that someone who loved you, your own father, would send you away without an explanation?"

"No, it doesn't make sense—it's never made sense."

"So, just for a few days, why don't you give him the benefit of the doubt? After that, be angry again if you want to. You were in more danger than you realize."

Bayla felt a surge of uncertainty and confusion.

"For now, Bayla, try to understand that Aatmanji did everything he could to protect you. Then and now."

"Now? So the person hiding in my apartment . . . that was . . . that was . . ."

"We believe Zed sent him to kidnap—or kill—you. We're not sure which."

Bayla stood, holding her stomach and gagging.

"I . . . I need a minute." Nauseated, Bayla made her way to the small lavatory at the back of the jet. Once inside, she began retching. Soon, she was crying.

How could Cartwright speak of this terrible threat so calmly? Why was he making light of the tragedy that had happened to her, one that had hurt and changed her so profoundly? And now he was whisking her across the globe without much explanation—again.

Thank goodness she didn't have family and friends at home wondering where she'd gone, except . . . maybe . . . Braden. She shook her head. He thought she was on vacation. *Anyway, why would he care about me?*

Once she felt calmer, she splashed some water on her face and stepped out of the lavatory. Jade was standing nearby, waiting for Bayla to reemerge, still rubbing her throat with a look of irritation.

"Are you okay?" Jade asked.

No, I need more information—much more. She nodded. "Where's the general?"

"He's up front—he needs to make some calls. Why don't you head back to your seat until he's done?" Jade turned and walked up the aisle without waiting for Bayla to follow.

Bayla watched her for a moment. Jade's irritation only seemed to be increasing, and she wondered why. Returning to her seat, she observed as Jade moved closer to the front of the jet and set up a laptop workstation. Jade snapped on the reading light, then seemed to notice Bayla looking in her direction.

"Need something?" she asked, her face blank, her voice curtly polite.

"No, thank you," Bayla answered, turning away, her own anger flaring. See, this was why she didn't reach out to people—they were impossible to figure out. She thought of the number of social engagements she'd turned down—or ducked out of early—at Environment Wire. She'd been relieved when the invitations had eventually ceased.

People only hurt you—or leave you—in the end.

Exasperated, she leaned her seat back a few inches and fumbled around with the scratchy blanket she'd found wrapped in plastic next to her, trying to get comfortable.

Finally, flinging the blanket away, she looked down at her hands and froze. For a split second, she thought she saw a mesh of light and fiber extending from them. *Threads of light,* she thought. When she looked back at Jade, the threads materialized again, stretching between the two of them. Then they vanished.

She needed to get centered. Bringing up her feet so that she sat cross-legged in the seat, Bayla began a simple breathing exercise, trying her best to stay fully present, trying not to drift into memories of the past or worries for the future. It took some time, but she found her way to stillness.

When she opened her eyes, she stood and walked toward Jade. Again, Jade looked at her with that indecipherable expression, without speaking. Bayla tried not to scowl.

"Jade," she asked, keeping her voice neutral, "do you have a problem with me?"

"No, why would I?"

"Look, I'm really sorry I hit you back at my apartment."

Jade looked a little embarrassed. "I'm not mad about that—I understand why you did it. In fact, it's good you know how to defend yourself."

"So, what is it, then?"

She didn't answer.

"Jade, Cartwright isn't telling me very much, and I think I have a right to—"

"*General* Cartwright," Jade interrupted, "is doing the best he can."

"Sorry—*General* Cartwright." Bayla knew how sarcastic she sounded and struggled to soften her tone. "Jade, you heard about my past. Can't you see why I'm desperate to know more? Maybe you could tell me what you know." Seeing Jade's unresponsiveness, she sighed. "Let me guess—you're not allowed to."

"Look, I get it, Bayla. But I can't help you."

Bayla dropped into the seat next to Jade, took a deep breath, then spoke again.

"How long have you known the general?"

Jade looked surprised by the question, or perhaps it was the change in Bayla's tone and demeanor.

"A long time—more than ten years."

"How did you meet?"

"Well, he helped me. A lot. I was a wreck after my last tour of duty—I attempted suicide twice that year."

Impulsively, Bayla reached out and took Jade's hand. "That's terrible—I'm so sorry, Jade."

Jade looked at Bayla for a moment, then withdrew her hand. But she seemed to soften.

"Yeah, the paramedics got to me each time, but just barely. It was the worst year of my life—almost worse than active duty. Almost." She turned to the window but continued to speak. "Flashbacks all day, nightmares all night. Panic attacks while driving in traffic. My baby girl . . ."

"Oh my God . . ."

"No, no, she's okay. She's with her dad."

"And then you met the general . . . ?" Bayla asked.

"I don't know how he heard about me, but he got me enrolled in the Army Research Center's CBTW program."

She looked at Jade questioningly.

"Cognitive Behavioral Treatment for Warriors," Jade explained. "An incredible program—virtual-reality tech combined with older biofeedback techniques. Not sure I would have survived without it. Anyway, it's a full-fledged military program now, but it was experimental at the time. He pulled strings, obviously. And then he gave me this job—no one else would hire me with my mental-health record."

She looked at Bayla again, as though surprised at what she'd revealed, and at what length.

Bayla leaned forward. "Thank you for telling me that."

Jade nodded, her face no longer perturbed. "He's a good person. I wasn't sure that you understood that."

"I can see that." They were silent for a minute. "Tell me about your daughter."

Jade turned to Bayla and smiled, at last without restraint. "Rosie? She's so smart; you won't believe what she said to me the other day. . . ."

After twenty minutes or so, Bayla returned to her seat and wrapped the blanket around her. She leaned back and closed her eyes, though she wasn't sleepy. *Interesting.* Jade's anger hadn't been directed toward Bayla but, rather, was in defense of the mentor for whom Jade felt so much gratitude.

When Bayla had put her own anger and confusion to the side, she'd been able to listen to and understand Jade. But how many things had she missed over the years, wrapped up in her own anger and confusion, shutting out the world, pushing away everyone she knew?

CHAPTER 25

CHAADI

Campsite, Prithvi Forest, near the former Tulā School grounds

"I've been looking forward to meeting you, Aatmanji! Professor Das says you knew my grandfather."

Aatmanji sighed. "Caveh was a remarkable man—and a good friend. Such a terrible loss." He gestured. "Come, let's have some tea while we talk. You must be hungry." Aatmanji led him to a shaded area with two caned chairs and a table holding tea, fruits, and biscuits.

Chaadi took the tea Aatmanji poured for him. "How did you know him?"

"We met in the '90s when I was traveling in Lebanon—in Shara Forest, actually. I'd been trying to locate a certain temple—an important one—and I'd traced it there. He was the archaeology professor I consulted, and we located it together."

"But what was so important about that particular temple?"

Aatmanji paused. "On your way here, did Mohan talk to you about traditional temples?"

"Oh yes. He said many of them were also energy centers, to help people feel balance and alignment before going about their lives again. The more I think about it, my grandfather always said that about the Shara temple, too. We'd sit and meditate, and each time he told me to concentrate and feel the energy inside." Chaadi paused. "But the Shara temple didn't look like the traditional temples I saw on the way here."

"Yes, it's constructed differently. I'd call it a yogic temple."

"The circular structure," Chaadi began. "The dome. The lotus on the ceiling."

"That's right." Aatmanji smiled and nodded. "Chaadi, I don't think your grandfather had a chance to tell you how special that temple is—*was*," he amended sadly. "It had a particular energy signature. Legend has it that the Seven Sages built multiple temples with that signature across the world, but this was the first one we actually discovered. And those temples were given a secret marking."

"Yes, the marking! My grandfather taught me how to find it." Chaadi paused, thinking. "So '108' designates an energy signature?"

"That's right—among other things. Your grandfather Caveh volunteered to guard the temple and to keep its secrets safe. He became its caretaker. Did he tell you about any of this?"

Chaadi frowned. "On the day he died, he said he wished he'd told me many things, but he only had time to show me the marking. He told me to 'find them,' but in the chaos, he couldn't explain. I deciphered the marking on my own, but I couldn't figure out what it meant. Then Professor Das led me to you."

A look of sadness came over Aatmanji's face. "I'm so sorry you had to witness your grandfather's death."

"Well, I didn't exactly—he pushed me out the back passageway and told me to run." Chaadi squeezed his eyes shut. "I should have stayed. . . . I should have tried to . . ."

"Then you would have died as well, Chaadi. What would that have achieved?"

Chaadi gulped and nodded.

After a few minutes, Aatmanji spoke again. "Mohan mentioned you saw someone at the site before the explosions—a woman."

"I did. She asked me if I was 'one of them.' What did she mean by that?"

Aatmanji frowned, but didn't answer. "Can you describe her?"

"An Indian woman—small, but so strong. She attacked me, and she knew what she was doing. She pushed her thumb into my neck at a weird angle; see, right here," he said, indicating the bruise. "And just like that, I collapsed."

"A *marma* point."

"A what?"

"A *marma* point is a pressure point in the body."

Chaadi felt wonderment—he was learning something new every minute.

"And then what did she do?" Aatmanji prompted.

"She obviously knew about the back passageway, because she escaped that way when the explosions began. Anyway, I gave the police a description, but as far as I know, they haven't been able to find her."

Aatmanji's brow furrowed, and he stared into space.

Chaadi understood. "You think this woman was responsible for what happened, don't you?"

Aatmanji paused before answering. "I don't know."

"What about the first explosion, back in 2025?"

This time, Aatmanji did not answer at all. He appeared to be deep in thought, and Chaadi didn't want to interrupt him.

Standing, Chaadi stretched, looked around at the temporary camp, then dropped his arms abruptly. "I've been having panic attacks over the past few years—horrible ones. It got to a point where I couldn't get through my day without having at least one. I realized it was because I was trying to push away everything that happened to me. When I decided to face everything and learn more, I thought I'd get to the bottom of things—that I'd feel better. And now I can't."

Aatmanji seemed to commiserate, shaking his head.

Chaadi sat and turned toward Aatmanji, who appeared to be examining Chaadi's face. "You know, you favor your grandfather. A lot."

"Yeah, I've seen some photos from when he was younger."

"Not just your looks—your manner, your presence. He made serious matters . . . lighter somehow."

"That's the nicest compliment I've ever gotten," Chaadi said, smiling.

Aatmanji smiled back, then laughed. "The jokes that man would tell!"

"I remember."

"It was helpful—a relief, to be honest—given the seriousness of our task and our purpose."

Chaadi looked at Aatmanji intently. "You know, Aatmanji, you haven't told me *what* your purpose is. Is it just to find these temples?"

"The temples are a means to an end. The Seven Sages predicted a catastrophe that would end human life on Earth—a catastrophe of humanity's making."

Chaadi's forehead wrinkled. *Wow.* "And you think that catastrophe is going to happen soon?"

"We believe so. But the Seven Sages also provided humanity with a key to prevent that self-destruction." Aatmanji paused. "Chaadi, 108 is that key."

CHAPTER 26

BAYLA

I am a child again, sitting below my favorite tree, reclining in a throne of roots. Those roots ripple and flow, and I ripple and flow with them. I look up and the dream-woman is approaching me again, calling for me. "Here I am!" I call back to her, but she cannot hear me. I reach a hand toward her, but it dissolves. Then the rest of my body dissolves, too, and I scream. . . .

Bayla jolted awake and blinked. How odd—another version of her earlier dream.

Jade was tapping her shoulder. "Hey, Bayla? Bayla, we're almost there."

She nodded and stretched. She'd been vaguely aware that they'd stopped to refuel, but they'd let her sleep for the duration of the trip.

"There's a small shower on the other side of the lavatory with some toiletries. We've got some breakfast stuff when you're ready—nothing fancy. We should land in about an hour."

She smiled at the change in Jade's manner toward her, then yawned and stretched again. "Okay. Thank you."

***

When the jet door opened, humidity immediately saturated the dry cabin air. Bayla inhaled the heavy moisture. She descended toward the tarmac and paused on the last step. Despite her long absence from India, she could feel her child-self reawakening and all the wonder of growing up surrounded by trees, plants, people. Closing her eyes, she remembered rootedness and belonging, but also the pain of abandonment and bereavement.

In her reverie, she forgot she hadn't reached the ground, and she pitched forward. Jade, who had preceded Bayla down the steps, caught her arm and steadied her. "Easy."

"Thanks." Bayla gazed into the surrounding forest, inhaling deeply. These were the sounds and smells she remembered so vividly. Her body tingled, as though emerging from deep sleep.

A few feet away, Bayla saw a shelter with a tin roof and the words "Agni Airfield" in faded red paint. Bayla looked around. There were no other buildings or people, except for a man wearing a sky-blue embroidered *kurta* over loose jeans, who was leaning against an electric jeep parked in the shade. She squinted at his face. His pure-white beard was cut close, trimmed with precision; his features were rounded, his nose long, his smile wide.

She took a deep breath. Was that . . . ? "Bose Uncle!"

He gave a whoop and a wave, and Bayla hurled herself toward him. Bose caught and embraced her in a bear hug, rocking her to and fro a few times before releasing her.

He leaned back to get a better look at her. "Look at you, Bayla—you're grown up," he said, his smile tinged with sadness.

"Bose Uncle, I can't believe I'm seeing you again. Where's Tante Sindhu?"

The man's eyes teared up, and he shook his head.

Bayla's breath caught. "When?"

"About five years ago."

"I'm so sorry," she whispered, taking his hand.

She heard General Cartwright clear his throat to signal her. Releasing Bose's hand, she turned toward Cartwright and Jade, both seated in the jeep and waiting for them. Jade beckoned, and Bayla climbed into the back next to her. Bose got behind the wheel and accelerated quickly, and they were all thrown backward.

Bayla wanted to ask exactly where they were going—and where they *were*, for that matter. The area looked—felt—so familiar. They couldn't be near the old Tulā School grounds, could they? She looked around her. It was impossible to tell, given the density of the foliage.

When synchronous-time satellite imaging became easily available some years ago, Bayla had momentarily lost her resolve to close the door to the past. Scanning the images of the forest regions near Vayu City closely and repeatedly, she'd found nothing resembling the school. After it had burned down, the forest had overtaken and covered it. In that moment, as she'd searched, she wondered whether her life there had been a dream.

Bayla sighed and leaned back in her seat. Was this really happening? Was she actually going to see her father again? She'd felt reasonably calm when she'd gotten into the jeep, even happy after seeing Bose again, but now her composure was diminishing. As they drove, her breathing began to accelerate until, soon, she felt like she was hyperventilating. Jade gave her a questioning look, but Bayla waved a hand to signal she was okay.

Slowly and deliberately, Bayla softened her breathing while

simultaneously lengthening it. After a few minutes, she could look around again as they drove the rough road directly into the forest. Suddenly, Bose turned the jeep, seemingly into a tree line, but it was actually a roughly hewn dirt pathway, cleverly hidden. The jeep now proceeded more slowly.

Bayla stood and angled her body through the jeep's open sunroof, looking back toward the turn they'd just taken.

"What are you doing?" exclaimed Jade.

Bayla swung back into her seat. "Just wanted to see that turnoff—there's a marker there if you look closely."

Cartwright's voice sounded from the front. "Bayla, would you please not launch yourself out of the vehicle?"

Bayla caught Bose Uncle's eye in the rearview mirror, and they both grinned a little. Then, sliding a bit forward on her seat, Bayla leaned her body back so that she could look at the view she remembered so well, directly into the sky, through the crowns of trees.

***

"*Namaste,* General Cartwright," said a pleasant voice. A woman dressed in a pale pink tunic and loose beige pants welcomed him with the customary palms-together gesture. "We've been expecting you."

Bayla looked searchingly at the woman's face, wondering if she was someone else from the past. *No such luck,* she thought, disappointed. This wasn't Tulā School after all, and fifteen years had passed. What were the chances she'd recognize anyone else? She watched the woman speak into a two-way radio as the jeep moved on down the dirt road.

Just when Bayla could not stand any more anticipation, they drove into a small clearing. A few people in simple garb stood waiting, and she scanned their faces as she exited the jeep. She caught sight of a lean and elegant man approaching, dressed in a simple shirt and slacks, and a full head taller than everyone else. She dug her fingernails into her forearm.

His figure was still limber, his salt-and-pepper hair still thick and wavy. She inhaled sharply and didn't think her legs would support her. Her hand groped for the jeep just behind her, and she leaned on it for a moment. She stood frozen as the man walked toward her, smiling.

Automatically, Bayla bent to touch his feet, the traditional gesture of respect and honor.

Her father placed his palms over her head in blessing, then raised her to standing, taking her face in his hands and kissing her forehead.

The past swelled open all around her.

She tried to summon her anger to resist tears, but couldn't. With his thumbs, he brushed them from her face, then enveloped her in his arms. Bayla's face dropped to his shoulder, and her body shook with sobs.

"Welcome, my Bayla," he said softly, his voice as warm and lilting as she remembered, like a song.

CHAPTER 27

AATMANJI

Campsite, Prithvi Forest, outside the former Tulā School grounds

Aatmanji led Bayla into the gathering tent and seated her next to him on a bench. How delightful, and how peculiar, to look at her now, after fifteen years of absence from her life.

He held her hand and patted her shoulder until her tears gradually ceased. Despite the redness in her eyes and the puffiness in her face, he could see how her childhood beauty had bloomed and contoured along adult lines. Her hazel eyes were still enormous, and her face still heart shaped. He smiled at the dark wisps escaping from the bun on the top of her head, remembering the wild and chaotic curls of her younger days.

Though she'd become predictably lovely, he knew what was currently missing from her interiority, what would have flourished by now if he'd been able to continue her training. What would she have become by now? Someone formidable. *What a shame.*

Finally, Bayla gazed up at him, her presence receptive. He

looked at her with tenderness, and he knew, in that moment, she felt his love and loved him back. He felt humbled, grateful.

Then he sensed the shift.

It was rage, pushing through her love for him.

Aatmanji released her hand and turned more fully toward her so that she could look directly into his face.

"Why didn't you tell me?" she asked, her voice shaking, reproachful. "Why didn't you come for me?"

"Did the general tell you about Zed?"

"A little—that you sent me away to protect me from him."

"Yes. He discovered my location at Tulā School, and he came to see me. He believed I set a fire that killed his brother."

"And did you?" Bayla whispered.

"No, of course not, Bayla. But a fire did break out later the same day I was on the premises. I think Zed needed someone to blame. Unfortunately, he learned you were my daughter. He threatened you and told me what he intended to do to you—horrible things." Aatmanji shuddered. "I was terrified."

"That explains why you sent me away—but not why you couldn't come with me."

"Bayla, Zed didn't threaten only you—he threatened every single person at Tulā School. Every adult living on the grounds was there because of loyalty to me and our work. And every child living there was entrusted to me by a parent or loved one. I owed all of them my presence; I owed each of them every effort to keep them safe."

Bayla looked as though a tumult was occurring within her—her hurt struggling with her comprehension of, and perhaps even agreement with, his decision.

"But why did you send me so far—so far from everything I knew?"

"At the time Zed confronted me, he'd become so powerful.

I had to send you far away. I turned to my friend, and he was able to provide an arrangement in the US."

"General Cartwright."

"That's right. And then, within days, Tulā School was attacked. Those of us who survived needed to disappear, not only for the sake of our personal safety but so that we could continue to do our work."

Bayla was silent.

"Bayla, it was a wrenching decision—one of the most difficult of my life. I was terrified that if any connection were discovered, you would become leverage . . . or you could be killed. These days, as you know, it's extremely difficult to disappear, difficult not to leave an electronic signature of some kind. I had to hide you completely and also make sure Zed could never find you through me. The general made the arrangements to sever all contact."

Bayla's eyes filled with tears. "And you just . . . just let me go? You never wanted to find me?"

"Bayla"—Aatmanji's voice broke—"that's not true. I wouldn't let Edmond tell me where you were. Because I would have come for you. I would have brought you back home—I wouldn't have been able to stop myself."

She looked at him, confusion and uncertainty in her eyes. He put a hand on hers. "I did the best I could, my child."

Bayla seemed to steel herself. "No. I still don't understand. It happened such a long time ago—surely the danger passed after a few years. Even if it hadn't, you could have explained . . . sent a note . . . or Cartwright could have told me. All these years, you let me think that my family and home were gone."

She looked at him with reproach, and his heart shrank. "You abandoned me."

"Bayla," he murmured, touching her shoulder.

She flinched and sprang up. "Don't. Please just—leave me alone." She pushed the flaps aside and exited the tent.

Aatmanji sighed and stood up to follow her. *This isn't going well.* As he approached the flaps, he stopped short. Aanvi stood in the entryway, her gaze following Bayla. She turned to Aatmanji. "My goodness. All grown up."

He nodded and explained what had transpired.

"I see. I'll get her. There's still a lot she needs to know."

CHAPTER 28

BAYLA

Bayla strode into the middle of the campsite clearing and stopped short, looking around her. The forest was pushing hard against the temporary settlement, with its tents and rudimentary facilities. Closing her eyes, she wrapped her arms around herself for a few moments. She needed to clear her head, but the magnitude of the betrayal she felt made it impossible.

"Oh—hey—hi there!"

Startled, Bayla opened her eyes to find a trim man about her own age, olive-skinned, with dark, wavy hair and even darker eyes. He was smiling.

"You must be Aatmanji's daughter. . . ." His smile disappeared as he looked at her more closely. "Are you okay?"

She gave him a look of exasperation. "No, I'm not okay—not remotely."

"Is there anything I can do?"

Who is this guy? "I'm sorry, I . . . I can't talk right now."

Bayla turned and stomped toward the forest edge, then past it. Within fifteen feet, the foliage seemed to close in behind her and swallow her. *Fine by me.* She wanted to be swallowed, to disappear from her strange life and the inexplicable actions of the people around her.

She sank to the ground and pressed her balled fists into her eyes, shaking her head back and forth.

After so many years, she was getting some of the information she'd long craved, but it wasn't making her feel better. Instead, she felt as though all her wounds had been purposely opened, and the promised salve wasn't working. She felt angry and ill.

"Bayla!"

She looked up. The voice didn't sound like her father's.

She heard it again, from just a few feet away. "Bayla!"

A tall and regal woman pushed through the bushes and stepped in front of her. Bayla got to her feet and stared into piercing green eyes.

She'd seen those unusual eyes before, and suddenly, Bayla remembered. "I-I know you." She'd seen her from time to time when she was growing up. A few years before Bayla's departure, this woman had relocated to Tulā School, and her younger sister and brother had joined her a bit later. Of course, the woman looked older now—Bayla noted the dramatic white streak in the black hair, worn loose and long—but the stateliness of her manner was the same.

"Aanvi," Bayla said aloud.

"You remember."

Bayla nodded.

"Aatmanji told me what happened," Aanvi continued. "I understand how difficult this must be for you."

Bayla bristled. "Really? How could you possibly understand?"

Aanvi looked at her for a moment. "I take your point, Bayla, but there's much more that you need to know. Why don't we go back to the tent together."

Bayla stepped away from her. "No—I . . . I don't want to see him. Why didn't he communicate with me all those years?" She paused, then spoke with some reluctance. "I guess I can get my head around why I was evacuated, and why he couldn't come with me. And I can understand that he didn't want to scare me when I was a child. But after that? It just doesn't make sense to me, and—"

"Bayla, stop. Stop. It's important that you listen to me. Fully."

Bayla turned toward the woman and waited.

"Once the immediate danger was over, Aatmanji wanted to communicate with you—many, many times. In fact, he was about to reach out to General Cartwright again and bring you back to the country." She paused. *"I'm* the one who prevented him."

Bayla looked at Aanvi, open-mouthed. "But why? Why on earth would you do that?"

"I couldn't allow it. . . ."

Indignation swept over her. "Couldn't *allow* . . . ?"

"So if you need to blame someone for that, Bayla, blame me. Aatmanji was only trying to keep you safe from Zed. But I had other things to consider as well."

Bayla shook her head in bafflement and disbelief. "What are you talking about? *What* other things?"

Aanvi raised a brow significantly and gestured with her hand, indicating the pathway back to the clearing.

"Fine," Bayla muttered.

Aanvi nodded once and began pushing through the foliage. After a moment, Bayla followed. When she stepped back into the clearing, she squinted, trying to adjust to the light. Aanvi walked toward her father, who stood just outside the gathering tent.

Bayla's anger reignited. This woman had interfered in her family's life and happiness and was now acting as though it had been justified. Outraged, Bayla ran to catch up with Aanvi, grabbing her arm and stopping her from entering the tent.

"How dare you?"

Her father and Aanvi looked at her. "Bayla?" her father asked.

Bayla glared at Aanvi. "You had no right to prevent Appa from communicating with me all these years. Why would you do such a thing? For what possible reason?"

He jerked his head toward Aanvi. "Aanvi, what did you tell—"

Aanvi placed a hand on his arm to silence him. "The sooner, the better, Aatmanji." She turned to Bayla, who looked at her, eyes ablaze.

"Well? Are you going to answer me?" she demanded.

"Come inside, Bayla, and we'll talk." Aanvi turned and entered the tent, followed by her father. Bayla heaved a sigh and went in after them. Aatmanji took a seat on the bench, but Aanvi stood next to a small folding table with two stools, indicating that Bayla should sit there. She did so but was surprised when Aanvi turned and walked to the front of the tent.

Bayla noticed that a small brass oil lamp lay there on a straw mat. She hadn't seen it earlier. A vibrant red hibiscus flower lay next to it.

As with almost every daily ritual of Indian life, there were multiple meanings, and layers of meaning, behind lighting a lamp. The light itself symbolized knowledge and wisdom, and the necessity of placing those at the front and center of one's life. The flame, by virtue of the chemical reaction it generated, changed the composition of the air around it, dispelling negative energy. And the act of lighting the lamp served as a reminder that a single lamp could illuminate an infinite number of others.

Aanvi stood before it for a few moments, as though in contemplation, before taking the chair across from Bayla.

"Bayla, what did Aatmanji teach you about the four yugas?"

"What does that have to do with—"

"Bayla, please," urged her father.

Bayla's brow wrinkled as she thought back. "That cosmic time is divided into four eras, called yugas, and that humanity's path is tied to those yugas."

Aanvi spoke. "Bayla, the first of those eras, Sat yuga, was a different time for humanity—a time of peace, because it was a time of *inner* peace. During Sat yuga, human beings understood their connection to one another, and to Earth itself. And during that time, human beings were not limited to the five senses we know today."

"What do you mean?"

"I mean that people could communicate differently and perceive life more deeply because they could tune in to the quantum realm of existence."

"The quantum realm?"

"Bayla, in your physics classes, you must have learned the rules of Newtonian physics, correct?"

Bayla nodded.

"Those rules describe the physical domain of life. That is, what you experience with your five senses—everything that's material, three dimensional, with boundaries you can perceive. But underlying the physical domain is the *quantum* realm."

Her father spoke up. "The modern-day quantum physicists

discovered what's already explained in yogic philosophy: that there is a domain composed entirely of energy and information that underlies the physical domain and influences it continuously."

Bayla felt something in her ignite, like a bodily memory, an inborn understanding of the nature of reality that her father and Aanvi were describing.

"And, Bayla," her father continued, "the ability to tap into the quantum realm is latent in every human being, but rarely finds expression."

Bayla turned to Aanvi. "Are you saying that *you* have the ability to perceive the quantum realm?"

"Everyone does," her father replied, answering on Aanvi's behalf, "but the ability manifests to a different extent in different people. And some people have abilities far beyond that of others. For example, Aanvi is able to perceive . . . possibilities for future events."

Bayla was speechless for a moment. "Predict the future?" she scoffed at last. "Are you kidding me?" But Bayla noticed her father looking at Aanvi with the utmost respect—and maybe more than respect. Were they in a relationship?

Aanvi spoke. "Well, I wouldn't call it *predicting the future.* In the quantum realm, all possibilities exist, and any one of them can emerge. Sometimes, I am able to see the likelihood of certain *scenarios.*"

Bayla regarded Aanvi with skepticism.

Aanvi looked as though she was choosing her words carefully to describe something that was entirely intuitive to her. "I'll do my best to explain. When I tune in to the quantum realm, each person seems to exist on a thin strand, interacting with hundreds of other strands. I can sense what might happen when those strands overlap."

"So when two strands—two *people*—come together, you know what will happen—with certainty?" Bayla asked.

Aanvi sighed. "Nothing is certain, Bayla. If anything, the quantum realm shows us that the physical realm can be influenced and changed. But sometimes—*not always*—I do see extremely high probabilities when certain people come together at particular times. Unless I feel sure, I don't share what I see, and we obviously don't act on it." Aanvi paused and squeezed her eyes shut for a moment. "And there are many times I'm *not* sure."

After a few moments, Aanvi continued. "But, Bayla, I was sure about this: any contact at all between you and Aatmanji during those intervening years would have led to your death."

Bayla's mind rebelled against such a concept. "But how could you possibly know that? How is such an ability even possible?" Bayla's voice was sharp. She turned to her father, who continued to look at Aanvi with admiration and awe.

"Bayla, Aanvi has guided much of our work over these decades. We trust her judgment. And whenever we disregarded her insights, the results were disastrous." Bayla glanced at Aanvi, who winced suddenly. Bayla wondered why.

"That's what I saw," Aanvi stated firmly. "Whenever there was contact between you and Aatmanji during those years, your strand just . . . disappeared."

"When Aanvi told me that, I couldn't risk it," Aatmanji murmured.

Bayla shook her head in disbelief and looked at Aanvi with narrowed eyes. "Do you get some perverse pleasure out of controlling people's lives—some kind of power trip? How do I know it wasn't jealousy—a way to get me out of the picture?"

"Bayla!" her father exclaimed.

Aanvi looked at him mildly. "It's okay, Aatmanji." She

turned to Bayla. "No, I don't take pleasure in it. Absolutely not. Frankly"—her voice choked, and Bayla looked at her, surprised—"it's been a hard burden to bear." Aanvi closed her eyes for a moment. "Those possibilities are always in front of me, always calling to me, and it's hard to put them aside. But I felt certain about you and Aatmanji. Just like I was certain about . . ."

Aatmanji cleared his throat.

". . . others," Aanvi finished.

Bayla regarded her in stony silence.

Aanvi's voice sharpened. "I sympathize with you, Bayla, and everything you've been through in your life. But the fact remains—your individual journey is not the only thing that matters. In fact, your journey connects to that of many others—and impacts them as well. And in your case, Bayla, it affects the whole world."

Bayla looked at her in puzzlement. "What do you mean, the whole world?"

"Just that. It's time you understood your own ability. Your own ability to perceive the quantum realm."

What was Aanvi saying? "But I don't see *strands*, like you do," Bayla said, with a hint of derision.

"There are different abilities, Bayla."

Suddenly, it became clear to her. The threads of light emanating from her hands and body, connecting her to everything around her. She'd seen them again on the plane, with Jade—interwoven threads connecting everything she saw in a web of life and light. She thought of her vision at Environment Wire—her perception of the people embedded in that web all around her, all of them intending the same action, all of them urging her to stop the liquid, trusting her to act.

Bayla felt a flash of wonder as she recalled the experience, but it collapsed immediately. She hadn't been able to do anything. In fact, she'd been frozen in place.

"No," she exclaimed. "You're wrong. I can't—I can't do anything like that."

"You can, Bayla," Aanvi insisted, "and you must do so soon."

"Stop it. You're both wrong about this. Trust me."

"Okay, Bayla. Okay." Her father spoke softly. He turned to Aanvi and spoke with a restraining tone in his voice. "Let's take a break. I want Bayla to rest and have something to eat."

Bayla almost protested but changed her mind. She was starving. The last thing she'd eaten was an apple and a packet of mixed nuts on the general's jet.

"Would you like to sleep for a while, Bayla? It will be an hour or so before dinner. As you can imagine, our facilities are limited."

She stood and stretched. More than sleep, she needed to move through some yoga postures. "Appa," she said, "we're close to the old grounds, aren't we? Of Tulā School?"

"Yes, my dear."

"I'd like to go there."

Her father hesitated. "It won't look like you remember it—there's very little left of it."

"I know," she said with sadness. "I just want to see it again."

He paused for a moment. "I have to meet with General Cartwright right now—he needs to leave shortly. But Bose can take you."

Bayla almost refused Bose Uncle's company, but it would be good to speak with him again, and she wasn't yet confident of the directions over the dirt roads.

"I'll find him."

CHAPTER 29

BAYLA

As the jeep jolted over the roughly marked trails, Bayla gazed around her with rapt attention, drinking in the landscape. When she glanced at Bose, he was smiling.

She smiled back. "What? What is it, Uncle?"

"You still have that way about you."

"A way about me?"

"Brightness—intensity." His smile faded suddenly. "Not joy, though. Not anymore."

Her smile faded as well.

"You used to bubble with excitement. We could hardly restrain you—you were so full of life—running and shouting and dancing all over the school grounds." He laughed. "It's good that Aatmanji taught you meditation early on, to channel all of that energy."

Bayla closed her eyes and leaned back on the seat. She couldn't imagine being described as joyful, excited, or full of life now.

Bose laughed again. "Tante Sindhu's daily job was talking you down from the trees—you always perched up there, out of reach, and she had to convince you to climb down for meals. Sometimes I didn't know if *we* were raising you or the forest was."

"How did she convince me?"

"Usually, a mango would do it."

They grinned at each other.

"Yes, I remember." She also remembered the amount of disciplining she'd needed as a child. "She took such good care of me."

They rode in silence for a few minutes. Bayla heard Bose sigh.

"Bose Uncle, are you okay?" she asked, concerned.

He glanced at her, then returned his gaze to the road. "It was such a shocking day when Aatmanji packed you up and sent you away, without even a chance to say goodbye. I always felt like you were my daughter, too—mine and Sindhu's. You were everyone's daughter, really. We all knew the danger you were in, and yet . . . and yet . . ." After a few moments, he spoke again. "How I wish Sindhu could have seen you again, grown into this beautiful woman."

"Oh, Uncle." She ducked her head in embarrassment.

"You know, Bayla, what happened to you was a tragedy, and Sindhu and I couldn't forgive Aatmanji for a long time. But . . . but at least you grew up safe and sound. And this chance to see you again—it is such a gift."

Bayla put her hand on Bose's shoulder, and her eyes filled with tears.

***

After about fifteen minutes, they pulled onto a patch of

ground only slightly flatter than the rest. Jumping lightly from the jeep, Bayla looked up at the rays of sunlight descending in lines through the trees, and then at her surroundings.

Predictably, the forest had overtaken the area, but Bayla could still make out the former locations of the dormitory buildings and gathering halls. Originally, Tulā School had been intended as a permanent place, so some of the foundations were still visible if she looked closely.

Bayla turned toward Bose, who was sitting in the jeep, giving her space to do what she needed. After scanning the area for a few minutes, she walked toward one of the old building foundations. Because the walls had been constructed of bamboo and the roofs of thatch, not a trace of those remained.

She remembered how her classes had usually been outdoors, remembered standing in the monsoon rains to learn about the water cycles, and crawling within a bush to examine a millipede's progress, and lying under the stars to identify the phases of the moon.

Living in Nevada after her evacuation had been an upheaval in so many ways. Due to the toxicity in the air, her school only had windowless indoor classrooms. Information was dispensed mostly via electronic screens.

She remembered how, during one lesson, a banyan tree popped up on her tablet, labeled as such at the bottom of the screen. Memories of the banyan trees near her former home had flooded her mind, when she'd sat for hours within the unusual root structures, gazing up into the branches and leaves. Looking at her tablet again, she'd heard the voice of revolt reverberating within her: *NO. This isn't a banyan tree. It's a* photo *of a banyan tree.*

Label, memorize, dissect. She'd eventually learned to

appreciate the precision and orderliness of this approach. But as she'd cut and divided and isolated concepts to study for the constant stream of written tests, she'd felt similarly cut and divided and isolated from everything she learned, as though it had nothing to do with *her* as a human being. She'd felt she was gradually losing her sense of life's rhythms and cycles and wholeness—the leaf on the tree in the forest, the seed in the fruit in the food chain, the water droplet traveling from ground to air to rain and back again.

Surely a person needed to do both—understand life in its deepest particularity and also comprehend how intimately she was connected to that life.

Bayla looked around at the old grounds, wandering until she suddenly recognized one of the trees. It had been the one outside her dormitory, the one featured in her recent dreams. Back then, she'd climbed it daily to read, sometimes with Appa, who would make a game of pretending to fall and catching himself at the last minute, making her shriek with laughter.

She smiled despite herself as she placed her hand on the bark, watching the red ants back away from her hand as she did so. How the tree had grown! She had been able to get close to the top branches as a child, but now she wouldn't even be able to reach the lowest ones to hoist herself upward. Closing her eyes, she felt the slow vibrations under the bark. These trees had been the background noise of her childhood years—leaves whispering stories, branches rustling songs, trunks hosting small creatures that chirruped and buzzed and twittered.

She sat under the tree and pulled her knees up to her chest, for once allowing the flow of memory without resisting. Even more than geographic and cultural displacement, she remembered feeling as though her heart had slipped out of its groove and would never find its way back.

As the past washed over her, she tried to banish the tightness in her throat, to grit her teeth against tears . . . *damn*. She'd cried more in the past week than she had in years.

After a childhood among a crush of people, her loneliness had been a torment. She'd tried so hard to connect with others, but every person she met seemed to be a separate island, closed and impermeable.

She'd adapted her accent quickly, taking on the cadences of American English, flattening her tones, retiring terminology like "frock" and "loo" and "trainers." She thought of it as another language, like the British English, French, and Tamil she'd learned simply by conversing daily at Tulā School. And she'd paid close attention to American culture, learned what to discuss, how to speak, how to dress.

Nevertheless, she'd been taunted relentlessly, and she hadn't been able to understand why. Luckily, her body was quick and lithe from her years of *kalaripayattu* practice, and she could anticipate when the students would throw softballs directly at her head in gym class.

But words couldn't be dodged.

She'd gathered the words they'd launched at her, built a shell for her heart, and then packed herself into it. The openness, the joinder she'd once felt with her environment and the people around her, began to diminish, her cells sealing off one by one.

From that time onward, only survival mattered—what her mind could do to make a future for herself, now that she was all alone.

The news agency had attracted her because it had seemed like a pathway to comprehension. But no matter how much information she collected, or how much analysis she did, she couldn't answer the relentless *why, why, why* in her head regarding her past and her family.

Bayla raised her head from her knees. All the pieces and parts of herself still seemed scattered on the ground all around her, unable to fuse.

She sighed. It was probably time to head back, so she walked toward the jeep to look for Bose. He was seated on the ground, eyes closed in meditation.

Finding a space close to him, she began the warrior series of yoga postures. Slowly, her tiredness dissipated, and she relished the strength and energy she felt. When she finished, she dropped to the ground and breathed inward to her very center, keeping that energy alive and aflame in the present moment.

She wasn't sure how long she sat, but when she opened her eyes, she saw Bose waiting for her, his expression tender. She gave him a smile, full of light.

CHAPTER 30

AATMANJI

Aatmanji looked up as the jeep returned to camp and Bose and Bayla got out. Walking toward them, he was pleased to see Bayla looking a bit . . . lighter.

"The others are all eating together, but I was hoping you and I could share this meal," he said, gesturing toward a small folding table. She looked uncertain, then nodded and sat on one of the campstools.

The attendant brought a platter, and for a while, he and Bayla were occupied with distributing *idlis* and *sambar*, freshly made and fragrant. He smiled at Bayla's obvious delight, remembering her voracious appetite as a child after all her running and climbing and playing, after being coaxed down from a tree by Sindhu's promise of mangoes.

Before beginning their meal, they said a mantra together:

brahmārpaṇaṃ brahmahaviḥ
brahmāgnau brahmaṇā hutam
brahmaiva tena gantavyaṃ
brahmakarmasamādhinā.

He thought of the food hall at Tulā School, the whole group chanting these particular words together before each and every meal—words acknowledging how food, and the people growing it, and the people eating it, had all come from one source.

When they completed the mantra, he saw Bayla eyeing the *idlis*, round rice cakes made from a blended mixture of lentils and rice, fermented, and then steamed. He gestured that she should begin eating. He watched her for a few moments before he himself began, knowing that she was appreciating the singular taste—ever so slightly sour, with a texture both soft and dense. Nothing could match their sheer wholesomeness.

They sat and ate silently for a few minutes.

"How was your visit to the school grounds, my Bayla?" he asked, when she'd slowed down a bit.

"I think it was needed." She paused for a moment, appearing to collect her thoughts. "I didn't realize how many memories I'd stifled from Tulā School and from those first months and years in America. I think I've always pushed them away, so they couldn't continue to hurt me."

Aatmanji closed his eyes, his face pinched with regret.

She looked at him. "I know you had your reasons for what you did, even if I don't agree with them, and even if I don't understand your reasoning. To be honest, I don't know if I can forgive you for everything that happened, but I know I have to try. I have to look forward."

"That's all I ask, my Bayla." For the first time, she looked at him steadily, without turning away, and he thought he detected some thawing of her pain.

After a moment, he spoke again. "You're still wearing your pendant."

Bayla touched the copper pendant—it lay at the hollow of her throat, so she couldn't look at it directly. "Oh. Yes. I never take it off, so it feels like a part of me. Sometimes I run my fingers over the etchings when I'm thinking through something." She unclasped and examined it. "You know," she continued, "when I got to America, there were days when I wondered whether I'd dreamed my whole life in India. The pendant felt like proof, I guess—like a totem, connecting me with reality."

Aatmanji nodded sadly and reached his palm forward. She dropped the pendant into it.

"Do you understand the meaning?" he asked.

"I haven't thought much about it—the tree etched on the front looks like the foliage around Tulā School."

Aatmanji held his palm upright so that he could point out the aspects of the design. "Notice how the tree has a root system and a branch system equal in size. That is meant to show the interconnectedness of nature, Earth, and people—it represents the web that connects us all. And the symbol on the back . . ."

He turned it over in his palm so she could see the reverse side.

"It's *śrī yantra*, isn't it?"

"Yes, indeed," he replied with a smile.

"A unity symbol, right?"

"A particularly rich unity symbol—a *maṇḍala* of nine interlocking triangles. Four are upright and represent Shiva, or masculine energy, or potential energy. Five are inverted and represent Shakti, or feminine energy, or creative energy. United, the triangles represent the entire cosmos, with all its forces in balance."

He closed his fist over the pendant and held it tightly for a few moments before passing it back to her. When she reached for it, he took her hand in both of his and bent his head. He felt his tears drop, and then hers.

CHAPTER 31

CHAADI

ALL INDIA NEWS

VIDEO TRANSCRIPT 8/1/2023

"I'm Reza Banai with *All India News*, coming to you from one of the most beautiful and biodiverse places in the world—the Prithvi rainforest, located near the point where the states of Tamil Nadu, Kerala, and Karnataka meet. But I'll be honest with you—whoa!—I'm having a hard time keeping my eyes open in this rain. Yes, indeed, monsoon season is well underway!

"I'm here with Aatmanji, a local environmental leader concerned about nearby farmlands. Phew, how do you handle this amount of rainfall?"

[*Laughing, turning face to sky*] "It's a gift, really—the monsoons are becoming irregular, so we've learned to take joy in them."

[*Laughing*] "Well, you'll have to train me later. In the meantime, talk to me about the problem you're trying to address."

"Reza, the world's soil is going extinct, and let's be clear—without soil, there's no food."

"How did it get to this point?"

"In this area, agrochemicals were used on local farmlands without limitation, without testing or quality control of any kind. Over the decades, those chemicals caused our topsoil to degrade and die by stripping away organic matter and killing the insect population that keeps pests at bay. We've been addressing this by teaching traditional farming methods to reduce chemical usage. But . . ."

"But?"

"There's a second interrelated problem."

"Which is?"

"The destruction of the forests. To sell more chemicals, agrochemical companies convinced governments to convert more forestland into farmland.

But forest root systems anchor topsoil and preserve natural water
cycles. With both topsoil and forests being destroyed, our incredibly
lush land began turning into desert.
Imagine that—*desert* in a tropical
land. It's mind-boggling! So we
started massive reforestation efforts
to gird up root systems and hold
topsoil in place."

"And have your efforts been
effective?"

"In this area of the country,
we've made progress on both fronts
and kept much of the zone safe and
productive. In the past, local industry leaders and governments didn't
factor collective resources and
public health into their decisions.
No payments or reparations were ever
demanded when business enterprises
took what belongs to all of us, to
every single person—clean land and
water, in particular. But now, local
industry leaders are listening, and
we have an educated populace willing
to advocate for the land and to keep
watch. So far, it's working."

"Well, that's good, right?"

"It's a large world, Reza, and
an interconnected one. If everyone

doesn't take these measures, and
quickly, what we do here won't matter. The world will not be able to
grow food."

***

Sitting on a small campstool just outside his tent, Chaadi looked up from the electronic tablet on which he'd been watching a video.

He was glad to see Aatmanji and his daughter approaching. He'd learned so much during just forty minutes of tea and conversation with Aatmanji. Then a woman had interrupted their discussion, whispering in Aatmanji's ear and causing him to brighten.

"Okay, Shanti." He'd turned to Chaadi. "I'll need to leave you for some time. My daughter is here."

"Your daughter?"

"We're being reunited after fifteen years." He'd waited for Aatmanji to elaborate, but no explanation seemed forthcoming. "I'll need some time with her," Aatmanji had continued, "and then you and I can talk again. Come, let me walk you back to your tent—I'll send for you later."

But, as of yet, Aatmanji hadn't. The people at the campsite had taken care of him, though, and he'd joined them for the most flavorful dinner he'd ever experienced—steamed rice cakes, some kind of lentil stew, and three different rice dishes—tomato, lemon, and tamarind. He'd even tried the pickled gooseberries—his mouth was still on fire, but it had been worth it. How had they managed to make so much delicious food with such limited facilities?

And, oh boy, the mangoes—the mangoes had defied description.

At dinner, he'd met Aanvi, who had intimidated him with her stern manner and seemed too preoccupied to speak. But Shanti, the woman who had summoned Aatmanji earlier, had been welcoming, explaining the food preparation and the ingredients and spices, even taking him to the cooking area to show him around. Bose, too, had been friendly, telling him about the unusual history of Tulā School and sharing the tablet full of video clips.

When Chaadi had bumped into the daughter earlier that afternoon as she'd rushed out of the gathering tent, their momentary meeting hadn't been an auspicious one. She'd seemed upset, traumatized even.

As he looked at her now, walking with Aatmanji, she appeared to be crying. Chaadi watched as she dashed tears away with the back of her hand. Reuniting with her father must not have been an entirely positive experience.

They veered off to the right, toward the gathering tent, but Aatmanji turned to him and beckoned. Chaadi hurried to them.

When Chaadi entered the tent, he saw the daughter in profile, sitting on one of the benches. Aanvi and Aatmanji were speaking in lowered voices, and he caught the tail end of the discussion.

"They'll keep us posted on the conditions in California," Aanvi murmured. Chaadi was intrigued. Everything he heard in this place made him hungry to learn more.

Aatmanji nodded to Aanvi, then turned to Chaadi. "Welcome. There's a lot we need to tell you, and it concerns both of you. I'd like you to meet Bayla, my—"

"Your daughter," Chaadi finished, a bit too eagerly. *What's the matter with me today?* "Yes," he continued, modulating his voice, "we met briefly a couple of hours ago." He turned toward Bayla and held out a hand. "Chaadi Darius."

"Oh. Hi," she said, taking his hand warily. Her serious expression didn't change.

"Chaadi is the grandson of a friend. He has a part in everything happening right now."

Bayla looked at Chaadi again. He nodded at her in a friendly manner, but she turned away.

"Bayla," Aatmanji said, "what do you think is the most important environmental issue, as it relates to human beings?"

Bayla looked at him. "Do you mean globally?"

Aatmanji nodded.

"How can I possibly answer that? I mean, there are so many areas of environmental distress." She paused. "I guess I'd say that we're short on the primary resources we need to live—and now people are killing each other for them."

Aatmanji nodded. "Most experts are saying that soil extinction has become our most pressing problem. The bottom line is that everyone needs to be fed. While you grew up at Tulā School, you learned about the importance of land and caring for it. But you didn't know that we were a base of operations for this whole area to reclaim topsoil and forests and to keep them intact. What's more, we helped units in nineteen other areas of the world to do the same—it's been the work of decades."

Decades? Chaadi thought of the video clips he'd been viewing on Aatmanji's work.

"So you helped twenty areas in all?" Bayla asked. "I read that there are only twenty viable agricultural zones remaining in the world. That's because of the work you did?"

Aatmanji nodded again.

"And this is one of those zones," Bayla said.

Aatmanji's face showed immense sorrow. "Yes, but one section of it has been irreparably damaged."

"FZ5," Bayla said. "FZ5 was released here."

Aatmanji nodded.

"What's FZ5?" asked Chaadi.

"In short, it's a dupe," responded Aatmanji. "ZedChem has sold the world a bill of goods, claiming that this agrochemical will double or triple production in those twenty zones in order to feed the world. But it's a lie."

"You mean it won't help production?" asked Chaadi.

"It will, but only in the short term—just a few years, in fact. And in those years, it will look miraculous. But a brave woman, Jala Sharma, studied the formula and told us the truth." Aatmanji paused and swallowed. "But she sacrificed her life to do it."

"What do you mean?" Bayla asked.

"We believe Zed had her killed and made it look like . . ."

"Suicide," Bayla finished, remembering the articles she'd read at her apartment.

"But," Aatmanji continued, "before she died, she did her best to tell the world how FZ5 will kill the treated topsoil."

"Appa?" Bayla asked quietly. "Is that what I . . . experienced?"

"Yes, it was."

Chaadi turned to her. *What did Bayla mean, she* experienced *it?*

"Bayla," Aatmanji continued. "Why don't you describe it— what you saw."

"But . . . ," she said, glancing at Chaadi uncertainly.

"It's okay, Bayla," Aatmanji reassured her. Chaadi nodded at her as well, trying to look trustworthy. She regarded Chaadi for a moment, then closed her eyes as though trying to picture something.

"I heard a voice calling me—*your* voice, Appa—to Prithvi Forest, and suddenly I was . . . *there*. I could recognize everything—the axlewoods, the banyans, the jasmine. It was the place where I'd grown up." She sighed. "And I felt connected to everything around me—like there were *threads* joining me to everything else. A web."

"The web of life," Aatmanji spoke.

"But there was some kind of black liquid pooling all around me." She paused, obviously finding it difficult to continue.

"Go ahead, Bayla," Aatmanji urged softly.

When she spoke again, her voice was shaking. "The liquid burned through the soil, and I thought I could see it eating through the roots. And . . . and . . ." Bayla gulped. "It was eating through me, too. And everyone—everything was screaming, and then it was just . . . silent."

She wrapped her arms around herself for a few moments, then turned to Aatmanji. "What happened?"

Aatmanji sighed. "As dense as these forests are, their underworld is far denser. Roots and fungal fibers interweave across the land, anchoring the soil and also serving as a communication system. When FZ5 is poured into the farmland, it saturates it instantly and then pushes outward rapidly—in this case, to Prithvi Forest. And it keeps going, acre by acre, farther and farther, through the interconnected subsoil structures, severing that vast underground communication system. Soon, the soil dies from literal disconnection." His face contracted.

"So it was real—what I saw?"

"I'm afraid it was. And now, FZ5 is going to be poured simultaneously in all twenty remaining agricultural zones at the end of the week. Five more days."

"We have to do something," Bayla said—just as Chaadi asked, "So, what do we do?"

"I think we have a chance—but it's a slim one. Our chemist, Jala Sharma, found a weakness in the dispensing system for FZ5, and we might be able to use it."

"A weakness?"

"FZ5 is actually a combination of two formulas that must be kept separate and airtight until the moment of dispensing. At that moment, they're mixed in specially constructed tubes to inject them into the soil. If we can expose those chemicals to air before they enter the tubes, then we can deactivate them both. The FZ5 solution won't be able to be synthesized for application."

"But how could you access the site?" Chaadi paused. "Wait a minute—are you saying that you have to gain access to *all twenty* sites to stop the FZ5 pour?"

"That's correct."

Chaadi couldn't believe what he was hearing. He threw his hands wide. "How is that even possible?"

"That's where 108 comes in."

"108!" Chaadi exclaimed. Aatmanji smiled at him.

Bayla looked perplexed. "I don't understand."

Rather than discouraged, Chaadi felt exhilarated. Clearly, Aatmanji's group was doing far more than seeking temples. They were actually tackling a global crisis. They had a plan.

A whole world was opening up to him, fold by fold. He hadn't felt this sort of wonder or exhilaration since the first time Grandfather had taken him to the Shara temple and taught him about the Seven Sages.

His past had led him to this place, this moment. After so many years, Chaadi felt he was exactly where he needed to be.

CHAPTER 32

AATMANJI

Aatmanji turned back to Bayla's puzzled face. "Bayla, 108 is a group of people that harnesses one principle: that our thoughts can affect our physical reality."

Bayla did not appear to know how to respond. Aatmanji then looked at Chaadi, who had seemed so excited when he heard "108," but whose enthusiasm now seemed to be waning.

"Wait a minute, Aatmanji," he interjected. "You're not saying that you can *think* this problem away, are you? Please tell me you're not—because that's just not possible. We can't think away climate change and school shootings and cancer and the billion other horrible things that are happening every day."

"Yes, Chaadi, I hear you—but between what *I* just said and what *you* just said, there are a number of degrees."

"What do you mean?"

Aatmanji closed his eyes, gathering his thoughts. "Let's start here," he said, turning a laptop toward himself and typing rapidly. "Have you ever heard interviews of people on the ground in New York City during 9/11?"

Bayla and Chaadi looked at each other.

"Watch this one," said Aatmanji.

TEN-YEAR MEMORIAL

VIDEO CLIP: INTERVIEW 9/11/2011

"And where were you when the first plane hit the World Trade Center?"

"So, I was jogging back to the NYU campus—I was an undergrad there—and a bunch of us were diverted to Battery Park in the chaos. The problem was, we couldn't leave the city from there. Everyone north of the attack site could access bridges to exit the city on foot, but we were trapped on the southern tip of Manhattan. And we had no way to walk off the island."

"How did you get out?"

"A lot of people don't know that there was a huge water evacuation from there. I'm not sure how it all came together—I heard that a few Coast Guard officials took charge and enlisted all the boats in the area—you know, ferries, police boats, recreational vehicles—anything with a motor, really."

"You're right—I never heard about that operation! So, what were you thinking when you got on your boat?"

"Besides freaking out, you mean?
[*five-second pause*] Well, I was trying
to figure out how to tell my parents
and my friends at my dorm that I
was okay. But cell phones weren't
working, and there was so much confusion. I didn't know whether more
attacks were on the way, or where
the boat would drop me off, or how to
get to safety, or where to stay the
night. [*five-second pause*] It's weird,
though—you'd think I'd have felt completely alone, but I didn't. I'm not
sure if this is going to make sense—I
had this sensation of being supported
and held, as though everyone in the
world was thinking of us in New York
City. Behind all the grief and shock,
there was something holding me up—the
only way I can describe it is as a
'wall of humanity.'"

Aatmanji paused the clip. They sat in silence for a few
moments, then Bayla spoke. "So are you saying that people's
thoughts actually affected this person—the person who was
interviewed?"

"Yes, I am. In fact, it was a *measurable* phenomenon using
devices called random-event generators—REGs."

Bayla's brow wrinkled. "Which are ... ?"

"REGs are machines that generate entirely random outputs
continuously—try to imagine a high-speed electronic coin
flipper. There's a network of them in sites around the world."

"What are they for?"

"Scientists analyze REG data to discover *when* their random output becomes mathematically *less* random and *more* orderly. In one study, they evaluated REG data to determine whether those less random periods correlated with global events. And they did—and the most powerful correlations happened on—"

"9/11," Bayla and Chaadi said together.

"That's right. On the morning of 9/11, we know for a fact that millions of people around the world were paying attention to what was happening in New York. The REGs actually *measured* the moments when all those minds were in sync. In other words, by just paying attention to a single event, our minds were having a measurable impact on the physical world."

"So all that attention directed to New York City influenced those . . . what were they called . . . REGs?" Bayla asked.

"Yes."

"Look, Aatmanji," Chaadi broke in, "I'm sorry to ask this— but, really, *who cares*? What difference does it make if there's some tiny effect measured by an REG? Why does it matter?"

"Ah, you see, Chaadi, that's what I meant by *degrees*. If group *attention* has some measurable impact, imagine what group *intention* does. That is, one group of people thinking one simple and directed thought." Aatmanji paused. "I've learned that directed intention *does* affect the physical world. And the more people involved, the more power generated. And the more *trained* people involved, even more so. That's what 108 is: a group trained in *intention*—focusing deeply and profoundly on a single action involving the physical elements."

"But—sorry—have you really been able to do anything?" Chaadi asked.

"At first, no. But we learned, over time, to generate small

effects. Sending a puff of air, igniting a tiny spark. But we had a problem: we could take these small actions, but we couldn't *direct* them where they were needed."

"So what did you do?"

"Not we—*Daksha*. Daksha was able to do it." He looked at Bayla askance for a moment.

"Is she a member of this group?" Bayla asked.

"That's a difficult question to answer, Bayla. Not exactly. But when she was with us, we had the ability to act *where* we needed to act. It was as though she could gather us together and move us en masse."

He glanced at Bayla. *Does she know she has the same ability?*

Chaadi looked confused. "But how . . . *how* did she do that?"

"I don't know the exact mechanism, Chaadi. Some of the Ancients had special abilities, and since then, those abilities have appeared among a few human beings. Daksha's was one of those abilities."

Chaadi looked at Bayla, who was looking more agitated by the moment. He turned back to Aatmanji. "So why didn't this . . . Daksha . . . help you stop the test pour?"

Aatmanji sighed. "We had barely thirty minutes to act. And when I called through the web, she seemed to respond. But then she was just . . . gone."

"What do you mean?"

"Just that. She . . . disappeared . . . from the web."

They sat in silence, then understanding seemed to dawn on Chaadi. "You're trying to do the same thing now, aren't you? When the pour happens in twenty locations in a few days." He paused. "But if you couldn't reach Daksha for the test pour, how are you going to find her now?"

"I may not be able to, Chaadi. Honestly, I don't think I will." Aatmanji took a deep breath. "But I can tell you this— when I couldn't reach Daksha that day, on the day of the test pour, I looked for . . . someone else. And I believe that person can help us now." Aatmanji looked at Bayla, who was shaking her head back and forth, not exactly in response to him but to herself, like a denial.

Aatmanji sighed. *She wasn't ready then. Will she be ready now? There's so little time. And we're not talking about one location—we're talking about twenty.*

Chaadi looked back and forth between Bayla and Aatmanji, as though trying to understand their silent interaction. "Are you saying there's someone else who can do what Daksha did?" he asked.

Aatmanji nodded.

"Who? Who is it?"

There was silence.

Aanvi, who had been sitting in the background during the conversation, spoke for the first time. "Bayla. We think Bayla can do it."

Surprised, Chaadi turned toward Bayla, who was sitting frozen, her hazel eyes wide.

"What . . . what are you talking about?" she whispered, though it was clear she knew.

Aanvi's voice was firm. "Bayla, we need you. This isn't just about you or the people in this room or a single group or a single country—this is about humanity. It's about the end of us all; 108 is our only hope—which means *you* are our only hope."

Aatmanji spoke. "Bayla, you *can* do this. And I believe this is what you were born to do."

After her long silence, Bayla's words seemed to burst from her. "No, Appa—I *can't*! I couldn't even *move* when you called me during the test pour. I just sat there on the dirt, writhing in pain. I was useless—I *am* useless."

Aatmanji moved next to her and took her hand. "Bayla, my Bayla, of course you're not useless. You just weren't expecting it. . . . How could you? But now you *do* know. You know what to expect. And you've done it before—as a child." Aatmanji had a sudden vision of flying, all the meditators together, gathered up by a beautiful, laughing light.

A school of fish.

A swarm of bees.

A flock of birds.

He looked at Bayla, who appeared to share the memory. For a moment, she looked free, open.

"You remember, don't you?" he said softly.

She seemed to return to the present, and her face fell. "Yes, I remember."

He felt her energy shift, just like before. Anger. Rage. She snatched her hand away.

"You shouldn't have brought me here. I told you. I can't do it anymore. Don't you understand, Appa—that ability is gone. I mean it, *gone*. And it's your own fault. When you abandoned me, you *broke* me," she exclaimed, bending over her knees, tears escaping her eyes.

"Impossible." Aatmanji's soothing voice turned stern, steely.

Bayla looked up at him in surprise.

"Impossible," he repeated, more gently. "Look at you, Bayla—look at what you've survived, what you've learned, who you are."

"You're wrong." She jumped up.

Aanvi stood as well. "Bayla, time is short, and—"

"No!" Bayla shouted, holding her hands out, palms forward,

as though pushing them away. "Stop it. Leave me alone—all of you. Leave me out of your plans."

"Bayla . . ."

"No, Appa, I'm getting out of here. I'm asking Bose Uncle to drive me back to Vayu City in the morning. I'm going home."

She turned and left the tent.

CHAPTER 33

BAYLA

I am a child again, sitting below my favorite tree, reclining within its mossy hollows. Fibers grow and weave around me, murmuring as they branch and thicken, and I hear those murmurs echoing in my own body. This time, I am ready when the woman appears. I jump up, grab her hand, and hold tightly, but a cavern opens beneath us both. We fall into gooey blackness, and I scream. . . .

Bayla sat up with a jolt. *Where am I?*

She touched the rough weave of the cot in her tiny sleeping tent. Sitting up, she said the Earth mantra, but instead of standing, she lay back again. She needed to get away from this place, away from the people raking up her past and then providing no resolution.

After the unnerving—actually, terrifying—conversation with her father, she'd run to this tent and cried until she'd fallen asleep. Now her eyes and face were sticky with old tears. Standing, she walked to the flap and poked her head out.

A woman seemed to have anticipated Bayla's awakening

and waited just outside with a fresh tunic and pants and toiletries, which she placed in Bayla's hands.

"Inge vaa, inge vaa," the woman said in Tamil. "Come here, come here."

She led Bayla to a small area enclosed by walls fashioned from bamboo poles, with buckets of water for bathing and a nearby latrine. When Bayla finished, dressed, and emerged, the woman was no longer there.

Bayla looked around the campsite, trying to locate Bose to ask for a ride to town. He was nowhere to be found. Spotting the meditation platform at the far edge of the site, near the river, she made her way toward it.

When she reached it, Bose wasn't there, but her father was. She frowned, though she supposed she should have expected it.

Despite her frustration with him, she watched and admired the smooth pace of his hatha yoga routine. Of course, hatha yoga was only one component of the full practice of yoga. *Yoga is not merely physical movements and postures,* he'd told them over and over again at Tulā School. *Physicality is just the entry point for yoga in its fullest significance.*

He'd explained that the word "yoga" meant "union," an experiential comprehension of the equivalence between individual consciousness and universal consciousness.

When her father eventually transitioned to a seated meditation, Bayla continued to watch, remembering how his stillness had always seemed tangible to her, as though it had its own form and heft.

Slowly, a few others occupied the platform and began their own practices, and she found a mat and an area for herself as well. Before she began, she sat for a moment, relishing the feeling of alignment and coherence in the space, generated by all the practiced meditators around her. It helped her put aside the turmoil within her, and she slipped into stillness.

As her concentration deepened, she witnessed a play of energy in front of her closed eyes, blooming in fractal patterns. As she sensed one meditator passing her a few feet away, Bayla watched how her own energy was impacted by his, and the wave they created together—a wave that flowed through the platform and then joined the entire ocean of existence.

***

When Bayla finished her practice and opened her eyes, the platform was empty. Noticing some activity near the cooking tent, she walked there and found an outdoor table with simple breakfast items, including individual portions of fruit. Chaadi stood nearby, eagerly spooning cut lychees and mangoes into his mouth from a little bowl made of melded leaves.

Given that he'd witnessed her breakdown yesterday, Bayla felt awkward and merely nodded to him. He smiled back, fully and without reservation.

I wish I could smile like that, she thought, wistfully.

"Honestly, in all my life, I've never tasted fruit this good," he declared, indicating his now empty bowl and reaching for another.

It was hard not to enjoy his enthusiasm—or take the suggestion. She, too, picked up a bowl of fruit and a spoon fashioned from husk, and began eating.

"How are you doing, Bayla?" Chaadi asked, after a pause. "That was rough yesterday."

This time, she gave him a crooked smile. "I'm not usually so . . . unglued."

"Seems understandable."

"If you really want to know, I'm exhausted. It's too much, and I'm not handling it very well. I want to leave, but I haven't found Bose yet. Have you seen him?" she asked, looking around the grounds again.

Chaadi shook his head.

"I'm hoping he can give me a ride to the airport—I don't know how else to get there." She looked at Chaadi again. "How long are you staying?"

"You know, I'm not sure—this has all been a huge detour from my regular life."

"Yeah, tell me about it."

"Bayla, I just want to say . . ."

She looked at him, his face suddenly somber.

"I want you to know . . ." He broke off and ran a hand through his hair. "Let me try this again." He took a breath. "I was surprised when you said . . . when you thought . . . you were 'broken.' When you used that word." He paused. "I don't know you very well, but I wanted you to know how I see you. I see a strong woman."

Bayla felt her ears redden. *That was unexpected.* She ducked her head and began to turn away, but stopped herself. "Thank you," she said gratefully.

"I don't really understand the ability you all were talking about yesterday, but I have no doubt you could wield it. None at all."

Bayla wasn't sure she agreed, but it warmed her heart to hear it. For the first time, she looked Chaadi full in the face and smiled at his earnestness. For a split second, she regretted that she was leaving.

They stood in companionable silence for a few minutes, eating and glancing at each other from time to time.

At last, she placed her bowl in the composting bin. "I'm going to keep looking for Bose. It was good to meet you, Chaadi—it really was. And in case you . . ." They both looked up as her father dashed toward them.

"Please, Bayla, please come with me. Chaadi—you, too."

Her brow wrinkled. "Appa, if this is about yesterday, I don't want to talk about it anymore. . . ."

"Just come with me—I won't ask anything of you again. And I'll get you to Vayu City right afterward. But come with me now."

Bayla looked at Chaadi, then nodded at her father, who turned and strode about ten feet away from them, then pushed through some fronds and leaves. A pathway appeared, one she hadn't noticed before. He turned back and beckoned.

Chaadi grabbed her hand, and they followed, trying to keep him in sight.

After twenty minutes, the three of them arrived, panting, in front of a large structure fully covered in greenery. When she squinted at it, she could make out the shape—a domed building, well camouflaged, about fifteen feet long in diameter.

Chaadi exclaimed, "It's another one—another yogic temple!"

A yogic temple? Bayla wondered.

"I don't understand, Aatmanji," Chaadi continued. "When—how did you find another . . . ?"

"I'll explain later, Chaadi." He waved them inside.

Bayla stepped into the chamber, followed by Chaadi, and she blinked in the darkness until her eyes adjusted. Cleverly disguised apertures allowed narrow shafts of light to enter. Aanvi was seated to the right of the entrance, and she waved Chaadi over to her and began to whisper what sounded like instructions in his ear.

Her father gestured. "Please, Bayla, sit. Sit here." She dropped gracefully into a cross-legged posture and looked at him, expecting him to tell her what was happening. He merely seated himself, eyes closed, his palms resting upward on his thighs.

Am I supposed to . . . ? Okay, then. She, too, closed her eyes and, after a few moments, thought she heard her father whispering something to her. "What did you say?" she asked, but there was no answer.

She felt a shift, a change. Opening her eyes, she found herself standing in a forest, surrounded by trees. *How did I get back outside?*

But no, wait, this was a different forest—not Prithvi this time. It seemed . . . North American.

I know this place!

It was Reston Grove, the oldest part of Walcott Forest, a few hours north of San Francisco. She'd visited often, sitting alone on the ground within the spiraling circle of redwoods, the branches and leaves weaving a cathedral overhead.

But this time, she wasn't alone. She felt the presence of a hundred people, maybe more, connected and intertwined in a web of life, a web of light, waiting for . . . her.

We need you, Bayla! Her father's voice directed her vision to a spot of forest floor covered in footprints and trash. And then she saw it: a few embers remaining from a campfire, inadequately smothered. Around those embers were miles of dried leaves and branches extending in all directions.

She felt the intention of every person around her: *Extinguish those embers.*

Anger rushed through her. Why wouldn't her father listen to her? She'd already told him that she couldn't move during the test pour. Why didn't he believe what she knew to the bottom of her core—that she was ineffectual, powerless?

She shouted her frustration.

She resisted and thrashed.

She pushed the orbs away, pushed herself out of the web, out of the tangle of energy. And there in the middle of the chasm between herself and all the others, she saw Aanvi.

Aanvi held up a palm, positioned vertically, fingers pointing upward. *Bayla, look here. Watch. This is your strand.*

Bayla looked into Aanvi's palm, and she could see the events swirl and accelerate around the strand that represented *her*—her own life. Images flashed.

Embers biting the parched leaves. A crackle. An ignition. A flame.

A roar.

A conflagration.

A devouring.

In all directions, air smoldering, creatures panicking, soil shrieking.

Somehow, Bayla knew. This was not a fire in the ordinary course, the type needed to renew the land. Instead, she was observing the largest North American wildfire to date devastate the forest. She was watching fire travel up, up into all the redwood trunks, immolating the branches.

The redwoods revealed the universe they contained— twisting branches, braiding roots, converging fibers—just before burning and burning and burning. She knew the burn would last weeks, then months. She knew the land would never recover.

Bayla screamed. *No, please, I can't—I can't bear this! I can't bear this loss.*

She drew a ragged breath and tore her eyes away from Aanvi's palm, from her own strand of life, from that vision of the future. Again, she looked down at the embers on the verge of igniting the surrounding detritus. She stared for a long moment.

No, she decided. *I won't bear this loss.*

Again, Bayla closed her eyes, turning inward, tuning into the web, feeling it around her and then within her, feeling its pulses and beats, hearing the music of her childhood, when she'd placed her ear to the earth and heard melodies, when she'd curled herself into the boughs of trees and heard stories.

She looked at the tangle of matter, then the tangle of energy within it. She was connected to all of it, her borders and boundaries thinning, her purpose expanding.

She felt the heartbeats of the people around her—each one encased in an orb of light within a web of light, each one a singular, inimitable warrior for this singular, inimitable Earth.

They were many. And they were One.

She called to them. They melded and moved.

A school of fish.

A swarm of bees.

A flock of birds.

They flowed through the forest interiors toward a riverbank, to a diversion held in place by a stone.

This. Here. Now.

A puff of air.

The stone fell.

The water burst through.

The soil drank and pooled and flowed to the embers, and the embers were extinguished.

They felt relief. They felt coolness. They made themselves

still and heard the music swell again. They saw cosmic dust and Earth dust, and all the stars above, and all the life below.

***

Bayla took a deep inhalation and opened her eyes. The others were watching her intently. Chaadi began to move toward her, but Aanvi grabbed his arm to hold him back. Bayla felt she was in an in-between state, watching the others but unable to interact with them.

After a minute, she emerged.

"What—what happened? What did we do?" she whispered.

"I think you know, Bayla. Tell us what you experienced."

Bayla closed her eyes, trying to verbalize what seemed un-translatable. "I-I joined everything—the matter, the energy. I was occupying the whole of space and, at the same time, the deepest interiors of cells."

Her father smiled. "Bayla, what you experienced was *life*, as it is, with all its interconnectedness and interdependence."

"And I felt the presence of people around me, but not ex-actly physically. And we all traveled together." Bayla gave a small gasp. "We diverted the water."

"We did, but we needed *you* to take us there."

"I . . . I couldn't move last time, but this time, I could. I felt all of you—I *became* all of you. And I knew what we had to do."

Bayla felt a profound sense of calm. All those discon-nected pieces of her life, the pieces that had seemed scattered all around her on the Tulā School grounds, the fragments that had never made sense, were now joining together, merging with who she was today, right now. Every part of her past had led her, inevitably and rightly, to this moment.

CHAPTER 34

AATMANJI

Aatmanji watched the play of understanding and peace on Bayla's face, feeling proud of his lovely daughter.

Aanvi rose and walked toward her. Aatmanji noticed Aanvi's look of relief as she knelt and embraced Bayla. "Wonderful, Bayla. You were wonderful."

He turned toward Chaadi, who appeared to be regarding Bayla with awe. Aatmanji felt pleased that Chaadi had been able to share in the experience—it spoke to his receptivity and willingness to embrace the unfamiliar. *Good thing, if he intends to join this cause.*

Aanvi rose to her feet again and nodded at Aatmanji. He returned the nod, knowing she had much to attend to. They all watched as Aanvi exited the temple.

Bayla still appeared to be collecting her thoughts and processing the experience. "Appa," she asked after a moment, "where does this ability come from?"

"We don't know, Bayla. We only know that what you did, and what Aanvi sees in the future, and how I call through the web—these were abilities some human beings possessed during ancient times."

"You mean during Sat yuga," said Bayla.

"Yes."

"Excuse me—what was that you said?" Chaadi's face looked confused. "What does that mean?"

Aatmanji answered, "Yugas are divisions of time as our solar system travels in an elliptical orbit around an anchor point in the middle of our Milky Way galaxy. Many say that the anchor point is a black hole of unimaginable density, essentially holding the galaxy together.

"When the solar system is closest to the anchor point, during Sat yuga, every human being feels a sense of connection, with everyone and everything. But as the solar system moves farther away from that anchor point, that feeling of connectivity diminishes, and human beings become gradually more disconnected, deluded, violent. At the farthest point in the orbit, truth is always under assault, people can't communicate with one another at all, and great fear dominates the collective. Does that sound familiar?"

Both Bayla and Chaadi responded at once, "Yes."

After a moment, Bayla spoke: "But . . . things can get better, can't they?"

"Yes, Bayla. As we turn the corner and move back toward the anchor point, humanity has tremendous potential to evolve again, to rediscover our connectedness."

"Okay," said Chaadi, shaking his head as though to clear it. "This is really new information for me. But bottom line—if things will get better as time goes on, what's the problem?"

"The problem is that we are now impacting the planet in such a way that it will no longer support human life. If humanity destroys its home, then turning the corner toward the anchor point and evolving as a species are irrelevant." Aatmanji paused. "We will not be here to experience it."

Aatmanji stopped speaking, and the others sat in silence for a few moments, digesting what he'd said and all it implied.

"Can anything be done?" Bayla asked at last.

"There *is* a great deal being done. There are advocates of all kinds, educating the public, fighting with governments, convincing leaders, arguing before judges. And there are grassroots movements, all over the globe, that have been taking small, incremental actions for decades."

"Like you, Appa," she stated. "You kept ZedChem out of this area of India—and out of those nineteen other areas in the world."

"Yes, but when we began that work long ago, we expected a wave of support to develop and grow. It never occurred to us that people would *continue* to harm the planet once they understood the damage they were causing. Now, even if every government on Earth cooperates, particularly the governments of countries that pollute the most, there's only a ten-to-twenty-year window to correct our current trajectory."

"So . . . there's no hope?" Bayla asked quietly.

"There is always hope. But FZ5 is closing that window—and fast."

Again, they sat in silence.

After some time, Aatmanji turned to Chaadi and gestured around him. "What do you think of the temple, Chaadi?"

Chaadi stood and began to walk the perimeter, his excitement obvious. "It's the same—exactly the same as my grandfather's temple—I mean, the temple at Shara Forest." He looked around and up. "The size, the shape. The lotus in the middle of the dome. The alcoves built into the walls. When did you find it?"

"Less than a year ago—it was right under our noses, but Prithvi Forest is extensive and dense. It took a long time to excavate. And given what happened to the Shara temple in 2025, very few have been informed of its existence."

Chaadi pointed to an area of the wall. "May I?" he asked, looking at Aatmanji.

Aatmanji gestured for him to go ahead. Chaadi held out a hand to Bayla, and she took it and stood. He gently pulled her to the wall. "Watch!" he said to her. Aatmanji smiled a bit at their interaction.

Chaadi spoke the Earth mantra at a particular spot, and Bayla gasped as the marking appeared. She got on her knees to examine it, but it disappeared in a few seconds.

"What was that?" she asked.

"It's a number," Chaadi responded with enthusiasm, "written vertically. Here, you do it—you'll see," he said, shifting out of the way. Bayla leaned down and whispered the same mantra—the Earth mantra she'd said every morning since childhood. The red marking appeared, but she looked puzzled as she tried to examine it before it faded.

"Do you know what it says?"

Bayla shook her head.

Chaadi spoke proudly. "It's three Sanskrit numbers in a vertical row—one, zero, eight." He turned to Aatmanji. "So why are the temples marked with that particular number? I mean, I saw references to all kinds of things when I was searching—about energy points and texts and beads—but I don't understand why the number is important in the first place."

Aatmanji looked at Bayla. "What do you think, Bayla?"

Bayla looked like she was concentrating, thinking back on her teaching and training, trying to find the right words. "In yogic philosophy, it's the number that illustrates the connection between humanity and the cosmos."

Aatmanji smiled. "Bravo."

"Okay . . . *how?*" Chaadi asked.

Bayla turned toward Aatmanji. "Shall I?"

"Go ahead," he encouraged, pleased that she remembered.

She took a breath. "Okay. Now remember, these calculations were made thousands and thousands of years ago. The diameter of the sun times 108 equals the distance between the sun and Earth. And the diameter of the moon times 108 equals the distance between the moon and Earth. Plus, the diameter of the sun is 108 times the diameter of Earth."

She paused for a moment, gathering her thoughts. "So, this number is grounded in humanity's home. But it's also grounded in the human *body*. There are 108 vital body points defined in Ayurvedic medicine. And there are 108 energy lines converging to form the heart chakra."

Aatmanji stepped in. "You see, Chaadi, the number '108' is a reminder that everything—humanity, Earth, cosmos—is tied to the same interconnected system. It reminds us to think on behalf of all life and all existence, at all times. If we can genuinely internalize that message, then the Sages have given us a way to preserve humanity. That is the secret of 108." He turned toward Bayla.

"Bayla, you asked whether there was hope. There is. The Seven Sages built temples around the world for various purposes. But they marked some of them with this number, because they were established in a certain way, with a particular energy signature.

"If someone within the temple directs her intention in a

certain way, with concentration and intensity, then the temple magnifies that intention. If the person in the temple is connected to others with the same intention, the power is even greater.

"We lost the Shara temple, but we found this one. We believe it was built by Agastya, one of the Seven Sages—the one who traveled through southern India to spread yogic teachings and philosophy. We are searching for others—here in India and all over the world—to help us magnify our intentions. But right now, Bayla, only you can *direct* our intentions."

"But I still don't understand—how do *I* have this ability?"

"These abilities of the Ancients have appeared in some people throughout the ages. But in your case, Bayla, I suspect it's because . . ." Aatmanji stood and walked toward Bayla. Taking her hand, he spoke. "Because your mother has the ability, too."

Bayla looked stunned. "What do you mean my mother *has* it? You told me my mother was dead."

"No, Bayla, I told you she was gone."

Bayla stared at Aatmanji. When she spoke, her voice shook. "Appa, are you—are you saying my mother is *alive*?"

CHAPTER 35

AATMANJI

Aatmanji winced. "I don't know for sure, Bayla. But I can tell you that I've had contact with her."

She pulled her hand away. "Appa, you lied to me! You've lied to me *my whole life*." He moved closer to her, but she jumped up and began pacing. Suddenly, she stopped and looked at him.

"Daksha," Bayla said quietly. "Daksha is my mother."

Aatmanji nodded. "She doesn't lead a typical life, Bayla. The only way I know how to describe her is *of Earth*—she wanders and takes whatever path calls her in the moment. But she has come to us when we've called. She's supported 108 all these years, helping us direct our intentions where they were needed. Much of our success in warding off ZedChem years ago was because of those abilities." He paused. "*Your* abilities."

Bayla's lips had settled into a firm line. "Tell me where she is. Right now."

"I don't know."

"Why should I believe you?" Bayla snapped.

He sighed. "It's a fair point. But as I told you, Bayla, she no longer answers when I call through the web."

Bayla seemed like she was teetering in place, and Chaadi lunged toward her and grabbed her arm to steady her. She didn't seem to notice. Instead, she was staring straight in front of her, her eyes unseeing.

"Bayla, she left you with me when you were an infant."

She pulled her arm away from Chaadi and looked at Aatmanji. "Then you're not even my father."

"Please don't say that."

"Why would she leave me . . . ?" Understanding seemed to dawn on her. "Aanvi. Aanvi saw something in our quantum strands, and she separated us."

"When Aanvi read the strands, they showed your death or hers if you remained together, in every combination of circumstances. We explained this to Daksha, and Daksha chose not to risk your life. She left you with us to raise you."

"How could you possibly know that for sure? That one of us would die if our paths crossed?" Her face hardened. "I don't think any of it is true. You wanted insurance. You suspected we both had this ability, and you wanted a 'spare.'"

"Bayla, please don't look at it that way. We thought—"

"And now your insurance is paying off, isn't it? Daksha is gone, and you expect me to step in."

"It wasn't like that, Bayla. Really."

Bayla simply stared at him.

"It was a great privilege of my life, to steward Daksha, to witness her abilities and her path. The forest came alive around her as she walked, the flowers would open—and they did the same for you when you were at Tulā School. My other great privilege was to raise you."

A sob escaped from Bayla, just one, a venting that seemed to prevent her from cracking into shards.

"Bayla, please listen. None of this matters. Nothing

changes the fact that this is your destiny—to fight for Earth and to avert the coming disaster, the one that the Seven Sages predicted and provided these temples for. It's time for you to join us—to join 108, and soon to lead it. This is your role for this lifetime."

Bayla extended her hands in front of her, again pushing Aatmanji's words away.

"No. No. Stop. I don't believe you. And I don't trust you. I told you—I'm going home."

"You witnessed it yourself—you saw what you can do. With the temple, 108 will have more strength and intensity. And with *you*, 108 will have precision and direction. Earth needs you. Humanity needs you, my daughter, my Bayla."

"I don't *want* to," she exclaimed.

Aatmanji stopped short, astonished.

"Did you just assume I would?"

"I . . . I suppose I did."

"Then you've made a mistake. I'm not the person you just described—that version of me is gone—*dead*. I'm not her—I'm just a girl you abandoned."

She angrily brushed the tears from her face. Aatmanji moved toward her, but she stopped him. Standing straight, arms at her sides, she faced him. "Appa—*Aatmanji*—look at me."

He met her eyes fully.

"I'll *never* forgive you. Don't call me your *daughter* ever again. You lost that right when you left me all alone." She paused and stared at him. "I wish I'd never known you."

Aatmanji bowed his head, realizing forgiveness was impossible. He looked at her, then placed a hand on his own heart, accepting her judgment.

Remorse flashed through Bayla's eyes for a split second, but she seemed to reconsider. Turning, she ran from the temple.

"Bayla, please, wait!"

"I'll go, Aatmanji—I'll catch up to her." As Chaadi ran to follow Bayla, Aatmanji sat again, head in his hands. *All my decisions have been wrong. All of them.* He felt flattened.

"Aatmanji!" He looked up. Aanvi stood at the entrance, her face ashen. She stepped inside, then leaned against the wall, as though she needed its support to remain standing.

"Aanvi, my dear, what is it?" Aatmanji exclaimed, alarmed. "Has something happened?"

She closed her eyes, with a look of concentration he recognized. The quantum strands had revealed something to her, something significant.

"Not . . . not exactly. Remember that odd bit of energy hanging in the background of the web—the one I've been watching . . . ?"

He nodded. She'd shared that detail with him over the past year.

"It's been growing larger by the day and taking on a more definite shape —almost like an electrical current. And now . . . it's moving toward us, toward our strands."

Aatmanji's stomach lurched.

"It must be Zed," she whispered. But her voice held doubt.

CHAPTER 36

CHAADI

Chaadi focused on keeping Bayla in sight—otherwise, he knew the forest would swallow him up. He burst after her into the clearing and saw her dash to the jeep. Her hands moved over the dashboard, trying to find the start button.

He reached her just as the vehicle began to move, and he managed to grab the window frame.

"Bayla! Where are you going?"

"Chaadi, not now."

"Please, just tell me where you're going."

"Leave me alone!"

He yanked the back door open and jumped in. "Let me stay. I won't bother you—I promise."

She huffed with exasperation and pressed the accelerator. The jeep lurched forward, and Chaadi threw his hands out to steady himself.

Bayla maneuvered the jeep skillfully over the pathway, but the trees around them were dense, and they often had to swerve to avoid them.

"Do you know where you're going?" Chaadi shouted

over the noise of the jeep and the crackling of brush and branches.

She didn't answer, but suddenly veered off to the right.

"Hey!" yelled Chaadi.

Bayla frowned at him, clearly irked that he'd followed her.

The jeep screeched as she braked.

Where were they? He looked around. Were these the old school grounds that both Bayla and Aatmanji had mentioned at different times? If so, nothing remained of them. Still, when he looked closely, he thought he detected the slight outlines of building foundations.

Bayla got out of the jeep and slammed the door. She put both palms on the vehicle and leaned over, breathing heavily. "How many times?" she shouted, the forest absorbing her words. She turned to him. "How many times, Chaadi?"

He didn't know what to say.

"So many lies, one after another. And the truth comes only on *his* schedule, according to *his* plan. I hate him. Do you hear me? I *hate* him!"

For a split second, Chaadi considered telling her that Aatmanji was trying to protect her, but he suspected she was tired of hearing it.

"How many times?!" she screamed.

Chaadi had no answer.

"What's the point of my career in research? No matter how many answers I get, no matter how much information, there are only more questions. I'll never understand my past— or who I am—or what I'm supposed to be."

Chaadi ached at the misery on her face. She shouted again, then stomped toward the interior of the forest, as though doing so could obliterate her anger. He thought it best to hang back and leave her to herself for a while.

But after twenty minutes had passed, he began to worry. Bayla seemed at ease in the forest, but what if she'd gotten lost? He knew she'd grown up right here, but what if she'd forgotten this terrain?

He looked up, hearing sharp noises in the distance. *Thwack! Thwack!*

Chaadi rushed forward, diving into the forest, following the sounds, not considering how he'd find his way back to the jeep. He pushed through some foliage and saw Bayla holding a pole of bamboo across her chest. She lunged forward, as though toward an opponent, and as she twisted, she deliberately hit the dead tree in front of her. *Thwack!*

He sighed with relief. As he stood panting, he tried to figure out what she was doing—some sort of martial art, it seemed.

"Hey," she called to him, her voice casual, as though this were the typical way to wrap up a fit of frustration in the forest.

"Everything okay?" he asked.

"Do you have a minute?"

"Pretty sure I do," he said with a wry smile. He gestured around him. "This is disturbing, by the way—being swallowed up by the forest like this."

"Really? I guess it still feels like home to me." She spun the pole to the right, then the left. "Ever hear of *kalaripayattu*?"

"Uh, no."

She scanned the forest floor. "There." She pointed toward a pole of bamboo on the ground near him. "Grab that one." He pulled and dislodged it. "Watch out for snakes," Bayla said, way too calmly.

He dropped it immediately.

The corner of Bayla's mouth turned up a little, and she

moved toward the pole and inspected it. "It's fine," she said, picking it up and handing it to him.

He hesitated.

She chuckled. "I promise. No snakes."

He took it from her.

"Here," she continued, "hold it like this, across your body. Okay, now try to block my advance."

She spun the pole and quickly brought it toward his head. He brought his pole up automatically. "Whoa, careful. I've never done this before," he exclaimed.

She advanced again, turned, sidestepped, and lunged, deliberately stopping just short of moving the stick against his throat.

"Huh—I've never seen anything like this."

"You've got good instincts. Try this move, right to left, back and forth."

Chaadi made the motions as Bayla moved the pole to dodge or counteract each one. After a few minutes, she brought the pole downward in front of her, as though to indicate the end of the sparring session, and she bowed her head. Chaadi gazed at her, taken aback by her look of sheer joy.

They stared at each other for a moment, then burst into laughter.

It was a relief to laugh after the tension of the past hour.

"These were the old *kalaripayattu* training grounds," Bayla said, gesturing around her. She sat on the ground, leaned back on her elbows, and extended her legs. Suddenly, she grinned. "I remember throwing tantrums as a kid, and they'd make me practice *kalari* to manage my anger, to use it productively."

Chaadi walked over and sat cross-legged next to her. "Looks like it still works."

She laughed again, jabbing his arm with her elbow in mock

anger. Sitting up, she looked at him, a question in her eyes. "Why did you get in the jeep? Why did you come with me?"

"I didn't want you to be alone, after everything you found out."

Bayla put a hand on his arm. "Thank you," she said softly. "I know I haven't been easy to be around." She paused. "And I'm not used to talking to anyone about my past." She looked into the distance, and Chaadi wondered if she was thinking of a particular person.

They were silent for a few moments, then Chaadi mused, "You know, this has been the experience of a lifetime for me. And I've found so many answers." He thought about the excitement of the last few days, about everything he'd learned. He wanted to be part of a solution, part of 108's work. And he wanted to help Bayla.

She looked at him. "I'm glad one of us is finding answers. I only seem to find more questions."

"Yes, I see what you mean." He hesitated. "Listen, I know I haven't known you very long. But after what I saw at the temple, I can safely say I have never, ever met anyone like you."

He saw her face redden, but she didn't look away from him. He leaned toward her and tipped her chin upward, moving his face closer to hers. Bayla closed her eyes for a moment, receptive, but then he felt something shift and change. She leaned backward. "I'm sorry—I'm sorry—it's just that, right now, I don't think it's . . ."

"No, no, it's fine—I understand." He knew his disappointment was obvious as he turned away.

Suddenly, both of them looked up.

"What was that?" Chaadi asked.

Explosions sounded in the distance, followed by a continuous *rat-a-tat*.

"What's happening?" gasped Bayla.

"Let's go—right now."

They ran to the jeep and leaped in. Bayla accelerated, and they tore back through the forest toward camp.

CHAPTER 37

BAYLA

Bayla floored the accelerator, pressing the jeep to go faster while simultaneously dodging branches and foliage in their path. Another volley of explosions sounded in the distance, in the direction of the campsite, and she looked fearfully at Chaadi, whose face was gray and soaked with sweat.

"Are you okay, Chaadi?" she asked, but another explosion distracted her.

The jeep burst into the edge of the campsite with a violent screech of tires. Bayla's mouth dropped. A fire had ignited all the smaller tents. She saw Aanvi in the background, gathering people into a huddle away from the flames.

Appa. Why wasn't he with them?

She looked toward the meditation platform over the river inlet and saw two figures standing there. Was he there? As she squinted to see, a mechanical scream sounded and an explosion landed on the platform, which began to tilt.

"Oh my God!" She began to run toward the platform, but Chaadi grabbed her arm.

"Bayla, don't!" he gasped, but she pulled free and took off running. Flames had erupted everywhere, intensified by all the thatching.

There! Is that him? She ran into the thickest part of the fire, choking and squinting to see through the smoke as she made her way toward the two men. When she arrived, the platform was empty. Where had they gone?

She bent over the edge of the platform and saw them by the river. "Bose!"

Bose was bent over another figure, who lay flat on the ground. *Oh no. Oh no.*

Bayla maneuvered toward the ground, waving her hands ahead of her to see, still choking on the smoke. She gasped as her hand hit a wall.

It wasn't a wall.

It was a man.

He, too, was trying to see through the smoke. Because of the uneven landscape, they found themselves eye to eye. She stared at him, her eyes watering, and saw the red-blue scar extending the length of his face.

It was the man from her apartment.

"Bayla!" a voice shouted. She turned toward it.

"Bose Uncle!"

She twisted away from the scarred man and ran toward Bose and the man on the ground, hoping beyond hope.

"He's dead—Aatmanji's dead!" Bose wept, shaking his head.

"Appa!" Bayla screamed, grabbing her father by the shoulders and shaking him. She collapsed over him, clutching his shirt. *"No, no, no, no, no,"* she repeated in a drumbeat.

"No, Bayla—run!" shouted Bose, pointing behind her and

pushing her away. But instead of running, she looked toward the group Aanvi had gathered, and Bose followed her gaze. "We'll be okay, Bayla. They want you, not us. Go now!"

Turning around, Bayla leaped up and barely eluded the hands reaching for her. She skidded away from him. She needed to get to the jeep. *Where is Chaadi?* Under the cover of the smoke, she climbed up the bank and sprinted back toward the clearing. At one point she looked backward, but no one seemed to be following.

She continued to run and almost thumped into a form in front of her. "Chaadi!" she exclaimed, grabbing his arm to keep him from falling.

Chaadi didn't answer. He didn't move.

She brought her face close to his and squinted at him. "Chaadi, what's wrong?" she demanded, shaking his shoulders.

Chaadi remained frozen, his eyes glassy. Suddenly, he dropped his hands to his knees and leaned over, vomiting.

"Chaadi, it's okay—you're okay," she said, crouching next to him and rubbing his back. "Come on—we have to get to the jeep." She took Chaadi's hand and pulled him forward . . .

. . . directly into the path of the scarred man.

Bayla began to move away, pulling Chaadi with her, but the man grabbed hold of her arm and twisted it upward. She gasped in agony, knowing that if she moved, her arm would dislodge from the socket.

After a few seconds, the man released her arm, and she gulped with relief. She began to shift away but looked up into the barrel of his gun and froze. Moving her eyes to the left, she saw Chaadi, motionless, drenched in sweat, as a second man brought a gun down hard on his forehead.

"Chaadi!" shouted Bayla. As she lunged toward him, she heard a sickening thud, and darkness descended.

CHAPTER 38

BAYLA

Bayla resurfaced to consciousness with her head pounding and an acute ringing in her ears. Groggily, she raised a hand to her head.

Where was she?

Looking around, she saw that she was sprawled on the floor in the back of a large van. It was in motion—she felt the roughness of the road under them as they pitched up and down. Though the vehicle was windowless, a few lines of light entered through the seams of the double door at the back.

What had happened? For a moment, she relaxed into that space between sleep and awakening.

Then the space burst open.

No, no, no, no, no. In grief and shock, she curled into a ball and wept, her entire body shaking.

Appa was dead.

She had lost him twice: first, as a child, and this time, after rejecting—indeed, disowning—him. The last thing she'd done was berate him and run away. That would be her father's last memory of her.

How could she have been so cruel, punishing him like that? She knew in her heart that he loved her deeply.

She closed her eyes, imagining what she should have said instead. *Appa, of course you are my father. I had the happiest childhood anyone could hope for. I know you did your best. I love you.* Instead, she'd . . .

Bayla couldn't bear the thought, and sobs shook her again for several minutes. At last, she sat up, wiping her eyes on her tunic, wincing at the pain spreading deeper throughout her body, and feeling a crushing headache.

She took a deep breath to calm herself. She needed to learn more about her situation. Squinting in the low light, she looked toward the front of the van and saw the profiles of two men—the driver and the man with the scarred face who had attacked them. They were speaking to each other in low tones, but she could not make out their words.

Again, she looked around at the large compartment in which she was sitting. There were boxes of machinery, some computer equipment, and a few sealed vats. She caught sight of a bundle in the corner and moved toward it for a better look.

It was a person, sitting stiffly upright and staring straight ahead.

Chaadi.

Bayla shifted, groaning from pain, and scrambled closer. She saw the bruise on his forehead and the blood surrounding it. His eyes were unseeing, and his face was streaked with sweat.

"Chaadi?" she whispered.

He startled and kicked her shin.

Oof! She clutched her leg and moved back a few feet. She spoke softly. "It's me—it's Bayla, your friend."

Bayla scrutinized his face. He did not appear to recognize

her, and he'd begun breathing in gasps. He would hyperventilate at this rate, she worried.

Again she moved toward him, this time at a safer distance, and leaned back against the same wall. "Chaadi, it's Bayla. I'm here with you, in a van. We're in India together, do you remember? We were with . . . with Appa . . . with Aatmanji." Her voice broke.

He turned toward her. She locked eyes with him to steady him. As she did, she gasped. Threads. For just an instant, she saw threads of light appear between them, and she felt herself inhabit the snarl of memory and emotion within Chaadi. Then the threads faded.

"Chaadi, whatever your mind is telling you—it isn't real anymore. It happened a long time ago."

Tentatively, she reached out for his shoulder. He jumped but did not pull away from her. "Chaadi, I want you to feel my hand on your shoulder, and I want you to listen to my voice. Just listen, you don't have to do anything else." She paused. "Chaadi, we're in a van, and we're driving on a road. Just breathe with me, in and out, follow my count. . . ."

Closing her eyes and breathing deeply, she counted aloud. After a few minutes, she felt an odd sensation and opened her eyes. There they were again—threads. This time, they remained longer, emanating from both of them and blending, as though her boundaries were overlapping with his. She felt his rush of panic and terror and tried to send her own strength toward him.

She was relieved to observe his breathing slowing down. When he relaxed against the wall, she thought it was safe to move closer to him. She looked into his face and held his hands in hers, joining him in the moment.

Finally, he spoke. "I'm—I'm okay now. I get panic attacks,

but I haven't frozen like that for a long time. But the fire, the explosions . . . it was just like before . . . always like before." He dropped his head into his hands, his despair obvious. "You're not the only one tangled up in your past."

"Chaadi, I understand, I do."

He nodded. "Thank you," he said after a few moments, without looking at her.

Bayla didn't respond—she didn't want to embarrass him. "Chaadi, I want to find something for that cut on your forehead."

She looked toward the front of the van again, but the two men weren't looking in their direction. Moving around the van's compartment on her knees, she again scanned the items piled around them. Some metal boxes appeared to hold supplies. Hopefully she could find a first-aid kit inside—or anything that could be helpful. But the boxes were locked.

Bayla turned and saw a plastic tub in the other corner, made her way there, and tried to pry off the lid.

"Bayla!" Chaadi's voice—a warning.

The scarred man, the one she'd come to consider as their captor, had entered the compartment, bending forward to avoid hitting the ceiling of the van. His eyes narrowed when he saw her in motion, and he lunged toward her. Bayla put her arms up and forward to signal that she wouldn't fight back. Nevertheless, he grabbed her arm roughly and threw her sideways. Fortunately, Bayla caught herself before she hit the van wall.

"Leave her alone!" Chaadi shouted.

"Ah, look, the crazy man is awake again." When he grinned, he revealed a mouth full of jagged yellow teeth.

"Tell us where we're going," Bayla demanded.

The man smirked. "Someone is waiting to meet you."

Bayla had a sinking feeling she knew who it was.

"Okay, then, you don't need *him*," she said, pointing to Chaadi. "Let him go."

The man looked amused. "No, there's a use for him as well." With a swiftness that shocked Bayla, the man threw an arm upward into Chaadi's chin. Chaadi slumped to the floor.

"Chaadi!" she screamed, trying to launch herself across the compartment toward him.

"No. Don't move," the man hissed, pointing a gun at her. She backed into her original position, looking at Chaadi in desperation, then sighing with relief when she saw his chest rising and falling.

The man sat on the largest plastic tub and stared at her, passing his gun from palm to palm. Bayla pulled her knees to her chest and dropped her head into her arms, not wanting him to see her weeping, overcome by fear and grief and frustration.

What was in store for them now? Again, she was being transported against her will, without any knowledge of her destination. Again, she was being maneuvered and manipulated without her consent.

Her father had believed she had a larger destiny in front of her, that her abilities were needed in the world. Bayla thought of his warning of the disaster bearing down on humanity. He'd assumed she would share his cause, join that fight.

But she'd refused outright. She'd told her father that she was broken, irreparable—and that it was his fault. She'd told him she'd never forgive him.

Bayla felt shame burning in her ears.

She lifted her head. Though their captor remained alert, his attention had shifted direction. As she stared at his profile, he seemed to encompass all the people who had controlled her life without her input, who had left her feeling powerless, frac-tured, and alone for fifteen years.

In an attempt to reassert control, she'd spent her adult years in America collecting and reporting information. But no amount of information she'd collected about the world, or her life, or herself, seemed to fill the holes inside her. And that path had only led her further and further away from self-awareness, from her own knowingness and wholeness.

Bayla took a deep breath.

She was done feeling shattered by the actions of others, done feeling damaged beyond recovery. And she was done be-lieving there were magical answers out there that would make her life make sense, that would fix her and everything that had happened to her.

World, people, Earth—they moved as they moved, and al-ways had, and always would. She might never know why, or agree with the reasons, or welcome the outcomes.

Her past, her pain, all her experiences—they were sim-ply part of the strange, cracked, imperfect mosaic of her. She might not understand why they'd come about, but they were *hers*—her own foundation, stronger than bone. She would draw power from that foundation, and understanding, and insight. She would face her future head-on, with clarity and without confusion.

A vision flashed through Bayla's mind, of a lone woman with eyes on the horizon, walking across the land, offering her strength and wisdom to the world.

CHAPTER 39

DAKSHA—AN INTERLUDE

She journeyed south.

She slowed as she approached Prithvi Forest, nearing the area that had been invaded by the black liquid. She had tried, without success, to absorb that liquid into herself, but the attempt had left her empty, surrounded by blankness.

Though she had not yet recovered her usual sense of her surroundings, she could still perceive the little flame.

She observed its rise and fall, its expansion and contraction, its motion and light. At times, the flame launched like a flare, lapping the air—then dimmed and softened. At times, it gleamed hot and incandescent—then folded into its own embrace, its embers diminishing but still awake.

She watched its movements and mutations as she made her way forward, step by step.

Wait.

The little flame erupted into a blaze.

She jerked her head upward. What happened?

She looked around her. Her nose wrinkled, detecting smoke

wafting from the distance. She stepped onto a pathway, and a gray van raced past her. She gazed down the path, long after the van was out of sight.

The little flame needed help. It needed her.

CHAPTER 40

BAYLA

Bayla paid attention to the van's motion, feeling the bumps and twists and turns of forest paths, then the smoothness of paved roads. Its pace slowed, with frequent stops and starts, and she heard the noises of people and vehicles around them.

Was this Vayu City? There were not many other cities close to Prithvi Forest. But soon even those city noises diminished.

She pretended to fall asleep, at which point their captor rose and returned to his seat at the front of the van. Bayla immediately moved toward Chaadi, still slumped on the floor across from her.

"Chaadi," she whispered. He turned his head and blinked at her. He was conscious again, thank goodness, and seemed calm, but his skin was gray, and his eyes were hollow.

"Are you okay? Can you sit up?" He didn't answer but struggled upward with Bayla's assistance. Suddenly, the van skidded to a stop, throwing them forward. She heard the driver and passenger doors open and slam. The back door opened, and the dim overhead light turned on. Bayla strained to see what awaited them outside.

"Out," their captor growled.

Bayla put her arm around Chaadi's waist to brace him and pull him forward slowly, but their captor grabbed him and dragged him out. Chaadi slumped to the ground, and Bayla gritted her teeth in anger.

Ignoring Bayla's hissed "Don't touch me," their captor seized her arm, then swore as she pushed the elbow of her other arm into his throat, using the motion of her descent from the van for momentum. He turned and hit her across the face, and she fell back against the open door. She grabbed it and pulled herself upright.

"Enough," he said, cocking his gun. Bayla turned toward him, assuming the barrel would be pointing at her. Instead, it was leveled at Chaadi's head.

She understood. Chaadi was there to ensure her good behavior.

Within seconds, both she and Chaadi began to cough. The haze permeating most of the world's urban air existed here as well, and it seemed to displace the breathable oxygen. Her nostrils wrinkled from the stench of chemical products in the air, exacerbated by heat that had not relented despite the evening hour. She noticed that the two men were wearing masks.

Through her watering eyes, she strained to identify their location. Gray buildings of varying sizes as well as a high compound wall of cinder blocks surrounded them, with guarded gates at opposite ends. Based upon the clang of machinery, some mechanical process was occurring. Giant vats lay in clusters everywhere.

Her coughing began to overwhelm her, and she bent over, gagging. The scarred man observed her in disgust. "Come here," he barked at Chaadi, who remained sprawled on the ground, unmoving. Bayla darted toward Chaadi to preempt additional rough handling and got him to his feet.

Bayla felt a push and began walking forward. She tried to calm her cough, but the air was unendurable. Chaadi, too, continued to hack next to her. "Shut up," snapped their captor.

They walked for several minutes on an uneven stone pathway, and she and Chaadi tripped several times. Each time, they were yanked upward. Bayla's shoulder, the one their captor had almost dislocated at the campsite, throbbed each time he grabbed her. She cried out in pain, unable to suppress it.

As she walked, she tried to keep her terror at bay. Their captor had said that someone wanted to meet her— presumably they'd be safe until then. Looking around, she took in more details. Even assuming they could surmount the walls and gates, she had no idea where they were or how to get to safety. And even if they could break away right now, Chaadi was in no condition to run or even comprehend instructions from her.

"Stop."

Bayla looked up. They were still within the compound walls but far from the other buildings, as well as the vats. In front of them was a low-profile building as gray and nondescript as the others, shaped in an elongated rectangle, about the length of two trailer homes end to end but lacking windows.

She was shoved toward the steel door at one end. As she walked down the two cement steps to access the door, she saw some kind of air circulation unit to the right; Bayla desperately hoped it was an air purifier, as she continued to cough and hack.

Their captor bent toward the door, which beeped after a few seconds and swung open. They stumbled down a dim hallway toward the open door of one of the rooms. At the threshold of that room, Bayla gasped—it looked like a jail cell. She stopped walking but was again shoved forward.

The door clanged shut behind them. Bayla heard the *click, click, beep* of a bolt mechanism. She began hitting her fists against the metal door but, eventually, hearing nothing, stopped and rubbed her stinging hands. No point—she was only hurting herself.

She looked around at the windowless cement walls. An old-fashioned light bulb swung from a cord in the middle of the ceiling, and a camera was mounted in a corner high above. A single narrow cot stood against the far wall.

At least she'd stopped coughing—there was indeed some air filtration happening inside, thank goodness. The room was even reasonably cool, despite the sultry surroundings. Perhaps this building was also used for purposes other than detention.

After surveying the room, she looked back toward the door. Chaadi was still standing by the entrance, his hand touching the wound on his forehead.

"Come on, Chaadi, sit down." She took his elbow and led him to the cot. His right eye was swelling, and the cuts on his face were still bloody. Bayla looked around again, hoping against hope there would be something she could use to bandage him.

Then she remembered the camera. She stomped over to it and shouted. "He needs medical supplies now—do you understand me? And water!"

Until she could come up with a better idea, that would have to do.

She sat next to Chaadi again. He looked at her with agonized eyes. Slowly, she put her arms around him, pulling his head to her shoulder, and rocked, hoping to comfort him.

"Oh, Chaadi," she said. "I'm so sorry—you shouldn't

even be here. They wanted me, not you." He slumped further against her.

After a few minutes, she insisted that Chaadi lie down on the cot, then surveyed the cell again. There was no way out but through that steel door they'd entered. She noticed something she'd missed before—an inset toward the bottom of the door, as though someone on the other side could shift a panel and create an opening. She walked toward it to see whether she could move or dislodge it, to no avail.

When she returned to the cot, Chaadi appeared to be asleep. She took Chaadi's hand in hers and squeezed it gently. Dropping lightly to the floor, she leaned back against the cot. The thought of her father burst forward. Resting her forehead on her knees, she wept in great, heaving waves. Eventually, exhaustion overtook her, and she slept.

***

I am a child again, sitting below my favorite tree, reaching my hands upward to the sky. It comes to greet me as a mesh of stars, a lace of lights, and when it reaches my face, it softens to silk. The dream-woman appears, and this time, her dark eyes lock with mine. "You can see me!" I gasp excitedly. She nods and speaks. I know her message is important, but I can't hear the words. She turns to go. "No, wait!" I cry. "I can't hear you!"

Bayla awoke with a start and winced.

Her neck felt strained from leaning against the narrow cot to sleep with her head buried in her arms. She hadn't wanted to wake Chaadi to ask him to make space for her. He'd seemed to be sleeping comfortably at last, after thrashing intermittently for hours.

Rubbing her neck, she shifted to sit against the wall, and

her eye caught something near the door. Standing and moving toward it, she found a stack of alcohol wipes, rolls of gauze and tape, and a sealed paracetamol bottle, all of which appeared to have been deposited through the panel at the bottom of the door. Next to those items was a twelve-ounce plastic bottle of water, on its side. *Not much, but something.*

Apparently, someone had heard her demand via the camera, so the camera was operational. And someone—maybe the same someone—had been willing to help them. Two useful pieces of information.

She gathered the supplies and walked to the cot, then used one of the wipes to clean her hands. This was not going to be comfortable for Chaadi, but she didn't want his cuts to get infected. She'd have to wake him up first, so that he would be ready for it.

She placed a hand on his shoulder. "Chaadi?" He stirred and looked at her. Bayla was relieved to see that his eyes seemed to focus on her, and not on something far away and long ago. Still, best to proceed with caution after he'd kicked her in the van. Her shin still ached from it.

"Are you okay?" she asked. "Can you sit up? I want to put something on those cuts."

Chaadi nodded and swung upward to a seated position. "Go ahead," he rasped.

Given his jumpiness over the past hours, Bayla was not sure how Chaadi would react as the alcohol stung his skin. However, he didn't wince—indeed, he barely moved.

"Impressive," she said with a hint of a smile as she proceeded to tape gauze over the wounds.

He didn't smile back.

Tearing the seal off the pill bottle, Bayla placed two tablets in his hand and handed him the water. He swallowed the pills and fell back on the cot. She sat on the ground next to him.

"Bayla, I thought . . ." His voice trailed off. He remained on his back, staring at the ceiling. She sensed his reluctance to speak further, and she didn't press. After a few minutes, he turned on his side, facing her. "I thought that if I could understand what happened in my past, these panic attacks would disappear."

"I'm no doctor, but I have a feeling that trauma is far more complicated than that."

"Trauma," Chaadi repeated, but didn't elaborate. Closing his eyes again, he spoke. "So, do you feel as stuck in the past as I do?"

"You know I do." She smiled to herself, remembering Braden's words at her apartment. "But I'm trying to remember that I'm much more than my past."

CHAPTER 41

ZED

ZedChem branch outside Vayu City, India
"Look," Zed barked. He swiped his fingers across the EtherScreen, advancing the photos:

Aatmanji lying flat on his back.

Aatmanji getting to his feet.

Aatmanji driven away in a jeep.

Velky had bungled kidnapping the man from the campsite and now stood hangdog in front of him.

"Why did you leave him there?"

"I thought he was already dead. Our local contacts were overeager—they launched the firebombs before I could . . ."

"Excuses."

"And anyway, we have the girl."

"What good is the girl without the old man?" Zed's plan had been simple: Aatmanji would watch his daughter suffer. Then both would die. It had been such an opportunity—both of them in one place. "Go. Get out," he barked at Velky.

"Yes, sir." Velky left the office, throwing a curious look

at the small and bony woman perched on Zed's desk as he passed her.

Without expression, the woman turned to Zed and sniffed her contempt. "Your people are incompetent."

Zed's anger ignited, but he knew the woman was right. Velky had botched his assignment.

"It doesn't matter. I have his daughter—and I'll get Aatmanji out of the hole where he's hiding."

After a moment, her growl cut the air. "The agrochemical pour. Is it on schedule?"

"Of course it's on schedule."

"You must kill both of them before the pour begins. Otherwise, 108 will stop you."

Zed sneered. "108 will never stop me again."

"You understand nothing."

Zed narrowed his eyes as he stared at her. Who did this woman think she was? How dare she tell him how to run his enterprise? She had always given him valuable information, but she doled it out bit by bit, always keeping the upper hand. He remembered their first encounter in 2025, when he'd walked into his office and found her perched on his desk, just as she was today.

***

"Who the hell are you?"

She ignored the question. "I know who set the fire—the fire that killed your brother. I saw it happen."

Zed looked at her expectantly. "Well?"

"His name is Aatmanji. He leads a group called 108."

"Why should I believe you?"

She regarded him for a moment before speaking. "Ever wonder why your ships were always turned back at Kannur? Why the trains carrying your vats were always canceled in Mysore? Why the S-305 regulation on chemical transport was passed?"

His brow furrowed as she continued to list the problems that had plagued ZedChem in southwestern India during those years. Obviously, she possessed accurate information.

"Aatmanji led that campaign. He turned the countryside—and the country—against you." She paused. "And he went to your factory that day, and he set the fire," she stated with finality.

Zed closed his eyes, remembering how the factory fire raged for more than three days, given all the chemicals on the premises. He recalled the precise moment he'd learned Matej had been inside that building.

His voice went cold. "I'm going to kill this man. Where is he?"

She slipped a piece of paper across his desk—coordinates for Tulā School in Prithvi Forest, outside Vayu City, India. In his mind, he was already planning. He would meet this man. If this woman's facts were accurate, he knew the appropriate vengeance for Matej: a fire in the dead of night.

She spoke again. "You must wipe them all out—the entire school. You must pull out the roots of 108."

Zed looked at her for a few moments. "Why?"

For an instant, he saw her blank face crease into rage before smoothing again. "Because they're trying to save humanity."

Was this woman insane? "So what?"

"Humanity isn't worth saving."

He shook his head in wonderment. "How do you know all this, about Aatmanji and 108?"

She paused before answering. "I used to be one of them."
"And now?"
"I'm a defector."

***

He watched as the woman jumped lightly to her feet from the desk and walked toward the single window in the office. She'd never revealed her name, so he'd always thought of her as "the defector."

"Remember. Kill the old man and the girl *before the pour.* If you can't do it, then I'll find someone who can."

Zed seethed. "Of course I'll do it. It's my right, my vengeance for Matej."

An image of Matej floated through his mind. Strange, whenever he thought of Matej these days, he remembered a blond-haired, blue-eyed child brimming with laughter, not a young man. He remembered his mother gently admonishing, *Protect him, my son. Protect his joy.* Zed had failed to do that in every possible way.

He looked up, and the defector was gone. He shrugged and walked to the window. This new chemical plant in southwestern India had been built in record time. Indeed, all twenty plants established for the worldwide dispensing of FZ5 had been built with astonishing speed. In a few short years, ZedChem had readied FZ5 for its grand launch, deploying extensive resources and workers, leveraging tax and legal loopholes, slicing through government bureaucracy by force, bribery, or exploitation of foibles and scandals.

Soon, he'd have what he wanted. He would avenge Matej

and prove his father wrong—after all, how could his father be ashamed after such a demonstration of global success?

Zed felt the twinge again at the back of his mind.

How can I prove myself to a dead man?

He pushed it away.

CHAPTER 42

CHAADI

When Chaadi awoke again, he felt more like himself. He turned to find Bayla and saw her sitting cross-legged on the floor with her eyes closed. He'd never seen anyone so perfectly still. And her stillness made him feel calmer.

He lay back again and watched her, riveted, for a few minutes.

What is it about her?

He knew the answer. She was so lovely—luminous, really—but her light seemed caught in a crystal of old hurts. Every once in a while, it broke free and made him catch his breath.

Chaadi's stomach knotted, remembering the moment they'd shared on the old Tulā School grounds after his first *kalaripayattu* lesson. He'd been disappointed when she'd pulled away, but he was glad there was no residual awkwardness between them from the incident—perhaps because she'd been taking care of him during the worst and longest panic attack of his life.

The minutes ticked by, and she remained seated.

When at last she opened her eyes, she didn't seem to notice he was awake. She began what was obviously a seasoned yoga practice. When she commenced the warrior series, she turned her back to the mounted camera, edged closer to the cot where he lay, and caught his eye. Chaadi watched curiously.

As she transitioned between postures, she spoke in a whisper. "Chaadi, I think they're observing us—and listening—through the camera. They heard what I asked them yesterday."

"What did you ask?" he murmured.

"For medical supplies for you."

Chaadi raised his eyebrows in surprise. Bayla continued speaking in low tones. "But it's strange they gave them to us, given the way we've been treated so far. I think there's someone out there who's sympathetic—and maybe even willing to help us."

He nodded.

"Chaadi, after everything Aatmanji told us, I have to assume Zed is the one behind all this. And if that's true, we're in terrible danger. He didn't hesitate to wipe out Tulā School fifteen years ago. We have to get out of here. So let's figure out what we're dealing with—what kind of a facility this is and how many people are guarding it and working here. I couldn't register much when they brought us here."

"I haven't been any help," he muttered. "I'm not sure I was even conscious. I have no memory of it, if you can believe it."

Bayla continued to transition between postures. "I *can* believe it. Don't be so hard on yourself."

She stopped and sat in front of him, with her back to the camera. She closed her eyes, as though trying to picture the details she'd been gathering. "I think we're at the new facility of ZedChem—the one they just built, the one that conducted the test pour. There are thousands of barrels outside; I think they're chemical vats." She paused. "And this building we're in—it's long and rectangular, with a door on either end. We're in a compound with two guarded gates. I saw a complex of buildings—factories, I think, and some offices."

"You saw all that between the time they pulled us from the van and the time we got thrown in here?" he asked, impressed.

"Yes, but we need to know more—a lot more. But I'm not sure how to find out, or what to do after that."

As if on cue, the door opened, and their captor from the van entered the room. Bayla spun toward him.

"You. Come here," he barked, beckoning to her.

"Leave her alone!" Chaadi shouted, jumping up from the cot.

The man ignored him and continued to look at Bayla. "Now."

She didn't move, lifting her chin in defiance.

Still staring at her, he removed a gun from his belt, turned his arm in Chaadi's direction, and, without looking, took a shot. Bayla screamed as the gun fired, and she ran toward Chaadi, who had fallen on the floor, groaning and clutching his shoulder.

"Come with me now, and we will tend to him. If not . . ." He shrugged and pointed the gun toward Chaadi again.

"No, stop!" Shaking, Bayla stepped forward, blocking Chaadi from the man's view. The man seized her arm and pulled her in front of him, indicating that she should walk out the door. Bayla turned her head and cringed at the sight of Chaadi sprawled on the floor. "You promised to help him."

The man ignored her.

As she got closer to the door, she grabbed the jamb with both hands, turned back toward the camera, and shouted. "You promised to help him!"

"Move!" The man pushed her out of the cell.

"Where are you taking her?" Chaadi struggled to shout. "Hey! Where are you taking . . . ?" His voice faded, and the room began to swirl.

He had to save his energy. Chaadi pressed his hand against his shoulder as firmly as he could to slow the bleeding. Luckily, it was a graze, but it hurt like hell.

Chaadi didn't know whether a few minutes or a few hours passed, but the cell door opened again, and a full-figured woman with bright blond hair and tight clothing entered, carrying a heavy bag. He watched her through a haze as she approached and bent over him.

"You will be alright," she said in a low voice, with a heavy accent.

He couldn't help it—he let go and lost consciousness.

CHAPTER 43

BAYLA

Bayla slowed her pace, scanning the hallway, trying to take in the details as her captor dogged her heels and gave her an occasional shove. Just as she remembered, the building consisted of one long hallway with a heavy metal door on each end. This time, she noticed the cameras mounted from the ceiling every ten feet.

Multiple interior doors lined the hallway on both sides. She tried to discern the mechanism used to open the doors—was it keypads, facial scans, something more sophisticated?

The man pulled Bayla toward a room at the end of the hallway, but she noticed that the large door of the adjoining room was ajar. The sign on the wall next to it read "Control Room 6." Taking a deep breath, she sidestepped her captor and ran toward it.

He grabbed at her, but Bayla dodged him, hurtled into the room, and fell to the floor. Sitting up, she looked around her: there were piles of electronic equipment and three computer workstations. A woman with spiky red hair and round wire-rimmed glasses stood at one of them, examining multiple EtherScreens at once. Seeing Bayla's lurching entrance, she seemed shocked.

Bayla caught sight of one EtherScreen currently showing the interior of their cell. Chaadi was lying on the cot, and someone with blond hair seemed to be tending him. *Thank God.*

Other screens showed the interior and exterior of the building at various angles.

Beyond the screens, a horizontal interior window provided a view into the adjacent room, which contained some kind of plank standing upright. *What is that?*

The man shouted at the red-haired woman, who was staring, mouth agape.

"Goddamn it, Petra!"

"I'm so sorry, Mr. Velky," the woman responded, visibly frightened. "I didn't realize the door was open."

The man—Velky—lunged for Bayla, but she twisted and rolled toward the back of the room. Velky bounded toward her, grabbed her injured arm again, and hauled her upright. She bit her lip to keep from crying out. He swung her out of the room, slamming the door shut and giving her a vicious look. He grasped her face in one calloused hand and squeezed. Bayla felt like her bones were cracking.

"Do you know what I'd like to do to your pretty face?"

Just as suddenly, he let go, shoving her to the side.

Bayla caught herself before she fell. Her jaw throbbed, as did her shoulder, which she'd fallen on yet again while in the control room. Velky grabbed her arm in a viselike grip. Bayla knew she wouldn't be able to pull away again.

He dragged her toward the adjacent interior door, positioning her in front of it. Bayla expected him to open the door and push her inside, but he didn't. What was he waiting for?

Petra stuck her head through the control room door. "He's ready for her."

Bayla was filled with foreboding. Still holding her arm, Velky leaned forward and spoke into the sensor next to the door.

A voiceprint! But she couldn't catch what he'd said.

She heard a *click, click, beep*, and the door opened. When Bayla entered, the door clanged shut behind them. She took a few more steps and looked around at the gray walls of a room only slightly larger than the cell that she and Chaadi were occupying. To her right was the horizontal window she'd caught sight of in the control room. In the left corner, she saw video equipment, and in the middle was the vertical plank.

But it wasn't a plank. It was an examination table—with straps and buckles.

Her mouth went dry. *An examination table? Video equipment?* What were they planning to do to her in here? She took a reflexive step backward into Velky's bulk. He shoved her forward, and she scooted away from his reach, to the far end of the room, with her back to the wall. In the silence, she could hear only Velky's open-mouthed breathing and her own accelerating inhalations. She held her hands together to keep them from shaking. She tried to slow her breathing but couldn't.

When the door lock clicked again, Bayla jumped in alarm. A man entered and approached, stopping just a few yards from the terrifying table and staring at her. He was Caucasian, of medium height and build, and broad shouldered. His dishwater-brown hair was badly cut, but his clothing was well tailored.

The man's unblinking eyes were an unsettling shade of yellow-brown, and they seemed to skewer her into the wall behind her. He stood with his arms crossed, his eyes traveling from her head to her feet. Bayla wrapped her arms around

herself, trying not to shiver, feeling a particular mixture of dis-
comfort and fear within her.

She remembered that feeling, and then the memory followed on its heels: her childhood encounter with this man at
Tulā School, when she'd run into her father's quarters with
flowers in her hands.

She recalled how physically ill at ease he'd been back then
as well. Looking at him more closely now, she observed that he
was scoliotic, the middle of his spine curving right, and that
his shoulders were hunched. Indeed, every part of his body
seemed to twist—his limbs, even his facial features.

"Welcome, Bayla Jeevan." She flinched as he approached,
took her chin between his fingers, and shifted her face right,
then left. "I remember you well."

She jerked her chin away, steeling herself and staring back
at him. Now she knew for sure: this was the same man who
had threatened her life, brought about her expulsion from Tulā
School, and destroyed her home and her family. The one who'd
torn the seams from her life.

"You're Zed."

"Such a bright girl. Aatmanji's daughter, all grown up."

He narrowed his eyes and dropped his gaze to the pendant
at her throat. Reflexively, Bayla reached for it and clutched it in
her fist.

"What do you want from me?"

He looked at her for a few moments. "So many things."
Bayla shuddered. "But mostly, your help."

"What makes you think I'd help you?"

Zed turned away from her as though uninterested and
spoke to Velky, his tone mild: "Show her."

Velky took three large steps forward and raised his

fist. In response, Bayla dropped to the floor and crouched. Grinning at her apparent submission, Velky towered over her threateningly.

Bayla shot upward and jammed her head into his solar plexus.

Velky fell backward onto the floor, gasping for breath. Zed laughed. "Velky, you're losing your touch."

The giant leaped up and lunged toward Bayla again, his face livid. She curled into a ball, protecting her head, bracing for the blow. At the last second, Zed held up a palm to stop him. Velky caught himself and backed away with reluctance, a look of fury on his face.

She struggled back against the wall, taking deep breaths, coaxing her abdomen to expand and her stomach to relax. She looked up at Zed with terror and loathing.

"As I was saying," Zed said, his voice calm, as though continuing a social conversation, "I need your help to bring Aatmanji out of the shadows where he's been hiding all these years, like a coward."

Appa? But Appa is dead.

An ember of hope sparked within her. Zed was a man of resources, likely to have current information. Was her father alive after all?

"When he sees you"—Zed gestured to the video equipment—"trust me, he will come."

She looked at him, taking in his twisted body and twisting mouth. Only the possibility of her father still being alive emboldened her. She spoke, making an effort to keep a tremor from her voice.

"Did you kill Jala Sharma?"

Zed seemed surprised that, of all questions, this was the

one she'd chosen to ask. Narrowing his eyes, he looked at her, taking some time before answering. "Jala Sharma was a disturbed young woman. She committed suicide."

Bayla gritted her teeth to keep herself from shivering. "I think you killed her because she exposed the truth about FZ5."

Zed appeared amused. "And what truth is that?"

"That it only works for five years. That it kills the topsoil. That we'll lose the last agricultural land in the world—the only way left to feed the population."

"Five years is a long time. And I have a right to my livelihood."

"But you don't have a right to harm what belongs to all of us."

"Listen to me, little girl," Zed said, his irritation evident. "If I didn't do this, someone else would. Why not me? Why shouldn't I be the one to profit?"

Bayla couldn't help herself. "But if all of the soil dies . . . if there's no food . . ."

"There's enough food for my lifetime. And if people don't have the competence to feed themselves, maybe they don't deserve food," he snapped.

Bayla gaped at him. How could a person think his own survival was independent of the planet's survival? What had caused him to see such a separation? And what had caused his disregard for—and his disconnection from—all other human beings, present or future?

Judgment and blame welled up in her, but she had a flash of realization. Did she truly live her life differently than he did, or was it just a question of degree—just a spectrum that she, too, inhabited?

After her childhood, how often had she placed her palms upon the earth; how much had she factored the planet into her decisions? Indeed, when her father had offered her a chance to battle on its behalf, she'd turned and walked—actually, *run*—away.

As a child, she'd been part of a loving community, but after all those connections were severed, how often had she reached out to other people? In her life in California, she had no friendships beyond acquaintances; she neither invited closeness nor offered love to others.

She looked at Zed. He'd said he had enough food for his own lifetime. Did the man not have any children, any family, heirs of any kind? Then she remembered the brother, for whose death Zed blamed her father.

She spoke up. "What if your brother were still here? What if he had a family? Wouldn't you want them to have . . ."

He lurched toward her, and she gasped as he slapped her. "Don't speak of him."

There was a tapping at the door. All three looked in its direction as Petra poked her head in.

"What?" Zed barked.

"Sir, the production team confirmed that they can move up the schedule. The pour will happen in twenty-four hours."

Bayla gaped. *Twenty-four hours? Oh no.*

"Out," Zed snapped, and Petra closed the door. He looked at Bayla. "Enough. You're boring me. Velky!"

"Yes, sir."

"You may begin."

Bayla cowered as Velky approached, grabbed her under her armpits, and hauled her to the table, as she struggled and kicked and screamed in terror.

"Quiet, child," said Zed, his voice emotionless again. "If it's any comfort, I don't necessarily want *you* dead. I'm really only interested in Aatmanji. I don't speak for the defector, though."

The defector? Who is that?

Clicking on the camera equipment, Zed held up a phone. "Here you see the date and time and the news headline," he stated.

Bayla realized that this video was intended to draw her father here so that Zed could kill him.

After the flash of hope that he might still be alive, Bayla felt despair. How could she prevent him from coming here and sacrificing himself? And how on earth could she stop the FZ5 pour?

The questions evaporated from her mind as Velky approached.

CHAPTER 44

AATMANJI

Town of Gudalur, India

Aanvi entered the room, her face somber. "No one has heard anything. We don't know where they are."

Terror gripped him. Where had Zed taken Bayla and Chaadi? None of their contacts had any information.

What if he'd taken them out of the country? But that was unlikely, he comforted himself. Zed wanted *him*, and Bayla would serve as leverage. If so, a message would be forthcoming. But in the meantime, nothing prevented him from harming her or Chaadi.

After the recent attack on the campsite, which had been eerily similar to the attack on Tulā School over a decade ago, firebombs and all, Aatmanji had been transported to the home of a physician in Gudalur, a small town outside Vayu City. This woman had helped their unit from time to time. With Zed searching for him, he could not risk a hospital. Luckily, he'd had only minor burns—painful but bearable. Bose's shouts declaring him dead had saved him from capture by deflecting Zed's henchman.

Unfortunately, Bose had borne the worst of the attack, and they'd had to hospitalize him in Vayu City, under the watchful eye of Shanti. By some miracle, all six people at the campsite had emerged safely from the blaze, and the fire had burned out due to soil dampness from the river's proximity.

Aatmanji closed his eyes, feeling through the web, seeking Bayla's presence.

At the Agastya temple, it had been glorious—and relieving—to see Bayla understand the web and her own power within it. But it also made the inability to reach her now feel excruciating. He concentrated on her, trying to visualize and send the memories they'd shared from her childhood.

A pond of lilies.

A cradle of branches.

A garden of jasmine.

He sighed. "Aanvi, I can't feel her within the web. I can't feel her presence anymore, just like I can't feel Daksha's. I'm worried it means she's in pain . . . or worse," he whispered. Aatmanji dropped his head as he thought of disturbing possibilities.

"We'll find them, Aatmanji."

Aatmanji nodded but did not feel optimistic. Distress and disconnection would limit Bayla's receptivity—she might not be able to perceive and respond. Abilities like hers were grounded in wholeness, rootedness, self-belief.

He remembered how she'd been able to move—almost dance—through the web as a child, and to carry all of them with her. By contrast, when he'd reached out to her during the test pour, she had heard him but hadn't been able to move, much less pull them all together for a single purpose. Ironically, the actions that he'd taken to keep her safe had suppressed her ability to access that part of herself.

But after witnessing her at the Agastya temple, leading 108's battle with the California wildfire, he firmly believed she'd recovered that knowingness.

He thought of Daksha, who had embodied the same knowingness, who had seemed like an extension of Earth, as though she'd been born directly from its depths. Aatmanji frowned, thinking of that identification with Earth. Had the test pour harmed Daksha when he'd called her to its location? Was that why he could no longer feel Daksha's presence in the web? Had it . . . had it killed her? *Oh God, no.*

And if Daksha was indeed still alive, where was she? Would her path cross Bayla's? If it did, would they be in danger— either of them, both of them? He thought of Aanvi's predictions, remembered her sad voice as she informed Daksha of the danger of remaining with her child.

Aatmanji took a deep breath; he could address only one problem at a time. *Remain in the present, remain in this moment.*

When he opened his eyes, he saw Aanvi looking abstracted, mournful.

He knew the reason.

Aanvi glanced up and saw him watching her. She sighed. "Fifteen years ago today."

Aatmanji took her hands. "I know."

"I miss them—I miss them so much."

Aanvi's much younger sister and brother, twins, had arrived at Tulā School in the 2020s, a bit later than Aanvi had. Kaali and Aakash were university professors of chemistry and biology, respectively, who had become increasingly disturbed by the ecological trajectory of Earth. They'd left everything behind to move to Tulā School and work with 108.

Aanvi, with her considerable height and larger figure, did

not resemble her smaller and more slender brother and sister, but all three siblings had been brilliant and magnetic, inspiring the group and serving tirelessly. Kaali in particular had possessed endless energy, her presence galvanizing everyone around her. It was no surprise that all three ascended to leadership roles.

Aatmanji looked at Aanvi, feeling the depths of her sorrow, knowing it was laced with guilt. She blamed herself for what had happened to the twins, but Aatmanji laid the blame on his own shoulders. Aanvi had encouraged Kaali and Aakash to stay away from Tulā School, but she hadn't felt confident enough in her reading of the quantum strands to insist. And Aatmanji had been swayed by the twins' vehement desire to join 108.

In the end, they'd all—even Aanvi herself—discounted Aanvi's ability, with disastrous results. The twins had been tasked with keeping the roads open between Vayu City and Prithvi Forest, so that 108 could obtain supplies and information. One day, as they'd entered Prithvi Forest, they were waylaid by a gang. Aakash had been slaughtered immediately with a machete, and Kaali had been beaten, raped, and left for dead.

Kaali had been located by a search party, and Aanvi had spent the better part of the following year tending to her injuries. Slowly, Kaali had physically healed, except for her vocal cords, which were permanently damaged by a blow to her throat.

But emotional recovery had eluded Kaali. She'd remained understandably disconsolate and lethargic, despite Aanvi's best efforts to support her. One day, shortly before Zed's attack on Tulā School and the first explosion at the Shara temple, Aanvi's sister disappeared. A note arrived for Aanvi after a few weeks: "By the time you read this, I will be dead by my own hand."

Aanvi had led multiple search parties of the surrounding cities and forests. After months of searching, she'd given up. Aatmanji remembered finding Aanvi in tears on that day. *Her strand—her quantum strand—I can't see it anymore.*

Aatmanji now embraced Aanvi, bringing his forehead to hers.

They came apart and looked up as a young man entered the room.

"Aatmanji, we've just gotten word of the ZedChem timeline."

"How long?"

"We have twenty-four hours."

He and Aanvi looked at each other. Would they have enough time?

The messenger spoke. "I have to go—there's more information coming in. I'll keep you posted." Aatmanji nodded.

Aanvi had emerged from her reverie and now spoke, her voice sure and firm, an undercurrent of support through Aatmanji's uncertainty. "I'll inform 108, all our units in all our locations. And I'll head to the temple myself." Her voice faltered. "The only thing is . . . without Bayla, what can we accomplish?"

"We'll have to assume the best, Aanvi—that we'll find her and Chaadi. And when we do, the rest of us will have to be ready."

CHAPTER 45

BAYLA

ZedChem branch outside Vayu City, India
Bayla stirred as images floated through her consciousness.

A pond of lilies.

A cradle of branches.

A garden of jasmine.

She opened her eyes, then closed them immediately—it was too bright. And there was too much pain erupting in a red haze under her eyelids. She whimpered.

Bayla!

Who was calling her? Still strapped to the table, head lolling to the side, Bayla blinked a few times. The room was empty.

Bayla! The voice sounded more distant.

She mustered her strength and strained to look around her. A web of light flickered in front of her and disappeared. She couldn't maintain the effort and simply collapsed, the straps still holding her body upright, her head tipped forward.

The door opened. She looked up in a panic, but it wasn't Velky. Instead, a full-figured woman with stooped shoulders and bright blond hair entered. She was carrying a large bag. More torture?

Then she remembered the EtherScreen in the control room, showing a blond woman treating Chaadi. She sighed with relief.

"Who are you?" Bayla croaked.

The woman did not answer but removed the straps from Bayla's ankles and wrists and then her waist, catching her firmly as she fell forward. Bayla, overcome with nausea, leaned away from the woman and vomited on the floor. The woman did not flinch. "It is alright. It will be alright," she whispered.

Bayla couldn't make out the woman's accent—like Velky's, it seemed Eastern European, but it also held a touch of some other language or dialect.

The woman lowered Bayla to the floor and propped her against the wall. Using a bottle of water and a washcloth, she cleaned Bayla's face, then removed some supplies from her bag to bandage Bayla's bruises and cuts. She took great care to move Bayla's clothing aside gently and touch her lightly. Bayla tried not to cry out from pain.

The woman opened a small juice bottle and held it to Bayla's lips. After Bayla took a few sips, she pressed the bottle into Bayla's hands, making sure that Bayla could lift it and drink on her own. The woman then tore open a small packet and gave two pills to Bayla.

"You will have headache," she whispered. Removing two ice packs from her bag, the woman placed one on each side of Bayla's face.

"Thank you," Bayla whispered to the woman, wincing and pressing the ice packs harder into her face with her hands. "What is your name?" Bayla mumbled.

The woman did not answer and, instead, gathered her supplies into her bag, strapping it over her shoulder.

"We will go to room." Putting a strong arm around Bayla's waist, the woman braced her firmly but took care not to press her bandages. Bayla cringed and cried out nevertheless. The lift to her feet and the first few steps were excruciating, but then it became easier to walk. "Here," the woman said, handing Bayla the ice packs, which had fallen to the floor. Bayla took them and, this time, pressed both to her abdomen.

Slowly, they approached the exit. Bayla tried again. "Please, tell me your name."

The woman glanced upward at the horizontal interior window, seemed to consider for a moment, then replied under her breath, "I am Marja."

Bayla wondered again at her accent, as well as her hesitation. She looked up at the woman's face for a few moments as they made their way down the corridor. Sadness and loss seemed to track their steps. "It's not your name, is it?" Bayla asked. "Marja is not your real name," she repeated.

Marja looked at Bayla, as though in shock. "How . . . how do you know this?" Bayla couldn't answer—she wasn't sure herself.

Marja spoke again, and Bayla could almost see her internal struggle. "I am . . . I am . . ." Lowering her voice until it was barely audible, she whispered, "Violette."

So *that* was the accent infused within the Eastern European tones. "Are you French?" Bayla asked.

Again, Marja looked at her in surprise. "My grandmother—my mother's mother." Marja's eyes lost their focus for a moment, as though she'd slipped into a memory.

"Violette," Bayla repeated softly. "I'm named for a flower, too—Bayla."

"Bayla," Marja repeated. After a few moments, she spoke again. "Violette was my grandmother's name, too. But she called me *petite fleur.*"

Little Flower.

***

Still holding Bayla, Marja bent toward the lock on the cell door, then leaned in and spoke a few words. Again, Bayla strained to hear but was unsuccessful. In a few seconds, the lock to the cell opened, and Marja helped her inside.

Chaadi jumped up from the cot where he was sitting and ran to them, moving to Bayla's other side and doing his best to support her, despite his bandaged shoulder. They maneuvered her to the cot and seated her. Marja pressed the ice packs, which had dropped again, to Bayla's face and abdomen until Bayla could take hold of them herself.

"Bayla, what happened to you—what did they do?" Chaadi exclaimed.

At the same time, Bayla fired questions at him. "How's your shoulder? Are you in a lot of pain?"

They smiled ruefully at each other.

Bayla looked up to thank Marja, but she'd already gone. However, she'd left a pile of items near the door. Chaadi followed Bayla's eyes. "I'll get them."

Because of his shoulder injury, he struggled to pick them up, but managed. "That was the same woman who came in to treat me. She seemed to know what she was doing. I'm lucky it was a graze. And look," he said, indicating his forehead, "she stitched up my cut."

Chaadi handed Bayla a water bottle that Marja had left for them. She took it gratefully and gulped it down. She felt a bit better, her nausea diminishing, but every part of her body throbbed. Chaadi helped her lift her feet and lie down on the cot. "This time, you rest." He sat on the floor next to her, with his back to the camera. After ten minutes or so, he asked, "Can you tell me what happened?"

Bayla suddenly pulled her knees up to her chest, shivering. Chaadi shifted and put a hand to her forehead, stroking her hair.

"I met Zed," she whispered.

"Do you want to tell me about him?"

She squeezed her eyes shut, shaking her head.

"Okay—it's okay."

After a moment, she whispered, "Chaadi, he's terrifying."

"I can imagine."

"It's not just *this*," she said, gesturing to her injuries. "It's his entitlement—that Earth is his for the taking, on his own terms, without responsibility. . . ." Bayla's voice trailed off.

They sat in silence for a few moments before Bayla spoke again.

"Chaadi—I think Aatmanji is alive."

"*What?* How do you know?"

"I don't, not for sure. But Zed's recording everything. . . ."

"Recording what?"

Bayla lifted her tunic a little, to show the bruises and bandages across her abdomen, and then her sleeves.

He looked at her in horror. "My God, Bayla—Zed did this to you?"

"Yes—well, it was the man who brought us here, the one with the scar. I found out his name is Velky. Zed told him to . . . hurt me." She paused and curled into herself again.

Chaadi clenched his fists.

Then the right side of her mouth tipped upward in a tiny

smile. "But I got one good punch in—right to the gut. Knocked the wind out of him."

Chaadi grinned. "You're amazing, you know that?" He looked at her arm outstretched on the cot. With the sleeve pushed up, amid the spreading yellow-green of hematoma, he saw four crescent-shaped scars in a line, on the inside of her forearm.

"Did Velky do that to you, too?"

"Do what?"

He pointed. "Those scars on your arm."

She looked. "Oh. No, that's . . . that's nothing. Just something I do when everything feels out of control—grab my arm and dig my nails in. Bad habit." She tried to smile again but couldn't.

Chaadi traced each crescent with the tip of his index finger as she watched, lying sideways, her eyes half-closed. He looked at her, then bent his lips to one of the scars, the one closest to her wrist. She watched in silence, her eyes filling with tears from the tender gesture.

After a few minutes, she whispered, "He said the video would draw Appa out. I'm assuming that means he knows Appa's alive."

"And what do you think, Bayla?"

She paused, considering. "Yes. I think he's alive. I think he's been trying to call to me, to reach me through the web. I saw images from the past—our past together at Tulā School. But the images don't remain long. And I saw the web flickering in and out—but I can't stay with it. Maybe it's because of the pain."

She lay back for a few minutes, and Chaadi stroked her forehead again.

Bayla groaned. "Chaadi," she whispered, "do you think they'll do this again? Hurt me?"

"No." His voice was firm. "We're getting out—I promise you." He looked up at the camera again, then turned back to her. "Can you tell me anything more about the building?"

Bayla nodded, trying to gather her strength. "Yes. The locks are run by voiceprint."

"Really?" Chaadi furrowed his brow.

"And I got into the control room for a few minutes."

"What did you see?"

"Three computer workstations, projecting more than a dozen EtherScreens. And this feed"—she tipped her head toward the camera—"shows up on one of them." She sighed. "But even if we get out of this building, Chaadi, there's a compound wall outside, remember? With guarded exits."

"But at least we know where we are now—like you said, this has to be the new ZedChem factory outside Vayu City."

Suddenly, Bayla covered her face with her hands. "The pour—the pour, Chaadi! Zed's moved it up to twenty-four hours from now, but I don't know how long ago that was—because I don't know how long I've been unconscious, and . . ."

"Bayla, Bayla, just breathe—one thing at a time."

She took a deep breath. "We can't even get out of this cell. How can we stop the pour?"

Chaadi looked at her, trying to project optimism. "We're going to figure it out."

She lay back, exhausted.

Chaadi paused. "That woman . . . the one who bandaged both of us up . . . what about her? She's been the one treating us. Maybe she could help. I bet I could figure something out if I could access their system."

"Marja. But she seems so scared."

"Yes, but maybe . . . maybe she wants to leave here, too."

Bayla looked at him. "I guess it's possible. By the way, Chaadi, what kind of work do you do?"

He grinned. "Computer network security."

CHAPTER 46

AATMANJI

Town of Gudalur, India

Aatmanji and Aanvi both looked up, hearing a gasp. The messenger had stepped out of the room, only to turn around again, staring at his phone.

"Aatmanji," he said, approaching them with urgency. "We've been scanning the internet for information. A video has been uploaded and marked with today's date and the headline of *India Southwest*."

"What's the message?"

The man's reluctance was apparent.

"Tell me. Right now."

"They want you to report to the ZedChem compound outside Vayu City alone. Or they'll . . . they'll . . ."

"Give it to me," Aatmanji said, pointing to the man's cell phone. The man moved the time track back to the beginning, pausing the video on the news headline.

Aatmanji felt he was looking at himself from a distance and in slow motion as he tapped the play button. He swiped to project the video in front of him, and the screams began immediately—Bayla's screams.

His heart froze. His stomach turned. Grabbing the container next to his bed, he vomited.

Everything he'd done to protect Bayla, all these years, had come to naught. She was in Zed's hands, undergoing physical torture. Aatmanji sat back, cringing. He wanted to turn off the video but felt he owed it to Bayla to bear witness to her ordeal.

"No, Aatmanji, you don't have to do that. You don't have to watch more," Aanvi said gently, as though he'd spoken the feeling aloud. She took the phone from him, closed the video, and handed the device back to the young man who stood waiting with a distressed expression on his face.

Aatmanji looked at Aanvi, who seemed to be anticipating his next words. "I have to go there—I have to follow Zed's instructions. Otherwise, they'll continue to hurt her."

She grabbed his hand. "No—we'll figure out another way," she insisted.

"I have to, for Bayla."

"Then I'm coming with you."

"No, my dear, 108 needs you—it needs your leadership. Be ready."

"But if . . . if Bayla can't lead us?"

"Then we'll do whatever we can with whomever we have."

Aanvi dropped her head and nodded assent.

He looked at Aanvi for a moment before speaking. "I'm going to call Cartwright before I go."

"You know what the price will be, Aatmanji. He won't do any more for you without additional information about 108. Cartwright's an honorable man, but you know he has his loyalties."

"I have to try everything."

Aanvi nodded and turned to go. At the door, she stopped and looked back at him, her expression disturbed.

"What is it?"

Aanvi closed her eyes. "It's that energy I told you about—the one that looks like an electrical current. It's dropped into its own strand—and it's begun to interweave with all of ours." She clenched her fists. "But I can't see what will happen."

Aatmanji could feel her frustration.

"I can't see it!" she repeated.

CHAPTER 47

BAYLA

Bayla attempted to emerge through the murkiness, thick and viscous, filling her head. When at last she opened her eyes, she was lying on her side on the ground, in a fetal position.

She'd survived her second session with Velky.

She remembered Velky entering their cell yet again, barely an hour after Marja had left her there. Her resistance had been fierce, considering how badly she was hurting. But again he'd turned and attacked Chaadi mercilessly until she'd screamed her willingness to comply.

Velky had strapped her to the table again. With the absence of anyone else in the room, his hands had wandered too freely. Her gut lurched and she began dry heaving.

What if they couldn't find a way to escape this place? How many more sessions would there be? She didn't know how much more pain she could endure.

Groaning, Bayla struggled to sit up. Who had taken her down from the table? Was it Marja?

Turning her head, she saw that Marja was indeed a few

feet away, returning supplies to her bag. Bayla looked down at herself—she'd been re-bandaged.

"Violette," she said weakly.

Marja startled. "Do not," she said in a strangled voice, looking around her even though they were alone. "Do not say that name." She stood. "Come. We must go back."

As Marja reached for her, Bayla whispered, "Please. Please wait a moment. I can't walk yet. Just sit here with me."

With a worried expression, Marja knelt next to Bayla after casting an eye at the door and up at the viewing window.

Bayla leaned back against the wall. "How . . . how did you come to be here, with Zed?"

Marja looked at her for a few moments before answering. "He took me from Marko."

"Marko?"

"Marko bought me when I was a young girl. . . ."

"Did you say he *bought* you?"

"Yes—so much conflict in my country—I lost my family. So many people—so many girls—on the street."

"Violette, I'm so sorry."

Marja's language took time to loosen, as though she was struggling to articulate a history she'd never spoken aloud before. "Marko was leader of cyber gang." She gulped. "I had to serve them."

"Oh, Violette . . ."

"It is okay, it is okay. Better than street. So much violence those days—shootings, pipe bombs. But I learned to treat their injuries," she said, with a shadow of pride.

"That's how you were able to help Chaadi—and me. But what about Zed?"

"Zed came to Marko. He wanted Marko to put . . .

information online. Marko said yes, but Marko did not know English—no one did, in the gang."

"But you did."

"Enough. Enough to do the work. My parents . . ." She stopped and squeezed her eyes shut. "My parents were teachers."

Bayla remained silent, not wanting to rush her. At last, Marja continued. "Zed told Marko he wanted *confusion* about ZedChem formulas. He wanted to . . . discredit people—to shame them. I worked so many hours, then Zed found out it's *me*. That I was the one doing this."

Again, she gulped. "He told me I would have better life, working for him. And I joined him—I still did same work for him, but I only had to . . . serve . . . one person."

Bayla's heart ached for her.

Marja looked abstracted for a few moments. "It is strange. When I came here, he said my name is Marja. I said, 'No, my name is Violette.' And he hurt me. He hurt me until I said, 'Yes, I am Marja.'"

Bayla touched Marja's shoulder, but she jumped up as though Bayla had burned her. Bayla withdrew her hand.

"You mustn't—I do not deserve."

"What do you mean?"

"I do terrible things. I am criminal like him—like Zed." She shuddered. "The chemist . . . ," she began, then hung her head, shamefaced.

"Jala Sharma?" Bayla asked softly. "That was you? You ran the smear campaign to discredit her?"

"Yes, I told so many lies about her. And then . . . then Zed sent someone—he killed her."

"I know, Violette."

Marja looked at her. "You remind me of her."

"You *knew* Jala?"

"She worked here. She spoke to me . . . just like you. *Kind.* And then she . . . she . . ." Marja's words trailed off. "I wanted to help you."

"Thank you, Violette."

"It was different, doing those things to Jala Sharma—hurting someone I knew, who was kind to me. Like hurting someone standing in front of me. Someone real." Marja covered her face.

"Violette, you know that Jala Sharma was telling the truth, don't you? About FZ5 killing the soil?"

Marja nodded, her face still covered. Bayla gathered her strength and tugged Marja's hands away. "Violette, listen, you can make it up to her—make it up to Jala. Help us stop the pour."

Marja's head snapped up, and she pushed Bayla away. "No! No. I cannot do that. Do not ask me." She looked up at the viewing glass again and stood up. "I will take you back now."

"Okay, Violette. Okay." Marja helped her to her feet, and she struggled forward. As they walked, Bayla turned to her a few times. When Marja appeared calmer, she spoke again. "Instead, maybe you can just help *me*—help me escape." She paused, seeing the uncertainty in Marja's face. "I won't survive this, Violette—what Velky's doing to me. It's too much." Bayla saw that Marja's look was sympathetic, and she pushed a little more. "I need your help to escape. Please, Violette. Please."

Marja looked like she was wavering.

"I will think," she responded at last.

"Okay," Bayla whispered. "Thank you."

In the middle of the corridor, Bayla stopped and looked at Marja full in the face. She could not begin to imagine the misery and desperation of such a life. Could she reach out to her through the web? Could she see the threads?

Bayla concentrated, but she was too weak. Instead, she cast through her memory for Tante Sindhu's French.

"*Je suis désolé pour ta douleur,* Violette." *I am sorry for your pain.*

"*Merci* . . . Bayla," Marja whispered.

Bayla put a hand on her arm, and this time, Marja did not flinch.

"Violette. You could come with us. You could escape this place, too. Escape Zed."

Panic returned to her eyes. "Do not—do not say this. I cannot—I cannot leave."

Bayla grabbed Marja's hand. Even if she couldn't avert the pour, she could help this woman. "Let's all get out together, Violette. Come with us. Please."

"I-I do not know. I do not deserve. It is bad . . . my past."

Bayla smiled, just a bit, as Braden's words came to her yet again. "Your past doesn't have to define you, Violette. You're much more than your past. And for once, you can choose your future."

CHAPTER 48

CHAADI

Chaadi paced the cell. It had been over an hour since Velky had returned for Bayla. He marveled at her courage, continuing to resist Velky despite her diminished strength. Only when Velky had turned on *him*, pummeling him with punches, had she ceased battling and submitted to being led from the cell.

Chaadi balled his fists. It was infuriating to be this helpless.

At last, he heard the *click, click, beep* of the lock, and again, Marja appeared in the doorway with Bayla. He flashed Marja a look of fury, finding it difficult not to associate her with Velky despite her assistance with Bayla's, and his own, injuries.

Chaadi held Bayla from the other side, and again they walked Bayla to the cot. Marja turned to go, but Bayla grabbed her hand. "Violette," she whispered.

Violette? he wondered, puzzled. Bayla had told him the woman's name was Marja.

"Will you help us? Help us to escape?" Bayla's whisper was hoarse.

Chaadi looked from Bayla to Marja, surprised by this turn

of events. But Marja pulled her hand away. "Please, Violette," Bayla rasped.

Marja closed her eyes and dropped her head for a moment or two. Her entire body seemed to waver with uncertainty.

"Alright," she whispered at last, looking at Bayla's grateful face and Chaadi's astonished one. "What do you want me to do?"

Bayla looked at Chaadi, who spoke immediately. "We need to record your voiceprint password so we can access the locks—you know, all the doors and the compound gates."

"Shhh," Marja said, indicating the camera with a tilt of her head. She bent forward, pretending to adjust Bayla's bandage, and shook her head. "No, it will not work," she whispered.

"Why not?"

"My voiceprint is not enough—my access is only inside building. Not outer doors, not compound gates."

Oh no, he thought, disappointed. "Then I need to get into the control room."

Marja looked doubtful. Bayla spoke up softly. "Chaadi understands computer networks, Violette. He'll find a way out."

"But if I do this . . ." Marja gulped. "If I do this, then Zed will learn I am the one who helped you." She paused. "I must come with you; I must leave here."

Bayla gazed at her, searching her face. "Do you *want* to, Violette?"

Marja nodded. "Yes. I want to go. Like you said—I want different future. I want to choose."

Bayla smiled weakly and dropped sideways to the cot. "I'm so glad. So glad you are coming with us," she said faintly, closing her eyes.

Chaadi looked at Marja. Willingness was one thing, but could this woman actually help them?

Marja seemed to be concentrating, working something out in her mind, and Chaadi felt the tension building in his body.

At last, she spoke. "There is one guard—the supervisor is his friend, so he sometimes leaves shift early, at three thirty a.m. If he leaves early today, I can freeze camera frames. I will come for you and open cell door. You must be ready. You will have only twenty-five minutes. Then next guard will arrive. Cameras must be turned on before that."

Chaadi's face fell. How could he obtain access to all the ZedChem grounds and get back to the cell in twenty-five minutes? It seemed impossible.

He looked at Bayla, lying limp on the cot. She'd endured too much. He *had* to come through for her. Chaadi took a deep breath to fortify himself. "I'll be ready."

Marja nodded. "Remember—I cannot be sure. If guard does not leave, then I will try again tomorrow."

Chaadi winced. *Tomorrow?* How could Bayla survive another day with Velky? Hopefully, luck would be with them tonight.

Marja's eyes were fearful as she studied his face. "Can you really do it? Find a way out? Zed will know I helped you. Do you understand? If I do not leave, Velky will kill me."

"Yes. Absolutely. I can do it," Chaadi stated, to convince himself as much as Marja, but he saw the doubt and reluctance on her face. *Oh no.* Marja was their best—and maybe only—chance. Was she changing her mind?

But Marja turned to Bayla lying on the cot, and her doubt seemed to fade. "She is beautiful person."

"Yes, she is." Chaadi marveled that this woman had agreed to put her own safety—indeed, her own life—on the line for them. She'd agreed to walk away from her entire world. How had Bayla convinced her?

He shook his head in wonder. Bayla did not seem to grasp how compelling a person she was. He thought of the name she'd called Marja—Violette. Did that have something to do with the woman's change of heart?

"Thank you for helping us . . . *Violette.* You're brave."

She looked at him, then stood straighter, as though embracing her decision with greater resolve. "Remember," she whispered, "if I come back tonight, you must be ready."

"I will be. I promise."

Marja exited after a backward glance at Bayla. Chaadi perched on the edge of the cot where Bayla lay shivering, eyes closed. He leaned over and embraced her. "You did it, Bayla."

Her smile was weak, her energy spent. "Chaadi," she said faintly, opening her eyes a crack, "I don't think I can come with you to the control room."

He stroked her hair. "Don't worry, leave it to me now."

Bayla began to whisper again, and he leaned closer as she relayed what she'd learned from Marja after Velky's torture session. After that, he watched her for a few minutes as she slid in and out of fitful sleep. When her body began twitching, he climbed onto the cot behind her, encircling her, hoping it gave her some comfort. She cried out at times, wept at others, and he held her until she stilled.

As he lay next to her, Chaadi crossed his fingers, willing Marja to return that night. His mind raced as he considered the possibilities the control room might offer. Marja obviously had some access to the ZedChem system—she'd said she could disable the cameras. Presumably, he'd be able to enter the network with her credentials. *Thank goodness.* ZedChem would have state-of-the-art firewalls, so hacking in from outside would have been impossible within these time constraints.

But past those firewalls, within the network itself, he'd

have options. As he well knew, securing a computer network from the *inside* was still a constant challenge for corporations. Of course, ZedChem would likely deploy periodic security scans to check which personnel were working in which areas of the enterprise, but he'd have to take that chance.

Impatiently, Chaadi felt minutes, then hours, pass. When he heard the *click, click, beep* of the lock, he maneuvered swiftly off the cot, trying not to disturb Bayla in the process. Just before the door closed behind him, Marja wedged something into the jamb and urged him forward. "Run!"

CHAPTER 49

CHAADI

Chaadi sprinted down the hallway, with Marja trailing behind him. In the control room, he surveyed the layout. As Bayla said, there were three workstations and dozens of EtherScreens, as well as boxes of electronic equipment and wires on the tables. As he walked forward, his hip caused one of the boxes to tip and crash to the floor.

"Shhh," hissed Marja, who had reached the room and now stood trying to catch her breath. "You must be quiet—Velky stays in opposite room." She scooted into the first workstation, spoke her credentials, then stepped away.

Chaadi took her place and, for a moment, felt entirely overwhelmed. He knew why ZedChem had opted for voice-print security. AI advances had allowed physical images and even iris prints to get hacked—he thought of the spectacular information thefts that had occurred just last month in the corporate world.

Now voiceprint technology had advanced by leaps and bounds, and the million nuances of workers' voices were being harnessed as cutting-edge corporate passwords. If Marja's voiceprint would not provide them complete access to the grounds, then he'd have to find someone else's. But digging for passwords in a high-security network would take hours, if not days.

Marja's fearful voice punctured his thoughts. "Nineteen minutes."

He glanced up. Marja was rooting around in the drawers, looking for something. He thought of the risk she was taking. Her fingerprints—actually, her voiceprints—were all over this breach of security.

Chaadi steeled himself and racked his brain. *How? How can I do this?*

Wait!

If he already *had* the exact verbiage of a person's password in hand, then he might be able to deploy a bot to locate it within the system and extract it.

"Violette," he called softly. She looked up, startled. The sound of that name still seemed to surprise her.

"Do you know *anyone* else's password at ZedChem? Someone with more access than you—like Velky?"

"No," she replied. "I only know . . ." Her body began to tremble.

Chaadi finished her sentence. "Zed's."

She nodded, distress in her eyes.

"Tell me," he urged.

Marja's voice shook. "He will know—he will know I gave it to you."

"Violette, you'll have to decide. There's no time, and there's no other way."

Marja looked anxiously at the clock, then fixed her gaze on Chaadi.

"Please."

Marja hesitated another second, then responded with a polysyllabic phrase that he couldn't catch: *"Sjeti se Mateja, ne zaboravi ga nikada."*

"Here, come here, Violette. Type it," Chaadi ordered, stepping out of the way. "As fast as you can. But you must be accurate."

Marja moved to the station and typed the words as he watched over her shoulder.

When she finished, Chaadi pushed past her and opened one EtherScreen after another, struggling to open an auxiliary bypass route to a WellSecure port using Marja's limited access. He dug further and further into ZedChem's network infrastructure, desperate for an entry point.

There!

He worked frantically, feeling sweat beading on his back, wishing he had more time. He took a deep breath. *It doesn't matter—this is the time I actually* have.

He launched the bot.

Marja whispered, "Eight minutes left."

Would his bot find Zed's password in time? Chaadi shook his head to clear it—he couldn't worry about that now. There was more he needed to do. Turning, he rummaged through the equipment until he found a pile of phones.

He selected an old—*oh geez, ancient*—model Hanaka, hoping it would be easier to bypass the password screen. Crossing his fingers, he turned it on and groaned. The battery life read only 45 percent.

It would have to do. He checked the connectivity icon and was relieved to see it brighten. Working swiftly, he disabled the password function.

"Five minutes."

Anxiously, he looked back at the EtherScreen and turned on the phone's recorder. *Come on, bot.*

"Four."

Come on.

Suddenly, Zed's voice growled from the speaker: *"Sjeti se Mateja, ne zaboravi ga nikada."* Upon hearing it, Marja jumped.

Got it!

"What does it mean?" he asked, as he double-checked that the recording had been captured.

She looked at him. "It means 'Remember Matej, never forget him.'"

"Who is—"

"You must finish—finish now," Marja cut in.

Wiping his forehead with the back of his hand, he used the recorded voiceprint to enter the ZedChem security system directly, locating menus for the locks, cameras, doors, and gates. He added his own passcode in order to access those systems with his phone during the time of their escape.

A thought occurred to him. "Violette, what about the guards at the compound gates?"

"I will change shift schedule for one of them. But one guard is assigned directly by Security Oversight—I cannot access that schedule." She began working frantically at another computer.

"Fine. We'll just have to make it work." But it was a worrisome thought. The remaining guard would likely be armed. "Yes, change the four thirty a.m. shift. And meet us at the front compound gate at that exact time."

"Okay, okay, yes. Now go—you must go!" she begged.

Turning, he caught sight of something—another computer workstation in the back corner.

"What is that for?"

Marja sounded desperate. "Please, please, there is no time.

You must go back to cell." Nevertheless, Chaadi maneuvered toward the back wall. It was a stack of EtherScreens. With a swipe of his hands, he separated them from each other. Twenty screens showing readiness for twenty simultaneous chemical pours. Was this room a backup station?

Chaadi replayed the voiceprint, then scrolled through the code controlling the dispensing machines, pulling up the timed instructions. *Got 'em!*

He knew what he needed to do, but he didn't have time. "Violette!" She looked at him fearfully. "You can stop this pour—you can do it." He pointed to the screen: "Look right here—you can enter contradictory time instructions. Just reverse this set of numbers on every other line. It'll produce an error and take the pour offline."

"Do not ask this of me! I told her—I told Bayla I would only help her escape."

"Violette, listen to me—"

"*No!* You must get out now. Here, take these with you," she urged, pressing something into his hand. "Now—run!"

"Violette, you can do this," he said, pointing to the EtherScreens. "I have faith in you. Bayla has faith in you." Turning, Chaadi ran out of the control room, then stopped in his tracks. He'd seen something important—what was it?

He stepped backward just as Marja was closing the door. "Wait!"

"No!" she exclaimed, trying to block him.

Chaadi pushed past her. *There!* A long metal stick as long as a broom handle, but heavier, lay on the ground—maybe used to seal a window or a door. He grabbed it and sprinted back to the cell, pulling out the wedge Marja had inserted in the doorway just as the cameras clicked back on. Panting, he bent over his knees.

Marja had reset the cell camera, and it was operating as usual. Nonchalantly, trying to control his breathing, he walked toward the cot, sank to the floor with his back to the camera, and leaned over his knees, as though attempting to sleep in that position. He opened his hand and saw something made of fabric. What had Marja given him? He examined it and smiled. Masks—high-quality ones. Good thing, or their coughing would give them away once they exited this building.

He slid the phone forward on the floor, continuing to block the camera's view with his back, and quickly double-checked his access to the various security obstacles they would face.

Less than thirty minutes till they had to meet Marja. He would need to give Bayla some time to transition to wakefulness, especially with her injuries and exhaustion. He looked at her, finally in a peaceful sleep. How he hated to wake her.

Bending toward her, he whispered, "Bayla."

She stirred and whimpered.

"Bayla, it's time."

She sat bolt upright, clearly in a panic. He wrapped his arms around her. "Hey, it's okay. Shhh."

She relaxed into him for a minute, and her breathing slowed.

"We'll have to go soon, Bayla."

Bayla focused immediately and nodded. "Yes. I'll be ready."

He looked at her, impressed by her snap to clarity, given all that she'd withstood. But he could see the effort it was taking from the dark circles under her eyes and the jerkiness of her normally fluid movements.

She scanned the room. "What's that?" she asked, indicating the stick he'd placed in the corner next to the door, hoping it would remain undetected there.

"It's the closest thing I could find to a *kalaripayattu* stick.

If we get attacked, I'll do my best to ward them off, but I think you'll be more useful than I will be. Assuming you're up for it, of course. I don't mean to push you."

"I'm up for it." She took a breath. "That is, I will be."

CHAPTER 50

ZED

Zed tossed in his bed, the pain in his body and limbs seeping into a dream.

As though from a distance, he could see himself writhing in pain on a forest floor, until a beautiful girl appeared. Dressed in a moss-green skirt and blouse, she almost blended into the foliage around her. With each step of her approach, he heard the chime of tiny bells. Kneeling, she passed a hand over his forehead, and the throbbing lessened and dissipated. She placed her fingers on his arm, and the searing diminished and ceased. He reached for the girl—he needed her to do *more*, to take away more of his pain—but she leaped to her feet. Taking the long stick she carried, she struck the ground—*thwack, thwack, thwack.*

His eyes flew open. It was a knock at the door.

"What?" he barked hoarsely, torn out of his dream.

"I'm so sorry, sir," an assistant said. "It's an urgent call."

Zed sat up, his entire body shaking from pain. He took a vial from the table next to him and injected himself, relaxing as the pain slackened enough to make him functional.

The assistant swept the call to the EtherScreen. The face appeared, the one Zed had been waiting for. He could tell the man was in a moving vehicle.

"Aatmanji. Look at you, alive and well. You managed to fool me for fifteen years."

Aatmanji didn't reply.

"I didn't know what would draw a coward out of the shadows, but torturing your little girl seems to have done it. I trust you saw the second session. Velky is very, very good at his job. Though I believe Matej suffered far worse than your daughter has—after all, your daughter is still alive. For now."

Aatmanji winced, but his voice was steady when he spoke. "You must stop what you're doing, Zed. I've answered you, just as you demanded."

"No. You were to report *here*, to the ZedChem compound, but you didn't. I believe it is time for session three. Velky!" he shouted. He turned back to Aatmanji and grinned. "Don't worry—we'll bandage her up before we start again. We find that providing a minuscule bit of hope generates even deeper despair."

"No. Stop. I am coming to you now, as quickly as I can. I'm willing to accept my death, for her life. But you must release her and Chaadi. I must know they are safe."

"You're not in a position to dictate terms, Aatmanji."

There was another knock at the door.

"Who is it?" he shouted.

The door opened a crack. "Velky, sir."

Velky entered, dragging a woman with him, bruised and disheveled, her clothing askew.

Marja.

CHAPTER 51

BAYLA

Bayla sat cross-legged on the floor, breathing deeply in and out, consciously pulling air into her lungs, then letting it inhabit and fill her entire body. Even these few minutes could be used to rest and reset her body and mind, to remind herself that pain didn't necessarily require suffering.

Opening her eyes, she glanced at Chaadi, who was still working on the phone, with his back to the camera. Moving toward him, she whispered, "What are you doing?"

"We can buy some extra time if I set up a subroutine stating that the locks are engaged, even when they're not," he whispered back. "I've almost got it."

She nodded, marveling at his skill, especially given how little time and equipment he had at his disposal. It was an escape possible only due to Chaadi's expertise, not to mention Marja's willingness to help them.

After another minute, he looked at her and said, "It's four twenty. Are you ready? We need to meet Marja at the front gate at exactly four thirty."

She nodded. "Ready." They bent over the phone, and Bayla watched as Chaadi accessed the camera menu and froze the images, just as Marja had done earlier from the control room. Reflexively, they looked toward their camera. Hopefully, it was off.

They approached the door, and Chaadi worked with the phone again, deploying the subroutine he'd just developed. Then he called up Zed's voiceprint. *Click, click, beep.* The cell door unlocked.

Bayla shivered—it sounded louder than usual at this time of night, due to the background silence. Chaadi pushed the door open an inch, then immediately closed it again. Bayla caught a glimpse of two men striding by, in the direction of the control room. She strained to hear them and caught bits of what they were saying: "Something's wrong with the pour. . . . They're saying someone tampered with the programming in Control Room 6. . . ."

Bayla looked at Chaadi questioningly.

"Violette—she did it! She stopped the pour!" he whispered loudly.

Elated, Bayla grabbed him and hugged him—they'd badly needed a victory.

"How did you convince her?" Bayla asked, her smile radiant.

Chaadi continued to hold her. "I think you're the one who convinced her, Bayla."

They stood looking at each other for a moment, then Bayla broke away. "Come on!" she said, pulling him by the hand.

She pushed the door open again, inch by inch. No one was in the hallway. They made their way down the corridor, to the exterior door farthest from the control room.

At the end, Chaadi entered another command on the phone and the bolt shifted, echoing through the corridor. Bayla and Chaadi looked at each other in alarm, but no one emerged from the rooms. They heaved a sigh of relief.

Bayla gripped the metal rod that Chaadi had found in the control room, then pushed the outer door open by a few inches. It was dark, except for a few electric lanterns on the ground. Pulling on one of the masks Marja had given them, she slipped out, followed by Chaadi.

They made their way through the dark compound until they caught sight of the front gate. There was only one guard there. Marja had indeed been able to relocate the other. Bayla was impressed by how much the woman had accomplished despite her fear of Zed.

"When Marja gets here, I'm going to open the gate. The guard will definitely see us," Chaadi whispered. "You just have to put him out of commission. Are you sure you're up for it?"

Bayla gripped the metal rod again. "Yes," she said, her voice firm.

"Don't worry, I'm going to help you."

Ducking behind a large metal utility box, they waited for Marja to appear. Chaadi eyed the time on his phone nervously. "Where is she? She should be here by now."

"She'll be here. She got the first guard out of the picture, so she's aware of the time."

"Yes, but . . ."

"Wait—please, just another minute, Chaadi." Bayla was worried, too, but wanted to give Marja every possible chance to join them, to escape this hell.

CHAPTER 52

ZED

"What is this?" Zed demanded.

Velky looked at the screen from which Aatmanji was observing the events transpiring in the room, and seemed reluctant to answer.

Zed turned to the screen. "Aatmanji, you have fifteen minutes to be at the ZedChem gate. As you can see, Velky is here and ready to continue his . . . *work* with your daughter." He chuckled. "Though for him, it's more like play." Zed enjoyed the look of terror on Aatmanji's face, then swiped the screen off.

"Well?" he said, looking at Velky.

"Security Oversight informed me that there was problem with cameras. There was no feed from three thirty to four a.m. When they checked, they found out that she"—he shook Marja by the arm—"entered control room at that time. It was her access code."

Zed strode toward Marja, bearing down on her as she cringed. "What did you do?"

"Nothing—nothing," she insisted, shaking her head back and forth, her teeth chattering.

Velky spoke. "When I went to find her, she was still there. She had programming screens open—ones for pour."

"Really?" Zed asked, surprised at this show of defiance—he didn't think she still had it in her. "Bring her here."

Velky hauled Marja closer as she whimpered.

"Marja, did you do this? Did you try to stop the pour?"

She inhaled deeply, looked at him, and raised her chin. "My name is Violette."

"Is that so?" Zed's voice was dangerously low.

She shivered. "Yes. My name is Violette."

The silence turned ominous.

"Velky, leave Marja here."

Velky nodded and pushed her forward. At that moment, his cell phone pinged. Reading the message, Velky turned to Zed in shock.

"Sir, the detention cell is empty."

Zed looked at Velky. "What?! Go—go now! Find them."

Velky dashed out of the room, and Zed narrowed his eyes at Marja. "What did you do?"

A strangled squeak emerged from Marja's throat. "She is safe. She is safe now," she sobbed, her voice a mixture of fear and rebellion.

He turned back to Marja, drawing out the time, taking pleasure in the woman's cowering, letting that pleasure mix with his fury, feeling the concoction flow through his veins.

"What is your name? Tell me again." He advanced, arm raised, ignoring the pain coursing through his own body.

"M-Marja."

The slap was instant and sharp. She fell to the ground.

"That's right." He looked at her, sprawled on the floor, and spoke with disgust. "Get up. Next, you are going to tell me everything you've done. *Everything.*"

CHAPTER 53

BAYLA

A sound blared from the compound, through numerous speakers throughout the property. They looked up. Guards emerged from the various buildings in the compound, entered the yard, and ran in their direction.

"Bayla," Chaadi urged, "we have to leave right now! We don't have a choice."

"We can't leave without Violette! We have to find her," Bayla said, looking around frantically.

"Bayla!" he exclaimed, desperately working on the phone. The gate began to slide, its noise echoing through the compound, adding to the noise of the sirens. He grabbed her hand and pulled her toward the threshold as the guards descended.

A voice rang out. "If you leave, she dies. Marja dies."

Velky.

Bayla turned toward him, enraged.

"Bayla, don't!" Chaadi's voice seemed to come toward her from a great distance.

Running back into the middle of the compound, Bayla swung the metal bar hard to her right, directly at Velky's legs, knocking him off his feet. He rebounded and lunged for her. She sidestepped and hit him across the back. He fell forward, momentarily stunned.

One of the guards rushed toward her. She brandished the rod again; it was heavier and longer than a traditional *kalaripayattu* stick, and she needed to adapt to that. Bayla swung the rod and caught the guard in the throat. He dropped to the ground.

She looked toward Chaadi, who was struggling with a man at the threshold of the compound. Another guard, some distance away, fired a gun, and Chaadi fell backward, outside the gate. The gate began to close.

"Chaadi!" she screamed. She ran toward the gate, then stopped short. A tall, elegant man stood just outside. Their eyes met. Was that—was that *Appa*?

Oh no, he'll be caught. She opened her mouth to shout at him, to warn him to get away, then squawked. Velky had grabbed her arm, causing the metal rod to slip from her hands. As she reached for it, he twisted her arm backward behind her. She froze, not wanting to dislocate her limb.

She gasped in relief when he released her arm, then kicked and screamed as he pulled her away from the chaos. Pulling her mask off, he shoved it into her mouth like a gag. She began to choke.

One of the guards ran to him.

"There's a police force outside, asking about the gunshots."

"I am coming. Do not allow them inside. And get the old man," Velky growled. "He's just outside."

Bayla!

Appa's voice. She could not see him, but the voice seemed to echo within her. *Bayla! Remember who you are.*

Her brow creased. *Remember who I am?*

She looked up as Velky appeared and shoved her toward the guard. "Put her in van." He turned and hit her square across the jaw. She blinked stars, and her head lolled forward.

CHAPTER 54

ZED

Zed gritted his teeth. His office was full of chemical engineers and computer programmers, all of them telling him they hadn't yet resolved the timetable problem—a timetable! And a problem created by Marja, of all people.

How had the stupid woman managed that? How had she found the nerve?

It must be the girl . . . Aatmanji's daughter. She must have encouraged Marja to defy him.

He'd abducted the daughter to draw out Aatmanji, but it hadn't worked. Velky reported that Aatmanji had appeared at the gate but slipped away yet again.

How surprising that Aatmanji had left his daughter behind to be tortured. If Aatmanji didn't care about his daughter, then the daughter was no longer useful. Velky could do whatever he wished with her—and with Marja, for that matter—before disposing of them, far away from ZedChem property, in the forest so that their bodies would be subsumed and irrecoverable.

And Aatmanji . . . he was still somewhere nearby, and Zed

had dispatched his best security officers to find him. It was only a matter of time.

Zed clutched his throbbing head and felt spasms travel up and down his spine. The chatter of the technicians blurred into a wall of words. "Enough!" he shouted.

The people around him snapped into silence.

"We are going to move up the pour—you have one hour."

A dismayed murmur erupted through the room.

"*One hour.* Figure it out. Fix the problem. Then start the pour. That's it—go."

As they filed out, Zed pulled a vial from his drawer to subdue the spasms shooting down his limbs.

CHAPTER 55

BAYLA

Bayla blinked awake, her head pounding.

A memory rose and surged—of the gunshot and Chaadi falling backward. *Was he . . . ?* She clutched her stomach. No, no, she could not think about that—not yet. Another image came to her: Appa's face, his eyes locked with hers. Had he been captured? Killed?

She struggled to sit up. The van was not in motion. The dim overhead light was still on even though the back doors were closed. She glanced toward the front—the passenger door was open. If she could get out of that door, she might escape after all. At least she might have more options here than at the next unknown location.

It could be her only chance. She clenched her fists and gathered her strength. *Just a little longer. Hold it together just a little longer.*

She would escape. She would find Appa and tell him that she'd forgiven him, that she loved him. And she would find Chaadi and tell him . . . Bayla felt her face flush.

Pushing aside the pain and exhaustion permeating every limb of her body, pushing aside the worry and terror about her father and Chaadi and the pour, she got to her knees and began to move toward the front of the van.

She heard a whimper.

She stopped and looked toward the other side of the vehicle.

Marja.

She was huddled in a corner, both of her eyes swollen shut, her nose bleeding. She had been brutally beaten.

"Violette!" she exclaimed, approaching and grabbing her hands.

"No, no, do not say that name," Marja insisted, shaking her head back and forth with violence. "Never say again. I am Marja. *Marja.*"

Bayla embraced the woman gingerly as she wept. "Tell me—tell me what happened."

"I went back to control room."

"But why? We were waiting for you."

"He—your friend—showed me how to stop the pour. I wanted to do this—for Jala Sharma, and for you. I thought I could do it. But Velky . . ." She gulped. "He found me—he took me to Zed."

"Oh, Viol—Marja." Bayla corrected herself to avoid distressing the woman further.

"You do not understand," Marja said, looking at Bayla. It was clear how painful it was to talk with the swelling around her mouth. "I told Zed. I told him everything—where to find you and your friend."

"You didn't have a choice."

"No, never. Never a choice." The woman collapsed against

Bayla and sobbed. After a few minutes, she grabbed Bayla's hand. *"Je suis désolé, je suis désolé,"* Marja whispered, over and over. *I'm sorry.*

Bayla glanced toward the front of the van. The door was still open, but she would not leave Marja behind. She wondered, could she carry Marja somehow?

"Don't give up, Marja. Please don't give up," she whispered.

The door slammed, and Bayla looked up. The ignition started, and the van began to move.

It was too late to escape.

Bayla waited until Marja's trembling and weeping ceased and she fell asleep against Bayla's shoulder. Carefully, she maneuvered Marja to the floor of the van and sat next to her, holding her hand and leaning against the wall.

The van was on the road, to God knew where, and accelerating. She pulled her legs close to her chin, curling into a ball.

Appa's words at the gate came to her. *Remember who you are.*

What did he mean? She was nobody. And she was powerless. Always powerless.

She'd told Marja not to give up, but she couldn't follow her own advice. Her throat constricted. She had no idea where she was being taken, and most likely, no one would be able to find her this time. Chaadi was probably dead from the shot she'd heard, as was her father, who had come to the front gate to trade his life for hers. Poor Marja had suffered for helping them escape.

And the pour!

Marja had been caught. The pour would still happen.

In the end, they'd accomplished nothing.

Nothing.

Bayla slid flat on the floor, sobbing.

CHAPTER 56

DAKSHA—AN INTERLUDE

She paused and gazed at her surroundings. She had followed the little flame out of Prithvi Forest, then through Vayu City, then into the agricultural lands at its outskirts, breaking her journey whenever the flame had faltered. Now, it was faltering again, becoming more and more difficult to detect.

She had to find it. She had to protect it. But, without her connection to the land around her, she didn't know where to go.

She closed her eyes and concentrated.

Concentrated.

The little flame was struggling to revive, but growing weaker by the moment—as though it had stopped battling its opponents and, instead, begun to extinguish itself.

It diminished to a single ember, too faint to guide her.

What now?

Her eyes snapped open. She'd heard something—felt something.

A strong thrum, like a heartbeat.

She placed her hand on the soil, but the beats did not come from the ground. Again, she concentrated.

They came from a person, but not from the little flame.

Who?

CHAPTER 57

CHAADI

Chaadi blinked awake and felt a surge of panicked adrenaline. "Bayla!" he shouted.

He struggled to sit up, but realized his wrists and ankles were strapped to a bed in an unfamiliar room.

"Hey!" he yelled. "Get these off me!"

No one entered the room.

He tried to keep calm. What had happened?

Chaadi remembered struggling with a man at the ZedChem gate, and then a gunshot originating from a guard farther away. In that moment, he was sure he'd die. Instead, he'd heard the shot pass him, just over his injured shoulder, and he'd fallen backward and landed with a sickening thump.

Now, as the fog in his mind cleared, he scanned his surroundings, everything clean and sterile. He saw a blanket at the foot of the bed with a logo stamped on it: "Property of Vayu City Hospital."

Hospital?

He looked down at his body, but he wasn't hooked up to

any monitors, and he could not see any bandages. Only his head was throbbing. All told, he'd been lucky. But why these straps?

"Hey!" he shouted again. "Get me out of here!" He continued shouting, to no avail, then leaned back, his voice hoarse.

Fear clutched Chaadi's stomach. What had happened to Bayla? He closed his eyes, thinking of how, even after all she'd been through with Velky, she'd shaken off her pain and weariness to make their escape. Their escape *attempt*.

He clenched his fists—he'd failed her. And he'd failed Marja, too—he never should have pressed her to interfere with the pour.

Bracing himself, ignoring the hoarseness in his throat from shouting for the last ten minutes, he yelled again. "Get. Me. Out. Of. Here!"

The door swung open, banging on the wall behind it. A tall, sturdy woman entered and walked toward him.

"What the hell? Get these off me. Now," Chaadi demanded.

"Sorry about that," the woman responded brusquely, moving to release the straps. "You were thrashing, and they were afraid you'd fall and hit your head again."

"Oh." He immediately pushed himself to sitting and swung his legs off the bed. As he attempted to stand, his head began to swim.

"Whoa, I've got you." The woman helped him sit back on the bed. "Take it slowly."

"I need to get out of here now—I need to find someone."

"You mean Bayla."

"Yes! How did you know?"

The woman's forehead creased. "He's working on that right now."

"He?"

"General Cartwright. I'm his assistant, Jade Sidaris. Give me a minute, okay?" Jade turned and left the room.

"Hey, where are you going?" Chaadi yelled. *Cartwright? Why was that name familiar?* Then he remembered—it was the man who had brought Bayla to India, but Chaadi hadn't had a chance to meet him before he'd left the campsite.

Chaadi looked up as Jade returned, followed by a bear of a man, stocky, strong, with blond hair and ice-blue eyes.

"Hello, it's Chaadi, isn't it? I'm General Cartwright."

Chaadi didn't want to bother with introductions. "We have to find Bayla! Do you know how dangerous Zed is?"

"As a matter of fact, I do. Who do you think evacuated Bayla in the first place, back in 2025? Not to mention less than a week ago."

"I don't care—what are you doing *now*?"

"Chaadi, listen—I'm not here in an official capacity. Aatmanji contacted me and asked for my help, and a colleague of mine in the country is providing it."

"Aatmanji? So, he's okay? Zed doesn't have him?"

"Yes, he's okay. He went to the ZedChem compound to turn himself in to Zed. But in the meantime, my colleague intervened and got the local police to show up. They couldn't do much—Zed is too powerful in the locality—but we did manage to buy some time, not to mention bring you here. We told Aatmanji that we'd look for Bayla, and that he should stay away."

"What do you mean? If Aatmanji turns himself in to Zed, then Bayla is safe."

"I doubt that, my friend."

"But why wouldn't Aatmanji . . . ?" Suddenly, Chaadi understood. Aatmanji must be trying to address the pour.

"The pour! It's happening even sooner than expected, isn't it?" Marja's interference must have spooked Zed. Chaadi sighed—he'd really screwed things up.

Cartwright looked surprised. "Yes, that's right. Aatmanji explained the effect of the chemical, but I'll be blunt. I can't get anyone to believe the truth—especially when they don't *want* to believe it. And no one wants to face down a global enterprise like ZedChem."

"So what are you doing?"

"I'm trying to get the pour halted, at least temporarily, but I have no authority here, and I'm in multiple bureaucratic tangles. I've been able to push a little in the European locations, but I'm not making progress in the other zones—there are twenty, after all." He sighed. "Frankly, I think it's impossible."

"Don't you understand? That's why you have to find Bayla. She can do it."

Cartwright looked at him for a few moments. "You're talking about 108, aren't you? I've known about the group for some time, from Aatmanji. But I'm not sure they can do what you think they can."

"Yes, they can! But they need Bayla. Find her—find her first, before you do anything else."

"Look, I of all people understand that there's more to life than what we can measure with the instruments available to us now. And Aatmanji has helped me in many ways—some of which I may not even recognize myself yet." He paused. "But what Aatmanji tells me about 108—I don't know. What can they do about a simultaneous chemical pour in twenty places? I've staked my reputation on a number of things, but I can't for this."

"But I've seen it—I've even been part of it—part of what 108 has done."

Cartwright looked at him skeptically. "Be that as it may, I have to tread carefully."

"Tread carefully? Are you kidding me?"

"I'll keep you posted on our progress. In the meantime, you're going to have to wait here. I'm sending someone to take a statement."

A statement? "General! Please listen to me—we have to find her and—"

"Chaadi, I am working on that, but there are different ways to get things done. Let me do this my way."

"But—"

"Jade," Cartwright said, turning to his assistant. "Take care of this," he said, gesturing toward Chaadi and walking to the door. Before Cartwright exited, he turned back and looked at Jade. Chaadi thought he caught a meaningful look between them.

Chaadi exploded at Jade. "What's wrong with you people? Doesn't anyone understand how dangerous this man is? You have to arrest him—he kidnapped us, and he's been torturing Bayla."

Jade looked at him for a moment. "It's not as simple as you think. Even getting the police involved at the ZedChem compound is causing trouble for the chief himself. And now the general and his colleague are getting a lot of flak."

"I don't care who's getting flak. And I'm not waiting here to give some statement. I'm leaving now, and I'm going to find her," Chaadi said, standing again and holding the bed as his head spun.

"Hey, hold up," Jade said, grabbing Chaadi's arm to steady him. "Stop—stop for a second." Chaadi looked at her curiously.

Jade turned her head toward the hallway, where Cartwright

was talking to several people. "We can give you some information. But it didn't come from us, do you understand?"

Chaadi nodded.

"His colleague has a possible lead to Bayla—drone footage of a van leaving by the back gate." Jade scrawled something on a piece of paper and handed it to him.

He looked at the digits. "Are these . . . ?"

"GPS coordinates. We're pretty sure that this is her location, but it hasn't been confirmed yet. And the general has to jump through a lot of hoops before he can get a team there. But *you* don't. So go find her—go find Bayla."

"So . . . you believe me—that she's the only one who can guide 108?"

"Can't say that I understand any of that. But the general does want to help her—he knows she's been through a lot. This is the best he can do for now."

Jade took a phone from her pocket, scrolled through some menus, then handed it to him. "Here. It's my personal phone, and I just removed the passwords. You're going to need something better than that," she said, indicating the obsolete Hanaka phone that Chaadi had lifted from the boxes at ZedChem, now lying on the table next to the bed.

"Call 'Jade-Work' by voice command if you find something. We'll do what we can to help."

"Thanks."

Jade nodded and left the room, and Chaadi turned to look for his shoes. Spotting them in a bag hanging from the bed, he pulled them on. When he glanced toward the door again, he gasped.

In the doorway stood Bayla.

How?

He gazed at the woman. No, it wasn't Bayla.

But a person of oddly similar height and frame stood there, with her dark, curly hair tied in a bun on top of her head. Her skin was darker than Bayla's, more bronze than gold. Her eyes were darker, too—chocolate rather than hazel. She appeared to be in her early forties, but there was no mistaking the resemblance to Bayla.

The woman seemed calm, but also exuded alertness and intensity. She held a large stick in a defensive manner, in a way that could become threatening.

"Who . . . who are you?" asked Chaadi, though he felt sure he knew.

She continued to appraise him without answering his question. Then she nodded, set her stick against the wall, and stepped toward him, palms open and extended, as though to show she meant no harm.

"You," she said. "I am looking for you. Because you are looking for *her*."

"Wha-what? I'm looking for whom?"

"I am Daksha," she said, as though that answered his question.

"You're . . . you're Bayla's mother?"

"Yes," she stated, and then her words became hesitant. "*Bayla's* . . . mother."

"But Aatmanji thought . . . thought you were . . ." He didn't want to finish the sentence. "How did you get here?"

Daksha closed her eyes and placed her palm flat across her chest, just under her collarbone. She bent her head slightly. "I can perceive her, and I was trying to find her. But the perception has been fading." She looked distressed.

She extended her hand and placed it over Chaadi's heart. "But then I felt her here. You love her."

Chaadi's face turned red. "I-I . . . well, yes . . . that is, I'm looking for her." He paused. "Wait, what do you mean, the perception's fading?"

"I think she's . . . she's losing hope."

Chaadi's heart sank. She'd been through too much. "But . . . but she's alive, right?"

Daksha's brow darkened. "I need to find her."

"Let's go—let's go now."

CHAPTER 58

BAYLA

Bayla lay with her cheek on the floor of a small shed, barely noticing the sweltering heat. The shelter was wet and dank, and she could only imagine the amount of bacteria in that stagnant water so near her mouth. But she could not lift her head, could not move away, could not take in her surroundings.

Velky had hauled Marja out of the shed moments ago, turning to Bayla before shutting the door. "Your turn next." He'd grinned, showing the full set of his crooked yellow teeth. Bayla's dread and revulsion and loathing seemed to coagulate in the air above her, but she could no longer feel them in her body.

No wonder her father had hidden her from Zed so long ago, and had kept her hidden without contact. Her father had understood the danger, but she hadn't—until now.

Bayla thought of the imminent FZ5 pour over the remaining topsoil on the planet, and she felt sick. She remembered the utter horror of the test pour, at the beginning of her journey. That same horror would be unleashed worldwide, entering every ecosystem and eating up humanity's food source and future.

What hope was there, when the forces arrayed against her were this mighty, this monolithic?

What hope was there, when the people threatening this bright and beautiful Earth were so impervious, so indifferent, so utterly untouchable?

Out of the corner of her eye, she saw a small, barred window near the ceiling, far too high to see through. She turned her head a few inches and stared at it from her vantage point on the ground. After a few minutes, she couldn't keep her eyes open. Or, perhaps, she didn't wish to.

I give up.

CHAPTER 59

CHAADI

Prithvi Forest

Chaadi and Daksha made rapid progress. They hadn't been able to summon an AutoCar, but a taxi driver had been willing to take them to the Prithvi Forest border, and even partly inside, until the dirt paths became impassable. After that, Jade's phone guided them toward the coordinates.

Without roads, Chaadi had difficulty navigating the forest. When the proper route became uncertain, or where there were multiple options, Daksha seemed to know instinctively which direction would be easiest to manage. Using the stick she carried and her own strong body and nimble hands, she cut pathways as needed, always going first, checking for animals and insects that might harm them.

He was astonished by her pace and often found himself scrambling to keep her in sight.

This is Bayla's mother, he thought, wonderingly—the mother she'd never known. How odd that he'd met her even before Bayla had. As Chaadi watched her, she seemed almost translucent, as though she were an extension of the leaves and limbs and brush.

He remembered Aatmanji's words—that Daksha was *of Earth*.

On occasion, Daksha would stop, eyes closed, as though straining to hear something, discern something. She would sigh afterward, clearly unsuccessful. Then she would turn toward Chaadi, lay a hand on his heart, and, after a moment or two, seem relieved. Chaadi blushed each time—was she really sensing Bayla through him?

They continued to close in on the coordinates, and worries proliferated in Chaadi's mind. What would they do once they got there? He was blindly relying on Daksha's confidence, and it now occurred to him that this might not be enough. It had been a relief to do *something*, after seeing General Cartwright somehow frozen in place. Now he wondered whether this had been the correct course of action.

He looked toward Daksha again. Would she mind if he asked questions? Would she answer him?

"Um, Daksha?"

She turned her head back to look at him briefly but continued to walk.

Clambering after her, he spoke. "Aatmanji's been looking for you. He said he needed you during the FZ5 test pour—*108* needed you to stop it. But he couldn't reach you."

She halted, and he almost ran into her. He looked at her and saw infinite sadness descend over her features. She knelt and touched the soil, then glanced at Chaadi. "The soil is dying here," she said sadly. "Something happened to me, too, when the liquid entered the forest—I lost my connection to the . . . web."

"The web of life," Chaadi said softly.

She looked at him. "You have felt the web, too." It was a statement, not a question.

"A little. When Bayla led us."

"Bayla," Daksha repeated.

Chaadi was surprised—every time she said Bayla's name, it seemed unfamiliar in her mouth. He remembered Aatmanji recounting how the infant Bayla had come to live with them at Tulā School.

Daksha looked at him. "After the liquid was poured, I could not sense anything at all . . . except my . . . my daughter. Except Bayla."

Suddenly, Daksha froze, then placed a hand over his heart as she had before. Her hand dropped to her side, and she slid to the ground with a gasp. Chaadi ran toward her and knelt next to her.

"Daksha, what's happening?" he asked urgently. She shook her head and remained crouching. "Here, let me help you up." Chaadi moved to wrap an arm around her waist to help her stand, but she held up a hand as though asking him to wait.

"She's given up."

Oh no, Chaadi thought. "What can we do?"

"I must find her. Right now. This moment."

CHAPTER 60

DAKSHA—AN INTERLUDE

Daksha turned inward.

She tried to keep her fear at bay, knowing that most of the time, fear was a trick of the mind. She witnessed her mind concoct scenarios that might never come to pass. She knew she must instead anchor herself in the present moment. If she could do this, then there would be no space for fear.

It was difficult.

After the gray van had rushed past her in Prithvi Forest, so close to the old Tulā School grounds, the little flame had taken on shape and form—the outline of a young woman, with a face similar to her own.

Since then, the waves of emotion emanating from the young woman had increased, and confusion, distress, and terror had surged into Daksha's body, often causing her to stop and catch her breath. At times, she'd leaned against the trees, heaving with nausea.

Sometimes, the emotions had felt like blows to her solar plexus, and she'd curl on the ground, arms wrapped around herself, trying to ride out those storms. She'd sit for some time afterward, recovering her breath, grounding herself in her current surroundings, pulling herself back to stillness so that she could continue forward.

Now Daksha cringed, intuiting the pain and abuse that had caused the extreme fluctuations, that had caused the young woman, at last, to give up hope.

Tears covered her cheeks.

Daksha slipped deeper, deeper within herself, into the source of her strength and power:

Mother Earth, help me. Help my daughter. Help your daughters.

CHAPTER 61

CHAADI

Chaadi paced impatiently. When Daksha said, "I must find her," Chaadi assumed they would increase their pace. Instead, she'd dropped cross-legged to the ground and handed him her stick.

"Don't let anything distract me," she'd said. "And keep a watch for animals."

For animals? If an animal did appear, what on earth was he going to do with a stick? Still, he'd nodded and stood watch. But more than ten minutes had passed, and his impatience was morphing into agitation.

What was Daksha doing? Had she stopped here to meditate, of all things? How was this helpful?

He was tempted to touch her shoulder, to pull her out of her meditation and urge her to continue their journey. *Should I? Yes, I'm going to do it.*

As he moved to tap her shoulder, Daksha opened her eyes and smiled. "I've found her."

Again, she closed her eyes.

"Wait . . . wait a second. Tell me where she . . ."

He sighed. He knew she couldn't hear him.

CHAPTER 62

BAYLA

As Bayla tossed and turned on the floor of the shed, dreams wrapped around her.

I am a child again, perched in my favorite tree, my cheek resting on the largest bough. Suddenly, the bough heats up, and the rest of the bark ignites. I pull my face back and look down for a place to jump, but there is only empty space, as though the tree is detached from the rest of existence, isolated and alone.

Alone.

I am shifting in the tree to keep my skin from burning. I look for the dream-woman, hoping for help. I see her in the distance, standing on nothing at all, just air. She walk-floats closer and closer, and today, at last, at long last, she remains standing before me.

Her face is beautiful and somehow familiar. The bronze skin is weathered, the black hair tinged with gray, the large eyes vivid and warm.

"Jump!" the woman calls to me.

"I can't!" I shout back.

"Jump!" the woman calls again, commanding this time. "Right now!"

"But there's nothing below me!"

"There is."

I release my hands from the bough, but before I can scream, I see them—I see the roots and fibers emerging from my feet, some as thin as hairs, others as thick as the tree branches that once held me aloft. They weave together and bear me up, providing solid ground. I feel their vibrations and pulses, echoed in my own body.

I look down. Those roots extend deep into Earth, drawing power from the iron core, and the layered rock, and the teeming soil.

I see.

I understand.

The woman and I sit together, facing one another. She places one hand on the ground and reaches the other toward me, to touch my heart.

"You are a daughter of this Earth, as am I. Her strength is within you. Her endurance. Her deep, wide love."

She looks at me intently. "You are powerful, my child."

The woman leans toward me, her mouth to my ear, and I expect a whisper.

"BAYLA!" the woman shouts.

Bayla gasped and opened her eyes, blinking and trying to remember where she was. Had someone called her name? She realized that she'd heard her name not as a spoken word but as a tone inside her own head.

Bayla!

She looked around wildly.

Bayla! Let me find you!

Was it—was it the woman from her dream? Bayla pushed herself up to a seated posture, cross-legged, palms up, eyes closed. She deepened her breathing and soon perceived the woman again, still seated in front of her, surrounded by a pulsing web, its threads of fiber and light weaving together and enfolding them both.

She reached for the woman's hand—and grasped it. She felt the energy of tenderness, protectiveness, and unconditional acceptance flow and flower through her.

The love of a mother.

***

Bayla opened her eyes. The shed was empty.

Still, she knew. For the first time in her life, she'd seen her mother. She'd come to Bayla in some form and they'd sat together, their hearts and energies joined.

She and *Daksha*.

Bayla sat for a few minutes, breathing in the experience, pulling it into her body. Realizations bloomed within her. Nothing that had happened in the past, and no person's actions, good or bad, could change the blazing core of her. She felt her rootedness. She felt her agency and capacity.

For a moment, she felt a flash of anger at her father, at the choices he'd made, how they'd caused her to lose that sense of herself. But the anger dissipated as quickly as it had emerged. Somehow, it no longer mattered in the same way. *All of us are imperfect. All of us are doing our best within the bounds of our own understanding. And because of this, we deserve forgiveness.*

Bayla felt a fusion within her. She felt her connection with life and Earth and humanity. And she felt her ability and wherewithal to act on their behalf. To fight for them.

Yes.

She could do it. It was what she was born and meant to do.

She could stop the pour.

Sounds radiated through her consciousness.

Bayla, we need you! Appa's voice. Appa's call.

Bayla concentrated, perceiving the threads, perceiving the members of 108 around the globe, their intentions projecting pure and true through the web of life, the web of light.

She delighted in how easy it was now, to see and feel it all.

This time, Bayla smiled.

This time, she knew what to do.

CHAPTER 63

CHAADI

Prithvi Forest

Chaadi felt relieved. At last, he and Daksha were on the move again.

After announcing that she'd "found" Bayla, Daksha had merely closed her eyes again, and Chaadi had thought he would burst a blood vessel from his heightening anxiety.

Now they were walking, and again, he was scrambling to keep up.

After another ten minutes, Chaadi looked at Jade's phone. They'd arrived at the coordinates.

Nothing—no one—was there.

Chaadi felt a surge of panic. He'd been worried about this. What if the van had moved elsewhere after those coordinates had been calculated? He peered at the phone, hoping information would somehow materialize there.

Daksha looked at his concerned face and extended her hand toward the phone. Chaadi thought she wanted to take it from him, but instead, she pushed it downward, as though dismissing it. She put her hand on his shoulder. "Chaadi, I can feel her now. I can see the web again. As we get closer to her, it becomes even clearer."

She closed her eyes for a brief second. "This way." Chaadi clambered after her, ducking the branches and leaves and critters. Just as he began to suspect they were heading into forested oblivion, they approached a clearing.

Daksha looked at him, put a hand across her lips to signal *quiet*, and motioned him to crouch. She scanned the clearing as well as the surrounding area. Chaadi raised his head an inch and saw a thin man, maybe a driver, standing next to a gray van and smoking a cigarette. It looked like the same van in which they'd been taken from the campsite near the Tulā School grounds.

A much larger man—*Velky!*—exited a dwelling that looked like simple living quarters and approached the driver. After they spoke for a few minutes, Velky reentered the dwelling.

About ten feet away and set farther back was a small and dilapidated shed.

Motioning Chaadi to remain where he was, Daksha took several steps forward. Chaadi marveled that she made no sound as she moved. He watched her face in profile. Daksha had closed her eyes, as though she was perceiving more that way than by using her eyesight.

The driver began to wander in the opposite direction, continuing to smoke.

"Now," said Daksha. She strode into the clearing, Chaadi at her heels, and approached the shed. It wasn't locked— apparently, Bayla's captors didn't expect to encounter anyone here.

Daksha pulled the door open by an inch or two. It squeaked

a little, and Chaadi looked around in alarm. Opening the door farther, Daksha stepped inside. Chaadi followed eagerly behind, then gasped.

Bayla sat cross-legged on the floor in the middle of the shed, her palms resting upward on her thighs, her eyes closed. He gazed at her beautiful face, its expression a combination of concentration and serenity and . . . *knowingness.* He started toward her, about to shout her name, but Daksha placed a hand over his mouth and an arm across his chest to restrain him.

"No," she whispered firmly. She had that same quiet strength that Bayla had.

Once assured that Chaadi would not move or speak, she pulled the door shut behind them and looked at him.

"Daksha," he whispered frantically, "we have to get Bayla out of here. That guy out there—Velky—you don't know how dangerous he is. We've got to leave."

"No. Don't disturb her."

"Daksha!" he exclaimed.

She eyed him sternly. "Quiet, child. What's happening in the world right now—it's bigger than you and me and Bayla. You must allow 108 to do its work. You must allow Bayla to lead them." She paused, seeming to register the frantic look in Chaadi's eyes. "Chaadi, I will protect her. I promise you. Nothing will happen to her."

Daksha stood strong and proud, holding her walking stick horizontally in front of her.

Chaadi took a deep breath. Despite his misgivings—*What good is a stick at a gunfight?*—he decided he had to yield, especially given everything he'd witnessed over these past few days. "Okay," he acquiesced, "but I'm contacting General Cartwright right now and telling him what's happening—I'll use Jade's phone."

Daksha closed her eyes, as though considering. "Yes. Do that. Watch for those men, return to the spot where we were observing, then walk at least twenty feet straight into the forest. Make the call from there." She looked at him for a moment, as though she sensed his dread of being swallowed by the foliage. "You will have to face your fears, just as Bayla is doing."

He straightened his spine. "Yes. Of course. I will." He returned to the door and looked back at Bayla, then at Daksha. Daksha nodded to him.

Chaadi turned, opened the door a few inches to observe the surroundings, then slipped out.

CHAPTER 64

ZED

ZedChem branch outside Vayu City, India

Zed watched as the defector paced his office. It was peculiar to see disturbance—or expression of any kind, for that matter—on her face.

"What do you mean, you moved up the pour?" she hissed. He could almost see her spitting venom as she spoke.

Zed glared at the woman. He was sick of her inexplicable commands and obscure threats. He'd had enough of wondering about the twists and turns of her agenda. She was no longer useful to him. This mere fact made her seem weaker.

"Don't talk," he growled. He watched her eyes widen in surprise, then narrow to slits. He turned to Stasia. "I want a heads-up at thirty minutes. Understand?"

"Yes, sir," Stasia responded, scooting out of the door.

He looked at the defector again. "Do not speak to me that way. Ever."

"Really? What will you do?" she challenged, approaching.

His rage ignited. He wanted to crush her face, beat her

black and blue, but his arms and shoulders already throbbed from administering Marja's punishment—a well-deserved one.

"Get out of here. I'm done with you. You have nothing else to give me."

The defector looked disbelieving, outraged.

"I *gave* you this formula—I *gave* you FZ5. You *owe* me," she rasped.

"What are you talking about? My chemists came up with FZ5 ten years ago."

"Idiot. I *gave* them the base formulation ten years ago. And they brought it to you."

"I don't owe you anything—*if* you gave me the formula, it's mine to use how and when I please. And ZedChem is the only enterprise large enough to dispense it so widely."

"I'm aware of that. Why do you think I gave it to *you*?" She approached and stood directly in front of him. "And it will bring you more money than you've seen in your entire life. All you have to do is kill one old man and one little girl before you dispense it—and you can't manage that."

Zed sniffed. "First of all, Velky's killed the girl by now. Second, my security detail will find Aatmanji."

She clenched her fists. "After everything I've done to make this happen—"

Zed cut her off. "Everything *you've* done?" he demanded, outraged.

"You're a fool. Delay the pour. Otherwise, 108 will stop you, just like they did years ago."

"ZedChem isn't what it was back then. It's too big now, too powerful to be stopped by some environmental group. I've tripled security at each of the locations."

"They *will* stop you." She stood up, her frustration

apparent. "If you don't kill the girl and Aatmanji first, then the pour won't work. They are the keys to 108."

"What difference does it make, *when* I kill them?"

She gritted her teeth. "You don't understand what they are—you don't understand what they can do. Have you forgotten the factory fire? Have you forgotten your brother?"

Zed responded, his words like ice. "Do not speak of him."

"And you couldn't even kill the man responsible," she taunted.

He launched out of his chair. "Shut your mouth!" He felt a flash of light behind his eyes, and his head throbbed harder. He sat, the pain overtaking him. "Get out. Get out before I kill you."

The woman moved toward the door. "You won't pause the pour?"

He turned away, not bothering to answer.

"Fine," she snapped. "I'll take care of Aatmanji myself, since you can't seem to do it." She walked to the door but turned before exiting. "Why can't you understand? This pour has to happen, and it has to be successful. Human beings are devolving, devolving into animals—worse than animals. Animals don't inflict pain on purpose; animals don't destroy their own homes."

He looked at her wonderingly. What the hell was she talking about?

She took a breath, as though trying to calm herself. "Soon it won't matter anymore." She left his office, almost bumping into Stasia, who was entering.

"Thirty minutes until the pour, sir."

"Good. Keep me posted."

Zed sat at his desk, pulled out a vial, and injected his pain medication. Staring at the door, he thought about this woman, the defector.

He'd dismissed her threats about 108 as nonsense, but

now a splinter of uncertainty had entered his mind. *Damn her.* Was there something to her warnings after all? Could 108 really disrupt the pour?

He remembered how ZedChem had tried to establish a beachhead in southwestern India long ago, and the series of problems that, like falling dominoes, had caused the entire branch to close. He remembered his operation unraveling and his father's contempt and condemnation.

No. ZedChem was a thousand times larger now. It was like comparing an infant's capabilities to . . . to an industrial magnate's. It was foolishness. It was madness.

Everything was under control. He had the best chemists, technicians, and programmers of any agrochemical enterprise— maybe *any* enterprise in the world. And he was launching the pour from the location that had defeated him long ago, to prove how far he'd come.

Zed stood for a few moments, trying to stretch his neck and shoulders forward, to get some relief from the spasms. The medication he'd injected wasn't working quickly enough. He sat again, staring at the wall, thinking.

A voice whispered in his mind: *Aatmanji slipped away from you.*

No matter, he responded to the voice. If his security detail didn't find him, the defector would.

Again, the voice: *Marja disrupted the entire pour schedule. . . . Marja, of all people.*

No matter, he responded to the voice. She'd been caught, and Velky would dispose of her shortly. The errors she'd generated had been sorted.

How can you prove yourself to a dead man?

"Shut up!" he shouted. He looked up at Stasia's startled face in the doorway again.

"Fifteen minutes, sir."

Zed nodded, rose with difficulty, and made his way to the primary operations building, where more than a hundred people were assembled. A semicircular room had been organized into twenty separate sections, one for each pour zone, with multiple EtherScreens within each section. He smiled to himself.

The world was watching.

He took the center chair in the last row, elevated slightly above the others, contained in its own booth. From this vantage point, he would watch the most powerful agrochemical ever to be developed enter the soil. Twenty simultaneous pours would activate thousands of contracts and fill his coffers with lightning speed.

The next few years would see his transition to trillionaire.

Trillionaire. He could almost taste the word, like a morsel.

He'd leave industry behind, go anywhere, do anything he wanted.

He'd won.

Zed visualized peppering his father's face with blows— right, left, right, left. *Take that, you monster.*

But, unbidden, his father's words rose to the surface and echoed in his mind: *You are weak—you are pathetic—you are unworthy of a company like ours.*

To calm himself, he tried to imagine Matej's face instead, then frowned. He couldn't seem to visualize his baby brother.

Instead, Zed turned to watch the EtherScreens channeling information from all over the world. He knew the media was watching, ready to report his triumph. His own ZedChem media team was standing by, ready to generate positive press and to silence—or slaughter—any naysayers.

He knew his rivals were watching, too—though ZedChem

had few these days. He'd absorbed most existing companies and plucked out any up-and-coming enterprise before it had a chance to gain a foothold, especially the "eco-friendly" ones. Those that remained were watching, jealously terrified of his peerless product.

Again, Zed scanned the live video of each area, showing the vats of FZ5 attached to long, intricately designed dispensing mechanisms with numerous spigots all in a line. These machines would combine two chemical solutions and inject the final product, FZ5, the culmination of his life and work, into the soil, all at once, around the world.

His chief chemist caught his eye and gave a thumbs-up. Everything was on schedule.

The vats around the world stood ready, and the countdown showed up on each screen.

Twenty seconds.

Fifteen.

Ten.

Five, four, three, two, one.

The spigots opened.

In that moment . . .

CHAPTER 65

BAYLA

Bayla gathered 108 in her embrace and set them in motion—spinning, spiraling, diving, rising. A collective consciousness and intelligence bound them together.

A school of fish.

A swarm of bees.

A flock of birds.

She laughed from the pure joy, the sheer beauty of their dance, their flight. Her laughter traveled among and through them, its music matching the music within them all.

It was frolic.

It was play.

Aatmanji's voice, rich and resonant, echoed through the web: *In the quantum realm, all possibilities exist. Your consciousness, your intention, your directed thoughts make them manifest.*

Bayla called to 108: *What is our intention?*

They answered: *Stop the pour before it kills the soil.*

She felt the intention within her. She felt the meditators in the Agastya temple, magnifying the power of that intention. She felt the meditators around the globe.

Aatmanji's voice: *In the quantum realm, physical distance does not exist.*

Bayla gathered the orbs around her and then threw her arms wide, sending pathways through the ether. Their intention flowed through the tributaries, invoking all the lands to be affected by the pour.

Aatmanji's voice: *In the quantum realm, time is not linear.*

Bayla reached upward, pulling the strings of time together, sliding her fingers down, then pinching the middle. There, the moment expanded, and meditators filled the time-space.

They were ready for her command.

Bayla held the strands steady.

Twenty seconds.

Fifteen.

Ten.

Five, four, three, two, one.

No.

Wait.

Bayla gasped. Something was wrong . . .

She sensed an electrical current.

CHAPTER 66

AATMANJI

He sensed an electrical current.

A tremor passed through them all, through 108, and discord crashed through the music, screamed through the laughter.

Aatmanji felt himself yanked out of the web, lying on his back, utterly immobile, with a bony woman sitting on his chest, a knife between her teeth, her long hair obscuring her face.

He struggled to emerge from the quantum state. Usually, he could do so quickly, but this intervention had been on a scale unlike any before. He was unable to move.

The woman shifted position, and he felt his hair jerked backward, his eyes staring at the lotus on the ceiling of the Agastya temple.

He strained his eyes toward the woman. Every time he blinked, the woman seemed to phase in and out, as a force, a burst, an electrical current.

Out of the corner of his eye, he saw Aanvi running toward him, panicked.

The bony woman held out her hand, palm forward.

"Stop, or he dies." The woman's growl sliced the air.

Aanvi froze.

Aatmanji knew the woman would kill him regardless. He tried to speak, to warn Aanvi, and at last his voice burst free.

He screamed as the knife pierced his skin.

CHAPTER 67

BAYLA

Bayla felt her father slipping away from 108, away from all of them, his presence dwindling and dissipating.

What had happened?

She kept her grasp on 108, trying to ward off her panic. *Hold the moment,* she told herself. *Hold it steady. Hold everyone steady.*

Steady.

Steady.

But disturbance tore through her body, as images tore through her mind: Appa sprawled on the floor of a temple. A bony woman hovering above him with a knife—her presence like a shriek, a howl across the sky. Her face phasing in and out, as a force, a burst, an electrical current.

Oh no! Appa!

Bayla shuddered in fear and shock.

She could feel the muscles of her body tightening with effort. She could feel the sweat soaking her.

Her grasp was slipping.

She couldn't do it. She couldn't hold on. She couldn't hold 108.

Around her, 108 was atomizing, dissipating.

Bayla's eyes opened, and she looked around frantically.

Daksha.

Daksha was seated in front of her, live, in the flesh. She was speaking, but her voice sounded within Bayla's mind. *Listen. Listen to me, Bayla. You don't need Aatmanji to do this.*

"But . . ."

Bayla. You don't need him. You don't even need me. You can do it. It has to be you.

They locked eyes.

You are powerful, my child.

Bayla felt her own strength reflected in the eyes of her mother. When Bayla closed her eyes again, she still felt Daksha's gaze fortifying her spirit, rekindling her vigor and resolve.

Bayla centered herself and felt the web open to her again, felt 108 all around her. They were holding on—they were waiting for her.

A school of fish.

A swarm of bees.

A flock of birds.

Bayla felt a tiny jolt, as though even Daksha was slipping away from the group. But it didn't matter. Daksha was right. She could do it.

She *would* do it.

In that moment . . .

She spoke, her voice reaching across the globe, to every person who had shown up for battle: *This. Here. Now.*

CHAPTER 68

AATMANJI

Agastya temple, Prithvi Forest

Aatmanji heard a *thwack*, and to his relief, the pressure of the knife was released. He looked up. Aanvi had hit the woman across the throat with a *kalaripayattu* stick, knocking her backward.

Aanvi reached for the fallen knife, but the bony woman lunged for it at the same time. This time, Aanvi swung the stick across the woman's legs, causing her to sprawl across the floor. Aanvi aimed the stick toward the woman's abdomen.

Aatmanji, able to move at last, looked at Aanvi. She was staring at the bony woman in disbelief.

"Kaali?" Aanvi's voice fell to a whisper. "Is it you?"

Aatmanji jerked his face toward the woman. He could see it now—behind the shriveled features, the haunted eyes, the emaciated body was the woman who had been a vital part of 108's mission long ago, who had been brutally attacked and had disappeared in 2024.

Aanvi's sister.

Aanvi's voice choked. "Kaali, you're . . . you're not dead. But your note said . . ."

"That note was true—I'm not that person anymore. She was weak and deluded, and she deserved to die."

Aanvi stared. "Kaali, what are you *doing*?"

"How does it look? I'm stopping you—all of you. I'm stopping 108."

Aatmanji spoke up: "But *why*? You left everything behind to work for our cause—you and Aakash and Aanvi."

"Exactly. I gave up everything to join your mission to 'save humanity.' And look what happened. Aakash was killed, right in front of me. Then they attacked me, and they . . . they . . ." She gagged for a moment, then squared her shoulders. "Don't you understand? Humanity isn't worth saving. I had to stop you. And I have. All these years, I've been working against you."

Aatmanji thought of 108's struggles after Kaali's departure—the destruction of Tulā School, the death of so many members, the slippage in their network of eyes and ears, the tasks gone awry.

"In 2025, it was *you* at the Shara temple. *You* set the explosives."

She frowned. "Yes. All of 108's leadership knew about the Shara temple. When I left you, I set out to destroy it. But I didn't find out about the intact chamber until later. I'd been monitoring Mohan Das's communications because I knew he was researching the temples. When I found out that the Shara temple was still usable, I went back during the new excavation. But somehow Mohan kept *this* place"—she gestured angrily around her—"a secret."

"And you tried to dynamite this temple, too," Aanvi said. Kaali looked at her defiantly, then cocked her ear as though listening for the expected explosions. Aanvi spoke again. "We were ready for explosives this time. I didn't want to take the risk, and I put people in place to defuse them if needed." Kaali shot her a look of anger and disgust.

"Kaali, Kaali, my dear," murmured Aatmanji. "I would have given my life to spare you what you went through. It was the worst thing that could happen to a human being, and it was perpetrated by the worst of the human race. But surely . . . surely you needn't condemn everyone on Earth, every single human being?"

"Why not? This is what human beings have done throughout history, isn't it? Rape and pillage, ravage and desecrate. They devour the land, and Earth, and each other. Shouldn't a virus like that be killed? Shouldn't it?"

Kaali's entire body was trembling, and Aatmanji felt overwhelmed with compassion for her.

"Kaali . . . ," he began, reaching a hand toward her.

"No. No!" she screamed, shoving his hand away. "Don't you dare feel sorry for me. Your compassion has spoiled your brain. But I . . . I can use my brain to its maximum capacity. I created FZ5. I figured out the formulation and gave it to Zed. I needed ZedChem's size and scale to dispense it all at once."

"You gave it to Zed?" Aanvi whispered.

Kaali shot her a look of contempt.

"Let me tell you what else. I made him attack Tulā School in 2025—to wipe you out."

Realization dawned on Aatmanji. "The factory fire—the one that killed Zed's brother."

"Yes, I lied," she declared. "I told Zed *you* were responsible."

Aanvi's voice was cracking. "But, Kaali, how could you do that to us—to everyone at Tulā School? We all loved you so much." Her voice dropped to a whisper. "And you're . . . you're my sister."

Kaali looked like she would spit. "Stop. Sentimentalism keeps you from seeing clearly—it keeps you from doing what's needed."

She turned to Aatmanji. "By now, Zed will have killed your daughter. And I just pulled you out of 108's intervention. You couldn't stop the pour." She threw her head up and smiled as though relieved. "FZ5 is now in the soil all over the globe. Don't you see? It's in the food, it's in the water, it's in the whole ecological chain. You just watch. Soon, people will turn on each other for resources—they'll all destroy each other."

Aanvi murmured, "Oh, Kaali . . ."

Kaali drew closer to Aanvi. "No, no, don't be sad, my sister. Think of it—think of it—Earth without human beings. Think of the land, rich and lush again. Think of species multiplying and growing. Think of balance restored. It's worth it—it's worth it." Her body suddenly shuddered, as though she'd gotten caught in a visceral memory. In a motion that seemed reflexive, she began wiping her arms and legs, as though cleansing herself.

"But that means death for you, too, Kaali."

"No, it means *peace* for me, my sister."

Kaali sank to the floor, tears on her face, and Aanvi reached for her. At that moment, Kaali grabbed the *kalaripayattu* stick and maneuvered behind Aatmanji, pulling it tight across his throat. Aatmanji began to gag.

"Kaali, no—don't do this—don't!"

Aatmanji couldn't move. He knew he didn't have much longer to live.

"Kaali, don't!" Aanvi screamed. "I love him!"

Kaali grunted in disgust.

Aatmanji felt the stick tighten, felt the imminence of his death. But his insides had already collapsed. All this time—all this time it had been Kaali working against them. As his mind shadowed and darkened, he gave thanks that Bayla was alive, despite what Kaali believed. He hoped beyond hope that Bayla had been able to lead 108 on her own and stop the pour.

Then, from the last corner of his conscious mind, he heard Aanvi's voice and the sweet notes of a folk song:

Nothing is stronger than our love for one another,
Nothing is stronger, nothing is sweeter!

He remembered. It was what Aanvi had sung to Kaali every night after she'd been attacked, during her long convalescence at Tulā School.

Kaali let Aatmanji drop, and he rolled away with an effort, gagging and trying to breathe deeply, trying to stay conscious.

Aanvi approached, her arms outstretched to embrace her sister.

Kaali, face furious, stared at her. "Nothing is stronger? *Nothing is stronger?*"

She leaped behind Aanvi, picked up the knife, and sliced left to right.

"NO!" Aatmanji screamed in horror. "Oh God, oh no, why—why would you do this?!" He scrambled toward Aanvi. Desperately, he tried to stanch the wound as Aanvi's blood pooled larger and larger.

Kaali knelt in front of him. "Do you see, Aatmanji?" she asked softly. "Do you see what is stronger than love?"

Aanvi's life was draining away. "Aanvi, no, no, my dearest,

don't leave me." He looked into her eyes until they dimmed. Wailing, Aatmanji threw himself on top of Aanvi, embracing her.

Kaali disappeared.

CHAPTER 69

BAYLA

In each place, and all at once, Bayla could see a puff of air mix with the two chemicals just before they were combined to create the FZ5 solution. The resulting liquid was both inactive and useless.

She felt a wave of relief—her own and the combined relief of 108. The worst crisis humanity had ever faced had been countered quietly and with little fanfare.

She sent her gratitude their way, to these warriors who had shown up for her and Earth and humanity.

It was time to emerge from the quantum realm and into the physical. Based upon 108's intervention in Walcott Forest, which she'd led from the Agastya temple just days ago, she remembered that her transition would take some time. But it was taking even longer than expected, probably because of the amount of space and time she'd occupied.

She tried to relax into the emergence, noticing how her lightness and expansiveness distilled into the solidity and structures of her physical body.

As her eyes began to focus, she felt shock, realizing why Daksha's presence had fallen away in the middle of 108's activity.

Velky was in the shed, and Daksha was fighting with him, using her stick. As Bayla watched, Daksha brought the stick up hard against his arm, making the gun fly from his hand, then maneuvered toward it, kicking it out of the way.

Still Bayla was frozen, caught between realms. Her vision of her surroundings had cleared, and she felt grounded within her physical body. Yet she still couldn't move. Her eyes darted wildly around the shed. Marja was cowering in the corner, her clothing torn to shreds. Velky had used her badly.

Suddenly, Daksha slipped, and Velky leaped on top of her, pinning her legs, ready to strike.

Nooooo! Bayla heard herself scream as though from a distance, projecting through something thick and viscous.

At that moment, Chaadi burst into the shed, looked at Bayla, then at Daksha. He ran at full speed and threw himself into Velky. Bayla winced internally, thinking of Chaadi's injured shoulder. Both men rolled to the side, while Daksha scrambled up.

Velky, a seasoned fighter, flipped Chaadi onto his back and hit him—right, then left—across the face, then pummeled his injured shoulder over and over, until Daksha maneuvered behind him and pulled her stick back across his throat.

Velky fell back but twisted away. Enraged, he sprang to his feet.

A gun cocked. All of them turned toward the sound.

Marja had picked up Velky's gun and now held it pointed toward him at close range, her hands trembling. Velky smiled, his yellow teeth gleaming, then made an abrupt upward cut with his arm, causing the gun to pop out of Marja's hand, spin, and land in his own. He grabbed Marja and spun her forward, holding the gun to her head.

"All of you, over there." Daksha and Chaadi backed up, trying to block Bayla from Velky's view, but Bayla could still see Velky between them. Velky moved the gun so that it pointed not at Marja but at her. Bayla struggled frantically to emerge.

"No!" she screamed, her voice free at last, but her body was slower to follow. The gun fired, and Bayla gasped. Was this how her life would end?

Marja fell to the ground.

Bayla stared at her, shocked. Marja's last act had been to jump in front of the bullet intended for her. At such close range, Marja must have known such a move would be fatal.

Again, she'd sacrificed everything for Bayla.

"Violette!" Bayla shouted, at last bursting from her transitional state.

Daksha, fury in her eyes, lunged at Velky and dropped him on his back, pinning him. Chaadi grabbed the fallen gun and pointed it at Velky, who froze at last.

Lurching, Bayla threw herself forward, pulling Marja's head onto her lap. "Why, Violette, why did you do that?" she wailed.

Marja's eyes were wide open. "It is alright," she spoke faintly. "I chose. Bayla, I chose." She gazed intently at Bayla as her life ebbed away.

"Hold on, Violette, please hold on!" Bayla sobbed.

No, I can't bear it—I can't bear this loss.

It was the same feeling she'd had during the test pour, trying to comprehend a loss that couldn't be measured.

From the corner of her eye, she saw Velky's sudden movement. She screamed to Daksha, but Daksha was ready for him. She threw her elbow to the pit of his throat, knocking his head backward, then hovered her fingers over the deadliest *marma* point in Velky's neck. As Velky shifted to shove her away, she pressed the point. *Hard.*

This time, Velky crumpled, unconscious.

Daksha looked at Bayla, locking eyes with her, and Bayla knew that Daksha was communicating something to her. In that moment, Bayla felt as though they were both pushing Velky's *marma* point together. Deliberately, at the final moment before Velky's death, Daksha relieved the pressure, sparing him.

She looked at Bayla pointedly, and her voice sounded in Bayla's head.

We are here for life, not death.

CHAPTER 70

ZED

ZedChem branch outside Vayu City, India
A red light flashed in the operations room. Zed's muscles began to throb along with it. He broke into a sweat.

What had happened?

He heard a murmur roll through the room, then the distinguishable voices of his employees, then the alarms from the computers. He felt like he was witnessing chaos approach from multiple sources and crash over him.

His father's face floated in front of him again.

Shame, said his father.

Shame.

The nerves around Zed's elbows and in his forearms ignited and began to spasm.

His chief chemist rushed toward him. But having arrived at Zed's booth, he now hesitated to speak.

"What is it?" Zed barked. "What happened?"

The man gulped. "We're not entirely sure, sir," he said, shuddering at Zed's look of fury. "The concentration monitors detected an alteration of the chemicals at the moment of dispensing."

"In *each* location?"

"Yes, sir, each one."

"How is that possible? If it happened in each location, then it had to be a sensor error."

"I'm afraid not, sir. The ground crews are testing right now. Whatever ultimately went into the ground in each location was not FZ5—it was altered."

"You're not making sense. Were the chemicals tested and confirmed when the mechanisms were loaded?"

"Yes, of course, sir, without question. Checked and double-checked by our own staff against the computer. Checked again by independent auditors."

Zed stared at the man, who had begun to shake in his shoes, then watched as the other EtherScreens awoke, showing news clips from around the world, in real time.

"Apparently, there was a problem with ZedChem's dispensing method, and . . ."

"All over the world, those awaiting the promise of ZedChem's savior agrochemical were disappointed. As you can see in this footage . . ."

"With the failure of the mechanism, the long-awaited and much-touted FZ5 pour did not occur, and it is no longer clear whether . . ."

He looked at his phone, which had begun to beep continually. Stasia, terrified, approached him on his left and bent to his ear. "Um, sir, there are a lot of calls that we need to return. Probably, we should start with the government leaders who contracted with us for—"

"No," he snapped, and she backed away. Zed stood up and

gritted his teeth, his whole body on fire with pain. He saw everyone's eyes on him and forced himself to straighten up. Turning, he walked back to his own office.

The spasms had reached his legs. He lowered himself into his chair and stared at the wall. How had this happened? All his meticulous planning—ten years of developing the defector's formula and building the dispensing mechanisms and constructing the chemical plants worldwide. Whatever force had stopped him had to be something extraordinary.

108.

The defector had warned him that 108 could defeat him if he didn't kill Aatmanji and the girl first.

Aatmanji. His rage reignited. Why hadn't he waited for his security detail to capture the man? Why hadn't he delayed the pour like the defector had insisted? He'd been impatient for success, tired of waiting.

At least Aatmanji's daughter was dead. At least Aatmanji would experience the pain that Zed had, upon Matej's death.

From the corner of his eye, he saw his office door open a crack.

"Stasia," he growled, "not now."

"Sir, I'm so sorry, but I really think you need to see this."

He nodded impatiently, and she set her phone on his desk in front of him and took a giant step backward. It was a message from his security detail:

> Velky and driver arrested. Bayla Jeevan
> rescued by local police—claims kid-
> napping by Krakun Zed and ZedChem
> personnel. Aatmanji still not found.

Stasia's phone dropped from his hand and hit the floor. His

pain had become unbearable. He reached out to open his desk drawer, seeking his vial of fentanyl, but he sprang back when he heard a banging on the door.

"Police!"

Police?

The Vayu City police chief burst through the door.

"Don't open that," the chief barked, indicating Zed's hand on his desk drawer.

"How dare you speak to me that way?"

"You're coming with us."

"For what possible reason?"

"For many, many reasons, but for now, kidnapping."

"You won't get away with this, Sanjeev. I made you what you are, and you turn on me like this?"

"I don't know what you're talking about."

Zed groaned as the chief pulled him up from his chair and pushed him out of the room, surrounded by police officers.

Fentanyl. He needed his fentanyl.

CHAPTER 71

BAYLA

Prithvi Forest

The shed door blew open, and four uniformed officers burst in with guns drawn, followed by General Cartwright. Two moved toward Velky, still unconscious. Cartwright issued instructions to the others, then approached the spot where Bayla, Daksha, and Chaadi were huddled over Marja.

Bayla looked up as two medics entered the shed and knelt next to Marja, examining her. The senior medic shook his head at Bayla, and her heart fell. She held Marja's hand until they bore the cot away.

"Are you all okay?" Cartwright asked.

They were mute for a few seconds, then Chaadi responded. "I think we're fine, but Bayla's gone through a lot in the last few days."

"So has Chaadi," said Bayla.

"Yes, I've arranged transport to the Tandon military base nearby. We'll get all of you checked out."

Cartwright turned to Daksha. "And this is . . . ?"

"Daksha," Bayla replied. "My . . . my mother."

"Ah, I see. It's good to meet you." He held out a hand, but Daksha merely looked at him. When Cartwright seemed to realize that no conversation would be forthcoming, his hand dropped to his side.

His phone rang. "Jade?" He listened for a moment. "Hang on. Let me open a conference." With a swipe, he put Jade's image in front of them. "Go ahead, Jade."

"So, I was just updating the general on the FZ5 pour. Something went wrong with the formulation before it hit the ground. There's a lot of confusion in all the zones, and the press is having a field day with it."

"And Zed?" asked the general.

"Arrested."

Bayla felt relief. "We did it!" she exclaimed, as loudly as her exhaustion would allow her. She turned and embraced Chaadi. When she released him, he pulled her toward him again, holding both of her hands in his.

He spoke firmly. "*You* did it."

They looked at each other for a few moments, then she extracted her hands. Chaadi seemed to know what she needed to do, and he stepped away.

Bayla turned to Daksha, taking a deep breath.

For years, Bayla had wondered why she hadn't pressed Appa for the identity of her mother, before it had been too late. Daksha had suddenly burst into her life, but their interactions had been on some different plane.

Now they were to have a conversation. In person. Bayla stood hesitantly, not knowing how to approach her, how to speak to her.

Daksha closed the gap between them, stepping toward Bayla and taking her face in her hands. She kissed her forehead, and Bayla began to weep. Daksha embraced her tightly for a few minutes, then stepped back and gazed at her in silence.

"You were the one in my dreams all this time," said Bayla at last.

Daksha nodded.

Bayla stared at her mother, drinking her in, marveling that they were exactly the same height, seeing her own face imprinted on Daksha's.

"The test pour—it hurt you, didn't it?" Bayla asked softly.

Daksha nodded. "I tried to absorb it—I tried to hold it all, and it broke my connection to the web of life."

"But . . . but then, how did you know how to find me?"

"I'm not sure. All those senses in me died, but somehow I could still see you—you were a little flame in the distance. You called to me—pulled me."

Bayla opened her mouth to ask a question, but stopped herself.

"Go ahead. Ask, my child."

Bayla took a deep breath. "Why? Why did you leave me?"

"Our strands could not mix."

Bayla looked at her. "Aanvi's prediction."

Daksha nodded. "Yes. Our lives could not intertwine. Yours and mine. I was told that one of us would die. And I could not risk your life. I couldn't take the chance it would be you."

"But how do you know that Aanvi's correct?"

"You know it, too, Bayla."

"No, I . . ."

For a split second, Bayla felt her perception join with Daksha's, and she saw it.

"Your life must be separate from mine," Daksha murmured.

"But you came for me now."

"Yes. The whole web was hidden to me after the test pour, but I could still sense *you*. And then I felt your pain—I felt the danger bearing down on you. I thought it meant there was only one pathway forward, that it was time for us to have this meeting, this . . . completion."

"So you can't . . . you can't stay now? Just for a little while?" Bayla asked wistfully.

Daksha looked at her and spoke gently. "No, Bayla. I believe that Aanvi's prediction is accurate. I will not take that risk. My path lies elsewhere from yours."

"I wish . . . I wish we could just have a normal life together."

Daksha took Bayla's face in her hands again and used her thumbs to wipe away Bayla's tears. After a minute, she stepped backward, and her voice was firm.

"When we are called, we must answer. *Especially* when Mother Earth calls, we must answer. She needs us now. Do you understand that? She needs us all desperately. She needs *you*."

Bayla looked down for a few moments, then looked at Daksha again. "Yes, I understand. What do I have to do?"

"When the time comes, it will become clear to you."

"But . . . can I speak to you while you're away?"

Daksha looked at her intently. "Yes. You have learned how."

She reached for Bayla and folded her into an embrace. Bayla heard Daksha's voice pulse through her.

I'm always a part of you, my daughter.

CHAPTER 72

ENVIRONMENT WIRE

AGROCHEMICAL FAILS TO DELIVER

NEW DELHI, INDIA. Formula FZ5,
ZedChem Corporation's newest agrochemical, encountered a fatal error
at the moment of its dispensing
worldwide. After ten years of
research and development, as well as
the construction of production facilities and distribution mechanisms at
the twenty remaining agricultural
zones worldwide, the formula did not
deliver on its promise to rejuvenate
topsoil. During the lead-up to this
massive event, ZedChem leadership
often touted FZ5 as a quick fix for
the world's failing food supply.

    According to experts, the two

chemicals to be combined at the moment of injection into the soil are required to be kept airtight. However, it appears that the chemicals were exposed to air, rendering the combined solution ineffectual. ZedChem spokesperson Lyn Tran stated that a comment was forthcoming, but nothing has been heard from the company as of the release of this article.

In an odd turn of events, Mr. Krakun Zed, the company CEO, was arrested soon after the unsuccessful attempt on unrelated charges of kidnapping. Now, preliminary investigations of the company—a company some considered impervious to accountability or responsibility—have exposed its seedy underbelly.

Police discovered a potential connection between ZedChem personnel and the death of Dr. Jala Sharma. The chemical engineer, once employed by ZedChem, was recently found dead in her apartment, having apparently recanted her statements condemning FZ5 and ZedChem.

Since then, an extensive collection of Sharma's research has come to light, revealing disturbing information about the nature of the

agrochemical. Specifically, FZ5 pro-
duces an immediate burst of agricultural growth. However, that growth
rapidly diminishes, then ceases, over
a period of five years. At the end of
that five-year period, the topsoil to
which the chemical is administered is
no longer viable.

According to that research, if FZ5
had indeed been successfully dispensed globally, it would have
destroyed almost all of Earth's soil,
agriculture, and food production
within half a decade.

When verified, these actions could
amount to a massive fraud perpetrated
against the governments of fourteen
different countries who contracted
with ZedChem to conduct this chemical
pour. Some are calling it a crime
against humanity and demanding a
joint international investigation.

Scientists are requesting immediate analysis of the agricultural land
bordering Prithvi Forest, the site
of the ZedChem test pour last week,
as well as the forest interiors, in
order to determine the extent and
nature of the damage caused by FZ5.

ZedChem operations have been sus-
pended worldwide while both civil and

criminal investigations are underway, and pending additional investigations of its CEO.

———

TRUTHSPEAK Blog

MOUNTAINS OUT OF MOLEHILLS

The campaign against ZedChem CEO Krakun Zed is a witch hunt. Kidnapping charges? Seriously? This is a man who built a chemical empire, and who is known globally for his ability and competence as a titan of industry. The question to ask is this: Who is truly behind the police investigation? Someone with a personal vendetta, that's who. *That's* what needs to be investigated, not . . .

———

MODERN FINANCE Blog

ANTI-WEALTH WINS AGAIN

Krakun Zed, the brilliant businessman known for tripling the size and reach of the ZedChem empire, has been

wrongly accused of fraudulent deal-
ings. Zed is the victim of the anti-
wealth movement, which refuses to
acknowledge the importance of working
for one's own survival and standing
on one's own feet. It's unclear why
this . . .

——

PERSONS OF INTEREST E-zine

ANOTHER REPORTER SEX SCANDAL

Environment Wire bureau chief Cecily
Barnes has a dirty secret. The news
agency reported on the recent ZedChem
"failures." But we have a source
revealing that Barnes is a woman
scorned, with a personal vendetta. Her
credibility is at issue, and no one is
asking the right questions about . . .

——

TRUE NEWS NETWORK Video Transcript

INDISPUTABLE: JALA SHARMA COMMITTED SUICIDE

The investigation into Jala Sharma's
death is completely unwarranted. Of

course it was suicide—she *admitted* that she made up her data. That's why you can't trust any data from any source—it's too easy to fake it. Better not to trust any numbers at all. Just trust your gut.

What people don't realize is that the ZedChem pour was in fact successful, and governments are now trying to appropriate the work of a great man. As we all know, men—particularly successful men—are under assault these days, and . . .

———

WAKE UP, WORLD E-zine

AN ALIEN INVASION?

Has anyone considered why every single FZ5 pour was affected at the same moment? I think we're dealing with aliens. There are close encounters all the time, and people just don't want to believe it. This was one of them!

Wake up, people. It's time to call for an investigation of . . .

———

DHEEPA R. MATURI

GET REAL: TRUE NEWS OF THE ENVIRONMENT Blog

ECOTERRORISTS AT LARGE

This is the problem with the so-
called environmental movement.
They're actually terrorists engaged
in smear campaigns, but they think
they have the moral high ground. They
don't. They don't follow the rules of
propriety or the rules of engagement.
In fact, they think they're above the
rules, above the law, and . . .

CHAPTER 73

DAKSHA

Prithvi Forest

Daksha felt the forest pull her back in and enfold her. She turned toward its interiors, arms wide, hands open—feeling herself reentering the natural cycles, feeling at home again. She slipped off her sandals and walked, letting the cacophony of the past week ground into the soil, letting it disperse from her body, feeling her breath become light and free.

Daksha closed her eyes and smiled. Still, the little flame burned in the background, bright and steady.

My daughter, Daksha thought, wonderingly.

How extraordinary Bayla was, with her intensity and brilliance and fierce courage. She marveled at Bayla's tremendous ability to move within the web—indeed, hers was far greater than Daksha's.

She was Daksha's unexpected and unanticipated gift to the future.

A little tremor passed through her.

She knew that something had changed within herself. In Bayla's presence, the web had become clear to Daksha again, and her connectivity had seemed to reestablish itself. But now, as she moved farther away from her daughter, its clarity was diminishing.

The test pour had done lasting damage to Daksha, to her ability to see and sense through the web, to feel her connectivity to life around her. She stopped for a moment, tears in her eyes, thinking of the test pour. *I would have absorbed more poison if I could have. But I was unable. I was unable.*

It gave her tremendous pain, that she couldn't do more for her fellow human beings. She felt like a mother to them all, and a mother possesses boundless forgiveness. A mother hopes that her child will awaken and regret its recklessness.

But, despite her desire to help her children, every mother has her capacity.

Daksha looked around as she went deeper into Prithvi Forest, heading north. She would need to find a way to recover this soil, to reawaken what was dying, but she didn't know how. She didn't even know where to begin. Regardless, this would be her work now.

She frowned.

Something was pushing into her awareness.

Everything . . .

. . . stopped.

When Daksha regained consciousness, she was lying on the ground, gasping, watching someone's feet retreat into the distance.

She hadn't seen her attacker approach—more significantly, she hadn't even *felt* the approach. Though Daksha's power had diminished, she still had some sensitivity. Who could have blocked her perception so thoroughly; who could have had the stealth to grab and clamp the *marma* point of her neck in a death grip?

Daksha realized that the danger had not been Zed all along. Rather, it had been *this* person, *this* attacker, a presence she hadn't seen and, now, would never know.

She had little time left. As her life energies drained, so did everything within her—the ancient wisdom, the old music, the truth-tale of humanity's meaning and purpose.

She could see the web of life shimmer brightly for a moment, before the threads began to thin before her eyes, before her connection faded.

Daksha looked into unseeing faces, and she begged.

*Please put your hands on Earth; please feel her beating heart; please do the needful. Please inhale the breath of trees; please feel the freshness of water; please see the rich green life all around you. When you see it—*really *see it—its beauty will break your heart . . .*

. . . and then renew it.

Please know you are all bound to each other, intertwined. Please see each other. Please listen.

Your pain is mine, too.

My death is yours, too.

Time is short.

Time is short.

In her last seconds, she thought of Bayla; her journey would be a difficult one. Did Bayla possess enough of the ancient wisdom? Did she understand it well enough to navigate the disconnection of humanity and the systematic annihilation of life on the planet?

Or would everything die with Bayla, ushering in the sixth mass extinction on the planet? If so, it would be the only planetary extinction perpetrated by its own victims.

But these were no longer questions for Daksha to ask or answer. She coaxed her awareness deeper and deeper into the forest, to a place still untouched by human hands. With gratitude, she rested in that space and drank the joy still bubbling there, whose source was the infinite heart of Earth.

Soon, her body would be reabsorbed by the soil, and her life by her Mother.

CHAPTER 74

BAYLA

Tandon military base

Bayla fell asleep off and on during the deluge of medical tests at the base. She'd tried to get out of them, but everyone had insisted. She guessed that Chaadi was undergoing his own medical tests, but she hadn't seen him since her brief conversation with Daksha. With her *mother*.

Bayla smiled.

As she sat up on the infirmary bed, she wondered about her father. Why had he dropped away from the 108 intervention? She knew that Daksha had left to protect her from Velky. Had Appa, too, encountered danger? She shuddered, recalling the images that had come to her at that time. But she'd been told that he was alive and recovering.

She thought about Appa, using her newfound confidence to find him through the web, but she felt some blockage, as though he didn't want to . . . receive her.

She'd caught Cartwright in the hallway and asked about her father's whereabouts, but he'd seemed distracted and directed her to Jade. Bayla hadn't been able to find her.

Bayla looked up as a nurse approached and spoke to her. "You're all done here. There's a room upstairs where you can shower and sleep, if you'd like."

"That sounds lovely. Thank you." She turned toward the door, and her eyes widened.

Appa.

She rushed toward him, touching his feet, then falling into his embrace.

"Are you okay, my Bayla?"

"Yes, yes, I am. Appa, I'm so glad you're here. And I'm sorry for everything I said, and . . ."

"I know, my dear. I know."

Bayla leaned back slightly and looked into her father's face. "Appa, what's wrong—what happened?"

She walked him back to the bed she'd just occupied and seated him there, then sat next to him. "Tell me."

Her father began to weep, dropping his face into his hands. "Aanvi. She's . . . gone."

Horrified, Bayla embraced him. "What happened?"

"She was killed—while she defended me at the temple. During the intervention."

Bayla's eyes filled with tears. "Who . . . ?"

"Aanvi's sister. Kaali."

Upon hearing that name, Bayla had a vision of an electrical current. This was the reason Aatmanji had slipped away from 108's battle during the FZ5 pour.

"Her *sister*? But, Appa, why would she do that?"

He related the story of the brutality Kaali had experienced long ago. "Her past has made her believe that all of humanity deserves to die—that Earth would be better off without us. She orchestrated the entire ZedChem operation; she even gave Zed the formula for FZ5."

Bayla marveled—she'd thought that all the danger had come from Zed, but Kaali's threat had been even greater.

They sat next to each other, unable to speak further.

Suddenly, Bayla felt an intense wave of pain and terror, as though something—someone—were cutting through her body, as though half of her were being torn away. She looked at her father in panic, seeking his reassurance, but his frightened face seemed to reflect hers. They clutched each other in distress.

After a few minutes, General Cartwright entered the room, his face somber. "Something's happened."

Appa looked at him. "Daksha?"

Cartwright didn't answer, but Bayla knew. She slipped to the ground. "Oh God, no, no, please . . . ," Bayla wailed.

She'd found her mother, then lost her again, within the space of a few hours. Appa dropped to the ground next to her, and together, they wept.

CHAPTER 75

CHAADI

Chaadi paused before knocking on the door. While Bayla was speaking with Daksha, he'd been whisked away for medical tests. Overall, he'd come through okay. His shoulder was healing well, and the rest of his bumps and bruises were, too. They would continue to monitor the head injuries.

He felt grateful to be alive and sent a silent *thank you* to Marja, who had done so much for them and who had traded her life for Bayla's.

Afterward, he'd been ushered to a small room at the base, where he'd showered and changed into clothing they'd provided. Then he'd located Jade, who had given him directions to Bayla's room and also informed him of the death of Daksha, attacked in the forest.

Shocked and concerned, Chaadi had made his way to Bayla's room immediately, but now, at her door, he hesitated for some reason.

At last, he knocked and heard movement inside, then the sliding of the bolt. When Bayla opened the door, he took a breath. Her hair was long and loose, the thick curls flowing richly down her back rather than pulled into a tight bun. The sadness and grief on her face made her seem younger than her years.

God, she's beautiful.

"How are you holding up, Bayla?"

Upon hearing his question, fresh tears flowed.

"C'mon," he said, entering the room, putting an arm around her shoulder, and seating her on the bed. Just like his room, hers was a tiny, military-style dormitory with only a bed and a dresser and a tiny, attached bathroom with a shower.

He sat next to her, and she leaned against him. As he waited for her tears to subside, he squeezed her shoulder and kissed the top of her head from time to time.

"Sorry—sorry," she said after a few minutes, lifting her head and wiping her eyes.

"Don't be," he said.

Bayla took a deep breath and nodded. She dropped her head back to his shoulder for a moment, then shifted on the bed to face him.

"I didn't think I had any tears left."

"Tell me, what can I do?"

The right side of her mouth tipped upward into a half smile, and she spread her hands, as though to indicate she had no idea. Sniffling, she spoke: "I'm . . . I'm glad I had at least a few minutes with her, to talk with her and hear my name from her lips." Again, tears escaped her eyes. "I'm going to stay here a few days with Appa. His loss is double." Chaadi felt shock as Bayla explained the circumstances around Aanvi's death, at the hand of her own sister.

Bayla stood up, walked toward the wall, then turned and leaned against it, facing Chaadi. "It'll be good for Appa and me to be together for some time. I feel I lost so much because of his choices. At the same time, I don't know what he should have done differently. Regardless, we've got to repair and restart our relationship, without all the secrets."

Chaadi felt protective of her. "Do you think you'll be able to do that? He hid a lot from you—and he hurt you badly."

"I know I have a lot to forgive him for, but I have to try. I do know that, whether his decisions were right or wrong, he did his best. After everything that's happened, I know that for sure." She sighed. "And frankly, the thought of leaving the area right away, the last place I spoke to my mother, feels agonizing."

"What happened, Bayla? What happened to Daksha?" He paused. "If you want to tell me."

"We just don't know. General Cartwright is investigating, but so far, he's found nothing, just some footprints leaving the area. He thinks it's a random act of violence."

"Do you believe that?"

"I don't know."

"I really do understand. I lost my parents and my grandfather when I was young. I know it makes the pain even worse—not being able to understand the circumstances around their death, not having any explanation."

Bayla nodded. "Thanks," she said tremulously. She returned to sit on the bed, and they remained in companionable silence for a few minutes.

"What are you going to do next, Chaadi?"

He smiled. "I've been talking to Professor Das about his temple quest. Aatmanji called him and asked him to come visit me. I'm going to join him—I think I've finally found the work I'm supposed to be doing. But we need to leave tomorrow."

"Tomorrow?" Bayla frowned. After a pause, she said, "I'm glad. That sounds perfect for you."

"And what about you?"

"I'm not sure. I'm going to talk to Appa to sort out what's next for me. The only thing I do know right now, based on my experiences with 108, is that my life feels bound up in everyone else's."

Chaadi looked at her. "What do you mean?"

"It's interesting," she murmured, almost to herself. "During the 108 intervention, I had a powerful sense of all the members who were sending their intentions. Every member was from a different background and place; each person was distinct from every other person, but I felt connected to all of them." She closed her eyes. "The whole experience felt like *opening* to those people. And now that it's happened, it's impossible for me to feel separate from them again. It's impossible not to identify with them, not to care about them. I don't know them personally, but they've become a part of me." She turned to him. "But I've been wondering if I'm capable of feeling connected to other people, too—the ones *outside* 108, especially the people with whom I disagree profoundly, or whose actions repulse me. People like Velky and Zed." She shuddered involuntarily.

Chaadi considered for a moment. "If anyone could connect with them, it's you."

She smiled a bit. "Thanks, Chaadi."

Chaadi chuckled and moved closer to her, taking her hands. "So . . . does that mean you can sense me, too? That you know what I'm feeling—about you?"

She looked at him, then tipped her head to the side and laughed a little. "That's a bit different."

He ran a finger lightly over the four curved scars on her forearm, the markings of her pain and fear and grief. Leaning in, he kissed them, one by one. She closed her eyes and shivered. When he looked up at her again, her gaze was direct, her hazel eyes enormous. She pulled him closer.

***

He awoke with her face close to his and brushed a curl away from her forehead. She opened her eyes and smiled at him.

Nothing, he thought, *nothing could compare to this.*

He thought of all they'd been through together and how much courage she'd shown, battling the demons of her past, then emerging to battle for him and the world. Such power and ferocity, but tempered with such grace and wisdom, compassion and love. *That's the sort of leadership the world needs,* he thought.

He leaned forward to kiss her again, then put his forehead to hers. "I know . . . I know you're meant to do great things, maybe even to save humanity, but the selfish part of me has to ask." He closed his eyes, channeling all of his longing. "Won't you come with me? Or let me come with you?"

With their heads together like that, he almost felt like he was absorbing her thoughts. His face fell, because he knew the answer that was coming.

"Chaadi," she said softly, "I have to be by myself right now. I need to learn what I am, what my capabilities are. I need to learn how best to serve the world." She paused, seeming to feel his disappointment, then touched his cheek lightly. "Humanity is worth fighting for, and I want to do just that. I want to fight that fight." She paused. "Can you understand that?"

Chaadi nodded, then reached for her, embracing her, pulling her into him. He knew her destiny was bigger than anything he could imagine. Still, the idea of letting her go made him ache.

He knew he'd always love her.

CHAPTER 76

ZED

Zed lay on the dirty cot, curled into a ball, eyes closed. He tried to moan, but his throat would no longer produce sounds. He had screamed in pain for hours.

He'd been elated when he'd been pulled from the Vayu City jail cell, convinced that one of his allies had gone to bat for him, but he'd merely been transferred here, to another cell, with no idea of its location.

He hadn't seen anyone since that move. If he had, he would have begged for pain medication. Without it, these spasms were going to kill him.

His surroundings were disgusting, but he barely noticed them as he lay there. He didn't know where he was—or in whose custody. Of course, the word "custody" implied something official, and Zed suspected he wasn't there officially.

He didn't know the time.

He didn't know the date.

He'd always relished aloneness—but on his own terms and with the ability to control his environment and to connect to information at will.

Zed thought of the events of the preceding weeks. What had happened to his people? Just before his own arrest, he'd learned that Velky had been detained. What about the others? They would likely bargain information about Zed for leniency. They would give Zed up. The old saying was true—no honor among thieves.

He thought of the people who had wronged him: Aatmanji, who was still alive. The daughter, who was also alive. *Oh, Matej, I've failed you. Everything I've done, all the money I have, and I couldn't avenge your death.*

Worse, his father's face appeared in his mind over and over again, tormenting him. Zed thrashed, trying to bat it away.

Zed assumed someone would appear soon, to begin a long session of questioning, probably the first of many—though they didn't need to torture him. His own body and mind were already doing that.

This was agony.

Agony.

He heard the clang of the cell door, but it took him a few moments to open his eyes.

A woman stood before him, wiry, sharply angled, in a fitted suit both elegant and nondescript. Her face was severe, its bones prominent. Her eyes were close together and deeply set.

The defector.

"It's you." His voice was weak.

She held a syringe and a bottle in her hands.

Inserting the syringe into the bottle, she slowly drew out the liquid, observing the vial fill. He cringed.

"Do you know what this is, Zed?"

Zed didn't answer.

"It's fentanyl."

Zed inhaled sharply. He wanted to lunge for it, grab it, but he couldn't make himself move.

"The amount in this syringe will take away your pain for twenty-four hours."

"What do you want for it? I'll do anything," he rasped.

"Good." She took his shaking arm to administer the injection and watched as his body gradually relaxed. When she seemed certain he could focus on her, she spoke.

"Your company is gone. The outside world thinks you've escaped custody. I've given the authorities enough information that you cannot show yourself anywhere without arrest or retribution. But I can get you out of here. Out of this cell."

"In return for?"

"We work together. We find them. Every last one of them. We kill them all."

"Find them?"

"108."

Zed gave a firm nod. "Done."

They looked at each other, sealing their agreement.

"By the way, you've never told me your name."

"My name is Kaali."

CHAPTER 77

AP WIRE

BREAKING NEWS

VAYU CITY, INDIA. ZedChem founder
Krakun Zed has disappeared from
custody. Though taken to the Vayu
City detention center for processing, he disappeared two hours later.
Vayu City police chief, Sanjeev Shah,
stated that the police are searching
for his whereabouts.

CHAPTER 78

JADE

Tandon military base

Jade began collecting her belongings from the small office she'd been assigned for their brief stay at the Tandon military base. It had been an exciting week. Cartwright and she had communicated information about FZ5's toxicity and other shortcomings to the governments and corporations that had signed contracts with ZedChem, launching law-enforcement investigations throughout the world.

A good week's work, she thought.

She looked up in surprise as the general strode in. Usually, he summoned her.

Cartwright took out his phone and swept a file to her. "Go ahead," he prompted.

As she scrolled, her eyes widened. Pages and pages of information on 108's activities, including Cartwright's provision of supplies to their operation for over fifteen years.

"I don't need to tell you this entire operation is off the books."

"Of course, sir."

"I trust you implicitly, Jade. You've been a loyal aide and even, dare I say, a friend."

Jade couldn't hide her pleasure. "I'm here for whatever you need, sir."

Cartwright nodded once. "Then get up to speed."

Jade turned back to the file, and her amazement grew; 108 was a global operation, their activities steadily increasing. How much of their work was sanctioned? How much was overseen?

And could they really do the things listed here?

Jade considered the various projects that Cartwright had prioritized over the last few years, particularly the black ops. She was starting to understand the bigger picture, especially given recent events.

A familiar name showed up, and she began to read.

Her mouth dropped.

What had the general done?

CHAPTER 79

BAYLA

San Francisco, California

Bayla awoke in her own bed and stretched luxuriously. After two weeks at the Tandon military base, Jade had arranged her transport back to the US. At home at last, she'd taken a long and glorious shower. After the minuscule bathroom at the base, her small shower had felt cavernous. Then she'd slept for over twelve hours.

Now she spoke the Earth mantra, then pulled her yoga mat out of the walk-in closet and placed it in the middle of the apartment. Opening the window shades, she relished the light and warmth on her face and body. Her practice felt sweeter and richer after rediscovering her past and finding her family and a new . . . friend. She smiled as she thought of Chaadi, off on his adventures.

She began packing her clothes and few possessions into boxes. She'd leave the furniture behind, transport almost everything else to storage, and take one suitcase with her.

After a few hours, she surveyed her empty apartment, struck by how dull the gray-beige space looked. A vision of Tulā

School popped into her mind, where the landscape made its own decor—vines and trees flowering, mountain mist wafting, waterfalls pouring into pools of lotuses. So much foliage, in more shades and variations than most people realized existed.

Foliage. It reminded her that she'd left the window box for last. The plants had done surprisingly well during her absence. She bent down and let the leaves touch her face. For a moment, she could picture her forest adventures of the last few weeks. She could picture herself as a child, running and dancing among the trees.

One by one, she carried the plants to a neighbor who had agreed to take them. The last was the formerly lagging hibiscus, now bright with blooms. Bayla was astonished—how lush and vigorous they were, as though the plant had intuited Bayla's journey. The flowers were fully open, as though clear about their purpose, sure of their strength. She touched the petals of one of the flowers, running a finger along the delicate veins.

Bayla felt a sudden ache inside her—one that she experienced from time to time, throughout her day. She recalled the woman who had taught her more in just a few interactions than she'd understood in her entire twenty-seven years. Her mother would always be a part of her, fused into her every action and choice and decision, melded into her body and cells. She placed her palm on her heart and bowed her head, feeling the spill of long curls over her shoulders.

"Bayla?"

Still holding the hibiscus plant, she looked up at the man approaching the porch.

"Braden!" It felt like years since she'd last seen him. She beckoned him inside.

"Whatcha got there?"

"It's a hibiscus," she said. Her eyes lost focus. "My father says it represents the divine feminine."

"The divine feminine?"

"A principle. He says that once your survival is taken care of, you should work on growing as a human being, becoming the best version of yourself. Not just surviving but *living*." She paused and looked at him. "He says that that flowering is the rise of the divine feminine in your life. It creates a life in balance."

Braden seemed to contemplate what Bayla had said. "Beautiful thought—but how do you know when your survival is taken care of?"

She paused, considering. "I guess when you understand you have *enough*. And that you *are* enough."

"Ah."

Braden gestured at the boxes. "You're—you're not moving, are you? At work, they told me that you're taking a leave of absence, but I didn't realize you were leaving town."

She nodded.

"Where?"

"For now? Back to India." She moved the plant to her hip, then reached out and grasped his hand. "Thank you, Braden, for encouraging me to face my past. I needed to do that to move forward again. To have a future."

"Wow. Sounds like you've had quite a journey. What have you been doing?"

Bayla leaned on the door and laughed. It would take hours to answer that question.

Braden watched her for a moment, his eyes sharing her amusement, then darkening into admiration. "Look at you, Bayla," he said softly.

She smiled at him, looked down at the plant she was holding, and passed it to him. "For you."

"Um, thank you." He paused. "You're full of surprises today."

They looked at each other for a few moments, then he ducked his head. "Hey, let me help you with those."

They took the boxes to her car, filling the trunk and back seat. She got into the driver's seat and lowered the window.

"Thanks, Braden."

"I'll . . . I'll miss you, Bayla. Will you be back?"

She smiled. "Yes, I think so."

"Okay, then, I'll just say goodbye for now."

"Yes. Goodbye for now." She started the car, pulled away from the curb, and headed down the road. When she looked through the rearview mirror, she saw Braden, hibiscus in hand, watching her drive away.

CHAPTER 80

BAYLA

Prithvi Forest

Bayla wore a tunic of rich red, symbolizing Shakti, the divine feminine at her most potent and powerful, in her fullest expression of creative energy. She sat facing Aatmanji in the Agastya temple.

Her father smiled at her. "They're ready for you."

She closed her eyes and felt the web emerge in her consciousness, the web connecting every living thing. She perceived them all, the ones who had dedicated their lives to the continuity of humanity, to the protection of Earth.

Together they rode the web, journeying over the land and water, through mountains and valleys. They dived deep through the earth, down to the iron core. From there, they rose upward, then dispersed outward, into empty space, into the cosmos.

Outward, inward, earthward, skyward. It was all the same, equal, One.

Aatmanji's voice resonated through the web. *Bayla Jeevan,*

do you join 108 of your own accord, from a deep desire to serve humanity and Mother Earth?

Yes.

We welcome you.

Bayla let herself emerge, opened her eyes, and embraced her father. She felt energized and alive.

At long last, all the contradictions within her had woven together and now coexisted without turmoil. Her past, her background, the traditions she followed, the philosophies of connection and rootedness—all staked themselves firmly behind her. Alongside her was everything she'd learned after departing for America: the knowledge of when things must break to emerge free and new, how to think and innovate without limitations, how to challenge assumptions and dogma to arrive at truth.

She felt an expansion, as though she was now occupying the full outline of herself—everything she was meant to be and everything she was going to become.

Of course, retraction from that outline was inevitable, part of the journey of her life. Regardless, she would strive to re-expand, to keep that outline filled, by accepting everything about herself—her mistakes and flaws and limitations, as well as her brilliance and intensity and compassion.

It was time to transcend boundaries and differences in order to heal Earth and preserve human life. This was her work for this lifetime, as it had been for her mother.

Bayla was ready.

EPILOGUE

Daksha hovered in the in-between, feeling herself disperse from her own body and mind into Oneness.

In this time-space, the physicality and thoughts and emotions that made her Daksha, *that distinguished her from every other person, evanesced. And as she approached Unity, she expected to feel that wave of bliss—*ānanda—*underlying all of existence.*

But something—one silken thread—kept her anchored to this plane of reality.

It was a question.

Why did humanity poison its home?

She tried to answer it: They know not what they do.

But the thread did not snap, did not release her.

Then she understood: They *do* know what they do. And they do it anyway.

She could feel the end approaching: the end of humanity's grand era on Earth.

What would it look like, she wondered—an Earth without humanity? Cosmic time was vast, and Earth would recover from the poisons and ravages and reckless disregard. In the grand scheme of things, it might not even take very long for Earth to regain its balance.

Daksha pictured the air reinvigorating, the water replenishing, the lushness returning. She visualized species reemerging, maybe even new ones igniting, the likes of which had never been seen.

She imagined the vibrant health of this exquisite blue-green planet.

Earth without humanity.

She thought she would sigh with relief, but she couldn't. Instead, she felt pain and despondency and wistfulness. How could she imagine Earth without its most interesting element, its most dazzling phenomenon—one with the ability to see widely and deeply, to love consciously, to seek meaning and upliftment, to choose its own destiny?

How could she imagine Earth without inhabitants able to transcend their animal behavior and reach with hope and longing toward divinity? Inhabitants who could view life through a multifaceted lens, then reflect back with art and music and sculpture, made of word and sound and stone?

No other piece of life, no other bit of existence had the potential to do all this.

Earth without humanity.

She could never, ever desire that. Her heart wept. How can a mother be reconciled to her children's passing—even if they are at fault, due to their own actions or indifference?

Words rose from the depths of her and diffused around her.

You still have time, my children. But just a little.

AUTHOR'S NOTE

I always love to learn why an author chooses to write a particular book—it feels like a peek behind the curtain! With that in mind, I'd like to share how the character of Bayla and the plot of *108* came into being, as well as notes on the story elements and my own background. Thank you for your interest!

THE STORY OF THIS STORY

Bayla's character came to me in inklings and images, long before I had a story to hold her. Instead, I wrote her in small sketches. Her memories, her emotions, her struggles—they bubbled up at random times, and I captured them in words whenever I could.

When I committed to a serious writing practice back in 2016, I began to write essays, poetry, and short fiction, and I particularly enjoyed exploring topics such as culture, identity, and diaspora. Soon, though, those topics began to intersect with ecological and environmental themes. As I wrote about parenting, I saw how my children had made me reenter the natural world. As I wrote about my mother, I realized I'd inherited customs and rituals that honored life and Earth in myriad ways. When I wrote about my love of classical Indian dance, I marveled how each session began with an apology to the ground I was stepping upon.

In retrospect, the character of Bayla was growing, and growing up, within the context of my curiosity about the human relationship with our planet, as I questioned why we feel and act as though we are separate from the home that allows us to eat, drink, breathe, and live.

Then I had three eye-opening, mind-shifting encounters, and a story took root in my mind, a story to hold the character of Bayla, with all her pain, potential, and promise:

- Lynne McTaggart's book *The Intention Experiment*, which brought scientific methodology and analysis to matters often considered unquantifiable, such as thought, attention, and intention (https://lynnemctaggart.com/intention-experiments/the-intention-experiment). The book also inspired Aatmanji's discussion of REGs in connection with 9/11.

- Fritjof Capra's class and textbook *The Systems View of Life*, which provided a vocabulary on the interconnectedness of nature within the framework of quantum physics, and which described how that interconnectedness can inform human-made systems if we choose (https://www.capracourse.net).

- The Save Soil movement, which highlighted the rapid deterioration and loss of organic content in the soil—one of the most pressing concerns of our time—as well as uplifting and inspiring stories of those taking the arduous and necessary steps of addressing it (https://consciousplanet.org/en /save-soil).

I began to suspect that writing Bayla's story could help me face my own "ecological grief," a term often used to label a personal, emotional response to environmental damage and loss. Perhaps writing that story would allow me to cultivate and share my own hope for the future of humanity and Earth.

The plot of *108* began to take shape.

WRITING THE NOVEL

I've often wished there was such a career as professional brain-stormer! Rolling out a long strip of butcher paper and mapping out *108*'s plot and characters and timelines felt energizing and incredibly fun.

After that wild brainstorming, I fully expected to sit down, outline a complete novel, and then follow that outline methodically—a path many writers take. In actuality, the road to *108* felt far more exploratory. I had to write *toward* the story, listen for it, and capture it in bits and pieces before it skipped out of my mind. I also had to examine and understand my personal "lens"—my own history and experiences through which the story focused and emerged.

When the joy and energy of brainstorming and draft writing leveled off into editing the final manuscript, I found it much harder to keep working toward completion. Self-doubt became a constant companion, as did loneliness. There is an invisibility to the act of writing, and writing the final version of this novel required all my brain power and every shred of discipline, without affording an opportunity to report results that made sense to others. There was no one to say, "Wow, you changed three paragraphs today? Wahoo!"

What helped me to stay put and dig in was a particular "ecosystem" that had grown larger and larger around me: books and other media addressing the environment, climate change, and the natural world. I read Robin Wall Kimmerer's *Braiding Sweetgrass* and *Gathering Moss*, as well as Richard Powers's *The Overstory* and *Bewilderment*. I read Aimee Nezhukumatathil's *World of Wonders* and Lyanda Lynn Haupt's *Rooted*; listened to podcasts such as Krista Tippett's *On Being* and Pádraig Ó Tuama's *Poetry Unbound*; and followed L. L. Barkat's *Tweetspeak Poetry* and Sara Barkat's *Poetic Earth Month* newsletters. I also read eco-fiction and eco-thrillers, all of which resonated, all of which echoed, *Yes, yes, yes, yes. I see you. I understand.*

But an unexpected and horrible event also occurred while I wrote. In a harrowing nine-month time span, my seemingly healthy and always energetic mother was suddenly diagnosed with pancreatic cancer and passed away soon afterward. Those months and their aftermath shook me profoundly, gouged holes right through me, and left me struggling for words.

From that experience came the most major revision to *108*. It brought the larger emergence of Bayla's mother, who embodied my own mother in so many ways: her quiet strength, her powerful endurance, her extraordinary intuition. My mother's presence had been deeply interwoven with my life, and afterward, her absence interwove with my novel.

MYTH, RELIGION, AND SPIRITUALITY

The Seven Sages

The myth of the Seven Sages can be found around the world, often relating how ancient knowledge was preserved during the course of cataclysmic global events. The stories vary, even the versions of the myth told in India. The version I heard most often was that the First Yogi taught the Seven Sages the science and philosophy of yoga, and they spread that knowledge throughout the world.

108 refers to that specific version of the myth, but the other story elements are fictional—for example, the Sages' catastrophic predictions and their provision of a cure, as well as the circular yogic temples they constructed around the world. That said, I have seen structures constructed in the manner presented in the book—round, with alcoves—in India as well as in the US. The lotus on the ceiling, noted by Chaadi, was based on a story I heard about a building in Lebanon that possessed that feature.

The Number "108"

In the novel, the number "108" is intended to demonstrate the connection between the human system and the cosmic system and also to illustrate the advanced mathematical comprehension of ancient India. Thousands of years ago, it was known that the diameter of the sun multiplied by 108 equals the distance between the sun and Earth. Similarly, the diameter of the moon multiplied by 108 equals the distance between the moon and Earth. If you calculate these figures, you will see that they're remarkably close to modern measurements.

The Yugas

The yugas are part of the Indian understanding of cosmic time, and Sat yuga is known as a time of ease in communication and connection. However, the story elements related to the yugas—Aatmanji's ability to call through the web of life, Aanvi's ability to read probability from "quantum strands," and Daksha's ability to move within the web—are all fictional.

The Web of Life

As for the "web of life" itself, it is a plot device that I imagined as I considered the interconnectedness in nature—notably, in tree-root systems. I wondered: What if the mycelium interwoven through tree roots could conceptually manifest in the ether as well, as "threads of light"? Additionally, the similarities between the composition of the cosmos and the human body, as related by Aatmanji, made me dream up this tangible demonstration of universal wholeness. I must admit, though, that the image of a web of life feels real to me, and I conjure it up in my mind whenever I walk through beautiful forested areas, and whenever I feel particularly grounded and in tune with what's around me.

My Background

I was raised in the Hindu tradition, with its interrelated cultural customs, always recognizing the Oneness of existence, the importance of pacifism, the multiplicity of paths to truth, and the end goal of self-realization. In my thirties, I learned more about yoga, meditation, and *kriyā*, which have become my primary spiritual practices. At all times, I am a seeker. I am always trying to understand, to keep my mind and heart open, to listen for truth.

Given all the overlapping influences present within this novel, it is important to note that what I've written does not represent any single religious or spiritual tradition, and it is certainly not a definitive narrative for any of them. Rather, it's a mixture of the myths and stories I've heard, as well as the way I've been raised and the practices I've adopted. Together, they are part of my personal lens on life and the world.

IMAGINING A SHIFT

If ecology and environmental concerns are at the forefront of your mind (I assume they must be for you to pick up a novel like this one!), I hope that *108* will feel uplifting and promising. Of course, there are many obstacles to environmental recovery, just as there are many opposing powers that seem (as they did to Bayla in her darkest moments) monolithic and impossible to surmount. There's no getting around that.

I do feel small. I feel inadequate. Writing *108* was a way to remind myself that, regardless of my shortcomings, regardless of my lack of power, I have a duty to witness what's happening around me and to respond in the best way I can. I must not turn away due to fear, dejection, frustration. And, just as I believe in the necessity and my ability to act, I believe there is power in our collective intention, directed with compassion, knowingness, and love.

Once we comprehend, deeply and personally, that the natural world is not separate from us but is, in fact, *us*, I believe a shift happens. Once the roots of a tree and the fins of a fish and the waves of the ocean feel like a part of us, an extension of us, I believe our consciousness changes. I have hoped to be a part of bringing about that shift in my own limited way, by telling this story.

I think of the oil lamp that Aanvi lit to usher in Bayla's knowledge and understanding. In an Indian household, that lamp symbolizes the power of one small flame: It can ignite an infinite number of others. It can light up the world.

108 BOOK CLUB DISCUSSION QUESTIONS

1. The story of *108* takes place in the future. Did you find the future environment and descriptions of Bayla's day-to-day life intriguing, frightening, or something in between?

2. Though the story of *108* is fictional, environmental pollution is obviously real. How did the environmental theme make you feel—empowered, educated, frightened, inspired?

3. At the beginning of the novel, Bayla holds certain beliefs that influence her personality and behavior; for example, *relationships only cause pain.* What other beliefs does she hold? Why does she hold them? Which beliefs, if any, change by the end of the novel?

4. In what ways do Bayla and Chaadi feel trapped by the losses, grief, and abandonment they've experienced? How do those traumas impact their ability to function in their day-to-day lives? By the end of the novel, do they overcome their traumas, and if so, to what extent? How do Zed's debilitating medical condition and emotional pain affect his philosophy of life?

5. At the midpoint of the story, Bayla is transported by van to the ZedChem facility—a pivotal moment for her personal journey. What realizations does she have in that moment, and how do they change her? What more does she need to learn before the end of the novel? Have you had similar moments of lucidity in your life that demarcate a significant change from your past behaviors and/or personality?

6. Bayla fears Zed because he threatens her safety and that of her family, but also because he willfully refuses to consider the long-term consequences of his actions and business policies upon the planet. Why does the latter inspire *fear* in Bayla?

7. Much of ZedChem's work is designed to drive sales while disregarding the impact of its products upon the environment. *Should* ZedChem have to consider its impact on human beings or the planet itself? In a capitalist society, is it possible to factor in the needs of the environment? What would *conscious capitalism*, which takes the needs of people and planet into account, look like?

8. Daksha is a powerful character operating outside typical social structures. Aatmanji has difficulty describing her and the source of her power, stating that she is "of Earth." What does it mean to be so deeply identified with the planet? In what ways does Daksha resemble Bayla, and in what ways do they differ?

9. Motherhood and mothering are complex topics in the novel. Bayla feels mothered by the Tulā School

community and indeed, by the forest itself. On the other hand, she doesn't experience Daksha as a mother while growing up, but she does feel mothering energy when they are reunited. What actions constitute *mothering*? Can mothering occur outside a one-on-one human relationship? Can one mother a landscape? A community? A planet?

10. The author deliberately uses recurring events—Aanvi's interventions, Kaali's actions at the temples, the fire-bombing of the Tulā School area, Bayla's multiple kidnappings—to evoke a sense of karma: actions repeating until true resolution occurs. What other recurring incidents can you identify in the novel? Which characters are able to find resolution to the repeating issues in their lives, and which are not? Can you identify recurring incidents in your own life that need attention or resolution? Do you feel there are lessons embedded within that repetition?

11. The heart of *108* reckons with ecological grief—mourning the loss of habitats, species, and ways of life due to climate change. How has the natural world changed where you live? How do you feel about those changes? Have you experienced ecological grief?

12. Honoring the earth is inherent in certain cultural and spiritual traditions. What is the importance of *ritual* in this context—for example, Bayla's utterance of an "Earth mantra" before stepping on the ground in the morning? Do you have a ritual related to the natural world—for example, walking in a particular park or speaking to the

plants in your garden? If not, how would you design your own earth ritual?

13. The novel discusses the interconnectedness of natural systems, particularly trees, topsoil, and rivers. Have you observed the interconnectedness of other systems in nature? Where do you see principles of interconnectedness at play in the world around you, either with respect to nature or to human systems such as health care, law, and education?

14. In the novel, members of a group are connected to one another via "threads of light" resembling root and fungal systems in the forest. Have you ever felt connected to another person across space and time? Have you and a friend or loved one ever simultaneously experienced the same thought or taken the same action? How did you explain those incidents to yourself?

15. Collective intention is a central concept in the novel. Have you experienced a feeling of collective energy when attending a concert, sports event, or other group activity? What was the source of that energy? What feelings did it inspire in you—excitement, fear, upliftment, awe? Did you ever think that your collective intention or energy could impact the events transpiring around you?

16. What happens to human beings who don't feel connected to others? How has Bayla's presence and personality changed since childhood, when she was living in a community? Does Bayla find community by the end of the novel?

17. Several myths—the Seven Sages, the First Yogi, etc.—are central to this novel and also inform its cultural context. Are there myths and stories that are part of your own life and that influence your way of seeing the world?

18. The principle of the divine feminine is mentioned at the end of the novel: when one possesses enough for one's own survival, one can concentrate on living fully and thriving. How does this principle illustrate the concept of balance? How can this principle be applied to planetary sustainability? Does the sacred feminine or divine feminine exist in your own cultural and/or spiritual background? What does it mean to you?

ACKNOWLEDGMENTS

Writing is such a solitary act, so I suspect every debut author is surprised by the number of people who must come together to publish a book and usher it into the world.

To *108*'s readers, I am truly grateful for the time you have spent with this story. Thank you for showing up for Bayla and rooting for her!

To Karen Upson, Abi Pollokoff, Reshma Kooner, Georgie Hockett, Paul Barrett, and the whole team at GFB, thank you for believing in this book and its message and making it a part of your 2025 slate. Your talents and efforts have produced a book that I'm proud of.

To the Indianapolis-area writing community, particularly the Indiana Writers Center and the lovely Barbara Shoup; to my outstanding critique group of Mary Redman, Marjie Giffin, Katie Simmons, and Elizabeth Nowak; and to all the writers on this wild adventure with me, thank you for your presence in my life. You are my comrades-in-arms and my role models. Every day, you show up to translate your ideas, musings, and stories into heartfelt words.

To editors Susan Fish and Nirmala Nataraj, thank you for your thoughtful and wise feedback, counsel, and mentorship.

To my friends Patti Freeman Dorson, Lori Fulk, Kaki

Garard, Maxine Houck, Surabhi Kaushik, Nicolle Nanasy Muehr, Lily Pai, Don Pape, Vibha Rajan, Bethany Rohde, Vani Krishnamurthy Sanghvi, Abhinav Singh, Vidhya Srinivasan, Monica Tewari, Seema Verma, Lisa Zeh, and so many, many others, thank you for your (multiple!) manuscript reviews, your generosity with your time, and your considered comments, as well as your constant encouragement and support. Over and over again, you've pulled me from the mire of self-doubt and taught me to trust myself and my voice.

To Ann Kroeker, who helped me launch my writing and publishing journey in earnest in 2016, who helped me press "Send" on the very first literary submission of that journey, who put me—and kept me—on the road that led to the publication of *108*, who helped me move through my fears and boundaries, I offer my gratitude.

To L. L. Barkat, who first gave me a platform for my voice via Tweetspeak Poetry, who provides a beautiful ecosystem for writers and poets who want to engage joyfully and whole-heartedly in making art, thank you for the beauty and light you provide the world.

To Samantha Shah, you are my example of how a person should exist in the world, with such grace, compassion, fortitude, and kindness. You've supported my book quest in so many ways, including week after week of phone calls, and I couldn't have completed it without your encouragement and excitement.

To Sumi Maun, ever since we met, I've watched you use your remarkable intelligence, capabilities, and energy to support all your friends in all their endeavors. Thank you so much for your steady counsel as I brainstormed, wrote, and rewrote *108*!

To Amie Rickels, my BFF, you made me face the hairiest

and scariest of goals by insisting, "You are writing a book." And then reminding me. And reminding me again. Along the way, you taught me the depth and breadth that friendship can have. I've leaned on you a lot these past few years, and I can't thank you enough. Your prediction has come true!

To my maternal grandmother, Thirilochani Sreenivasan; to my father-in-law, Subba Rao Maturi; to my mother-in-law, Vijaya Vani Maturi; and to my ancestors past, I offer my great- est respect. To my sister-in-law, Laxmi Naik; my brother-in- law, Narayan Naik; as well as my scores of aunts, uncles, and cousins, thank you for your interest and support in this en- deavor and in all things.

To my boys, Vikas and Jay, you were witnesses to *108*'s entire journey, and you brought laughter and lightness to a challenging road. You're both wise beyond your years and have become extraordinary people in every important way. Your father and I love you wholeheartedly and possibly beyond reason.

To my husband, Raj, I could not have done this without you. You are, as always, the most interesting of my friendships and an endless source of fun and joy. Thank you for seeing the best in me, even when I'm at my worst. Thank you for cheering me on, every day. How did I get so lucky?

To my father, M. Rammohan, you are a man who knows how to use his voice for good. You are still my hero, for your principled view of life, the passion behind your beliefs, your knowledge of exactly who you are, and your regard and respect for your heritage. You are an example to us all.

To my mother, Sunantha Sreenivasan Rammohan, I have to believe you can perceive these words somehow. Thank you for being my first and best friend; for your kind, steady, and loving presence in my life; and for your honesty, sincerity, and utter reliability. How I wish you could have seen *108* come to fruition, out in the world at last. How I wish you could have read about Bayla's mother and recognized yourself in her. This book is yours.

Finally, I offer my profound gratitude to my guru, who opened my eyes and changed my life.

ABOUT THE AUTHOR

Dheepa R. Maturi is a New York–born, Midwest-raised Indian-American writer who explores the intersection of identity, culture, and ecology. Her essays and poetry have appeared in numerous literary journals, so imagine her surprise when her first novel came to her as a thriller! *108: An Eco-Thriller* was her way of writing through ecological grief and toward hope, optimism, and a renewed connection with Earth and her communities.

Before turning to writing full-time, Dheepa worked as a lawyer, entrepreneur, and education-grant director. She received her BA from the University of Michigan and JD from the University of Chicago. She lives with her family in the Indianapolis area.

www.ingramcontent.com/pod-product-compliance
Lightning Source LLC
LaVergne TN
LVHW042036060625
813235LV00004B/463